THE LAST LIGHTNING

"The love of money is the root of all evil…"

1 Timothy 6:10

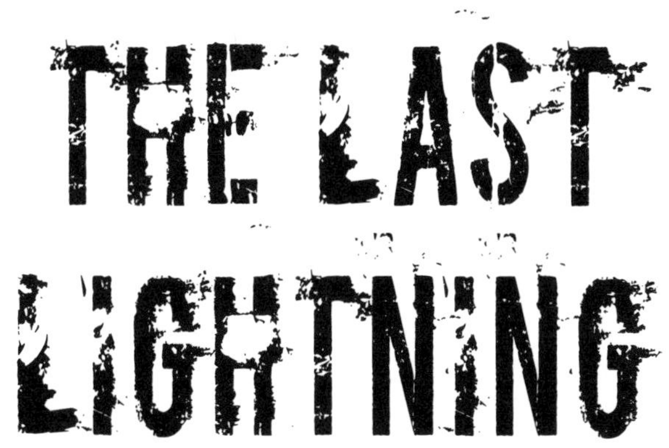

BY CRAIG MACINTOSH

ISBN: 978-1-59298-509-8
Library of Congress Control Number: 2012916822

Book design by Ryan Scheife, Mayfly Design
Typeset in Janson Text

Printed in the United States of America
First Printing: 2013

17 16 15 14 13 5 4 3 2 1

Beaver's Pond Press, Inc.
7108 Ohms Lane
Edina, MN 55439-2129
(952) 829-8818
www.BeaversPondPress.com

To order, visit www.BeaversPondBooks.com
or call (800) 901-3480. Reseller discounts available.

For Bryan Moon

ACKNOWLEDGMENTS

I continue to be grateful to a small army of people who have invested their time in helping me write this story. Foremost is Bryan Moon who created his MIA Hunters to fulfill his vision of bringing the missing home. It was his enthusiasm that compelled me to accompany him to Papua New Guinea. I also salute my fellow MIA Hunters of Team Four, enthusiastic and uncomplaining, who shared privations and adventures on my Papua New Guinea trip.

By organizing my words and offering invaluable suggestions, my talented editor, Cindy Rogers, brought her usual gift of clarity to the project. Support from Amy Quale at Beaver's Pond Press was welcome, as well proofreader Molly Miller's critical input throughout my manuscript. My brother, Kent, contributed his design talents as did Ryan Scheife.

Throughout the writing process I was aided by the following: Military aircraft historian Terrance Geary, veteran sailor Richard Aubrey, publicist Rachel Anderson, friends Marcia Herbster and Ken Wolf for initial reads and fellow author Marilyn Jax for her encouragement. I'm grateful to Greg Gibson and Ron Fagen, curator and founder respectively, of the Fagen Fighters WWII Museum. Special thanks to Dr. Mike Vogt for his enthusiasm in keeping alive the memories of those who served.

A debt is owed to the gracious and welcoming villagers of Papua New Guinea who are always willing to help the visitor. Their aid to the Allies during World War Two was incalculable, as was their suffering.

The brave young Americans who flew the legendary P-38 Lightning in the Southwest Pacific achieved a mythical status in aviation's pantheon. Their stories continue to excite admiration seventy years after their exploits.

Finally, I thank my wife, Linda for her decisive support in bringing *The Last Lightning* to print.

PROLOGUE

At 310,000 square miles, New Guinea was far too tempting a prize to be ignored by an Imperial Japanese Navy flush with its surprise victory at Pearl Harbor. Anchoring the strategic southwest perimeter of the Pacific, New Guinea sat astride the northern tip of Australia. An adjacent necklace of scattered islands—New Britain, Guadalcanal, Tulagi, and Bougainville—would gain infamy in coming months. The emperor's military needed them to guard its expanding empire.

On January 23, 1942, Japan took Rabaul on New Britain's northern tip and immediately transformed it into a fortress from which to threaten New Guinea, and beyond that, Australia. Japan appeared unstoppable.

Only the Battle of the Coral Sea on May 7–8 thwarted Imperial Navy plans for a seaborne conquest of New Guinea's capital, Port Moresby. Instead, Japan made a fateful decision to launch an attack from the island's north coast by going over the mountains via the Kokoda Track.

What followed was a protracted, bloody overland drive fought in some of the earth's most inhospitable terrain. In the end it was the Japanese who were driven from coastal outposts their generals and admirals once thought impregnable.

Without American control of New Guinea's skies the outcome on the ground would have been far different.

PART ONE

Chapter 1

New Guinea, April 10, 1944

In late afternoon, following a brief violent shower, a flight of four American P-38J Lightnings crossed the Owen Stanley Range, heading south toward Port Moresby, the island's capital. Twenty thousand feet below the fighters, mountains smoked as if on fire. Volcanic peaks, wreathed in clouds, rose thousands of feet above primeval jungle in torturous vertical walls and razor-sharp ridges. Swift-flowing rivers cut deep gorges in forested slopes and steamy vapors hovered, cloaking hills, setting mountaintops adrift in a sea of fog. When the sun finally appeared, wind scoured the peaks and retreating clouds defiantly released drenching rains in a biblical deluge. First Lieutenant Lloyd Peterson, the flight's lead pilot, glanced down at an unbroken carpet of jungle suffocating in humidity, a primordial hothouse where man was an alien. For two years, men have been predators, stalking and killing each other in this tropical abattoir. Japanese and Allied soldiers continue their murderous business with unmatched ferocity.

War in New Guinea has been a close-run affair and only recently has the tide begun to run against the Japanese. The balance now shifting in favor of the Allies was bought at horrendous cost. As Australians, New Zealanders, and Americans push northwest along the coast, contested trails slick with blood are strewn with thousands of corpses. The natives—caught between the belligerents—suffer as well.

Cruising at 20,000 feet, Peterson could only imagine struggling to survive in a punishing environment that made no distinction between combatants. Peterson and his wingmen—all aces with at least five aerial kills apiece—lived with memories of friends whose last airborne minutes had been marked by plummeting ribbons of flame. Over the vast ocean surrounding the island, losers in these deadly aerial ballets disappeared forever. On land—if his plane plunged into the jungle—a pilot was equally lost. Peterson and his fellow pilots had witnessed more than one fatal duel; knew the downed flier had already become an enemy's trophy; and looked to their own survival. If a pilot safely parachuted to earth, rescue was almost always impossible given the terrain. On the ground, he faced an entirely new enemy: the jungle, where he began his own terrifying struggle to survive. Were he to fall to earth injured, chances for survival were even more dismal. Each passing day without rescue would be followed by despair, festering wounds, madness, and finally, death—all under the eye of a seemingly distant Creator. God's eyes are not the only ones watching. To Peterson, New Guinea's unforgiving landscape resembled a bolt of sodden green felt abandoned in a harsh tropical sun—wrinkled fabric twisted into barriers like the Owen Stanley Range. Relieved to leave the mountains behind, Peterson led the others toward the southern coast of the island.

Banking over malarial swamps fed by mountain streams, the twin-engine Lightnings lined up single file for their final approach to Jackson's Field. Villas, colonial-era buildings, and a sea of rusting tin roofs came into view. Coiling smoke from hundreds of cooking fires nearly obscured the capital city.

Beneath the inbound P-38s, rows of shiny Quonset huts ringed the airfield, competing with maintenance hangars, taxiways, and sprawling tent villages for available space. Near the runway, parked bombers and fighters sat in earthen, horseshoe-shaped revetments bulldozed from a vast ocean of saw-blade kunai grass. Rugged foothills and steep foreboding mountain spines rose in the distance. Across the base, armies of bronzed mechanics crawled like ants over large aluminum bodies, patching wounds in fuselages or cannibalizing engines.

Slowing his big fighter to 125 mph, Peterson lowered his Lightning's tricycle landing gear and lined up his plane's nose with the middle of the airstrip. Seconds later, the P-38's wheels gently kissed runway. Peterson let his plane run nearly to the end of the pavement where he braked and trailed a jeep with a "Follow Me" sign to a taxiway. A second Lightning came down as easily as the first and was followed in turn by two more. Ground crews ushered the big two-engine fighters to shelter behind high earthen berms. After a final revving of motors, the four pilots cut power and popped hatches. The props slowed, then coughed, sputtered, and died.

Each man climbed from his plane on a metal stepladder lowered from the rear of the cockpit pod. The quartet retrieved personal belongings from cramped space in the tail booms and did a quick inspection of their fighters before gathering by the nose of Peterson's plane. Stripping off goggles, Mae Wests, and parachutes, the pilots sought precious shade under the Lightning's wings. The men traded sweat-stained leather headgear for billed peaked hats or went bareheaded.

A crew chief in a rumpled, oil-stained jumpsuit and jaunty cap roared up in a jeep and leaped from the rear bench. A thin captain in sweat-stained khakis slid from the passenger's seat with effort. Steadying himself with a wooden cane, the officer walked with a noticeable limp. The mustached captain joined the waiting men in the shade of the wing. The pilots saluted.

"Lieutenant Lloyd Peterson, sir."

The captain returned the gesture and offered his hand.

"Keith Phillips, here. Welcome to Port Moresby, Peterson. How was the ride?"

"Little bumpy over the range, but pretty routine, sir."

"Good. I've got crews lined up to take care of your birds." Barking orders over his shoulder, the captain summoned the crew chief loitering on the fringe with a knot of enlisted men. "Sergeant Perkins, get your boys on the job right away!"

"Leave it to me, sir," replied the noncom, touching his cap's brim. "We'll have these ships refueled and rearmed in two hours."

"Okay, let's get you settled then," said the captain, waving them to his jeep.

Peterson and the others followed Phillips to the waiting vehicle. "Any idea what the skinny is on this meeting, Captain?"

"Can't say, Peterson. Won't say, really. What I can tell you is that you've got a whole lot of brass hats waiting for you and your boys."

Climbing into the jeep's rear seat, Peterson—"Pete" to his squadron mates—grumbled aloud about special missions always being dreamed up by headquarters planners. Tired from the long flight, he was in no mood to face a crowd of senior officers. "When's the briefing, sir?"

Their host dismissed the weary grumbling with a smile. "Actually, you caught a break, Lieutenant. It's set for tomorrow morning. Zero nine hundred hours. We're still missing some people, so it's been delayed until after chow." The jeep's driver, a nervous private with a scrawny neck and bad haircut, sat silently, eyes straight ahead, an invisible man. Scrambling aboard, the aviators shoehorned themselves and their gear into the rear seats and the driver took off, trailing a cloud of dust along a road paralleling the runway. Lieutenants Roger Herman, a tanned Californian with matinee idol looks, and John Rippinger, a perpetually grinning Chicago native, braced themselves as they bounced along the track. Only John Lane, the squadron's newest ace, seemed blissfully unconcerned. Youngest of the four officers, Lane, a husky, round-faced Midwesterner with a loud sense of humor on the ground, was, like the others, a killer who was all grim business in the air. At twenty-four, Peterson, a Minnesota Swede known for grumpy cynicism, was the "old man" of his foursome. Together, the quartet had scored twenty-three kills and were, according to Peterson, "mighty sore" about having their hunting interrupted to come to Port Moresby for "some mysterious briefing." Feeding off Peterson's suspicions, his fellow pilots were equally wary of the upcoming briefing. The captain got an earful of the usual griping as they drove past parked aircraft.

Skidding to a stop in front of a row of Quonset huts, the driver waited as his passengers unfolded themselves from the jeep. Easing from the front seat, Phillips told the private to wait while he oriented the flyers.

"You'll have the front half of these quarters to yourselves. Nothing fancy but at least it has bunks and a roof, gentlemen." Pointing his cane at a low wall of sandbags running between the buildings, he continued. "Slit trenches if you need them, but we don't see much of the Jap these days. Not like old times from what I've been told."

Glancing at his watch, the officer wrapped up his introduction. "Mess hall is in that end building with the white door. Chow in two hours. Damn fine cooks if I say so myself. Best donuts this side of San Francisco for breakfast. Showers and sinks behind your quarters, latrine beyond that. I suggest you familiarize yourselves with the lay of the land while it's still light. Any questions?"

He nodded at a mammoth isolated Quonset with a chest-high sandbagged skirt. "Your briefing will take place over there. Be on time. Better yet, be early. Anything else?"

Peterson and his men snapped salutes. "Thanks for the tour, Captain."

Phillips settled himself in the jeep's front seat, cane between his knees. "I'll go back to the field later and check on your birds. I want to make sure everything's taken care of."

"Appreciate it," Peterson said.

The jeep roared toward maintenance sheds in the distance.

"Well, boys," grinned Peterson. "I don't know about you, but I want to see if the showers work. Then I'm going to catch some shut-eye before chow."

Lane piped up. "And I'm going to familiarize myself with the latrine." The four men howled with laughter and swept into the Quonset hut to claim their bunks.

....

Chapter 2

Jackson's Field, April 11

"ATTENTION!" A booming voice echoed off the walls of the briefing hut. Peterson, his fellow pilots, and a handful of uniformed men leaped to their feet.

A blast of humidity followed a phalanx of high-ranking officers into the building. Four floor fans tried their best to stir the morning air in the windowless Quonset.

Catching a glimpse of three silver stars on the leading man's collar, Peterson thought, *Must be something big*. He nudged Rippinger, whispering, "It's the Old Man himself." The stars belonged to Lt. Gen. George Kenney, commander of the Fifth Air Force, and MacArthur's ranking airman. Peterson had met the short, pugnacious Kenney twice before during awards ceremonies. Trailed by a retinue of brigadiers and bird colonels, the general reached the lectern and nodded at Phillips standing at the end of the front row of benches. "Take your seats!" bellowed the captain. Two-dozen airmen sat as one.

Dressed in khakis damp with perspiration, Kenney peeled off aviator sunglasses, tossed them into his hat, and handed it to Phillips without looking. "Good morning, gentlemen," he barked.

"Morning, sir," his audience parroted.

Clasping hands behind his back, the general swept his eyes over the ranks. Flashing a quick smile, more of a grimace, Kenney spoke rapidly. "You men have been hand-picked by staff for a special mission. What you are being asked to do is vitally important to the fight still ahead of us." Kenney turned, nodding to a colonel who perched by a large easel draped in gray cloth. A quick tug and the fabric fell away, revealing a blow-up of the island's northern coast. Kenney continued, the colonel following the general's briefing by tracing a long pointer across the map.

"We need allies in this fight, gentlemen. Not just Aussies and Kiwis. Some of our most dependable allies are the original inhabitants of this island. We cannot bring the fight to the enemy without native help. That's where you come in."

Stepping from behind the lectern, the general paced in front of the benches and singled out Peterson and his lieutenants. "I had my people get me top-notch flyers for this mission. Told 'em I wanted only aces, pilots who knew how to deal with the Nips. Men with a proven record." Kenney returned to the podium and wheeled on his audience. "Lieutenant Peterson!"

The Minnesotan jumped to his feet. "SIR!"

Kenney grinned, softening his voice into fatherly tones. "I know you and your boys would rather be out hunting Japs, am I right?"

Peterson stammered. "Well, truthfully, sir…yes."

Kenney waved him back down to the bench. "Don't worry, son. I'll get you back into the fight in a few days. But right now I need you for this mission. Don't fret about running up your total, Peterson. You and your boys will be in the thick of it soon enough. There are still plenty of Japs to go around."

Low chuckles swept the briefing room.

"But first, we've got to secure the north coast." As Kenney spoke, the colonel's pointer scratched across the chart, tracking with the general's words. "Clean out the little bastards, so we can sweep up into Dutch New Guinea and from there, into the Philippines. We won't disappoint General MacArthur will we?"

A throaty roar filled the room. "NO SIR!"

"He's counting on us to do just that." Kenney wrapped up his pep talk by raising his arm at the map behind him. "Colonel Wolf will give you mission details. He'll brief you on all the particulars but I will say this much: what's on that cargo plane has to end up in the right hands. It's the heart of your mission. It's vital that you succeed in its delivery. I know you won't disappoint me. What's said in this room stays here. It's top secret, men. This just might be one of those peculiar turning points in the war. Consider yourselves privileged to be part of it." Holding out his hand, the general plucked his hat and sunglasses from Phillips's grasp and stormed to the aisle. His audience rose as one. On his way out Kenney paused, bulling his way into the second row to shake hands with Peterson and his three pilots, along with several others. With a flourish, the general was gone, the door banging behind him, brigadiers and colonels in his wake.

Wolf, a gray-haired bird colonel wearing wire spectacles and a somber face, took center stage with an announcement. "Anyone not actually involved with flying this mission is now dismissed."

In minutes, the group thinned and the doors were locked,

guarded by a pair of armed MPs posted outside. Only P-38 pilots Peterson, Rippinger, Herman, and Lane were left along with four strangers—a captain, two lieutenants, and a sergeant—the crew of a C-47 that had landed an hour earlier. Facing the eight men, Wolf introduced Peterson and his pilots to the transport's airmen. That done, the colonel recited the heart of the upcoming mission, then delegated a weather update to his meteorologist, a sour-faced major wearing ill-fitting khakis. Part science, part mumbo-jumbo, the officer's confident forecast would be disproved in one of New Guinea's volatile downpours that would postpone the mission for four days. All that was yet to come. When the briefing ended, the men were reminded of the secrecy of their assignment. Released for chow, they were ordered to avoid contact in the mess hall by dining as a solitary group. Forestalling any gossip about the missions, Peterson launched into a favorite topic: baseball. He kept the conversation alive throughout the meal by repeating stories about close games he had witnessed during his war-shortened amateur career as a catcher. His wingmen had heard them all.

....

Chapter 3

April 15

Dawn of the fourth day brought the narrow weather window forecast by the meteorologist. Great towering pillars of storm clouds closing in from the north coast weren't expected to cause any problems for at least two hours. "By then," crowed the meteorologist confidently, "you'll be over the Owen Stanley Range and on your way to Nadzab. Shouldn't be a problem."

"Easy for him to say," grumbled Peterson, "he's not flying, is he?"

He and his fellow Lightning pilots debated the wisdom of betting against the island's notorious weather but in the end yielded to the C-47 pilot's impatience. The hushed predawn consultation in the briefing hut ended with an uneasy agreement to fly the mission. Fitted with twin drop tanks, each P-38 would take off after the C-47 was airborne and take up station to cover the transport as it climbed to 18,000 feet. Rippinger and Lane would shadow the cargo plane at 2,000 feet above and behind. Peterson and Herman were to provide cover 2,000 feet above them. Flying S-shaped routes, each pair of P-38s would weave back and forth in order to stay with the slower transport cruising at 185 mph, its maximum speed at the higher altitude.

Ten minutes behind the loaded C-47—which used up most of the runway to struggle into the air—Peterson's Lightning lifted off. Moments later, Herman's fighter roared down the runway in the gray light, followed by Rippinger and Lane. The four silver-bodied Lightnings easily caught up with the C-47 that had reached 12,000 feet and was still climbing. Jockeying alongside the transport, Peterson keyed his mike. "Hardware One, this is Blue Leader, how do you read me, over." Glancing at the P-38 off his port wing, the big plane's pilot flashed a thumbs-up sign at Peterson, answering, "Everything looks good, Blue Leader. Where are your boys?"

"Everybody's in position. You're covered, Hardware One."

"Always good to know. See you upstairs."

"Roger," replied Peterson. "Heading upstairs. Blue Leader out."

Waving at the face in the C-47's cockpit, Peterson waggled his plane's wings and climbed left before circling back to join his wingman trailing the transport 4,000 feet above. Heading north, the five planes approached the Owen Stanley Range's unforgiving knife-edged ridges and were met by a wall of clouds rapidly closing from the coast. Menacing anvil-shaped clouds, their glowing cores crackling with thunderbolts, swept across the mountains threatening everything in their path. The meteorologist's promised "window" had suddenly, and irrevocably, slammed shut. Behind them, Port Moresby abruptly vanished in a curtain of heavy rain.

"Hardware One, this is Blue Leader. What do you want to do?" Static sputtered in Peterson's headset. All he caught was, "Can set…down…Dobo."

"Roger," bellowed Peterson in his mike. "Understand you want to head for Dobo, correct?" No answer. *Did I hear that correctly?* He wondered. Beneath them, mountains disappeared, covered by ugly scudding clouds smothering every peak.

Herman's voice broke in. "Blue Leader, this is Blue Flight Two. Can't see anything in this damned soup. I'm having a hard time keeping you in sight. What's our plan, over?"

Peterson called his pilots. "Blue Flight, this is Blue Leader. Hardware One wants to head for Dobo. I agree. Can't get over this stuff. Can't see the deck. Blue Flight Two and I will stick close to Hardware. See you in Dobo. Acknowledge, over."

Clicks of static filled Peterson's ears. He tried again but heard nothing except hissing noise. Even his wingman, Herman, was lost to sight. Peterson called the cargo plane but got no answer. Gambling, he slowly dropped to catch a glimpse of the transport. Spotting what he thought was the big plane's tail below him, he came down another thousand feet and was rewarded with the sight of an olive drab aircraft just ahead. Pulling closer, Peterson angled for a better look.

The plane was a Jap fighter! A "Hamp"—a clipped-wing Mitsubishi Zero painted with the familiar meatball insignia.

Miraculously, the lone enemy pilot had not seen him.

Shaken, Peterson throttled back, dropped his external fuel tanks, and let the enemy fighter pull ahead. At this range he could not miss. When the drifting Hamp filled the lighted circle of his gun sight, Peterson fired a three-second burst of machine gun fire. Exploding in a fireball, the Jap broke apart in flaming scraps. No parachute.

Pulling away, Peterson throttled to 300 mph and went into a shallow climb.

"Blue Flight! Just ran into a bogey! Don't know how many there are! Skin tanks and stay alert! Do you read me? Over!" Two burps of static, a fragment of voice, and then more radio noise. Unbeknownst to Peterson, his fellow Lightning pilots were battling their own problems.

Feeling his way down through the ugly storm clouds to 16,000 feet, Roger Herman ran head on into two Zeros. Flaming one with cannon fire, he turned to pursue the other only to find a Zero on his tail.

"Where the hell did you come from?" he yelled in his mike.

Accelerating, the Jap pilot poured a long burst into the American plane. Herman felt heavy 20mm fragments thud into armor plate behind his seat. Slipping left to throw off the Jap's aim, his plane shook violently, his cockpit filling with thick oily smoke. He fought to regain control of the Lightning. Staying glued to Herman's six, the shooter ripped short bursts of cannon fire at him. The P-38 went screaming into a dive and slammed against a mist-covered mountainside.

Jumped by three A6M5 Zeros from above, Rippinger's canopy was shattered in the first pass. He was hit in the neck and shoulder. Machine gun fire raked both engine booms. No one answered his radio calls for help. With his port engine trailing smoke and oil, Rippinger put his Lightning into a shallow dive to flee, only to find himself at right angles to a pair of Jap fighters feeling their way through the soup. Rippinger stood his crippled P-38 on its port wing and turned into the Zeros. Righting his plane, he started shooting, his guns tearing apart one enemy. Rippinger flew through flaming debris and pulled his twin-engine fighter into an impossible right turn that put him back on the tail of the surviving Zero. Light-headed from loss of blood but determined to finish the Jap fighter, Rippinger fired a long burst from his guns, giving him a second score. Another Zero dove to attack the crippled P-38. Rippinger threw his fighter into a dive to outrun this new foe, but it was no contest as the Zero intersected him for the kill. A long burst of 20mm cannon fire and the Lightning tumbled into the jungle below, exploding in a column of flame.

Isolated and unaware of the aerial combat, Lane listened to snatches of radio talk and decided to find his way home. Setting a new heading, he tried calling the others without success and began running for the coast. Dropping toward what he thought was Dobodura, he spotted two Jap fighters during a break in the rain clouds. One of the planes, a Nakajima K1-43 "Oscar," spewed a thin ribbon of oily smoke from its cowling. Lane went into a dive, firing at the crippled aircraft on his first run. His 20mm cannon shredded the Oscar, breaking it in half. Pulling up to gain altitude, Lane found the other Jap on his tail, climbing with him, firing short bursts. Lane's P-38 easily outdistanced the Zero and he came around again for another try at the enemy. As Lane zoomed toward him, the Japanese pilot kept coming, guns blazing. Lane's bullets found their mark but the Zero was steady, its paired 7.7mm machine guns and cannon spitting fire at the Lightning.

The distance closed to 1,000 yards, both planes heading toward each other at 250 mph. Lane's guns jammed. Cursing, he pulled right. The Zero screamed left.

Both fighters collided, exploding in blazing scraps of wreckage, plummeting into a deep, forested gorge that immediately swallowed any evidence of a fight.

Cruising at 15,000 feet, Peterson cautiously probed ahead of him, wary of surrounding mountains obscured by clouds. Alert for more Jap fighters, and with no sign of the C-47, he tried his radio. Still dead. Dobodura did not answer. Finally spotting the lumbering transport several hundred feet to his left and heading away from him, Peterson turned and easily overtook the plane.

What he saw shocked him. The cargo plane's port engine was out, its big three-bladed prop feathered. Oil streaks and scorch marks covered the dead Pratt and Whitney engine—evidence of a fire. The plane's ninety-five-foot wingspan was riddled with gaping holes. *Cannon fire*, thought Peterson. A second look also confirmed that the C-47's fuselage had also been stitched with rows of bullet holes, its rudder shredded.

Dropping closer, he drew abreast of the cockpit, looking for signs of life. The pilot was slumped over, his shattered head splattered with blood behind smashed windows. The big plane flew steady and level, giving Peterson hope the co-pilot was handling the controls. Dancing his Lightning over to the right side of the transport, Peterson was relieved to get a wave from the man at the controls. Peterson signaled back and tried his radio. Nothing. He wiggled the P-38's wings, motioning for the big plane to follow him down. Turning, he was pleased to see the C-47 mimic his move. Heading for a ragged hole in the towering thunderheads, Peterson led the cargo plane lower.

Out of nowhere, a lone Jap fighter swooped down, guns blazing.

Cannon fire and machine gun bullets tore through the radio compartment behind Peterson. Two slugs nearly took off the top of his head. Bullets hit his back, piercing both lungs. Blood spurted from head wounds, blinding him. The enemy fighter hosed both planes with deadly fire and turned for another run. Ripping the bloodied flying cap from his head, Peterson wiped blood from his eyes, struggling to control the Lightning. Knowing the Jap would be back for another go at its wounded targets, Peterson craned his neck only to find the predator gone. To his left, and below him, the C-47 droned on, its useless left engine on fire again from tracer rounds. Sparks popped from the right engine where growing flames ate at the big 1,200 hp radial. The transport dropped quickly and Peterson followed it into dense clouds, hoping for merciful cover. Mountains, always a worry in bad weather, loomed somewhere ahead unseen. Disoriented, Peterson was unsure where he was.

Suddenly, the hunting Zero rose in front of him, obviously as lost as its prey. Reacting instinctively, Peterson pressed the gun tit, flaming the enemy plane. Exhausted by his effort, he slumped forward, his bloodied gloves gripping the half-wheel. Despite his pain, Peterson managed to emerge from a low ceiling of heavy rain. He throttled back to stay with the C-47.

A deep mountain cleft opened before them. Hemmed in by trees on both sides, the narrow canyon, bisected by a swollen stream, wore a wide blanket of tall grass. A few thatched huts huddled in a distant forest at the base of the mountains.

Straining to focus, Peterson drifted dangerously close to the transport. Dropping toward the open area, both crippled American planes glided in, wheels up. The C-47 bellied in slightly ahead of Peterson and to his right. Shearing off both props, the transport, its back broken, twisted sideways, shuddering to a stop in a line of trees where jungle-clad ridges rose abruptly from the valley floor. The engine fires sputtered, then died in pouring rain.

Seconds later, Peterson's twin-engine fighter bounced across the stream, broke through a wall of vines, and lost part of its starboard tail boom. Plowing a deep furrow in the sodden ground, the P-38 skidded to a stop. No fire. Peterson, unaware his plane had landed mostly intact, was dead before the Lightning came to rest.

....

Chapter 4

Oro Province, Papua New Guinea, present day

Emerging from a green wall of foliage, three shadowy figures cut their way through a curtain of tangled vines. The lead man's frenzied slashing of the rope-like tendrils revealed a tiny clearing bathed in a shaft of light streaming from an opening high in the canopy. Lowering his machete, a slender black man in ragged shorts and sleeveless T-shirt gestured to a stocky white man behind him.

The silent trio stood together on a sloping jungle floor carpeted with rotting vegetation and brittle fallen palm fronds. With the exception of echoing calls from a few crying birds, the surrounding jungle was strangely quiet.

The white man took off his bush hat to fan himself. Slipping out of his backpack, Brad Wood knelt in exhaustion in the sunlight. Sweat soaked every inch of his clothing. Holding a GPS skyward like an offering, Wood took a position reading and made a note in a small book. Rooting in his pack, he found a bottle of water and greedily gulped. He rinsed the sting of salt from his eyes and tossed the bottle to his nearest companion, a muscular, shoeless black man in khaki shorts.

"Drink up, Joshua," barked Wood hoarsely, "you need it."

Staring blankly at the sky, Wood's colleague, his head

wrapped in a red bandana, caught the bottle and drank, then passed the bottle to the point man who sat on his haunches watching quietly. Younger than the other two, the guide, like Joshua, was shoeless, his splayed toes planted in the dark earth. He finished the water, the last drops spilling down his ebony cheeks like tears. Renewed, he sat upright against his pack.

Fanning himself with a topographic map, Wood broke the silence. "This two-hour walk of ours has turned into another half day. Ask Simeon how much farther we have to go." Wood spread the chart across his knees.

While the black men bantered, Wood studied the map's version of the terrain, knowing they were somewhere in the lines resembling fingerprints. The three had been hiking for two days. Crossing a quilt of tribal lands had cost them money in addition to small gifts such as a knife or fishing line each time they entered another village's territory. Their goal was a narrow ravine the map showed to be within five hundred meters of their present location. There, close to his village, promised Simeon, they would find the wreckage of an airplane. Wood, a missionary with what his wife, Dorothy, called "an obsession" for World War Two aircraft, ministered at a small isolated station high in the rough hills southwest of Popondetta. During travels to villages in his assigned area, Wood had found a half-dozen aircraft crash sites from the Pacific war. Two of those planes yielded bones and Wood, with the help of a stateside contact, had alerted a U.S. Army recovery team from Hawaii's JPAC—Joint POW/MIA Accounting Command. A successful excavation at both sites and two years of painstaking forensics work had later closed the circle for families of the missing airmen.

Sitting on the forest floor, map in hand, with enough food for just three more days, Wood made up his mind to give up the chase in the afternoon. It wouldn't be his first fruitless search.

To Wood, it seemed as though they had been over some of the same ground yesterday without having found the hidden ravine or the supposed crash site. *How could we have missed it?* he wondered. Given the thick jungle and near vertical hillsides, meandering was understandable but frustrating. And dangerous.

Despite a GPS and map, Wood knew their success depended more on young Simeon's recall than on technology. A villager from these same hills, the man had pledged to lead Wood to a downed aircraft. It was not the only one he knew about, he promised the missionary. It took very little persuasion to commit Wood to the search. At the insistence of his wife, he had taken along Joshua, a trusted mission worker, as interpreter and security.

But two days in nearly impenetrable jungle was wearing on Wood. For the last four hours, the men had hacked their way through unknown terrain solely on the promise of the villager's memory.

Conversation between the two natives ended and Joshua cocked his head at Wood. "Pastor, he say we almost be there now. This place, not so far." Opposite the missionary, Joshua rocked on his heels, busily shaping three new walking sticks with a machete.

Wood glanced up from his map. "You think he really knows?"

Joshua's heavy eyebrows rose and fell like nervous caterpillars.

"What's that supposed to mean?" Wood scoffed. "Should we keep going?"

The eyebrows danced.

"Okay. You get out in front with Simeon. But stay in his back pocket."

Joshua tilted his shaggy head, not understanding.

"That means you stick with him. You savvy?" Wood rose, shouldered his backpack, and gripped an offered pole. He pulled

Joshua to his feet and helped him with his pack. Simeon stood, his machete pointing at a wall of foliage.

Mimicking the gesture, Wood said, “Be my guest, Simeon. Lead on.”

Following the scout, they stepped off single-file and were immediately swallowed by the jungle. After an hour of tortuous descent, they came across a hard-packed footpath and followed it toward the sound of bubbling water. At the edge of a narrow brook, they stopped to fill empty bottles and rinse sweat-soaked bandanas in the cool water. Wood dropped chlorine-dioxide pills into each makeshift canteen. They pushed on, following the stream.

Winding between tangled roots and over-sized ferns, the shallow creek wandered, dropping over moss-covered rocks in a series of waterfalls. At the mouth of a yawning ravine, the stream widened. Screaming from the canopy, startled birds filled the air with raucous calls. Unseen creatures of all sizes slithered or fled at the trio’s approach. Brush and trees choking the bank slowed their progress. Simeon left the path for the water, hurrying the pace. After thirty minutes of slogging in the streambed, Wood called a halt.

Joshua slashed at the undergrowth, clearing an opening along the bank where they could stop. As they rested, Wood plotted their location with the GPS and consulted his map. “Might be what we’re looking for,” he announced. “It seems to match! Okay, so far, so good, Simeon.”

A hint of a smile spread across Simeon’s face. He promised they were very close. After a ten-minute respite, he returned to the stream, his companions splashing behind him. The water led them to a forested valley hemmed in by steep hills cloaked in trees. Ugly bald patches dotted the hillsides with slash-and-burn scars. *Someone’s farming*, Wood noted to himself.

Simultaneously, Simeon and Joshua alerted Wood to large metal fragments embedded high in the crotch of a mature tree. Twisting matted vines partially obscured long strips of aluminum held fast in strangling vegetation. Metallic scraps were strewn everywhere. Wood paused in awe. He knew what they had stumbled into—a virgin site. Drawing the guide to him, he threw an arm around the young man's shoulder. "You've done it, Simeon!"

Wood spotted a slab resembling a wing in dense undergrowth covering the jungle floor. In the undisturbed foliage, Wood came across a twisted tubular shape overgrown with knotted roots like some grotesque sculpture. It was an upended landing gear, its tire rotted long ago, wheel spokes still recognizable. Kneeling, he shook off his backpack, snagged a small digital camera from his shirt pocket, and began snapping pictures as if afraid the evidence would disappear.

His two companions probed among jagged spires of twisted metal rising from the jungle floor. Wood, his heart racing, followed Simeon along the length of the debris field. What looked to be an engine had buried itself vertically, leaving three telltale feet of prop blade showing. Possibly a bomber, more likely a fighter, he guessed.

Joshua began chopping saplings to free a hulking cylindrical shape. His booming voice shattered the scene. "Hey, Pastor, come quick!"

Tripping over fallen limbs and grasping vines, Wood staggered to the man. Joshua had severed a mat of saplings and was busy pulling debris from what was obviously a cockpit. As more of the aircraft emerged, Wood stepped back and took a series of pictures of a smiling Joshua leaning triumphantly against the wreck. Peering inside a shattered, detritus-filled cockpit, Wood took more pictures. Putting aside his camera, he joined Joshua in slicing matted tendrils clinging to the plane's crumpled front end. As fast as the two cut, Simeon pulled the stubborn vines free, dragging them to one side and flinging them into a growing pile.

In thirty minutes of frantic slashing, the airplane's nose emerged. Raising his hand, Wood halted the pruning. He had seen enough. Tossing a bottle of water to each sweating man, Wood crabbed his way through tangled boughs to crouch at the front of the aircraft. Straddling the rounded bullet shape, he leaned forward, reverently brushing away leafy debris. His efforts revealed five blackened, rusted stumps poking from the fighter's nose.

"Gentlemen," he said, hushed, "we've found ourselves a Lightning."

....

Chapter 5

Oakdale, California, November 18

Five miles east of the self-styled cowboy town, past orderly rows of almond trees and cattle pastures, the Central Valley yielded to undulating grassy slopes that gave way to rugged, pine-covered hills of the Stanislaus National Forest, one of Yosemite's gateways. Beyond that rose the majestic snow-covered Sierra Nevada.

Just past the city limits, a gravel spur split from two lanes of merged highway and twisted to the top of a balding knob where a large rectangular, one-story stone house sat overlooking the valley. On nights without fog, the valley became a black velvet cloth sewn with precise rows of glittering diamonds marking Oakdale, Modesto, and the distant university town of Stockton.

Sunday evening. The husband, a tall, lanky man crowned

with a white leonine mane, burrowed fitfully beneath a thick down comforter. Unable to sleep, he squinted at the digital clock and surrendered to his restlessness. Swinging his long legs from under the warm covers, he sat on the edge of the bed listening enviously to his wife's measured breathing. Finally, he rose, stepped into slippers, and wrapped himself in a threadbare wool robe. He crept across the tiled floor, gently closed the door behind him, and shuffled down a hallway to a paneled den dominated by a wide desk spilling over with stacks of paper, files, a scanner, printer, and answering machine. A coffee mug, half-filled with yesterday's sludge, sat next to a keyboard belonging to two large flat computer screens in sleep mode. A pair of polished brass 20mm shells jammed with pencils and pens guarded a tower of newly burned CDs. Four metal filing cabinets lined one wall, hemming in a tall bookcase jammed with bound Army Air Corps unit histories and ragged rows of aircraft books. One wall was covered from floor to ceiling with signed aviation prints. Under glass, a pair of P-38s chased a quartet of Japanese Zeros through pastel clouds. A P-51 Mustang poured a stream of tracers into a ME 109 alongside art of B-24s dropping bombs on a smoking refinery. Award plaques and a framed honorable discharge from the U.S. Air Force lay propped on a long shelf. In the den's frosted, ten-foot-wide window, winter's inky sky sparkled with millions of stars above a valley glowing with lights.

He sank into a high-backed leather chair and tapped the keyboard to wake the computer. Both screens, synchronized as one, came to life.

Ten email messages queued for reading. The first six were solicitations from charities and an aviation magazine subscription offer. He trashed them. One was from a Las Vegas dating service he had never heard of. Gone. Another was the weekly political screed from an uncle in Los Angeles. Gone. The ninth was the usual soft-core picture from an old air force buddy. He dumped it without looking.

It was the last message that made him put down the mug and sit up straight.

A missionary in Papua New Guinea was asking for his help. Though familiar with the name, he had never met the man but had supplied critical information matching missing aircrews with wrecks the missionary had found. To searchers in Papua New Guinea and elsewhere, the Californian was a human encyclopedia about all things military—particularly airplanes. The message filling his computer's email window made him pull the big chair close to the desk. Brushing aside bulging folders, he propped both elbows on the mahogany surface to study the text.

Have found remains of a P-38 in the hills southwest of Popondetta. Local came in to mission station with information on site. Hard terrain. Not easy to find. Crash site not too bad, better than most. Good-sized pieces. Scattered pattern but lots of stuff. Pilot nacelle surprisingly intact despite impact. Mapped it with my GPS. Locals not overly friendly. Almost hostile. Not helpful. Will have to do some evangelism outreach to sweeten them up for future trip-maybe. Three of us cleaned site as best we could. Weather lousy last day. Found some serial numbers. Check attachment. Local guide says bigger plane nearby. Description sounds like bomber or cargo. Says it's definitely American. Not sure. Check details for info on this Lightning. Found small bone fragments. Might be animal. Not sure what I have. Left all in place. Can go back if need be. Maybe do a check on the bigger plane. Exciting find. None of our pilots have mentioned this before. Know you can help ID this site. Will stay in touch. As usual, wife not as excited but she humors me. Terry, as usual, you're the man on this one. If anyone can run this down, you can like you did others. Thanks for help in advance. Blessings, Brad Wood.

Eyes locked on the monitor, Terry reached left without looking, powered up the printer, and slipped a stack of paper into the feed. In front of the flat screen, a smile spread across his face. "Well, how about this? Our friend in PNG has found himself a P-38!" Leaning over the keyboard, chin cradled in both palms, he addressed the screen. "It's been a while, hasn't it, Reverend Wood?" Hitting the print button, he read the message again, his smile growing wider.

Immediately, he began tapping a reply to a man he had never met, halfway around the globe in a part of the world he had never visited, about a missing pilot he did not know…yet. All that would come later. It always did. Like a challenging puzzle that would be solved. Finding the numbers, the mission, the terrain, even the weather for that long-ago day, would take time, but his knowledge of missing aircrews was as good as the Pentagon's…maybe better. The hunt was on.

Terry clapped hands, musing, *No wonder I couldn't sleep. My instincts wouldn't let me rest. I am going to put these pieces together and find this pilot. If he has family, I'll contact them. We WILL bring this man home! And to think…a P-38. A Lightning. My favorite war bird.* Above him, a beautifully detailed model of a P-38 Lightning turned slowly at the end of a nylon tether anchored in the ceiling.

• • • • • • • • •

Chapter 6

Washington, DC, December 5

At eleven-thirty in the morning, senior researcher Russell Hightower emerged from the National Archives onto Pennsylvania Avenue, a bulging folder tucked discreetly under his right arm. Momentarily blinded by the sunlight, he pulled clip-on sunglasses from his overcoat and snapped them over thick spectacles. He headed southeast on Pennsylvania Avenue. In the distance, the Capitol dome floated like a pale mirage above rushing traffic.

Despite his Russian lamb's wool hat and bright sunlight, the day's chill chased him down Pennsylvania Avenue to the Seventh Street crosswalk where he waited impatiently for a light to change. Three cars crossed in front of him, heading toward the Capitol Mall, leaving an empty street. A bundled pair came up behind him, then charged across the street against the light, leaving him alone on the curb clucking disapproval at their boldness. Hightower stomped his feet to keep warm and only when the light changed did he step into the crosswalk. Ironically, despite his rigid adherence in life to such things as the District's traffic rules, Hightower was on a reckless personal mission that belied his monastic existence.

Money had become Hightower's private failing. For the past nine years he had provided a secretive collector of antique Americana with rare documents belonging to his employers—the people of the United States. He started with a few presidential letters. Civil War field orders followed, along with rare maps and, more recently, minor forgotten manuscripts penned by Longfellow and Poe. His accomplice in the thievery—"selective culling" was what Hightower preferred to call his thefts—was a private middleman and dealer named Harrington who owned one of the nation's largest collections of autographed first editions and rare documents signed by historical figures such as Napoleon, Stalin, FDR, and Lincoln.

By design, Hightower and his confederate met only twice a year to lessen the chance of their pilferage being discovered. What the archivist carried in his hands had excited the collector when Hightower first signaled him via their arranged method—cryptic anonymous ads in *The Washington Post* classifieds.

Hightower's route paralleled the looming Federal Trade Commission building for an entire block and at the corner he turned right. Shielding his eyes, he squinted at the neoclassical silhouette of the National Gallery where Sixth Street intersected Constitution Avenue. A black Lincoln town car with tinted windows and vanity plates reading "Talon 2" idled at the curb in a prearranged spot. Though Hightower did not recognize the vehicle, it sported the correct strip of orange tape on its right rear bumper. The scent of money in the cold air quickened his pace. Harrington was not one to linger and would not appreciate tardiness.

Forty steps from the car, a figure in a black leather jacket left the FTC's plaza on Hightower's right and fell in behind him. Hightower, unaware he was being tailed, approached the vehicle and was suddenly startled by the presence of a large man behind him. Hightower hesitated. The stranger gripped the smaller man's elbow, reached past him, opened the long car's door, and sent him tumbling into the rear seat. The door slammed, locking behind him. Retreating to the plaza's steps, the man lit a cigarette and began pacing, his raptor's eyes locked on the car.

Sinking back in the soft seat, Hightower removed the clip-ons and polished his fogged spectacles with a handkerchief.

When he replaced his glasses, he studied the man seated opposite him—a man in an expensive overcoat, dark suit, and pale blue tie. The man slowly pulled a white silk scarf from around his neck and folded it across his knees. A shaven head, fighter's nose, and trimmed goatee added to his menacing look. Glancing across the seat at Hightower, the car's occupant disarmed him with a smile, offering his hand.

"It's about time we met, Mr. Hightouter."

"Hightower," corrected the archivist, refusing to shake. "It's Hightower."

The bearded man quickly withdrew his hand. "I beg your pardon. Of course, Hightower."

"Who are you? Where's Harrington?" snapped Hightower, alarmed but irritated.

Toying with the silk in his lap, the man smiled. "No names just yet. Your friend Harrington and I have done business before. He'll vouch for me if need be."

Hightower had a fleeting thought of bolting, but outside the tinted window the big man who had helped him into the back seat still hovered on the walk.

"Let's just say he sent me in his place. He thought what you were offering would be more to my liking than his." Smoothing the silk, the man held up his hand to silence any interruption. "Think of it this way. You and Harrington have an understanding, a contract of sorts." Nodding at the manila folder, he continued.

"I bought your contract from Harrington for a modest finder's fee. Now you are obligated to do business with me. It's quite simple. You see, I'm curious about what you've found."

Hightower disputed the logic. "I don't have to agree to this."

"Of course not, my dear fellow. It's your choice. But at least hear me out," he purred. "I repeat, Harrington said you found something that might interest me rather than him." Relaxing slightly, Hightower shifted in the soft upholstery to eye his questioner. "Do you have something that will interest me?" the man asked.

"Perhaps." Pushing his glasses up against the bridge of his nose, Hightower patted the manila envelope. Knowing its contents emboldened him. "This is very valuable information. One might be tempted to say it's worth a goodly sum of money."

"One may say a lot of things, Mr. Hightower," soothed the stranger, holding out his hand for the envelope. "Might we have a look?" Hightower gripped the folder, hesitating, the hand in front of him. More purring. "Oh come, come, Hightower, surely you can understand that I at least need to see what you have before I can decide whether or not I'm interested."

Hightower clutched the envelope to his chest. "I know what I've got here."

The man's tone changed by degrees. "I understand your reluctance to part with your find. But be reasonable, man. If I'm to invest in what you claim to have uncovered, then wouldn't you agree I'm due a look?"

"Perhaps one peek." Hightower handed over the manila folder and the man spilled the contents in his lap. Quickly scanning each document, the reader arranged them neatly on the seat as he studied them.

Facing Hightower, the man waved the final yellowing sheet as he talked. "These are all stamped top secret. Highly classified documents, are they not?"

"Correct."

"Can you guarantee that these reports, these papers and maps, have been under lock and key all this time?"

"I can. My guess is that these somehow ended up on the wrong shelf."

"Filed in the wrong place? I find that hard to believe."

"It happens," snorted Hightower. "Things get moved around. End up in a corner gathering dust for years. Some records are never discovered. We hold millions, you know."

"Even so, I was under the impression all combat reports from the war were de-classified quite some time ago."

The scholar in Hightower warmed to the subject. "True. The vast majority of the reports have been open to the public for some time now. We get requests from authors, academicians, and the like. Even family members have access to fill in the blanks for servicemen if they want. A handful end up like these."

"Fascinating. But how did you find these? What brought them to your attention in the first place?"

"A month ago, a fellow I know called from California asking about them."

"This very mission?"

"Well, details about one of the planes involved. My guess is he doesn't know the particulars. He was looking for information on this one flyer who was involved. He got his hands on a copy of a MACR, a Missing Air Crew Report, for this specific pilot. I've helped him over the years with requests like this. The National Archives is just one of his many sources."

"What did you tell him?"

"I rooted around for the better part of two weeks before I found what he was asking for. It wasn't easy. But once I identified the material I told him the reports didn't exist. They had been classified top secret and I knew why once I read them."

"Did he go away?"

Hightower shrugged. "For now. He's very thorough, has other resources."

"You think he's going to cause us any trouble?"

"Not really. He doesn't have the documents you hold."

"And yet this fellow in California knows about one of the pilots. How odd."

"Not really. Someone in Papua New Guinea got in touch with him. They located one of the planes from that mission, asked him for help in identifying it.

He found a name and, in turn, went looking for the pilot's family members. It's a process of elimination. Some identification plates, some numbers on a fuselage, maybe a painted name on a fuselage and before you know it, you have a particular airplane. That leads to a pilot's name and eventually a hometown. One matches it with Missing Air Crew Reports. It can be that simple if one has a few pieces of the puzzle. After making a few calls he found a family member. The relative will probably contact him to corroborate the man's family history. It happens all the time. Believe me, it's coincidence, nothing more. It shouldn't be a problem."

"I don't suppose you have this relative's name?"

"It's scribbled on the top envelope. Along with address and phone number."

"Ah, yes, so it is," said the man, sifting through the stack of paper. "Very efficient, saves me the trouble. Thank you, Mr. Hightower. I appreciate how helpful you've been." Returning the stack of paper to the folder, the interrogator frowned.

"I take it you either knew what you had or discovered its value soon thereafter. Which was it?"

"When I read the reports, I knew they were special."

"Oh, they're more than special if what I've read here turns out to be true."

Bristling, Hightower flashed a scowl. "It's authentic. I did some cross-referencing and what I found validates what you have in your hands." The pair sat in silence for several minutes. Reading his watch, Hightower declared, "I'll have to be getting back."

Ignoring the plea, the man tapped the files. A minute passed. "A few more questions. You're positive no one's looked into this in all these years?"

"All the participants were MIA, missing in action. No witnesses. No survivors."

"Why," mused the stranger, "didn't the government bother to look for them?"

Sighing as though the answer was obvious, Hightower explained. "You can tell from those charts that an exhaustive search was done. Several searches, in fact. The terrain is hellish. Weather was a big problem. The very next day was 'Black Sunday' when the Fifth Air Force lost thirty-seven planes returning from a raid on Hollandia. I'd say headquarters was a bit busy at that point. Did you know some of those planes have never been found? One can't just stop the war. They had to keep moving. After a while, people just forgot."

"Probably a drop in the bucket overall," said Hightower's interrogator softly.

"Most likely. Look, I really do have to be getting back. I'll be missed."

"Of course. Here's what I'm going to do, Mr. Hightower." Stirring in his seat, the man faced the archivist, suddenly clamping a vise-like hand on his reluctant guest's knee. "I'm going to pay you five thousand dollars…"

Squirming in his questioner's grip, Hightower interrupted, "We agreed on ten. I want my ten thousand."

Releasing his hold, the man with the goatee added, "You and Harrington agreed on ten thousand, not me. I make my own rules. You'll get another five thousand if this information pans out."

"Look, I'm risking a lot here. I could get in a lot of trouble for giving you this material. I want what I was promised."

"Be reasonable, Russell. You don't mind me calling you Russell, do you? You'll get your money. If what you have here is solid, you might even get a bonus." Leaning toward Hightower, the man's eyes hardened. He pointed outside. "Don't forget my friend there. He's not the kind of person you want to fuck with, Russell, believe me. He has a particular fondness for hurting people. He's bent that way. Why, I don't know, but there it is. So my advice, Russell, is to take the five thousand now and watch your mailbox. You might find another envelope. I'll contact you through Harrington if we need to meet again."

A rap on the window brought the pacing sentinel to the car. He leaned over, staring menacingly at Hightower through the tinted glass. In the back seat, the man wound the silk around his neck, smiling malevolently. "Are we good, Russell? Do we understand each other?"

Hightower nodded in surrender. In response, the bearded man motioned to his watchdog. After opening the door, the sentry plucked Hightower from the rear seat. Producing a thick white envelope from his jacket, he thrust it at the researcher without speaking. The driver got behind the wheel and the town car pulled from the curb, leaving a visibly shaken Russell Hightower alone in the cold.

Hightower hefted the thick envelope, stuffed it inside his coat, and jammed the wool hat on his head. A glance at his watch told him he had fifteen minutes left of his lunch hour, but he had lost his appetite. Leaning into the wind, he drew his overcoat tighter, turned right, and began a hurried walk up Constitution Avenue.

PART TWO

Chapter 7

Upsala, Minnesota, December 10

Spotting a familiar bundled form and trotting dog at the curve in the snow-covered road, the driver of the silver pickup slowed. Tapping on his horn, he drew abreast of the plodding figure and lowered the passenger window. The man's only escort, a placid hound in the cab's rear seat, poked its head into the cold, sniffing a greeting at the hiker and dog.

"Hey, Becky," hollered the truck's owner. "Need a ride?"

The woman walked across the road and leaned in the window, her elbows resting on the door, her dog barking at the animal in the cab. Hushing her pet, she rubbed the driver's dog and smiled at the man behind the wheel, a neighbor. "Hey, Mr. Soderlund. On your way home?"

"Yeah. You want that ride? It's pretty nippy out here, young lady."

A weary smile flashed from under the hooded jacket. "Nah, I'm okay. It feels good, actually." Nodding at her heeled dog, she added, "Besides, Buddy and I can use the exercise." Becky's breath came in small bursts of steam. "We're almost home," she said, waving at the dark woods behind her. "But thanks for asking."

"Have it your way. Stay warm."

"Will do." Giving the man's dog a last playful pat, Becky pushed away from the cab and waved as the truck's lights disappeared around the bend. She whistled Buddy to her side and resumed walking. Darkness dropped over the snow-blanketed cornfields on both sides of the road. Another quarter mile and she traded gravel for her own tramped footpath through deep snow. The trail led into a stand of dark pine. Ahead of her was the silhouette of a house on a bluff overlooking a lake locked in ice. Breaking from the tree line, her dog romped ahead to the darkened home.

Inside, Becky shucked her boots and hooded jacket to rub the dog's feet with a large towel. She struck a long match at the base of a pyramid of kindling in the hearth and went into the kitchen to make dinner. Outside, wind scoured the lake ice, sending bursts of snow onshore, rattling the windows.

Becky ate quietly as Buddy devoured his meal in a corner of the kitchen. When dinner was finished, she fed two logs to the fire and slipped into her pajamas and punched up her computer to check emails before bed. Poised to turn out the lights, Becky noticed the blinking red eye of the answering machine on the kitchen counter. *How did I miss that?* she wondered. *Probably Darryl again*, she fumed.

Darryl had made himself a nuisance since their divorce six years ago. Actually, she thought, he had always been a nuisance, an asshole really, even before they married. Two years out of high school, she had originally set her eyes on Darryl's older brother, David. Like many a young man pursued by an infatuated small-town girl, he had been cavalier with her affections. His abrupt joining of the army after two years of college left her feeling betrayed. In the wake of his absence she panicked, marrying his younger brother out of spite. It was a mistake. Becky had been a year older, a tough survivor of a blighted childhood and battling self-loathing but no wiser than Darryl, the man-boy she married.

She hadn't seen the telltale signs then, didn't want to. Truthfully, she had ignored the signs of a classic alcoholic. After two DWIs, Darryl had been kicked out of law enforcement classes at nearby St. Cloud State. A switch to vocational school had taught him welding skills and he learned enough to hold a job repairing farm equipment around town. The worsening economy had dealt another blow to their shaky union. Verbally abusive, alcoholic, and stifling an inner rage, Darryl seldom found work. Adrift, possessive, and in the same town, he was the proverbial accident waiting to happen. Not a good combination. Becky got out of the marriage but not out of town—her second mistake. Working four days a week at Paul and Kathy's Supermarket on Main Street was a temporary lifeline for now. The Pine Lake house, a roof over her head and a refuge, had been a godsend.

Even there, in her newfound sanctuary, Darryl haunted her, phoning constantly. She had considered, and then dropped, the idea of a restraining order. Rural women had a bad track record where restraining orders were concerned and Becky thought it more prudent to wait him out. Just in case, she had Buddy and a .22 pistol loaded with hollow-points for protection. Small comfort.

Darryl's tearful, slurred, late-night phone calls had become part of her routine and she dreaded them. His monologues ricocheted between whining apologies and beery mumbling. Becky knew she needed a new start.

"Honey," counseled Ida, a gray-haired, doughy cashier at the supermarket, "we all have a clock ticking inside of us that will tell us when it's time to give up on someone."

"You mean Darryl?" Becky had misunderstood the woman, a weary, battered survivor of her own one-sided domestic wars.

"No, darling. I mean YOU. You'll know when the time is right to move on. Go somewhere. Change your life. Meet someone else. Get on with things."

"He'll never let me go," Becky had said.

"They never do. You just don't tell them," the woman said. "One day you're here; the next day you're gone. For good."

"So why haven't you left?" It seemed a logical question to Becky.

"'Cause I can't, honey. I'm too old to change. My legs would give out on me halfway down the driveway. Lord knows what Otto would do if he found me crawling in a ditch to the highway. No, I missed my chance. Didn't listen to my clock when it ran out. Ignored it. But you're still young enough."

"I'll think about it," Becky had answered.

"Listen for that timepiece in here," said the older woman, tapping her ample bosom. "Don't say I didn't warn you."

"I appreciate what you're saying, Ida. Really, I do."

Smiling sadly, the woman had shrugged as if her warning was chaff in the wind. "You turn around and a year's gone by. Turn around again and it's two years. Then five, then ten." Their conversation had ended when Ida's husband had barged into the store, heading for the meat cooler at the rear of the store. He stomped back to the two checkout counters, barking all the while about something the older woman had failed to do at home. After he stormed out, Becky's eyes met Ida's. She nodded.

Now, it was just a matter of timing. Timing was everything. The long walks after work had helped focus her thinking about the warning. It had been six years since the divorce and Becky was closing in on an unspoken deadline. Men like Darryl had their own deadlines. That's what frightened her. One thing she did know. Having made up her mind to never go back to him, she stalled him by listening to his weepy calls. She calmed his boiling, impotent rage by feeding him morsels of hope. "We'll see, we'll see." She was playing a risky game and knew it. "One day you're here," Ida had said, "the next day you're gone." *But which day?*

Becky tapped the steady blinking red button of the answering machine.

A beep, followed by a gravelly voice booming from the speaker. "Hello, my name's Terry. I'm calling from California. I'm trying to locate the family of a Second World War pilot named Peterson. Lloyd Peterson. He was an Army Air Force lieutenant. Flew P-38 fighters in New Guinea; went down in April '44. If this is the correct Peterson family, please contact me at the following number. I'll also give you my email address as well as my Facebook page if you prefer that." Becky listened to the rough voice rattle off numbers and an address. "Either way, please contact me if I've reached the right household. Thank you." The call ended. She hit the save button to store the message for later. *How odd*, she thought. *I wish him well. Right name. But there are a lot of Petersons in Minnesota phone books, especially around Upsala of all places.*

After re-checking the doors, she punched in the alarm code and slipped into bed. Buddy curled at her feet, his body heat warming her. In ten minutes she was asleep, her dog snoring softly on the thick quilt.

....

Chapter 8

At 2 a.m., Becky sat upright, her eyes wide open. Buddy awoke with a start, alarmed. "It's him!" she cried to the dog. Leaping from the bed, the big Lab began pacing rapidly beside the bed, its tail swatting the quilt. She patted the covers and the dog jumped into her lap, nuzzling her. "Why didn't I get it? The call, Buddy! Grandpa Lloyd Peterson! Lieutenant Lloyd Peterson! That call was about him!"

Throwing back the covers, she slipped out of bed, taking a flashlight from her nightstand. Reluctantly, the dog followed her down the stairs to the home's lower level. Two bedrooms and en suite bathrooms flanked a large tiled living room dominated by a fireplace sealed against the cold. French doors, etched in frost, looked out over a drift-filled deck and beyond that, the frozen lake. Becky opened a utility room door and hit a switch, bathing the room in blinding light. She attacked a pile of suitcases, snowshoes, and cardboard boxes shoved in a corner.

A small, dust-covered wood box sat under a fire marshal's nightmare of yellowing newspapers, paint cans, and carpet scraps. Becky wrestled the box onto an overturned wardrobe and blew a layer of fine dust from the top. Backing from the storage room, she ordered her dog from under her feet. "Back upstairs, Buddy. Good dog." She hit a switch, plunging the downstairs into blackness, and carried the box upstairs. Tossing a towel on the kitchen table, she gently placed the wooden box on top and wiped away the years of dust. Becky washed her hands at the sink, boiled water for tea, and, while it steeped, pulled a chair to the table. A pair of carved initials—LP—marred the wooden top. Slipping the tarnished brass clasp, she carefully lifted the lid to reveal a small gray felt bag, binoculars, a pair of aviator sunglasses in a chipped leather case, and several bundles of musty-smelling letters bound with frayed string.

All the envelopes were addressed to Mrs. Betty Peterson, Rural Route 1, Upsala, Minnesota. The return address on the top bundle was Lt. Lloyd Peterson, APO 471, Postmaster, San

Francisco, California. Becky pursed her lips in a low, reverent whistle. Though she held history in her hands and knew it, World War II was a fuzzy memory from some high school class she had suffered through. She set the letters aside, poured boiling water in a mug, added one bag, and returned to the table. The box yielded a collection of colorful ribbons attached to stars and a pair of dull pewter-colored wings. At the bottom of the box a slim, tattered green book, four inches square, lay hidden in the corner. On the cover, inked in strong, clear script, was the name "Lt. Lloyd Peterson" along with a serial number underneath.

Becky set down her mug and paged through the book, obviously a diary.

A brittle photo of a group of handsome young men in khakis, standing next to a plane's nose, fell from the pages along with a faded telegram of sympathy. She studied the earnest, anonymous faces. Words of the war department's wire were blunt and obtuse, the condolences sterile. She put it aside and picked up the photo to use as a bookmark. The journal's lined sheets, with dates at the top of each page, were covered in the same masculine scrawl as the cover.

Jan. 1 *Finally going to get our planes into action. Good! Thought we were going to sit out the war the way things were going. Saw Rippinger and Roger Herman. They came in yesterday. I've missed those two. Felt like the old man. Hot, humid all day like yesterday and probably tomorrow. How do people live in this place? Believe it or not, machines have a harder time. Japs tried to come by to welcome us but were shooed away by the boys. Would love to hold you tonight. Know you feel likewise. Love, L*

Jan. 9 *Two of our ships came back today shot up. Nobody hurt. Close call. Rumor is we'll get our turn this week. Can't wait. What did we train for? All the mechanics gripe about lack of spare parts. They patch everything. The natives aren't the only cannibals here. Ha, ha! Don't worry, just a joke. Miss you. Hope all is well. Take good care of my sweetheart. Love forever, L*

Becky went to the fireplace, added two birch logs, and gently blew on the embers, coaxing the fire to life. The flames licked hungrily at the fuel, warming the room. Wood siding popped in the cold and frost grew in the corner of the windows. She pulled her robe tighter and went back to her kitchen perch to read.

Jan. 12 *Place full of rumors. It's a local industry here. Nothing else to do. Big storms came through today. Had to repair our tents and bunks. What a rat's nest this becomes after too much rain. Ducks would love this. Wouldn't it be fun to be feeding ducks on Pine Lake right about now? Ha, ha, forgot, the lake is probably solid ice. Some of that cold air would feel pretty swell. So would a kiss from you. Love, your favorite earthbound lieutenant, L*

Buddy wandered into the room and sprawled under the table, keeping her company. Flipping open the diary to a page she had marked with the photo, Becky continued a young pilot's tale of loneliness, boredom, scotched missions, weather.

Feb. 20 *Got your wonderful news about our baby. Oh, my darling. Would trade a whole squadron for a weekend with you during this time. Miss you so much. You must take special care of yourself and the baby. Boy or girl, I don't care. We'll* *make up for it when this is all over. Want to be home, just the three of us. Love, L*

Feb. 25 *Still over the moon about our baby. Heavy downpour all morning and afternoon. Does it always rain like this? We'll need an ark soon if it keeps up. Place is a mud hole. Not healthy. Don't mean to sound so down, I'm not, after your wonderful news. What I would give to be home. Love you, little mother-to-be, L*

Fascinated, she kept on, her untouched tea growing cold beside her. Though nearly seventy years had passed, the tender thoughts and longing of a man for his wife touched her. She became part voyeur, part confidant, caught up in the writer's mixture of intimacy and thoughts about life at the edge of the world.

Mar. 1 *Wonderful day! Got three letters from you, darling. One from mother. She worries. She's not the trouper you are, sweetheart. Write and tell me if any of my letters come through. This will make interesting reading when we grow old together, don't you think? I miss you soooo much. Keep me in your prayers. You and our baby are always in mine. Love, Your L*

Mar. 9 *We're socked in. I plan on returning to read your earlier letters. Keeping them locked up. I've read each one a dozen times. Oh, I can't believe how much one person can miss another. All the married guys feel the same. Love you, L*

She read until a sliver of dawn announced morning in the windows. Despite the rosy sky, winter's long purple shadows still covered her tip of the lake. She quit reluctantly and repacked the box's contents. Carrying it to her bedroom, she cleared space for the wooden container on a shelf in her closet.

In the room's full-length mirror she studied a bedraggled image of herself. Brushing her dark brown hair from her forehead, she frowned at puffy eyes and pale winter skin. *Not a pretty picture, are you, Becky? You need a hot bath and more sleep. Crazy to stay up all night reading.* Sighing, she let her hair fall over her eyes. *I'll finish reading later today and maybe call that California guy Sunday night. Glad it's the weekend. I need the time off.* After letting her dog inside, she fell across the bed, exhausted.

Becky awoke refreshed despite only three hours of rest. Sunlight streamed through her bedroom window, bathing the room with warmth. At the foot of the bed, her dog stirred, lifting his big head to stare at her. She tousled his ears and slipped from the bed. Becky showered, dressed, and headed for the kitchen, diary in hand.

Two messages had come in while she was sleeping and she knew the source.

"How come you're not answering, babe? You don't have someone with you, do you? Hope not. Pick up the phone… okay?" She dumped the message and listened to a second one. "Becky, pick up the damn phone! I know you're there. What the hell? You haven't called me back. Don't be a bitch! Talk to me!"

She trashed that one as well.

Ten o'clock on a weekday morning—much too early for Darryl—and he was already off and running, in a blue mood. *Huh, how could I forget? The big baby's always whining.* She got a bagel, zapped it in the microwave, and ate while sitting on the couch, the diary in her lap. Brooding, she stared at the frozen lake. Darryl could wait until the afternoon, after he calmed. The next call would be his usual babbling apology tinged with intimidation. *Years of this and no end in sight*, she thought. *I have got to do something soon.*

Buddy followed her to the couch, chased his tail in a circle, and plopped down on a rug in front of the sofa. After settling a blanket over her legs, she continued reading. Two more boorish calls from Darryl came in but she ignored them. His voice had mellowed, as she knew it would. The last message was contrite and she told herself to return his calls before dinner. There was more diary to read.

> **Mar. 14** *Finally got my first kill. Caught a Zero on the other side of the mountains. Can't believe it! It was all training, start to finish. My Lightning is such a beautiful ship. One short burst and the Jap was a fireball. Too excited to think about him. Roger got one too—a Hamp. A great day! Love, L*

The boasting entry caught Becky off guard. She reread the passage, afraid she had misjudged Peterson but there was no mistaking the joy in what he had written.

> **Mar. 19** *You can be proud of me, sweetheart. We hit a flight of Japs making a strafing run on our boys on the deck. We scattered them and I got myself two! Another pair and I will be your own ace! Hugs, your L*

By the time she closed the book at March 26, Peterson had attained his coveted ace status, plus one. She put aside the journal, calls from Darryl on her mind. After four rings he picked up, mangling his greeting as usual. "Wha…huh. Yeah, whassup? Oh, her highness finally calls. Where the hell were you? You deaf, Becky? I left at least a dozen messages, you know."

She pressed her right hand against her temple. "I heard 'em.

I was busy. Figured I'd let you blow off some steam before I called you back."

An angry rattle came back at her. "Yeah, well, you figured wrong. What the hell is it with you? A man can't call his wife? You ain't working every day. You can pick up the damn phone."

"Ex-wife, Darryl. Whadaya want?"

"I want to see you, babe. Talk. Work some things out."

"We have nothing to work out right now. I told you, I need time, space."

"What's with that time and space bullshit?"

"I'm thinking things out, Darryl. You know that. We agreed."

"Agreed, my ass! You're the one who wanted a divorce, not me!"

She took a deep breath, gazed at the lake framed in the window. "I know. You have to be patient. Give me…us…some more…time. We can work this out."

Resignation mixed with anger poured through the receiver. "Well, damn, I don't know what you're doing out there by yourself. You don't need six years to make up your mind. That's a helluva long time, Becky."

She soothed him with another of her delaying tactics. "Maybe we can talk next weekend. I'm off Saturday. We can meet at Bullfrogs in the afternoon for drinks." A risky step but she won the round. He backed off immediately. "Oh, yeah? Okay, if that's what you want."

"Yeah, I think that would be good. Just to talk over some things."

"Okay. You gonna call me then?"

"Sure. I can do that. I'll call you."

"Right." His voice dripped syrup. "See you next Saturday. Love you, babe."

Becky stayed neutral. "Sure, Darryl. I know. Goodbye." Hanging up before he had a chance to answer, she rang off, put her head in her hands, and wept.

....

Chapter 9

December 13

With Buddy at her side, Becky took a long, cleansing walk halfway around the lake. Cold air bit at her hooded face as she pounded along the gravel road, clearing her mind of Darryl's depressing phone calls. She turned back, letting Buddy run ahead of her through the tree line to the house.

Dusk arrived, and with it snow squalls filling the air with sparkling ice crystals that made the security light on a pole in the yard glow. Shadows sent long blue fingers through the surrounding woods as the sun died.

Dinner was a hurried affair: hot soup and bread. Comfort food. Buddy padded out, only to scurry back to the warm house after a few hurried moments in a snow bank. Becky built another fire and drew a hot bath to pamper herself. Soaking in the tub relieved the day's anxiety and she stayed until the water turned tepid. Afterward, she stoked the fire and doused all lights save one by the couch where she cocooned herself in a wool blanket to read the last few pages of Lieutenant Peterson's diary.

> **Mar. 28** *Might move our squadron up the coast. Japs are cornered but still dangerous. Some of us sat down with Tom McGuire, one of our top aces. You've probably read about him.*

He and Dick Bong are swell guys. Bong's from Poplar, Wisconsin. Both of them are great shots. McGuire cranky but full of good advice. I'm at seven kills, looking for my eighth...and more. Tell me about your doctor visits. I want all the details. I miss you, Love, L

April 9 *Feeling blue. We have orders to return to Port Moresyb tomorrow. Rippinger, Lane, Roger and me. Some special mission. Why us? Hunting slim on the coast. Not enough Japs to go around. Never thought I'd hear myself say that. Don't know what they have for us. Everyone sore about Port Moresby. Missing you, L*

Becky got up, threw more wood on dying flames, poked in the glowing coals to keep the fire going, and heated yesterday's tea. Returning to the couch, mug in hand, Becky scanned the diary's last three entries. After that the pages were blank. She picked up where she had left off, the picture of the pilots marking her place.

April 11 *We got a hush-hush welcome yesterday. We now have bunks with real sheets. I could get used to this life. Forgot how nice it felt. Earlier we had a briefing with the Old Man himself—Gen. Kenney. Turns out he selected us because we're aces! We're to escort a C-47 to Nadzab. They want the usual four-plane formation. SOP—we don't go up without four of us. Safety in numbers. We're to leave tomorrow but weather not looking good. That's the way it works here. Weather first. Cargo plane crew are nice guys, isolated along with us from others. Pretty special, huh? Unfortunately, we get the same chow. Not like yours. Love, L*

April 13 *Socked in. Supposed to be the coming dry season. Ha! Got to know the C-47 crew. Played cards. Shared a bottle with a lieutenant. Can't believe this, sweetheart. They are loaded with crates of ammo, clothing, machetes, tarps, rations, building supplies and a half-ton of gold! Shouldn't put this on paper. It's too fantastic. 1,000 pounds of gold. He showed me one of the small gold bars they're shipping. Made a sketch. I'm no artist but this is close to what they look like. Bars packed in sawdust, inside ammo cans. Lashed to the floor. Took me on board and gave me a look. Both of us a bit tipsy. Shouldn't have done it. Pray for me, love, L*

Leaning toward the lamp, Becky brought the book inches from her nose and read the entry again. *A half-ton of gold? Why would they ship gold in the middle of a war?* Peterson's simple sketch showed a small bar the size of a stick of gum, only slightly thicker. Jotted measurements on the drawing read two and one half inches long by one inch wide. Each bar, he had written, weighed two ounces. A hastily scribbled footnote indicated a small eagle and "U.S." stamped on one end of the bars. *A half-ton of gold? And why,* she wondered, *pen this in his diary? Was he allowed to do this? Wouldn't this be top secret?* Lowering the small green book, she stared into the flickering flames, smiling, trying to imagine what a thousand pounds of gold would look like. *How many tiny bars is that? How big a pile would that be?* Putting aside the thoughts, she finished reading.

April 15 *We go at dawn. Can't sleep. Talked with that lieut. this morning. He's scared to death about showing me the stuff. Promised to keep my mouth shut. Don't want my career to end because of this. Wish I had refused his "tour" but it's too*

> *late now. See what I get for being a nice guy? I'll keep these notes separate in case I get called on the carpet. Hope no one finds out. My fault. I'm wiser now, I hope. OK, clouds clearing. We leave in one hour. I'd rather hunt Japs than play nursemaid to a cargo plane loaded with you-know-what. Just following orders. Want to put this behind me and find myself back in your arms once again. I am so lonely for you and baby. Love flying, but miss you more. XXXXX, L*

The remaining pages were blank. Closing the diary, Becky ran her hands over the cover, smoothing the wrinkled linen as she stared at the smoldering fire. *Now the call from California made sense. Or did it? Did the caller know about the gold? He hadn't mentioned it. He was looking for family members for Lieutenant Lloyd Peterson, nothing more. Or was he? Was that all there was to it? Only one way to find out what the mysterious caller wanted. Phone him tomorrow and confirm the identity of First Lieutenant Lloyd Peterson.*

Whistling Buddy to her side, she shuffled down the hall to her bedroom, pinning the wartime diary to her breast. She slipped into bed, tucked the journal under her pillow, and drifted into deep sleep, pictures of small gold bars tumbling end over end, filling her dreams.

• • • • • • • • •

Chapter 10

In the morning, Becky walked her dog through the woods to her neighbor's. She spent several minutes next door chatting with Judy Soderlund before heading back home. Light snow drifted down through the bare trees, the morning air frigid. Coaxing the Honda into life took ten minutes. She went south on the newly plowed road, winding along the west side of Pine Lake until she picked up Highway 238. She drove through Upsala, automatically glancing behind her as if expecting Darryl's pickup to appear in her wake, tailing her. Town was buttoned up and she found herself alone on the road. In ten minutes, she was in the outskirts of Albany. Weekend traffic was light. Turning right on Railroad Avenue, she went one block, turned left on Second Street, and crossed the Lake Wobegon Trail, a bike path buried in snow on both sides of the cleared road. On her left, early mass was letting out of the massive brick Catholic church. Ahead of her was the entrance of Mother of Mercy, a nursing home and rehabilitation center. Becky parked and made her way to the front door where she signed in before heading for the second floor—the long-term care unit. After greeting familiar faces at the nurses' station, she went down the tiled hallway to a room at the end. An aide, a slight, pale blonde in her 20s, met her in the doorway, her arms filled with used linens. Becky stood aside and greeted her warmly. "Hello, Abby."

"Morning, Becky."

"How is she today?"

"Resting." After dumping the linens in a canvas bin, the aide added, "She just got back from morning therapy. They worked her over pretty hard. She's tired."

Leaning into the doorway, Becky asked over her shoulder, "Sleeping?"

"Just drifted off. It's okay if you wake her. She'll know your voice."

In the room, two beds, parallel to each other, took up most of the available space. Heavy, high-backed vinyl chairs, both empty, faced the foot of the beds. The one closest to the door was stripped to its plastic-covered mattress, a curtain drawn down the middle of the shared room. Morning sunlight poured through a window.

Nodding at the aide, Becky put a finger to her lips and slipped into the room. On the bed next to the window lay a sleeping woman, thin beige quilt drawn to her chin, both legs encased in soft walking casts. Lowering herself into the empty chair, Becky quietly took up a post at the end of the bed. The dozing woman shifted beneath her covers, opened her eyes.

"It's Becky. I'm here."

A slow rustling under the sheets. "I don't…see you."

Rising from her chair, the younger woman squeezed between the wall and the bed, lowered the safety rail, and reached for a frail outstretched hand. Hovering over the patient, Becky gently stroked the woman's forehead. Breaking into a smile, the prone woman groped for words. "Tired," she wheezed. "Too tired…to sit up."

"Don't worry about it," soothed Becky. "I hear they put you through a lot of hoops today. But they said you're getting stronger each day."

A quick knowing smile acknowledged the comment. A moment went by without further response. Then five minutes passed and sleep overtook the woman in the bed. Becky drew a heart with her name and the date on a white board on the wall. A nurse padded into the room, nodded at Becky, and busied herself with checking her patient's vitals. "She's actually better than she looks right now," she whispered. "Her therapists have increased her regimen. She's doing quite well considering."

"Any idea of..."

Interrupting, the nurse gave her stock answer. "When she'll come home? No timetable on that, I'm afraid. But you have to have hope. Barbara's strong. A fighter. She'll be dancing before the end of summer. You'll see."

Becky kissed the sleeping woman's forehead. "I'll be back on Sunday, Barbara. I'll come after lunch."

The nurse raised the bed a few inches, adjusted the pillows, and raised the guardrail nearest the wall. She followed Becky into the hall and chatted as they headed to the nurses' station. Becky took the stairs.

....

Chapter 11

December 15

For an hour Becky sat staring at the phone. More than once she picked up the receiver, started to dial the number in California only to pause and hang up. Next to the phone, Lloyd Peterson's war diary lay opened to the first page. Propped against the answering machine was the faded wartime photo of the Lightning pilots.

Earlier, Becky had composed an email but for some reason had not sent it, deciding instead to hear the man's explanation firsthand. *You're just nervous*, she told herself.

At her feet, Buddy rolled on his back, staring at her, begging for a tummy rub. "You're thinking, why don't I call, right?" The big Lab yawned, swatted the rug several times with its tail, and rolled again to resume its nap, oblivious to its owner's plight. "This is crazy," mumbled Becky. Holding the receiver, she read the numbers, punched the buttons, and sat back.

After five rings a deep, growling voice answered. "Morning, Terry here."

She froze. The gravely voice repeated the greeting. "Hello? Terry here."

"Uh, this is…this is Becky…Becky Peterson returning your call."

"Say again. Who is this?"

"Becky…from Minnesota. You left a message about Lt. Lloyd Peterson. You know, something about finding his plane in New Guinea."

The voice in the receiver came to life. "Oh, of course. Forgive me. I was in the middle of something else when you phoned."

"I can call back on Monday if you'd like."

"No, no. You're good. Let me pull up some information, Miss…"

"Becky…ah…Becky Peterson."

Papers rustled in her ear. Loud tapping on a keyboard as she waited.

"Okay, sorry about that, Becky. Thanks for returning my call. Let's see, you live in…Help me here."

"Upsala," she said.

The man mangled the town's name and she repeated it twice.

"Got it, thanks."

"What's this about?" she asked. "The reason for your call, I mean?"

"This will sound a little bizarre so stay with me, okay? A missionary I know in Papua New Guinea contacted me, emailed me about finding a plane in the jungle there. After comparing some things in my database, cross-referencing information in my files, and doing some other noodling around, I narrowed down the search. Got lucky. Squadron records had a hometown listed. Started calling all the Petersons listed up there. Had a couple of dead ends. Only had three people call me back to take themselves out of the running."

"There are a lot of Petersons in this state."

"So I've learned." The voice paused. "Upsala looks tiny, Becky. Classic American small town, huh?"

"Yeah, it's not very big. Maybe four hundred people. We like to joke the size of Upsala depends on which end of town you enter."

"Real Norman Rockwell, huh?"

"Who?"

"Uh, never mind. Anyway, once I pinned down the aircraft and the right name I kept going. And, I may not have mentioned it, but there may be...and I emphasize may be...some remains at the wreck site. This missionary fellow is going to try and get back there. He told me there's apparently another plane nearby. Said it was a big plane."

The comment made her sit up. "Really? What kind of plane?"

"Not sure yet. Could be a bomber or a transport."

"Is it what they called a C-47?"

A smile crept into the man's voice. "You've been doing some reading."

"Yeah. I have a diary."

"Well, that's a precious find. You've obviously paged through it."

The big Lab stirred under the table, rose to rest its muzzle in Becky's lap. She stroked the dog's head. "Yes, I didn't know much about the war but I dug around, found a diary after your call. Spent a couple of nights reading. A lot of it's boring."

A rough laugh erupted on the other end of the line. "I've read enough of those. I know what you're talking about. It wasn't all about shooting, you know."

"He mentioned lots of planes. I remember the C-47 being one of them. Could that be the other plane the missionary found near my grandfather's?"

"Maybe. He'll have to go back to confirm it."

"Well, what should I do now that you've called? Do I have to do something legally? I mean, his wife Betty—well, his widow really—remarried after the war. She died in 2003. They had a daughter, Barbara. She's still alive but in a nursing home recovering from a bad car wreck."

"Sorry to hear that, Becky. Maybe she'd like to know about her father's airplane being found. But only if she's up to it at some point. It brings closure to most people. Sometimes it comes as a shock after all those years. Wouldn't want to be the bearer of bad news. Know what I mean?"

Nodding, Becky added, "I understand. She's not really with it right now. Maybe someday. But she's got a long way to go before she can come home."

"How old is your mother, if I may ask."

"My mother? Oh, Barbara is…she was born in '44."

"And you?"

"I'm 35."

"You sound a lot younger."

"People say that."

"I'm not surprised. Look, if you'd like, I'll email you information about your grandfather's outfit, his plane, what his service record looks like. Maybe I can find some abbreviated history for you."

"Sure, I'd like that. Do folks go to New Guinea to visit these wreck sites?"

"Absolutely. There are groups that do that. It's part history, part tourism. Haven't made the trip myself but I've worked with folks who have."

"Like this missionary?"

"Well, that's different. He lives there, ministers to the people in the hills. But I can email you some of the websites for these search groups if you'd like."

Becky leaned back, the dog by her side begging for more attention. "Thanks. I think that might be interesting."

"There used to be a search outfit right there in Minnesota, you know."

Curious, she poised a pen over a note pad. "I didn't know that. Do they make those trips often?"

"They used to. The founder moved to Florida but you can check their website. Got a pen and paper?" She told him yes and scribbled the information. After trading small talk about the advantages of California's weather versus Minnesota's they finished the call with a promise to stay in touch.

That wasn't so hard, she told herself. *Yes, I have been doing some reading. Some of it very interesting.*

....

Chapter 12

With all the enthusiasm of a condemned woman, Becky crossed the newly cleared parking lot between the supermarket and Bullfrogs, the bar where Darryl waited. Despite her down vest and wool cap, the afternoon's damp cold seeped into her bones. Great depressing mounds of gritty plowed snow crowded the gravel lot, reminding her of prison walls in old movies. Bullfrogs was a classic Midwest rural bar—a long, utilitarian, one-level metal shed that in another life might as easily have been a two-lane bowling alley, storage facility for farm equipment, or a hog barn. Only the Old Milwaukee and Miller Lite signs on its sides hinted at its real use. Four pickups, a van, two snowmobiles, and Darryl's pathetic white Toyota with crumpled front fender sat next to the building.

Becky pictured Darryl ensconced in his favorite corner booth from which he could survey the bar's lone pool table, hurling snarky comments at missed shots "a blind man could make!" Burrowed in like a snarling ferret in its den, his back to the paneled wall, Darryl would have a forest of empty beer bottles lined up in front of him by now. He would have commandeered the jukebox just inside the door, next to the electronic dartboard and the big chest freezer. Having jammed several dollars worth of quarters into the machine, he'd be cycling the playlist through his favorites: sappy, tear-jerking, heart-breaking country ballads alternated with screaming heavy metal standards.

Knowing all this, Becky had still agreed to meet. Theirs was an odd bargain. Paying attention to Darryl assuaged him, gave Becky the right to hold him at bay, to delay what he wanted most and she wouldn't give—a reconciliation. With Darryl, the risk of eruption was always there, but so was the reward of trading a couple hours for her right to more time and distance. Today her goal was to buy time.

Resigned, Becky sighed wearily, stamped snow from her boots, and went inside, trailing a blast of arctic air. Standing in the entry, she faced the familiar mirrored wall of off-sale liquor shelved behind a long Formica counter. The bar had the usual stools and neon beer signs; there was a pair of taps handles by the register and an army of booze bottles lined up like soldiers. Flat-screen TVs hung on walls everywhere, playing muted news or sports. A mummified retired farmer in greasy overalls and a crumpled seed cap sat at the end of the counter nursing a beer. He tipped his hat at her in the mirror and got a bored stare in return.

The bartender, a burly, bearded, former high school football star in a red plaid shirt, put down his Sudoku puzzle to greet her. Becky waved, her mouthed hello drowned out by Aerosmith screeching from the speakers. A knowing tilt of the server's head toward the back of the main room prompted Becky to peek around a floor-to-ceiling partition built as a windbreak. Square pub tables draped in red and white checked tablecloths took up the front half of the long room, five booths and the pool table the rest of the space. Three of the tables were occupied; the booths were empty except for the last one.

From the corner, Darryl's watery eyes locked on hers. Hoisting a bottle, he beckoned. Shrugging in sympathy, the bartender went back to his puzzle, the farmer to his beer, and Becky to the last booth. Willie began crooning "Blue Eyes in the Rain" as she approached.

Darryl was drunk. Short of courtesy as always, he remained seated, slurring his words. "Hey, baby, whadaya drinking?"

"Hey, Darryl." She slid into the seat opposite him. "I'll have one of those."

"Don't bother your pretty self. Lemme get it for you." Grasping the table's edge with no little effort, he belched, pulled himself from the booth, standing unsteadily. Leaning over her, he planted a sloppy, beery kiss on the top of her head before staggering off. She turned, watched him weave toward the bar then abruptly take an exaggerated right turn, hurrying with mincing steps into the narrow corridor where the bathrooms were. Two florid-faced snowmobilers sat at a pub table, stuffing popcorn in their mouths, smirking at the floorshow.

Darryl returned to the booth empty-handed and flopped down. “Oh, shit, babe. Forgot your beer.”

“It’s okay, I got one myself,” she lied, holding one of his empties aloft.

“Oh, okay. Wanna nother?”

“Not finished with this one yet. You wanted to talk, remember?”

“What about?”

“Us,” she answered. “You called, said you wanted to talk about…us. I agreed to meet you.”

Gazing at the red tiled floor, confused, his face darkened as if the act of thinking hurt. “Oh, yeah, right. Uh…what about us?”

Regretting mentioning the reason for meeting, Becky tried steering the conversation in another direction. “Visited Barbara today. Her nurses think she might be able to come home in a couple of months.”

Feigning interest, he said, “Oh, that’s a good thing, right? Hey, you wanna beer or sumpin’?”

“Nah, I’m good. You can if you want.”

Darryl didn’t answer. His head dropped to his chest; his eyes closed and he began to snore softly. Becky kept talking, gradually shifting to a monotone then lowering her voice until she was whispering. Easing slowly from the booth, Becky stood over Darryl, gazing down at the snoring man. In his condition he didn’t seem so threatening. Mercurial maybe, but certainly not threatening, maybe even amusing in a way. *Don’t kid yourself, he’s hasn’t changed one bit. He’s just drunk. When he awakes he’ll return to form. He always does. Count on it.* Becky backed from the booth, turned, and marched to the door past the buzzed snowmobilers and grizzled regulars. “I’ll see him home when I close, Becky,” said the bartender without looking up, his eyes glued to his puzzle.

"Thanks, I know he'd appreciate it." She went out into a cold, starry night, reprieved, a different woman from the one who had come in.

"Man can't hold his liquor," wheezed the farmer on the bar stool as Becky passed. "What the hell kinda man is that I ask you?"

"Refill?" asked the bartender, working his eraser yet again.

"Damn straight," barked the wrinkled face in the mirror, sliding the empty glass across the bar.

....

Chapter 13

Maple Grove, Minnesota, January 6

Being early came naturally to Dale Morris—an old habit from the service. Arriving fifteen minutes ahead of time at a chain restaurant on the northwestern edge of the Twin Cities, he sat in his truck watching a parade of diners come and go. The popular eatery was just off I-94 in a complex of shops—a halfway point where Becky had suggested they meet.

Ten minutes passed with no sign of the woman. Morris got out of his truck and headed for the restaurant. Six feet tall, broad shouldered with a thick thatch of gray hair, Morris carried forty extra pounds over his wartime weight of 145, most of it muscle. Dressed in work boots, jeans, and heavy jacket, Morris looked more like a construction boss than a retired military pilot. Walking briskly in the cold, he trailed a young couple into the restaurant.

A beaming hostess spotted him. "Mr. Morris?" she said hopefully. Wary, he nodded. "Please follow me." Obediently, he trailed her to a corner booth where a pony-tailed woman in a leather jacket sat sipping a draft beer. She radiated confidence with just a touch of wariness.

"Miss Peterson?" he asked hesitatingly.

The woman offered her hand. "Becky, please. You must be Dale Morris."

"I am." Removing his coat, he sat. "You got here first. I'm impressed."

"Didn't want to be late. Sorry to get you out on a night like this. Cannon Falls is a long way from here."

"No problem. You had a long drive yourself. From St. Cloud, right?"

"Yes, but the roads were dry."

"I came because I was curious about why you called. That, and I prefer putting faces with a voice and a name."

"So do I," she shot back. "Do I fit the image you had in mind?"

"Wasn't sure," he mumbled. "You sure look a helluva lot more grown up than I expected. I mean in a good way, of course. I mean, your voice sounded so young."

"I've heard that since I was a kid. I take it as a compliment."

"It was meant to be one." A grinning waiter scooted to their booth and Morris rattled off a drink order, then buried his nose in the menu. "How did you find me?" he said without looking.

"I went online to find groups that search for missing airplanes in New Guinea. I don't know if you're aware of this, but there are a lot of them."

Morris snorted, put the menu down. "I know most of them. But keep in mind not all search groups are created equal."

"I found one called MIA Hunters. I emailed the guy who started it."

"Bryan Moon?"

"That's him. He's moved to Florida. Said the last time he took a big group was back in 2010."

"I know. He probably also told you it's a young man's game. Wouldn't know it from the folks who went with him. Most of the people were older...like me. I did two missions with Bryan. Didn't make his last one though."

"How come?"

"Couldn't fit it into my schedule at the time. My wife and I were busy planning our dream house in Ft. Myers, Florida. It was her idea. She's a Florida girl. Turns out while I worked on the house, she was building a divorce. She waited until after the house was finished...and furnished. We tangled in court. A blind man coulda seen that coming; not me, though."

"Sorry to hear about your divorce. Anyway, Mr. Moon gave me several names of people here in Minnesota, yours among them. Said you might be helpful. I googled you. Saw your photos of the 2008 trip. Impressive."

Morris shrugged. "You're lucky you caught me. I'm selling my house and heading south as soon as I can. No more winters for me."

"Hard to beat Minnesota for summer and fall."

"There is that. But I've got friends in Jacksonville who are putting together a nice condo development on the St. Johns River despite the economy. I'm a silent partner in the project. They're optimists, as am I. It's a safe bet I won't be doing any ice fishing AND I'll be on the opposite coast from my ex. That's gotta be a plus. Okay, enough of my lonely hearts profile. Back to the business at hand. You called me and now we're sitting here having dinner. You were a little bit vague on the phone. What exactly did you have in mind?"

Digging in her purse, Becky produced a picture of smiling airmen clustered around a big twin-engine fighter and handed it to Morris. "I want to find my grandfather." Taking the yellowed photo, Morris turned it reverently in his hands. Reading the faded penciled lines on the back, he asked. "Which one's your grandfather?"

"Standing on the right, holding one of the propellers."

"He's probably what…about twenty-three or -four, huh?" An agreeing nod from across the table. Smiling in admiration, Morris said softly, "Boy, they were so young. So cocky. So damn good at what they did. Hell, Dick Bong was twenty-five when he died."

"I'm sorry, who's Dick Bong?"

"Top ace from your grandfather's war. Forty kills. Probably a lot more. Flew a Lightning in the Pacific. Back when your granddad was flying." He handed back the faded picture and folded his hands in front of him. "If what you said on the phone is true—that his plane's been found…"

"It's true," she interrupted excitedly. "A missionary found it. A guy from California named Terry called me to confirm it. He's done all the research about it. Apparently, he's an expert about these kinds of things. And he knows Bryan Moon."

When his drink arrived Morris motioned for Becky to order, then did the same. When their server left, he resumed talking. "First things first, Becky. Just so you know, I'm not looking for another trip overseas right now. Been there, done that. I'm here strictly as a courtesy call to learn about who you are and what you want. I'm being up front with you, okay?"

"I understand completely."

"Okay. With that out of the way, let's say that what this missionary claims to have found really does turn out to be your grandfather's plane. It's no picnic to go into the jungle over there and find wreck sites that are almost seventy years old."

"I know. But don't they have GPS locations and everything?"

"It's still a crap shoot to know exactly where a plane went

down; getting there is another thing. You have any idea what kind of terrain we're talking about?"

"I was told it's pretty rugged."

A low whistle escaped Morris's lips. "Rugged is an understatement. There are places so remote you'd need a chopper to get in and out."

"They have helicopters there?"

"Sure. Most of them are based out of Lae, Goroka, or Port Moresby. Those jockeys really know their stuff. They know the hills and jungle like the back of their hands."

Becky asked, "Why do they need helicopters?"

"I told you. They can get into spots where it's impossible to land a fixed wing aircraft. Everything from sightseeing to construction, mining, missions, and medical. Those eggbeater boys know what they're doing. No offense, Becky, but just how old are you exactly?"

"Thirty-five."

Running a hand through his gray hair, Morris chuckled. "Geez, I'm having dinner with someone young enough to be my daughter. Now don't take this the wrong way and don't give me any of that politically correct feminist crap, but you look to be in pretty good physical shape."

"I jog some, walk a lot. I quit smoking long ago. I don't drink any hard stuff."

"All in your favor. Shame about the drinking though."

"I'm serious about this, Mr. Morris."

Softening, Morris studied the woman across from him. "Call me Dale. And that was a joke about the drinking. You do seem determined."

Morris resumed his questioning. "Be honest. How much do you really know about Papua New Guinea?"

"Not much," admitted Becky. "Well, actually, pretty much nothing."

"No shame there. I doubt most Americans could find it on a map. Hell, even the natives there couldn't find it on a map if you asked them. And they're standing on it." The two laughed.

"I know it's somewhere near Australia," she offered eagerly.

"You're close." Plucking a marker from his shirt pocket, Morris sketched on a napkin. In quick strokes he outlined Australia and the big island north of it. "This is Papua New Guinea," he said. "Used to be called New Guinea." He drew a dotted line down the middle of the ragged isle. "These days the west half is Papua, part of Indonesia. It's Muslim. Used to be called Irian Jaya. The eastern half is Christian, Papua New Guinea. Missionaries have been hard at work there since the 1880s." Rotating the napkin, he pushed it at her. "Oh, yeah, the people are animists too, but mostly Christian."

"Animists?"

"They worship nature spirits. Ancestors, stuff like that. That and go to church."

Becky studied the napkin, then put it down. "I can do some reading about the country. New Guinea, I mean."

"Papua New Guinea," he corrected her. "PNG for short. Even in the third world, it's a two-point-zero country. People there are lovable but poor as church mice. Some say it's Australia's basket case. So, tell me what you know about your grandfather's war. What exactly did they teach you in school?"

"I wasn't much of a history student. It always kinda bored me."

"Huh," grumped Morris. "You must have had a lousy teacher. Boring it's not. History's a great way to understand how the world works." Weaving his hands in the air, Morris gave a six-minute summary of the Pacific war. When finished, he sat back to gauge her reaction but the woman was hard to read. His tutorial seemed to have floated right past her. "Do not pass Go," he clucked. "Do not collect $200. You've got some studying to do, Missy. You can't expect to go half way around the world without knowing the history of the war or the why of it."

She flashed a rueful smile and glanced away, embarrassed. "Maybe I should have paid more attention, huh?"

Morris nodded. "Yes, you should have. But now you're older and hopefully wiser. Time's a'wasting. You'll have to play catch-up. Make up for those years the locusts have eaten." He produced a scrap of notepaper. "I took the liberty of making you a list of books you might want to read before making up your mind." Holding up a hand to cut off a reply, Morris added, "I know, I know, you're set on going. But you have to do some soul-searching. Best start with the history there."

Becky eyed the list. "Do all the people you take with you have to do this?"

"Most of the folks I've gone with," he scolded, "paid attention in history class. They know this stuff. It's second nature to them." Leaning forward, Morris locked eyes with her. "It's why they want to go there in the first place. It's holy ground."

She leaned back, wary. "That sounds a bit…I don't know… intense."

Letting the comment pass, Morris explained. "It can sound that way. But it's kinda like visiting Gettysburg. You're familiar with that, I'm sure."

She shook her head. "Vaguely." Another failure from her high school years.

Morris lectured. "When you read the history of that battle the ground comes alive for you. It's the same for Papua New Guinea. You'll see."

Grasping at his comment, she brightened. "Does that mean you'll take me there?" Smiling paternally, he pointed at his list of suggested reading. "Before I'd even start thinking about being part of this you have to study those. After that we can talk seriously about going, not before. Feel free to find someone else if you like. Bryan gave you other names. All good men, I'm sure. But this is the way I operate. You still game?" Scanning the note, she nodded in agreement.

Their food arrived and they ate in silence for ten minutes.

"I have a diary my grandfather kept," she offered later, between bites.

Morris paused, intrigued. "Really. Have you read it?"

"Yeah. Some interesting things in it. Mostly about how bored he was. How he missed his wife. How lousy the weather was."

Laughing, Morris spoke through a mouthful of burger. "Oh, it surely is. Did he write about how hot and humid it was? About the rain?"

"Mostly about the rain. How he kept getting flooded out of his tent."

"That's Papua New Guinea for you." He stopped chewing. "I'd like to take a look at that diary if you're willing."

Becky looked down at her plate. "Uh, well, sure. I guess I could copy the pages and send them to you if you'd like."

"Do that. You have my address." At the end of the meal, Morris signaled for the check, paying over Becky's protest. "Not kosher to have a lady pay on the first date." Embarrassed, she laughed. They finished their drinks, got refills, and declined dessert. Out of questions, he invited hers.

"How did you get involved in all of this MIA stuff?" she asked.

"In the interest of time I'll give you the short version. I was air force. Flew Skyraiders in Vietnam." Cocking an eyebrow, Morris teased. "Did they teach you anything about that in high school?"

"Vietnam?"

"Yeah," he shot back. "Vietnam. You know, ancient history."

"We had a veteran come talk to our class once. I know a little about it."

Rolling his eyes, Morris grimaced. "Public education, it's a wonderful thing to behold. Okay, here's the short version. I drove an A-1E Skyraider. It's a prop plane." He fluttered both hands at her. "You know, propellers. We called it a Spad. Carried a big payload. Four cannon and 8,000 pounds of hardware. Brought a world of hurt to the bad guys. I loved it, I truly did. Kinda like what your grandpa and his buddies did with their P-38s." Furrowing his brow, Morris lowered his voice. "Got shot down in 1971 near the Cambodian border. Not pleasant for a former Boy Scout to wander in the woods for a day like that. I'm not ashamed to say I asked God to get me out of there. Promised I would do something noble if I was rescued."

Morris slapped his hands on the table, startling his companion. "Damned if a Jolly Green Giant didn't appear from heaven and pluck me out of that jungle hell. I was so damned thankful. Once I got out of the service I spent the next thirty-five years doing things to hold up my end of the bargain. Then one night at an American Legion dinner in Rochester, I heard Bryan Moon talk about his MIA Hunters."

Raising his arms, Morris exulted. "That was perfect! I was between projects. Looking for those missing pilots and planes from that war was a good fit. I had some of the necessary skills, so I signed on and did a couple of missions. End of story." Becky was motionless, her eyes glued on Morris. "Course that's the short version. Give me a campfire and good whiskey and I just might give you the long version." Laughing, Morris threw a last verbal jab at her. "Of course, if you had paid more attention in class you would know the long version."

Blushing at the reminder, Becky sank back in the booth.

"Just kidding. C'mon," directed Morris, "let's blow this joint, Missy."

He tossed a tip on the table. Rising together, the pair made their way outside.

"Don't forget your reading assignment," admonished Morris in the parking lot. "Take a few weeks. Call if you're still interested. No guarantees. We'll talk."

Holding the paper aloft in the frigid air, she promised, "Library tomorrow."

They shook hands. He got into his pickup, waved, and was gone. Pocketing the book list, Becky slipped into her rusting Honda and let it warm. She headed home, confident her meeting with Dale Morris had gone well.

Her next task, besides the reading assignment, wouldn't be as easy—convincing the Lindquists to join the expedition. To succeed, her cobbled-together plan depended on a pair of strong backs to carry the gold once she found it. She couldn't risk strangers. No, she needed both brothers to accompany her to New Guinea. "Papua New Guinea," she corrected herself aloud a half-dozen times as she drove west.

....

Chapter 14

St. Cloud, Minnesota, two weeks later

The books on Dale Morris' reading list devoured Becky's evenings. Her disdain for history during her school years vanished, replaced by a newfound curiosity about the Pacific war's New Guinea campaign. A second read of Lloyd Peterson's war diary renewed her determination to find the missing treasure.

On a Friday, Becky drove through Upsala to Albany, picked up I-94, and headed southeast toward St. Cloud, pushing the ancient Honda as fast as she dared. Twenty minutes later, she exited on Highway 15, took a right on Division Street up to Thirty-third Street, and turned into a mini-mall's lot. She parked at a UPS Store.

In the shop, she filled out paperwork for a rental mailbox and paid a six-month fee. "I'm new in town, just renting an apartment for now," she told the clerk at the register. With keys to her new mailbox in her pocket, she drove a few blocks and stopped in front of a Granite City franchise. David Lindquist's pickup parked in the lot meant he was likely working. The noon rush hour had peaked. With the exception of a few lingering couples, the place was nearly deserted. Friday's happy hour was still four hours away. She got a corner booth, ordered a bruschetta salad and a Diet Coke.

"Is David on duty?" she asked her server.

He was.

"I'd like to see him. Would you tell him his sister-in-law is here?"

When her food was delivered, Lindquist showed and dropped down across from her. He was dressed business casual: dark slacks, shirt and tie, brass nametag pinned to a pocket. Lean like his younger brother, but taller, David's brown hair was short, flecked with gray. A lopsided smile showed uneven teeth in a small mouth. There was a hint of menace about him she had always found attractive, still did.

"You want anything, David?" asked the waitress.

"A tonic water with a twist of lime, please." The server headed for the bar.

"Tonic water and lime? Not the David Lindquist I know."

"I'm working." The crooked smile flashed. "Hey, Becky,

always nice to see you. You're looking as foxy as usual. What brings you to town? Please don't tell me my brother's done something stupid again."

"Nah, he's cool…for now." She sipped her cola, stabbed at her salad. "I've got a proposal for you, David. Something…different. Pretty exciting, really."

His drink arrived and he sent the server on her way with a wink, and then turned to Becky, his voice silky. "Haven't seen much of you lately," he said. "Where you been keeping your beautiful outrageous self?"

Ignoring his remark, she arched an eyebrow. "Hear anything I just said?"

He sipped his drink, fished out the scrap of lime, and nibbled. "Sure, I heard you. A proposal. Different. Exciting. What? You gonna tell me you got religion? Or are you pushing Amway?"

"None of that," she laughed. "It's about Grandpa Peterson."

Pushing his drink aside, Lindquist leaned forward. "What? You found a will and it says he left you the lake house after all?"

"Be serious, will ya?"

"Okay. You got smart. You're moving somewhere where that asshole brother of mine can't find you."

She sank back. "Ugh, don't I wish. Nothing like that. But I do want to set up a meeting with him, the three of us."

"Oh, I don't know about that. Remember the last time we got together? It didn't go well, or did you forget that night?"

"Hard to do. No, I haven't forgotten." She reached across the table, put a hand on his arm, and left it there. "If you hadn't been there he probably would have killed me. I owe you, David."

"What did you expect him to do? He's always been jealous. Besides, no guy wants to hear his wife tell him she's divorcing him. Wants her space, or some feminist crap like that. You sandbagged me on that. I coulda used a head's up, you know."

Becky withdrew her hand, stared at her salad. "Sorry about that. I thought Darryl would listen to his big brother. You're the only one he'll talk to, you know."

A bartender signaled and Lindquist excused himself. "Hold that thought, I'll be right back. Have another drink on me if you want." She watched him solve some problem with a register at the bar and sign paperwork before returning to the booth. "Okay, where were we," he said, slipping into his seat. "Oh, yeah, you were apologizing to me for putting me in the middle of your little domestic war with my crazy younger brother." Stony silence and a glare followed his remark. "Okay, sorry, bad choice of words." Propping his elbows on the table, he told her to continue.

"I have a chance," she said. "We have a chance—at something big. I'm talking about making a complete change in all our lives. You, Darryl, and me. This is the kind of opportunity that only comes along once in a lifetime."

Holding palms up, Lindquist sat there confused, waiting. "I'm all ears, Becky. But I gotta tell you, I'm not exactly flush with cash flow if you're looking for a loan or investment money."

"I'm not asking for either."

"Good, because I'm living on the edge right now." He sipped his water, and then launched into an uninterrupted defense. "This job is the best steady gig I've landed in a long time. I don't want to screw it up. I'm working my way back from a ton of debt. I'm down to one credit card and I'm dating a beautiful grown-up girl who actually has her own bank account."

"Sorry to hear about the girl," purred Becky. "Should I have a talk with her?"

"Hey, we're ancient history so don't even go there."

Jabbing a forefinger into the table, he kept on. "My bike's almost paid for and I'm current with my rent. Best of all, I'm not living in the same town as my screw-up brother and having to clean up his messes. Hell, even the IRS loves me. I'm a regular citizen with responsibilities and I get respect here at my job."

Leaning back, he threw an arm across the back of the booth. "Did you know I'm in line for a manager's slot? So what could you possibly offer me that's better than that?"

Flashing a feline smile across the table, she cooed, "How nice for you."

"And did I mention," he added in a low voice, "that for the first time in years, I'm getting laid on a regular basis? I'm sitting pretty good right now. Top that."

"Twenty million dollars, give or take a few million."

"What?"

Smiling at him, she recited the figure. "Twenty million dollars, David."

"What have you been smoking?"

"Nothing. It's just sitting there waiting for someone to come along."

David sat back, not sure he had heard his former sister-in-law correctly. "What in the hell are you talking about?"

"I know where twenty million dollars is hidden. We can walk away with more than two million of it."

"Oh, really? Is it some Nigerian prince who needs seed money to get his hands on his family's Swiss bank account?"

"I'm serious about this."

"I can see that. Who does the money belong to?"

"It's not cash, it's gold. And it belongs to whoever gets there first."

"Look Becky, if you're cooking up some armored car thing with Darryl, I don't want to hear about it. I don't want any part of it."

"Darryl's not part of this…yet. And it's not an armored car. Not a bank. Not a casino. Not a gold dealer. It's better than that."

"If it involves drugs it's not my thing. Do you hear me? Not for me."

He started to rise from the table. She reached out and held his wrist. "Please, just hear me out."

David sat back down, leery but curious. His eyes narrowed with suspicion but he listened. Speaking quietly and rapidly, Becky made her argument with her hands, constantly touching his arm to emphasize her story. When she finished sketching the New Guinea mission, she sat back, knowing she had just narrowly won the first round. Seconds passed before he spoke.

"Pretty wild. So what do you do next?" he asked. "Why talk to Darryl?"

"I have to," she said conspiratorially. "If I find the gold…" She corrected herself. "No, when I find the gold I have to move it. We're talking about heavy lifting. I can't do that by myself. I need muscle. Where am I gonna find that? Who else can I trust but you and Darryl? I've got nowhere else to go. You're family. I can't ask anyone else."

"Darryl? Geeze, you're absolutely certain about this?"

"It's a gamble but yes, I think it's a reasonable risk," she said.

"Okay, talk to Darryl. Set up a meeting. I'll come. But do some peacemaking with him first," he cautioned, "for both of us." She saw a light go on behind his eyes. "Matter of fact, here's a better idea. Don't tell him we've discussed this. You're gonna have to pitch it to him as if you and I never talked. Otherwise, he'll go off on us. He'll think we've been talking behind his back. You know how paranoid he gets about the two of us. And be careful with how much you tell him. Darryl's got a big mouth. He's an accident waiting to happen."

She agreed, nodding at his warning.

"Got to get back to work," he said calmly. Picking up her tab, he said, "I'll get this. You buy the next time."

Throwing her arms around him, she said, "I married the wrong brother."

"I could have told you that if you had bothered to ask," he whispered hoarsely. He walked her through the restaurant's double doors into a fading afternoon sun and waited as she coaxed her ancient car into life. A wave and she was heading to the highway.

David held the door for a couple, early birds for the happy hour. After following them inside, he signaled for a hostess to show them to a table near the fireplace.

"Well, that was certainly an interesting show you put on," chirped a voluptuous blonde—his girlfriend du jour with the bank account. Turning to face his accuser behind the register, Lindquist pleaded. "What? A guy can't talk to his sister-in-law?"

Arching a painted eyebrow, his girlfriend yawned to a grinning coworker. "That's a first. I've never heard the sister-in-law line before. Have you?"

Both women broke into giggles. Embarrassed, he waved them off in mock disgust and busied himself clearing tables alongside a busboy. His mind played the conversation with Becky over and over. *We can walk away with more than two million in gold. Manager would be nice*, he thought, *but two million?* The amount, he knew, didn't matter. Reasoning with Darryl would be the key.

. . . .

Chapter 15

Northwest Washington, DC

Russell Hightower threw on a fur-lined overcoat and tucked a nervous ball of fur under his arm. Dressed in a quilted vest, the bichon frisé resembled a furry toy. "All right, Princess," he cooed, "let's get you some air. Have you missed Daddy? Been bored, sitting in your apartment all day?" He pocketed the keys and took the elevator to the condominium's lobby for his nightly ritual.

Hightower went through the security door, locked it behind him, and stopped at the bank of mailboxes. Tugging at the leash to keep the dog close, he opened the box and quickly sorted the day's mail. The hoped-for envelope with his additional five thousand was not among the bills and junk mail. He shut the box, locked it, pocketing the key and mail. A frown crossed his face. *Maybe tomorrow*, he thought. *Best not to dwell on it.*

Hightower went out the front door and turned right as usual for the block-long walk to Gompers Memorial Park. At the corner of Tenth and L streets, Hightower reached down, scooped up the animal, and hurried across the street. On the opposite sidewalk, the two strolled along a diagonal walkway bisecting the park. He let the leash play out as his pet explored the grass near the park's namesake sculpture. Hightower stomped his feet impatiently in the cold, waiting for the dog to do its business under the stern bronze gaze of a seated Samuel Gompers. Hightower jerked the leash to signal a return home via the Eleventh Street crosswalk.

Mid-block on L Street, a hooded figure sat at the wheel of an idling black van, watching Hightower approach the crosswalk. Pulling from the curb, the van coasted to a stop just short of the intersection's right turn lane. Waiting for the light to change, the driver kept an eye on the man with the dog.

When the "walk" light flashed, Hightower stepped into the street. The dark vehicle, its orange signal blinking, crept forward, its high beams blinding man and dog. Raising an arm to shield his eyes, Hightower gave his bichon frisé the lead.

With a squeal of rubber, the van suddenly accelerated, slamming into Hightower as it roared through the crosswalk. His airborne body struck a passing car and rolled into the street, lifeless. A woman screamed.

Fleeing, the black van's front wheels crushed the crumpled form a second time and headed north on Eleventh Street with no one in pursuit.

Pedestrians ran into the street toward the bloodied heap of clothing. Witnesses pulled out their cell phones to call 911. A couple corralled the panicked bichon frisé, which ran in circles, dragging its leash behind it.

Two blocks from the accident scene, the van's driver took a left on N Street, went west for one block to Twelfth Street to shake anyone following him. Turning north, he drove one more block to O Street where he turned left and found the alley he had scouted two days earlier. The hooded driver pulled into the alley and killed the engine. Taking the keys, he walked briskly to the street and tossed them in a storm drain opening.

At the alley's mouth, Hightower's killer got into a parked, unlocked dark blue SUV with a single key in its ignition. After stripping off the hooded sweatshirt and gloves, he started the car and eased from the curb. Driving calmly to the end of the block, he turned right on Thirteenth Street and joined a line of cars heading north toward Logan Circle. Behind him, sirens wailed in the distance.

Keeping one hand on the wheel, the driver pulled a cell phone from his pocket and punched in a number. Speaking in clipped, emotionless tones he said, "Afraid our friend won't be able to make dinner tonight. He's been delayed. No, I don't think he'll be able to reschedule. Sorry about that." Smiling, the driver snapped the phone closed and waited patiently as the queue of cars in front of him took turns jockeying for an opening in the traffic circle's unending stream of cars. Waving at a car to his right, he let a woman caught in the turn lane slip in ahead of him. She flashed a smile, nodding gratefully at his unexpected courtesy. He waved politely and broke from the pack at the top of the roundabout to pick up Thirteenth Street again. The dark blue SUV headed north toward Silver Spring.

....

Chapter 16

Upsala, January 13

Shivering in her Honda, Becky huddled, waiting for the engine to warm. Luke-warm air from the car's fickle blower fan flowed across the dash, battling a windshield opaque with frost. Flipping open her cell phone to check on missed calls, she found three consecutive messages from Darryl topping the list. Not in the mood for his harangues, she frowned, scrolled past them to the most recent call—one from the Soderlunds, her next-door neighbors at the lake. She pushed the talk button and waited for the ring. A deep baritone filled her ear, Soderlund's voice. "Becky, that you?"

"Yeah. Saw you called. What's up?"

"Where are you?"

"At the market, warming up my car in the parking lot."

"You expecting anyone today?"

"No. Why?"

"You have a visitor," he said.

She answered warily. "I hope it's not someone from Mother of Mercy."

"Doesn't look like a nurse or a priest. More like an undertaker actually."

That's worse. Something's happened to Barbara, she thought. *Please, no.*

"You still there, Becky?"

"I'm here."

"Can't tell from here but he might be a cop. White guy. Been pacing on your porch. He tried knocking. Looked in windows. Walked around at first. Good thing Buddy's with us. He'd be going nuts by now if he were still in the house. The guy came in an SUV."

"How long has he been there?"

"Pulled in about a half hour ago. Gets in the car from time to time to stay warm. Can't blame him, it's pretty raw out."

"You said he might be a cop, right?"

"Could be. Not in uniform, though. He looks more like a fed or military. Maybe he's a plainclothes guys, or a business type. You want me to go over and talk to him? Find out what he wants?"

She voiced a fear. "I wonder if this has something to do with Darryl."

Soderlund sighed. "Is he in trouble AGAIN?"

"Not that I know of."

"What do you want me to do, Becky? I could phone the sheriff."

"Nah. I don't need that. How about I see what he wants first? I'll call you if everything's okay."

A pause. "Sure, that works for me. When you show, I'll let Buddy out."

"Thanks. I'm leaving the lot now."

"We'll be watching." The call ended. She pulled from the parking lot, the windshield cleared of all but a stubborn margin of frost at the edges.

As she drove, Becky's mind ran through possible scenarios.

Something with the house? A legal issue perhaps? Mortgage problem? It had to be something with Darryl. He probably screwed up something…or somebody. It would be like him.

A wild thought occurred to her, prompting an outburst of maniacal laughter. *The Publishers Sweepstakes guy! He's sitting there with a million dollar check and a car full of balloons, just waiting for me to show up.* Her laugh died. *Maybe her neighbor was right. A cop or a fed. But that didn't make sense. No, the answer had to be Darryl.*

In fifteen minutes, she went to parking lights, turned into her driveway, and parked the Honda in the garage. She got out of the car and studied the idling SUV's cab where a figure hunched over, cell phone buried in his ear. Her dog bounded through the deep snow, greeting her arrival with loud whimpers and wagging tail. She playfully cuffed his ears. "As long as you're with me I'm not worried." She clipped a short leash to Buddy's choke chain and waited.

The SUV's motor died and the driver got out. Bundled in a heavy overcoat with upturned collar and a wool watch cap, the visitor, leather briefcase in his left hand, shielded his eyes from the glare of the garage's security light.

Her big Lab erupted. After quieting Buddy, Becky faced her caller who held out a gloved hand. "Geoff Timmons. I'm really hoping you're Becky Peterson."

She reined in her dog and took the offered hand.

"Terrific." The man smiled. "Would it be possible for us to talk inside? Out of the cold?" Leaning forward and lowering his voice, the visitor added, "I'm here about the discovery of your grandfather's plane."

Becky stammered, "Oh, that. Okay, follow me." She led the way into the front hall and hung up her coat. Behind her, Timmons stomped his feet to remove traces of snow. He set the briefcase on a pine bench in the entry and removed rubber overshoes. Becky shooed Buddy into the kitchen, took the man's coat, and ushered him into the living room where he stood, towering over her. In a black suit, white shirt, and tie, Timmons looked out of place. She offered him coffee.

"Yeah, sounds good," he said, rubbing his hands.

Becky paused to strike a match under a pyramid of kindling in the fireplace, and then went into the kitchen. Without asking, her guest crossed the room and sat down at the dining table, placing the briefcase in front of him. At the stove, Becky studied his reflection in the window above the sink as coffee brewed.

A faint patina of stubble covered Timmons's shaved head. Even in a suit his muscular frame was obvious. Hard eyes and a nose set slightly to one side as if pushed there long ago in a fight defined his face. His voice had a clipped, vaguely eastern accent. When he talked, he flashed a nervous grin.

She poured steaming coffee. "Sugar, cream?"

"Black." He took the mug and blew on the scalding liquid.

"Sorry you had to wait."

"Been colder." He grunted. "Didn't mind waiting."

She sat down across from him and signaled Buddy to her side. The Lab ambled next to her chair, big brown eyes on the stranger.

Flashing a robotic smile, Timmons opened the leather satchel, withdrew a file, and opened it. "We understand you've been notified about the discovery—in New Guinea—of what may be Lt. Lloyd Peterson's missing World War Two airplane."

"Papua New Guinea," she corrected him.

An eyebrow rose. "I stand corrected," he said, smiling. "Papua New Guinea. As I was saying, we understand..."

"Who is 'we'?"

A pause across the table. Timmons raised the mug for a long

swallow of coffee. “My mistake. I should have said, my employer understands…”

“Okay,” demanded Becky, “but who’s your employer?” Sensing the tension in his master’s voice, the sentinel at her side muffled a low growl.

Glancing at the nervous dog, Timmons answered. “Fair enough. My employer, who wishes to remain anonymous, happens to be president of one of the nation’s larger private military contractors.”

“You mean like those hired guns who served in Iraq and Afghanistan?”

“His people are professionals, not hired guns,” snorted Timmons. “Anyway, my employer heard rumors about your grandfather’s story and was intrigued.”

“Rumors?”

“Water cooler talk among those of us in the defense industry.”

“How does he know about my grandfather, and how did you find me?”

“Good questions. Let me back up a bit. I realize it must be a bit unnerving for a complete stranger to show up on your doorstep. My apologies. It wasn’t my intention to barge in like this.” She got up to spoon more sugar in her coffee, his voice following her into the kitchen. “The discovery of your grandfather’s airplane attracted my boss’s attention. Correct me if I’m wrong about the sequence. Some missionary stumbled across a long-lost P-38 Lightning in the jungles of New Guinea…Papua New Guinea. Unsure of what he found, this missionary contacted a gentleman in California with access to government documents about downed aircraft. This person in turn searched in dozens of different places for answers. You can’t turn over that many rocks without eventually attracting attention. I wouldn’t have driven all the way out here without knowing I'd get a chance to talk with you. Fair enough?"

Shuffling back to her chair, Becky shook her head in agreement. "I suppose so. I think I follow you," she said.

A sip of coffee, followed by Timmons's mechanical smile again. "This person talks to that person. Pretty soon word got out about a possible genuine find overseas. Mind you, these kinds of discoveries are becoming rarer all the time. Question is: where exactly did the plane go down and under what circumstances? Adding to the mystery, no records of the actual mission are known to exist."

Sifting through the papers in front of him, Timmons lifted a letter-sized sheet.

"This is a MACR, Missing Air Crew Reports. Every time a plane went down reports like this were routinely filed."

Becky leaned forward in her chair. "I still don't know why you'd come all the way out here to talk to me about my grandfather's plane. If you know where it is, why don't you just go over there?"

"Good question. Why don't we just—as you say—go over there and find it?"

She paused, coffee mug halfway to her mouth. "Well, why don't you?"

Steepling his hands under his chin, Timmons's eyes bored into Becky's. "That's exactly why my boss sent me all the way out here to talk with you."

"And the reason is…" she prodded.

"Ms. Peterson, are you familiar with the market for World War Two aircraft?"

"Not really."

"I'm not surprised. Most people don't know about it. It's a rather unique culture. A select fraternity. It's a very expensive hobby for wealthy collectors. It can be quite profitable. We're talking about authentic war birds from your grandfather's war. Bombers and fighters."

"But what's that have to do with me?"

"Regrettably, my boss is not privy to the entire story of your grandfather's airplane. For starters, he doesn't know exactly where the wreck site is. He could probably locate it eventually, but that would take too much time and a lot of money. He has the latter but not the former. In addition, he would not enjoy access to the same information you would have should you decide to go to Papua New Guinea."

"I don't understand. I was told there are groups that go over there all the time to look for old airplanes in the jungles."

"Quite true," explained Timmons. "But in your case, our missionary friend operates under a rather archaic set of rules when it comes to wreck sites."

"What does that mean?"

"Remember the collectors I mentioned? These are people who are willing to go to great lengths to get their hands on actual combat planes from the war. They are powerful men obsessed with finding planes such as your grandfather's Lightning. These men are used to getting what they want, one way or another. Some of the aircraft are retrieved in large pieces; some are cannibalized for their original parts. There is a lucrative market for both."

Becky sat quietly, prompting Timmons to fill the silence.

"Frankly, people like my employer are addicted to collecting these planes. It's not a hobby for ordinary people. Restored war birds are works of art to those who can afford it. We're talking very deep pockets. Getting the picture?"

"Okay, yeah. How much do you think this plane might be worth?"

"Depends on its condition. If it's salvageable enough for restoration, you could be looking at hundreds of thousands of dollars. But that's just the start. A rebuilt Lightning might sell for as much as four million."

Sitting upright, Becky repeated the quoted sum. "Four million? You've got to be kidding. He'd pay that much for an airplane?"

"Not just any airplane—a Lightning."

"I had no idea it might be worth that much."

"As I said, even parts are potentially worth a lot of money. Depends on their condition. That's why we need to move quickly. If this plane is worth saving the reward could be quite handsome."

"Which makes me wonder why your rich boss just doesn't hire someone to find it for him. Why come to me?"

"Good question. This missionary—the guy who found your grandfather's plane—has quaint ideas about whom he will share his discoveries with. He prefers talking only to family members of those pilots whose aircraft he finds. Have you given any serious thought about going to Papua New Guinea?"

Becky's eyes widened. "Me? Are you serious?" she said softly.

"Absolutely, Ms. Peterson. Would you consider making such a trip?"

"You're really that interested in my grandfather's plane?"

Eying her from the rim of his coffee cup, Timmons said, "Without question. We want your help to get access to that P-38. My employer might make it worth your while to make the trip."

Leaning forward, she locked eyes with her visitor. Baiting him, she coyly said, "This will sound weird. I mean, with you showing up and all, but I've already talked to someone who's been there several times."

"Really?" Timmons stiffened. "How did that happen?"

"I got a call from some guy in California who knows all

about missing planes from the war. He knows the missionary who found my grandfather's Lightning. He also gave me the name of one of the groups that made some trips over there. I ended up calling one of the guys who's been on those trips."

"I'm impressed. This sheds a whole new light on the subject. And who might this gentleman be?"

"Just a local guy. He knows a lot about those airplane wrecks. I met him for dinner once. We talked about a trip over there. He didn't say anything about how much planes are worth to guys like your boss. He's not a collector or anything."

"Interesting. But this could complicate things. My employer might be disappointed to hear you've already contacted someone about this."

"It's a free world," she shot back. "It's not like I committed to go."

Timmons probed carefully. "Have you thought seriously about going?"

"I dunno. Maybe. He said May would be a good time to go."

"I'm curious," said Timmons, "why May?"

"He said it was the dry season."

"Huh, well, that makes sense."

"But I'm not sure I can afford to go."

"Believe me," brightened Timmons, "my employer is aware of the expense of such a trip. But let me remind you that his would be the bigger risk when it comes to money. The plane might be worth recovering or it could be a pile of useless scrap at this point. It's been almost seventy years."

"Or it could be worth salvaging," she responded. "You said that yourself."

"So I did. I take it you understand why time is crucial in this case."

"You need me, don't you? Maybe I'll go, maybe I won't."

Leaning forward, Timmons's expression hardened, the smile absent. "Since you seem so damned sure of yourself, let's both lay our cards on the table. Yes, we would need your cooperation. And yes, we're interested in your grandfather's plane. I believe we can reach an accommodation if you're willing to listen."

"No harm in listening."

Timmons threw up his hands in a surrender pose. "Finally. We're getting somewhere. Excuse me while I make a phone call." Backing from the table, Timmons threw on his overcoat and slipped out the front door.

Scratching sounds at the kitchen door prompted Becky to let Buddy out. While she was up, she added birch logs to the fire. Her phone rang. Soderlund's voice whispered in her ear. "Everything going okay over there? Judy and I are watching in case you need us."

"It's cool. I've got some papers to read. He's outside making a phone call."

"I see him on your porch. Call us when he leaves, okay?"

"Thanks," she replied. "I appreciate that."

Becky ended the call and returned to the table. A rush of cold air followed Timmons into the house. He snapped his phone shut, pocketed it and sat on the couch, wearing an enigmatic smile. "I have an interesting proposal for you."

"Was that your boss?"

"Yes," nodded Timmons. "He wants you to have the opportunity to visit your grandfather's resting place. He can help make that happen."

"Could be expensive."

"Believe me, the gentleman has ample resources to support your venture, Ms. Peterson. He's a patriot. Quite the amateur historian when it comes to World War Two. He'd love to get his hands on a P-38 Lightning. But he wants to be the first to look over that plane. He's given me authority to offer you an arrangement."

"Oh, so now it turns out I am going?" she said sarcastically.

"You sounded intrigued. And it certainly might be worth your while."

"All I have to do is share my access to the crash site, right?"

"I should think that's fair. After all, underwriting your trip gets closure for your family at no cost to you. He'll advance you more than enough money to finance your trip."

"And the catch?" she said, taking a seat on the couch.

"No catch. As I told you, just work with us to gain access to the wreck."

"That's it?"

"Those are the terms. Shall I continue? It's a very generous offer. Take it or leave it." Wary, she shifted on the couch, cornered. *I'm on my own*, she thought. *Can't call David. Can't tell the Soderlunds. What should I ask for? How much?*

"I want one hundred fifty thousand dollars," she demanded.

Saying nothing, Timmons reddened, boiling at her quoted price. He stood over her. "You're quite the avaricious little bitch, aren't you?"

Bristling, Becky sat back, her arms folded, certain she had overplayed her hand but not about to show her panic to him.

"You're an amateur playing a dangerous game here," he finally growled.

"I know my boss. You're this close to screwing this up. He'll give you half that and not a penny more. That's a princely sum. Pay for your trip with it and keep what you don't spend. Final offer. Yes or no? Do we have a deal?"

Fighting to keep her composure, Becky's mind raced. *What was I thinking? Can't let this get away from me. Don't completely trust this guy but what can I do?*

"I'd say your silence means you're turning him down." Timmons stomped to the table and made a show of stuffing papers in his briefcase.

Becky marched across the room, threw open the kitchen door, and whistled Buddy indoors as a precaution. "Don't put words in my mouth," she shouted to Timmons. "I'm just thinking here."

"I want an answer before I leave," he snarled without looking.

"Okay, okay. Fine! It's a deal!"

Slowly turning, Timmons faced her, paused, said, "Really."

"Shouldn't you phone your boss? Tell him we have an agreement?"

"I'll call him from the road," he snapped. Before Timmons shut the briefcase, he withdrew a thick manila envelope and tossed it on the table. "Seventy-five thousand. Our part of the deal."

"How did you know that…"

"That you'd take the deal? In my business I'm paid to read people. You, little lady, are one lousy poker player."

"And you're a real asshole, you know that?"

"I've been called worse," he said, eyes narrowed, "and by smarter people. Couple of things to remember. One, if you're using a bank, don't deposit more than ninety-five hundred bucks at a time. Banks have to report deposits of ten thousand dollars or more to the feds. Save yourself and my boss being asked embarrassing questions."

"I knew that."

Timmons smirked. "I'm sure you did," he said dismissively. "Second thing, let us know when you firm up your travel plans. We're going to send a couple of Australian TV cameramen along with your expedition to record everything."

"I didn't agree to that."

Dismissing her objection with a wave, he continued. "Not negotiable. We need eyes on the ground to protect our investment."

Clutching the thick envelope of cash, she waited as he slipped into his overshoes, retrieved his coat, and paused to warm his hands in front of the fire.

"Okay I'm done," he said. "Plan on going in May if you want. We'll be in touch with you before then."

She followed him to the door. Timmons hustled to the SUV without acknowledging her. From the porch, Becky watched the vehicle's taillights float along the lake road toward Upsala until the car was lost in the pines. She turned in the circle of light and waved across the ravine at the Soderlund's house where a single kitchen window glowed. A porch light winked twice in response to her signal. She shooed Buddy inside and locked the door. Tossing two more logs on the fire, she wrapped herself in a voluminous down comforter in an effort to still her tremors. The visit from Timmons had flayed her nerves and sleep was not an option.

....

Chapter 17

Maple Grove, Minnesota, January 29

Things were falling into place for Becky. Confident about facing Morris again, Becky phoned him before the end of the month. They met at a restaurant in the same suburban shopping mall where they had dined earlier. Morris made sure to arrive first. He took a corner booth opposite the bar where he could watch the door. He shucked his denim jacket and waited.

Becky strode in, wearing a heavy down vest, fashionable wool turtleneck, and felt boots. Drawing admiring glances from the bar drones, she was in high spirits. Morris stood to greet her, then let her settle opposite. "You look different somehow," he said, baffled.

"I cut my hair and lightened it. I'm entitled to change if I feel like it."

"Doesn't make you look any older though if that's what you wanted."

She peeled off the vest, crossed her arms on the table, and threw him a caustic look. "Now that we've discussed my hairstyle what should we talk about?"

"Fair enough. You said you had a lot to talk about. Let's start with your homework." He threw a question at her. "You think you've got a handle on the Pacific war now?"

"If you mean, did I read the books you had on the list, yeah."

Morris propped both elbows on the table and leaned forward. "Good. It's a start. Okay, you've got the floor. Tell me what you learned."

"A lot. The men who fought there—in the Pacific, I mean—were on the end of the pipeline. The first few years were tough. MacArthur had to scrap for every piece of equipment, every airplane, and every infantryman. Japan ran wild in Asia and the Pacific. Australia thought they were next. And they might have been if it hadn't been for the Battle of the Coral Sea. That was the first time the Japanese got their nose bloodied and it shocked them. From what I've read, Roosevelt and Churchill said fighting Germany came first, Japan second." Talking non-stop for twenty minutes, Becky recited what she remembered of the New Guinea campaign, the air war, and the grinding campaign of island hopping that followed. She won over Morris with her recitation.

Grinning, he slapped a palm on the table. "Outstanding! You got it! I'm impressed. See what you missed in high school?"

"Okay, sure. Now I'd like a drink."

"And I'll buy to celebrate your newfound scholarly status, Missy."

Rolling her eyes, Becky sat back. "You've ridden that schoolgirl theme long enough, don't you think?"

"You're absolutely right. That will be my last word on the subject." Waving a server to their table, Morris ordered beers and pushed a menu across the table.

As Becky studied the specials, he lowered his voice. "You said on the phone you had something important to tell me." He waited as she scanned her options. "Well?"

Calmly folding her hands, Becky announced, "I think I'll have the pasta. What are you ordering?"

"A steak. Now about your phone call..."

"Let's order first," she said, determined to control the conversation's pace.

He yielded. When the waitress returned with the beer, they recited their choices and sent her away. Morris nursed his brew, waiting on Becky.

"I've done what you asked. I've read the books," she said. "I even reread Grandpa Peterson's diary to get a better feel for what he was going through. Did you read the copy of the pages I sent you?"

"Yes, thanks. Interesting. Did any of this homework help?"

"Yes. I still want to go to Papua New Guinea and find his plane."

Morris took a long swallow from his glass and set it down. "Maybe I haven't made it clear enough how tough a trip like that can be. You'll be miserable hiking through the jungle. The heat will sap your energy. Rain will turn everything to rust and mold and you'll be courting a dozen diseases. You'll have to sleep on the ground and you won't be pampered."

"I'm tougher than you think, Dale."

"And did I mention snakes, leeches, bats, spiders the size of dinner plates, and crocs? You ought to put all this aside and be grateful for clean sheets and a roof over your head that doesn't leak."

"You left out lions, tigers, and bears," she deadpanned. "Are you done?"

He answered with a shrug. "For now. So, what's your news?"

"I want to start planning to go in May. You said it was the best time to do it."

Rubbing a calloused hand through his hair, Morris stared at his beer. "I had a feeling you'd say that. From our first meeting I knew you were determined to go."

Salads arrived, briefly interrupting their exchange. Picking up where he left off, Morris pushed ahead. "I have a couple of questions. Have you thought about how you're gonna finance this? A plane ticket will set you back at least twenty-five hundred bucks. You'll have hotel costs, meals, transportation, and carriers. In PNG, everybody has a hand out. Plus, you need the right gear. Thought about that?"

Unfazed, Becky pounced on his query. "My turn for a surprise. Since we last talked I had a call from a distant relative. A nephew of Grandpa Peterson's who lives out east. Somewhere in Virginia, I think. He was one of the Petersons that guy from California found while looking for family. This nephew led him to me."

Pausing, fork in mid-air, Morris waited for the rest of the story. "And?"

"And…get this! He's fabulously wealthy. Wants to pay for

my trip and anyone who's going with me! That means you could come along all expenses paid, AND get a bonus for being my guide. You won't have to pay a thing."

"Hmm, nice relative to have in the family tree," mused Morris. "You sure he's legit?"

Pouting, she pushed away her salad. "Of course he is. He shared stories only a family member would know. He's quite old," she added, "in his seventies. Said he only wants me to bring back evidence that we actually found his uncle's plane."

Their food came. Morris attacked his steak while Becky nibbled her pasta, expecting more questions. The enthusiasm she had expected from him was missing. Morris was subdued. His reaction troubled her. "You don't seem overjoyed."

"It's a lot to absorb all at once," he muttered. "I actually didn't think you had a chance in hell of finding a way to make this work. Now, all of a sudden you tell me some long-lost uncle pops from the woodwork and agrees to foot the entire bill."

"A nephew, not an uncle. Maybe he wants closure. The guy in California said that happens with family sometimes. They want an ending to a story they never thought they'd see. It's probably like that with him."

"You must live a charmed life to have this drop in your lap."

Deliberately avoiding Morris's stare, she dropped yet another half-truth on the table. "I've asked two friends to come with me on the trip."

Dropping his knife on his plate, Morris stopped carving his steak. "What?"

"I asked two guys I know to come along."

"Why? What the hell for? All of a sudden you're going hog wild on a thing you know nothing about! Damn!" he flared. "Who are these friends you're talking about? They have any experience?" Chastened, her eyes finally met his across the table. "Just two brothers I know from St. Cloud. I met them in college. The older one was in the army, First Gulf War. They're okay guys. Said they'd be willing to go along."

Waving his hands, Morris stared at her, incredulous. "Ka-ching, ka-ching! You've just quadrupled your airfare and hotel bill. Did you think about that?"

At first defensive, then increasingly combative, Becky challenged him. "But this rich relative is willing to pick up the tab. What do I have to lose? He said I could write my own ticket, take anyone I wanted. I couldn't go over there alone. Didn't you tell me that the first time we met?"

A visibly upset Morris, dark brows knit together, shoulders hunched, set aside his half-eaten steak. Gripping the table to calm himself, he reasoned with her. "Yeah, I said that. But you can't just go over there with amateurs and expect to waltz into some village. I told you, it's no picnic. Be reasonable!"

"Reasonable? All of a sudden I'm not being reasonable? Wait a minute. Am I missing something here? You were the one who got me to do homework on New Guinea and the war. I read every damn book you told me to. I got guidebooks about the island. I've looked at maps. I did research on the Internet. I talked to these friends and they thought it was a great idea, an adventure. At least they're willing to help me. I was hoping you would come along to show me how it's done but you seemed reluctant. I didn't know if you were going to agree to this or not."

Morris buried his head in his hands. "I can't believe you really want to do this. Look, reading books and studying maps is one thing, but…"

"But what? Actually hiking into the jungle is no place for a girl. Is that it?"

"Didn't say that."

"No, but you were thinking it," she chided. "You were, weren't you?"

A pause followed her comment. Morris, quiet, slumped against the booth. Becky picked at her pasta, holding her last bit of news until she had Morris where she wanted him. Her eyes darted from her plate to the brooding Morris. He was about to commit and she could feel it. *I can wait,* she thought confidently.

"Now it's my turn. I've got something to tell you," he said.

"Go ahead, I'm listening."

Morris stabbed at his food. "Hell, this is so damn anti-climatic it's pathetic. I've decided to go along. I did my best to persuade you not to go. I'm a sucker for damsels in distress."

"I'm NOT one of those," she shot back.

"Well, consider me intrigued then. I guess I have one more trip in me."

"That's fantastic!" she squealed. Reaching across the table, she took his hands in hers. "You won't regret it. That's great news! Great news!"

Blushing at her enthusiasm, Morris waved her into silence. "Okay, okay. I'm in. Actually, I sorta made up my mind earlier. Didn't want to tell you right away because I thought another trip was a pipe dream for me. I figured if you went over there you wouldn't last two days without someone who knew the ropes. Now that I got that off my chest don't think I won't take your bonus money, little lady. My fee is five thousand, plus expenses. Think your relative will balk at that?"

"Not at all. He's to send money as I need it."

Morris shook his head. "I can't believe I've agreed to this."

Reaching across the table, Becky took Morris' hand again. "Thank you, Dale. I'm excited you're going to come. You'll be in charge, I promise."

Frowning, Morris summoned his best irritated face. "I want to meet your two Boy Scouts as soon as possible. Maybe I can scare some sense into them."

"Oh, one last thing," she said. "This nephew insists on arranging for a pair of Australian TV guys to tag along and film the discovery."

A string of expletives escaped from Morris. "What? Television people? We haven't even talked about what the trip entails and you've already saddled us with a damned circus! You paying them too?"

Becky threw her arms in the air. "No, no. They'll pay their own way in exchange for our cooperation. They thought it would be a wonderful human-interest story. You know, 'flier found after nearly seventy years' or something like that. They'll meet us in Papua New Guinea. It's not like they have to travel thousands of miles to get there. And we could end up on the National Geographic Channel for all we know."

Sarcasm coated Morris's voice. "Oh, great, that's always been a goal of mine." Propping both elbows on the table, his appetite suddenly gone, Morris stared at his dinner companion. "Any other bombshells? I don't think I could take one more."

"That's it," she said, smiling. "I'm so grateful for your agreeing to do this."

As their server cleared dishes, an elated Becky scribbled notes dictated by Morris—tasks he wanted done in the next few weeks. He rattled off passports, tenting, tropical clothing, footwear, rain gear, and camping supplies. Writing quickly, she finally closed her notebook with a solemn promise to start immediately on his requests. Meeting with Darryl and David Lindquist topped the list. Morris had surprised her by his acceptance of the mysterious benefactor and the idea of being shadowed by Australian TV. She knew the next hurdle would be convincing

Darryl. Getting him to travel halfway around the world on a wartime diary's promise of treasure would not be an easy sell.

....

Chapter 18

Albany, Minnesota, two days later

Darryl Lindquist agreed to meet Becky and his brother, David, for dinner. She suggested Albany, a neutral location south of Upsala on Highway 238, just blocks from Interstate 94. Albany was far enough away from Upsala to afford privacy, but close enough to make the drive a short one for all three. David would be coming from St. Cloud. Becky was to pick up Darryl. That way she wouldn't be at his mercy, depending on him to get her back home.

Running ten minutes late due to her balky Honda, Becky pulled in front of Darryl's trailer in the woods behind the welding shop. She tapped her horn twice. He crossed the mobile home's tiny deck wearing a Rush concert T-shirt and ripped jeans. He lurched unsteadily down the sagging steps. In the car, Darryl leaned over to plant a sloppy kiss on Becky's cheek.

"You smell like beer," she scolded, pulling away and wiping her face.

"Man's gotta right to enjoy a beer."

"Or two," she chided.

"Or three...or four," he said, grinning.

They drove in silence, Darryl breathing on his window and drawing lopsided hearts with crooked arrows. Glancing at his child's art on the glass, Becky rolled her eyes. Darryl flipped on the radio, played with the dials until he found a station playing vintage heavy metal, and cranked up the volume. Smoldering, Becky kept her eyes on the road all the way into Albany. Spotting the restaurant's green awning, she parked in front and shooed Darryl out of her car.

From his perch in a corner booth, David heard the couple squabbling in the restaurant's entry and braced himself. Darryl, wearing a benign expression, nodded at his older sibling and slid across the seat facing him. "David. Long time no see. How you been, man?" The two did not shake hands.

"Been doing okay. How about you? Getting any work?"

A shrug and a mumble. "In this economy? At this time of year?"

"Arne Thompson asked you to fix his rigs, didn't he?" asked Becky.

"Yeah, so what? That's good for about a month, then what?"

David added his encouragement. "But that's still good news, Darryl. Oughta be decent money. Thompson always paid up front as long as I can remember."

"Still does," answered his brother.

A shy teenage waitress came to their booth and took drink orders. Darryl asked for a beer but was told they didn't serve alcohol. Throwing a disapproving look at Becky, he settled for a Mountain Dew. David measured the tension in the air and handed out menus to move the conversation in another direction. The trio gave their orders to the girl when she returned with drinks.

"Okay, Becky," queried David, "you dragged us all the way out here for some mysterious meeting. What gives?"

Frowning, Darryl snapped at his ex-wife. "Looks like I'm not the only one who doesn't know what the hell's going on. What are you up to?"

Folding her arms, Becky smiled conspiratorially. "What I'm

going to tell you is strictly between the three of us. Understood?"

Pushing himself into the booth's corner, Darryl nursed his drink, suspicious eyes darting between Becky and his brother as she laid out her plan. When their dinners arrived, the three ate in near silence. Darryl wolfed down his food as Becky went over her idea again.

Darryl was working on his third Dew as their server cleared the dishes. Dinner had loosened his tongue, a full stomach turning him cooperative. Becky hurried to conclude the conversation. She sat back, inviting questions.

Darryl started. "So, you're saying this gold is still there?"

"Yes. Never been found by the government."

"How can you be so damn sure?"

"Because the plane carrying it was never located. It's there, Darryl."

"Well, shit, Becky, that's a big leap to make."

She was defiant. "I know it's there."

"Why not tell somebody in Washington and get a big reward?"

"Not that simple," interjected David. "Sounds like from what Becky says, they had their chance. They gave up almost seventy years ago. Now it's our turn."

"You sure there's twenty million?" asked Darryl.

"There is," she explained. "The worth depends on the market. But three of us couldn't possibly move that much gold. My idea is to carry out ninety pounds between us."

"How much is that worth?"

Playing with a tiny calculator in her palm, she said, "Like I said, it all hinges on the market for gold. Could be over two million, could be less."

Staring at the table, Darryl's lips moved, mumbling the sum over and over.

Becky spotted the waitress heading their way and waved her

off. They were at a delicate moment. The negotiations could still go awry. *You never know with Darryl*, she thought. *I have no idea how many drinks he had before I picked him up. Have to answer these last few questions and get him out of here.*

"I'm not dumb, okay? I get the numbers. But why me and David? What's the catch? Our pop used to say there's always a catch."

She deliberately placed a hand on his arm. "No catch. I told you, we have to move the gold to a spot where we can get it out. That's where you two come in. There's no way I can do that by myself. I need your muscles, both of you. The three of us can make this work."

"But how do we eventually get it out of the country?" asked David. "You can't fly it out. Too heavy, too many customs checks."

"I'm working on a solution," she said confidently. "I'll figure it out soon."

"Nothing illegal, I hope."

"I told you. I'm working on it. I may have a solution. If it doesn't work out, we don't go. I'll let you know when I'm sure."

A crooked, boyish grin spread across Darryl's face. "So, you want me and David, huh?" Wagging a finger, he chuckled triumphantly. "See? I told you you'd need me some day."

"You were right, Darryl. I do need you. Don't you see? This is our best chance to start over." Edging closer, their legs touching, Becky pressed her argument. "If we do this, things will be like they were before. Only we won't have to worry about money anymore. There won't be any reason to argue; to fight about where we're gonna live; what we're gonna spend." David watched, fascinated as his former sister-in-law drew his brother into her dream. Her silky voice worked magic.

"And how we gonna pay for the trip? Hell, Becky, you don't have that kind of money. Neither does David. I sure as hell don't."

Patiently, she repeated her rehearsed explanation. "An elderly nephew of Grandpa Peterson's lives out east. He's a wealthy businessman. He's agreed to finance everything. He's even hiring an Australian film crew to document our trip. All he asks is that we bring back evidence that the plane is Grandpa Peterson's."

"That film crew could be a problem," said David.

"By the time they realize what's happened," answered Becky, "we'll be long gone. We'll have disappeared off the face of the earth. This can work, believe me."

Throwing up his arms, Darryl surrendered, looking to his sibling for help. "David, whadaya think? Even if the gold is there, is this fucking crazy or what?"

Leaning across the table, David lowered his voice, whispering, "Yeah, it's crazy. But if Becky's right about the gold I think it's a no-brainer, little brother. At today's prices we could split almost two million dollars worth of gold. Cut three ways, the math works for me. I like the numbers. I'm signing on."

Becky moved even closer, her lips next to Darryl's ear. "Think of it. That's probably seven hundred thousand dollars for each one of us. Could mean a million plus just for us, Darryl."

Something clicked. "Hell, if David's good to go so am I. When do we leave?"

"Third week in May. It's the dry season over there. Best window of weather we'll have all year."

"That's five months away!"

"Can't be helped. We need time to get in shape. Can't get through the jungle if we're not fit. Plus, we have to get passports, buy camping stuff, and do some reading about where we're going."

"There's the catch! See, our old man was right!"

Laughing, David said, "She's right. We have to read up on

New Guinea. Find out what to expect. And we definitely have to get in shape."

Becky leaned back against the booth, drained from the conversation. "One more thing. There's this guy who will be running the show for us. Name's Morris, Dale Morris. He's gone over there twice before. Knows his stuff. Older guy. Former air force. We need him to take us into the jungle where the planes are."

"Is he part of this gold thing?" asked David guardedly.

Shaking her head, Becky assured the brothers. "No. We're the only three who know about this. And it stays with us. Not one word about this to anyone. If the shit hits the fan because one of you talked, I'm out."

"Don't worry, Becky," swore a solemn David. "I'm not gonna blow a chance at a couple million dollars."

Shifting her gaze, Becky waited for Darryl's promise. He said, "Me too. I ain't saying nothing to nobody."

"You'll have to watch the booze," warned David. The warning prompted a scowl from his brother. Raising his right hand, Darryl shook his head as if affirming an oath. "No problem."

"Okay," said Becky, "I'll call you when I know more. You'll have to meet Morris at some point. I want him to know you're coming with me. He'll probably ask you some questions. That's where the reading comes in. It's sorta his thing."

Digging into her purse, she pulled out two identical paperback guidebooks and put them on the table. "Go through these. Get a handle on what Papua New Guinea is all about. Do the homework."

"Huh, Papua New Guinea and the Solomons," said David examining the travel guide. "This your idea or this Morris fella?"

"My idea. Morris had me do it. I learned a lot. You do the same."

Each man took his book, studying the cover, flipping through the pages. Becky plucked the bill from the table, fished two twenties from her wallet, and scooted from the booth, followed by the Lindquists.

"Hey," crowed Darryl, holding an opened page aloft toward Becky. "I think I'm gonna like this place." Giggling, he waved a picture of a topless native maiden wreathed in flowers. Ignoring his adolescent gloating, an embarrassed Becky hurried to the register and paid the bill. *Hope I haven't made a mistake by including Darryl,* she asked herself. *David and I will have to take turns keeping him corralled. If he gets out of hand...* She left the thought unfinished.

Outside, a light snow was falling, coating streets, sidewalks, and windshields. David caught Becky's worried look and quickly steered his brother to his parked car with the excuse about wanting to discuss their role in the New Guinea trip. Grateful for the gesture, Becky mouthed a "thank you" to David, rushed to her car, and was gone before Darryl realized what had happened. By the time David's car headed to Upsala, Becky's taillights were distant red dots in swirling snow.

....

Chapter 19

Ala Wai Marina, Honolulu, Hawaii, February 6

Huddling in a hooded warm-up jacket against the predawn chill, Kalani Souza sat astride a sports bike, sipping hot chocolate from a foam cup. One of the feral "harbor rats" haunting the marina, Kalani listened to surf booming offshore at Ala Moana break. As forecast, a rare wintertime south swell had built during the night. Within the hour, the parking lot would fill with eager surfers taking advantage of the waves and he longed to be out there before the crowds arrived. But there was a nagging conflict. To earn some cash he had promised to help one of the marina's sailboat owners. For now, Kalani was content to straddle his bike and enjoy an early morning treat while observing the ocean theater.

Behind Diamond Head's iconic silhouette, thin streaks of light were setting clouds on fire, revealing barely visible lines of gray-green breakers from Queen's all the way to Kaiser's Bowl and Ala Moana. Traffic hummed along the boulevard, crossing the canal, a stream of lights curving toward Kalakaua Avenue and the glass wall of hotels lining Waikiki.

Talking excitedly, three surfers emerged from a battered pickup, lifted their boards from the truck's bed, and crossed the parking lot, passing in front of the bike's loitering rider. The lead surfer, an alpha male with a short board tucked under a tattooed arm, acknowledged the hooded figure. "Hey, Kalani, you comin', brah?" The trio of muscular youths clustered around the bike.

Gripping the handlebars, Kalani Souza nodded at the surfers. "Later, huh? Looking good out there, brah."

All four gazed seaward at perfect, long dark walls peeling toward the edge of the channel. Sloppy chop swatted the rock seawall, spraying salt mist in the air above the parking lot.

"Mebbe we see you out there later then, huh?"

Kalani shrugged. "Yeah, mebbe. Catch some for me, eh?"

The two bumped fists and the surfer led his companions over the rocks in the growing light. Out beyond rushing lines of incoming whitewater, a dozen surfers clustered at the take-off point. A set hit the reef, rising into steep menacing walls. Two figures paddled into a peak and crouched, dropping quickly into bottom turns, their boards carving white trails as the wave curled, chasing them. One of the riders disappeared, caught in a thundering explosion of foam. The remaining surfer shot across the wave, then went airborne over the back of the wave as it collapsed in a crashing roar. Kalani lost track of his friends in the swirling foam as two more sets poured through the break. Tossing his empty cup, he reluctantly turned away. Pumping his legs, he stood on the bike's pedals, nimbly gliding between parked cars, looking for unlocked vehicles. No luck. The early birds had been vigilant. Kalani gave up and headed for the marina piers, rehearsing a plea to avoid chores in exchange for several hours of surfing. With any luck he would be able to talk his way out of work and join the others enjoying the unexpected gift of the freakish south swell.

Coasting halfway down a dock, Kalani pulled up next to a 42-foot Alden-designed sailboat moored stern first. Dismounting, he leaned his bike against a locked storage bin and climbed aboard the two-masted schooner, *Sunshine*. Drifting gently against soft white bumpers on its port side, the boat's topside was deserted, quiet, wet with early morning condensation.

Kalani stepped down into the cockpit and rapped on the main cabin's closed teak hatch. "Hey, Skipper Rick! Morning! You awake?" Sliding back the hatch, he thrust his head inside and repeated his wake-up call. "Skipper! You up?"

Muffled snorts and a roar came from a darkened berth somewhere below, the boat's owner stirring in the gloom. Bare feet slapped on the ladder's varnished teak steps as Kalani lowered himself into the cabin. Wedging his body into the galley near the hatch, he snapped a dial on the propane stove and filled a small pot with water from a plastic jug. Blue flames danced as he made coffee in the dark.

Kalani went forward, heading for the source of the snoring as the morning coffee brewed. A single naked foot protruded from under a ragged quilt in the forward berth. A hand draped over a mahogany rail, knuckles resting on an engine handbook. Next to the manual's oil-stained pages sat a pizza box with a curl of crust and an empty upright wine bottle. Laundry scattered on the deck completed the cabin's still life. *Just the captain. A good sign*. No lingering partygoers like usual. *Must have been a dull weekend*, thought Kalani. He waited for rhythmic breathing to resume and then quickly rifled the sleeper's bulging wallet for a pair of twenties. Pocketing the bills, he stood a foot away, speaking to the quilted mound. "Skipper? Making coffee. You want some?" He shook the bedding and was rewarded with a low growl. A strong aroma of coffee wafted from the galley.

Rising from the covers, a bearded figure in khaki shorts stumbled into the head. Emerging moments later, the man shuffled to the edge of the bunk, snagged a T-shirt, and pulled it on. Kalani poured a steaming mug of coffee and offered it to Rick Crandall. Crandall ran a hand through a bird's nest of unruly auburn hair salted with gray and mumbled a thank you into the cup.

Taking a berth opposite the skipper, Kalani leaned against the bulkhead on one elbow and pitched his idea. "Big south swell coming through this morning. You should check it out, Skipper. Maybe we go out, eh?"

Crandall squinted across the passageway. "Big?"

Kalani grinned. "Eight feet and glassy. Perfect. Not that many folks now. We go for a couple hours, eh? Before da wind comes up."

"Too much to do today," grimaced Crandall, sipping his coffee. "Remember, Tony Chun's coming to help us put the motor back together. Sorry, no can do."

Kalani deflated, shoulders slumping. Rolling from the berth, he retreated to the galley to sulk. Reading his deckhand's face through sleepy eyes, Crandall followed him, clamped a hand on his shoulder. "Hey, no reason for you to stay around. Go on. Surf til noon if you want." He held up a hand, adding, "IF…you promise to come back by then to help Chun and me."

Raising both arms in triumph, Kalani wiggled past him, heading for the ladder. "You got it, brah! Mahalo!"

"NOON!" bellowed Crandall from the galley.

Ignoring the reminder, Kalani scrambled topside, ripping at tattered Velcro straps securing three surfboards amidships. Emerging from below, an amused Crandall, his forearms propped on the hatch, watched Kalani hop across the deck, one leg tangled in his surfing shorts. The half-naked youth buttoned up and leaped to the dock, a short board under one arm.

"NOON!" Crandall repeated, raising his mug in salute. Grinning, Kalani waved over his shoulder as he headed to the breakwater.

Finally severed from the horizon, the sun floated free, turning the harbor to rippled copper. Trade winds shifted the marina's forest of masts, sending sailboats tugging gently against their lines. Purring quietly, a small dinghy slowly passed the moored hulls on a coffee run. Ala Wai harbor came to life. Stroking in unison, two outrigger canoe teams set a punishing pace into the mouth of the Ala Wai Canal in an early morning workout. Across the harbor at the members-only Hawaii Yacht Club, clattering china announced breakfast for early risers. A large white-hulled catamaran, motoring from the club's dock, got underway, moving toward the channel to brave incoming swells, something Crandall had no desire to chance.

Shaking morning dew from cushions, Crandall stretched out in the cockpit by *Sunshine*'s wheel. A nylon tarp, tied over the naked boom, provided shade from the morning sun. Leaning back, he contentedly surveyed his watery realm like some indolent commodore. Living aboard a boat agreed with Crandall. Occasional charters to the other islands in the Hawaiian chain provided extra income, and a comfortable inheritance from his late father added enough for his modest needs.

A couple of years earlier he would have gambled on Tony Chun's notorious tardiness and joined Kalani in surfing Ala Moana. Not today. Getting *Sunshine*'s engine operating took precedence. *A sign of advancing age?* he mused. *No, more like common sense.*

Crandall rubbed his eyes, scratched himself, and yawned. First things first, he told himself. A shower, shave, and food. Though a third set of hands might be useful, he and Chun really didn't need Kalani's help to put *Sunshine*'s motor back into action. The sailboat's power plant—a four-cylinder, 75 hp motor Crandall had cannibalized from his ex-wife's '83 Mercedes—was in need of Chun's magical touch. One of Oahu's best marine mechanics, Chun was constantly in demand either at the marina or across the harbor at the island's private yacht clubs. Crandall had been waiting patiently for two months to get Chun to visit *Sunshine*. Once the engine was back in action, Crandall thought, his options would improve markedly. A return to northern California's Bodega Bay, *Sunshine*'s home port, maybe the coast or a run south to Central America and the Canal. Chun would have to lay his healing hands on the engine to make those options possible. *First things first.*

Startled by an incessant beeping, Crandall fumbled for his cell phone. Chun was calling. Probably late, groused Crandall. "Yeah, Tony. Where are you?"

"Howzit, Rick. Running late, brah. Had to drop the kids at my auntie's. Da traffic killing me, brah."

Grinning, Crandall accepted the expected excuse. "Okay. No problem. I'm going over to the yacht club for breakfast. Call me when you get here, yeah?"

"Will do, brah. Hey, my nephew said Ala Moana's pumping. Dat for real?"

"Yeah, I had to turn Kalani loose. He was drooling all over the deck."

"That little 'aihue still hanging around your boat, Rick? You oughta cut that kid loose before he cleans you out. You way too soft-hearted, brah."

"My little thief, as you call him, is a project. I'm trying to break those bad habits before he does something stupid."

"You won't be the first bleeding heart to try dat, brah. Don't say I nevah warn you, eh? Later." Chun's hearty laugh rang in Crandall's ear as he ended the call.

Rousing himself from the piled cushions, Crandall went below to pick out a decent aloha shirt. He grabbed his wallet, came topside, stumbled into *Sunshine*'s rubber dinghy, and started the outboard for the short trip across the canal. The yacht club's chef, a marina neighbor, had invited Crandall numerous times to pay back various favors. Never one to turn down a good meal, Crandall aimed for the club's dock. He took a table in the shade where he could keep an eye on his boat in case Chun surprised him by arriving on time. As Crandall ate, Cruz, the club's chef, stopped by to chat, informing him his tenure in the kitchen would finish at month's end. The members' palates were jaded, he said. A hazard of the trade. No hard feelings according to Cruz. He'd find another job in one of Waikiki's hotels.

"Try Kauai," Crandall said. He'd heard they were hiring at some of the island's bigger resorts. Cruz thanked him and disappeared into the kitchen to prep for the lunch crowd. At the same time, Crandall's cell phone came to life. Chun had arrived and was starting on the engine. Crandall finished his breakfast, left a five-dollar tip, and took his inflatable back across the harbor to

Sunshine. Wiggling from the hold at the stern, Chun pushed a plastic bin filled with oily rags and engine parts across the deck. The front of his T-shirt was filthy. "Hey, how was breakfast?"

Crandall finished tying off the dinghy. "Fantastic as usual. Might be the end of my meal ticket though. Cruz is getting laid off."

"Those rich folks changing chefs again?"

"Yeah. He says they get in a rut over there and like to shake things up."

"Money does that to you, huh?"

Crandall hunkered down against the closed hatchway. "I wouldn't know."

Chun tossed a rag in the plastic container and sat. "Got some good news and some bad news. Which one you want first, brah?"

"Go with the good for now."

"Okay. I know dis guy over Kãnohe. Got an almost-new engine. I can get it for you and put it in for fourteen."

"Geez, fourteen. I dunno. What's the bad news?"

"Ain't that bad. I pulled all the injectors. Gonna take 'em back to da shop. Gotta clean 'em and check the spray pattern. If I need to change out anything else it'll cost you extra. Benz parts ain't cheap, you know."

"Don't I know. So how much time we talking about here?"

"Couple of days. You in a hurry?"

"Not going anywhere without an engine, am I?"

"Nope. And you oughta think seriously about dat new engine, Rick."

"Not interested. Maybe if I won one of those Asian lotteries."

"Gotta play to win."

"Minor detail. Okay," sighed Crandall, "get back to me as soon as you can."

"You got it, brah." Chun muscled the bin to a waiting wheelbarrow on the dock, leaving Crandall with a gutted engine. After tightening the awning over the cockpit, Crandall wiped palm prints from the hatch and stretched out in the shade with an unfinished Patrick O'Brian paperback. In the evening he would paddle out at Ala Moana if the swell was still pumping. Propping the novel on his chest, Crandall drifted off to sleep.

....

Chapter 20

"You're AWOL." Crandall shot a scolding look at Kalani who had quietly slipped on board the *Sunshine*. "As captain I have the right to have you keelhauled and shot."

"Sorry, Skipper, I forget da time, eh?"

Crandall dropped his mask. "Waves pretty good, huh?"

Kalani's wide smile was the answer. "Da best. You should go out later. Plenty good ones still coming in. Not too crowded. Tony Chun come by yet?"

"You planned that well," grunted Crandall. "He's come and gone." Tossing the youth a rag, he pointed to scuffmarks on the deck from the dismantling of the boat's engine. "Better make yourself useful, Kalani. Clean the spots I missed."

Pushing back the hatch, Crandall had one foot on the ladder when he spotted a young woman with long black hair waving to him. Climbing back on deck, Crandall ambled to the rail. Mamo, one of the harbormaster's go-fers, pedaled along the pier toward *Sunshine*. Braking to a stop, the woman straddled the bike, hiking her muumuu to her thighs. She held out a folded piece of paper. "Hey, you got a message."

"Finally, an invitation to your prom?"

"Funny man. Don't you wish," she shot back. "Somebody called the office for you. Probably one of your ex-wives, eh? How many you got anyway?"

Leaping to the dock, Crandall plucked the note from her hand and stuffed it in a shirt pocket. "Thanks for bringing it over, Mamo. Now about prom night."

Blushing, his messenger giggled. "By the time I'm old enough to go out with you it will be too late. You gonna be in assisted living."

"Always worth a try. Mahalo, eh?"

Mamo waved, tossed her long black hair, mounted her bike, and rode away. Kalani had stopped work to watch the exchange. He grabbed his crotch, leering at the girl. Disgusted, Crandall barked at the crude display. "What, you never seen a beautiful wahine before, Kalani? Put your tongue back in your mouth and finish your job!"

Crandall came back aboard, pointed out some spots Kalani had missed, and went below. Grabbing a cold beer from the fridge, he sprawled in the forward berth. Unfolding the scrap of paper, he smoothed the sheet and took a long pull on the beer. Running the icy bottle across his forehead, he began reading.

Rick Crandall, Hoping you will respond to my note. I have been calling every marina on both coasts hoping to find you. Gave up on the mainland and thought of Hawaii. Knew your dad had been stationed there when you were a kid. Remember you talking about it. Office at the marina said you were there. You don't know how happy I am to find you again. Please call me or email me as soon as you get this note. I have never forgotten you, Rick. I hope you still have a soft spot in your heart for me as I have for you. Fond memories of Florida. Love, Becky

Stunned, Crandall sat back against the bulkhead. Slowly sipping his beer, he flashed back to senior year of high school. Spring break. Last chance for freedom before the approaching hell of plebe summer at the Naval Academy. Crandall's fealty to a male family tradition had predestined him for Annapolis. Closing his eyes, Crandall imagined his week of infatuation with the girl from Minnesota.

Becky was one of a dozen high school seniors who had driven non-stop to Ft. Lauderdale. If there is such a thing as love at first sight, the two of them had experienced it. Days of sun, beer, sand, the ocean, and laughter. Deep meaningful conversations. Nights like silk. Passion, sealed with multiple solemn pledges of love made the inevitable separation even more heart wrenching when the week ended. The usual promises to write and call had been exchanged.

Rising from the bunk, Crandall helped himself to a second beer and returned to the note. The memory of ten-page letters and two-hour late-night phone calls came flooding back. Hell week at the Academy swept all that away. There was no room for sentimentality in a plebe's life. His letters, when he wrote at all, were truncated versions of earlier ones. The academy redirected his focus.

His commitment changed from love to duty. Eventually, the letters dried to a trickle, died. He went on to flight school, lost track of Becky, as she did him. Clumsy cursory attempts to reconnect were derailed by both of them. Monastic sea duty finished it. But he had never forgotten his first love. Lost in his reverie, Crandall did not hear Kalani's voice booming through the forward hatch. "Hey, Skipper, you awake? I'm done. Check it out!" Snapping out of his daydream, Crandall stared up at Kalani's brown face framed in the hatchway.

"Okay, be right up." He rinsed his beer bottles, left them in the sink, and went topside to inspect the cleaning job. No grease spots showed, the brass glowed. Nodding approval, Crandall handed Kalani a ten-dollar bill and sent him on his way so he could be alone with his thoughts. *Not ready to talk yet. Need to think this through. Why now? After all these years? What's going on in her life? I need to write first, not talk. I have to be very careful with my words.* Unlocking an overhead cabinet, Crandall took out a laptop to compose a reply to the address Becky had furnished. He went on deck and sat in the shade under the canvas rigged on the stern. Starting and stopping a half-dozen times, he threw away words until he was satisfied with a beginning. From that point on he wrote for two hours until emotionally drained. Hesitating over the keyboard, he took a deep breath and sent his heart on its way.

. . . .

Chapter 21

County Highway 21, south of Upsala

Two joggers in hooded sweat suits, towels around their necks like prize fighters in training, crested a rise on a winding farm road that snaked past dark pine windbreaks and isolated farmhouses. The lead runner stayed a good twenty or thirty yards in front of the second one. A honey-colored dog darted between the pair like a four-legged cheerleader, joyously nipping at their heels.

Pounding through slush, Becky, the first runner, glanced over her shoulder at Darryl, the distance between them growing with each step. Slowing, she dropped back until he drew abreast of her. "Too fast for you?"

"I'm pacing myself," he huffed.

"Like hell you are. You're out of shape, Darryl."

Glowering at the insult, he sprinted ahead, only to falter on the downside slope. Becky stayed on Darryl's heels to spur him. When his pace slackened she slowed to let him keep the lead. When she lengthened her stride, threatening to overtake him, he turned on a quick burst of speed to stay in front. They ran this punishing accordion-style contest for twenty minutes until Darryl ran out of steam on the outskirts of town. "Walk!" she ordered. For once he obeyed, grateful for the chance to suck needed air, to let his leg muscles work out the crippling cramps from the last quarter mile. Holding a hand to his side, Darryl grimaced in pain as they cooled down.

They walked in silence until reaching the farm lane leading to a white, two-story clapboard farmhouse. Darryl's trailer perched on concrete footings in a grove of aspen and pine behind a barn-cum-welding shop wearing a coat of peeling red paint. Becky's Honda sat in the driveway next to his white Toyota.

Becky put a hand on his back, offered him her towel which he refused, preferring his own which he draped over his head. "You're doing better, Darryl. Each day gets you closer to the goal."

Taking a seat on the trailer's porch, he shucked his sweat-soaked jacket. Steam rose from his body. "Your goal, not mine," he said.

"Your goal too," Becky reasoned, toweling her face and neck. "You can't walk out of a jungle if you're not in shape."

"I'm tired of you giving me that same old bullshit. I'm out here busting my balls while David does squat."

Hands on hips, she faced him. "You don't know shit about what David's doing. Matter of fact he's been working out three, four times a week at a club in St. Cloud. So don't give me crap about your brother."

Shelving his complaining, Darryl switched strategy. "Wanna come in for a beer?"

"No beer," she scolded. "You're in training, remember?"

"Hell, Becky, Babe Ruth trained on beer. Did you know that?"

"I seriously doubt that."

"It's true." Grinning mischievously from the trailer's sagging deck, Darryl tossed out a clumsy lure. "Okay, how about we share a bottle of water?"

"How about I go home to shower. You do likewise."

"The two of us? Your place? I'm up for that."

She shot him a well-practiced drop-dead look. "You know what I mean, Darryl. I'll see you tomorrow before work. We'll do the same run."

"Five miles?" He draped the towel over his head, buried his face in his arms. "Ahh, shit, how about we take a break and do it the day after. You're killing me here. This ain't the frickin' Olympics, you know."

Becky started the Honda and threw him a bone. "Okay, tomorrow we'll just do three miles. See you at nine."

"Three miles, five miles. Nine o'clock. What the hell, you're still killing me."

Backing down the driveway, she rolled down her window, saying, "You'll survive. Just think, you'll be in great shape by the time we're done."

As she drove away Darryl stood, bellowing defiantly, "I'm going inside and I'm GONNA HAVE A BEER!"

....

Chapter 22

Ala Wai Marina, February 12

Monday morning Chun arrived, reassembled the *Sunshine*'s engine, and had it purring by noon. Crandall was pleased with what he heard and felt. Smooth and steady, no hiccups, no problems starting, and no oil leaks. He killed the motor and paid Chun in cash. "Sounds beautiful. You just gave it another ten years of life. May your tribe increase, brah. You are one fantastic mechanic."

"Ah, you, my friend, are a good judge of talent. What you gonna do now? Back to the mainland or what?"

Crandall kept his mask on. "No big plans. Maybe keep running charters for a while. Do the South American thing again. Maybe Australia. It's just an idea I've been kicking around. Long way, though. Mainland's closer. Might just stay on here. Hate to get too far away from you. Who else could baby my engine like you?"

"That guy in Kãnohe still get that motor for sale, brah. You change your mind and…"

"Not gonna happen," said Crandall, patting the Mercedes. "You saved me money in the long run. Mahalo, eh?" The two shook hands. Chun loaded his toolbox in a wheelbarrow parked on the pier and pushed it to his pickup. Crandall went below. After making himself a sandwich, he opened a cold beer and booted up his laptop to open a saved cache of Becky's most recent letters.

He lay back in a berth, opened a desktop folder with her photos, took a bite of sandwich, read, ate some more, drank beer, and re-read her latest email. It had arrived two days ago. What she had proposed was unbelievable. The stuff of fantasy. Reading her proposition a second and third time intrigued him. Like Becky, the plan was outrageous. Passionate. Compelling.

After two hours of hesitation, Crandall worked up his courage, went topside with his cell phone, and called the number she had given him. He dialed twice, panicked and hung up both times before finally connecting on his third try. Hearing one another's voices after eighteen years electrified them both. Becky said she had known it was him calling. She had patiently waited for him to decide whether he would let the call go through. They talked for thirty minutes, then connected on Skype. Crandall was stunned at Becky's seductive beauty, she at his handsome ruddy face, sailor's beard, and easy smile. It was Florida redux. Spring break interrupted, now resumed. Forty minutes flew by. As they talked, she shared images behind her—frosted windows, a log fire, and an ice-locked lake reflecting a dying sunset. Crandall went topside, gave her Oahu's Ko'olau Range, a flawless sky, and Waikiki's skyline. When they reluctantly signed off, each had surrendered to the other.

....

Chapter 23

Ala Wai Marina, one week later

The tantalizing aroma of steak drifted from a charcoal grill on *Sunshine*'s stern. Crandall turned a pair of filets over white-hot coals while silently rehearsing the proposal he was about to make to Kalani. He thought about the FedEx envelope with thirty-five thousand dollars squirreled away beneath his berth. The package had arrived within days of his conversation with Becky. Along with the cash was a detailed plan in which Becky revealed the reasons for her upcoming trip to Papua New Guinea. Her audacious proposal, plus follow-up calls explaining her reasons for the expedition, had won over Crandall. All he lacked was someone he could count on for the long trip to the South Pacific. Kalani would be a less-than-perfect fit but he was impressionable and available. At sea, there would be no thievery.

"Coming down!" bellowed Crandall, descending the teak ladder with a platter of sizzling meat. He slapped steak on their plates, opened two beers, and slipped a slack key CD in the player. Layered guitar chords and Led Kaapana's lilting falsetto floated through the cabin. Lifting his bottle in a toast, Crandall said, "Beer and steak. Does it get any better than this? Here's to a terrific meal."

"Pau hana time, brah." Kalani tapped his bottle against Crandall's and got an "Amen" in reply. Both men attacked their dinners, eating in silence. When they finished, Crandall pushed away the empty plates and drained his beer. Opening two more, he stared at his dinner guest. "I have a proposition for you. I want you to give it very serious consideration, okay?"

"Sure, Skipper."

Taking a long swallow of beer, Crandall locked eyes with Kalani. "I'm thinking about sailing to Australia and Papua New Guinea. I'd like you to come along. It's a big decision so take time to think about it."

Lowering his bottle, the youth took a deep breath. "That's a long way, brah."

"Yeah, I know," agreed Crandall. "It's a big decision. I've got a couple of friends who are going to be down that way in May. They're looking for a ride back. Could be a great time."

"You mean we'd go down there just to bring them back?"

"Hell, yes. Ever been to Australia or New Guinea, Kalani?"

Shaking his head, the Hawaiian youth answered, his expression serious. "Been to California once but that was a couple of years ago. Didn't like the cold water. Too many haoles. No offense, Skipper."

Crandall chuckled. “No offense taken, Kalani. Nah, this would be something completely different. We’d head south; hit some of the island chains. Maybe Tahiti, Samoa, Fiji, the Marshalls, the Solomons. Papua New Guinea. Australia.”

“Gee, but, I dunno, brah. How long you figure something like that take?”

“Maybe a month-plus to get down there. Two months back. See a lot of places.” Helping himself to another beer from the refrigerator, Kalani returned to the small table where a smiling Crandall leaned against the bulkhead, a dish of pudding-like Haupia balanced on his stomach. Between spoonfuls of dessert he resumed selling the idea. “Think of all the places you’ve never seen,” he said. “All that ocean. All those islands. Kinda like following the footsteps of your ancestors.”

“’Cept for the mainland I never been that far from home, you know.”

Crandall pressed in. “Yeah, but what’s really home? You’re living with your auntie, right? With all her kids you have what, one room to yourself in her house in Manoa? How long you want to live like that? What’s a room in Manoa compared to having the whole world? I’ve been up and down the mainland coast, through the Canal twice, and across the Gulf. I’ve seen both coasts of Florida and the Keys.

I’ve sailed the Caribbean and visited South America. I’m kinda curious about the South Pacific, aren’t you?”

The meal, or maybe the beer and Crandall’s salesmanship, was working. Sensing it, he moved in to close the deal. “Whadaya think? We make the run, pick up my friends, and get back in time for winter surf on the North Shore. You game?”

“Just the two of us? That’s a lot of ocean, brah.”

Crandall got another beer for both of them to help his case. “We’ll need to drum up another body. Maybe two. Backup.

Maybe some folks you know might want to taste a little adventure, eh?"

"I can ask around," said Kalani, weakening. "I know plenty guys, Skipper."

Crandall wagged a finger. "They have to know something about sailing."

"Right. Too much ocean for just us two, eh?"

"Exactly. Ask around, Kalani. I'll do the same. See what we come up with, eh? Sound like a plan to you?"

One more beer and Crandall had him. "Yeah. I'll do that, Skipper. When we gotta leave?"

Tugging on his beard, Crandall put on his best thoughtful face. "Have to leave in the next two months for sure."

"Gee, not much time, eh?"

Ignoring the comment, Crandall tossed out a hook instead. "We can check out surf spots everywhere we go, eh? Papua New Guinea has some nice spots. Fiji's got good reef breaks, you know. Kinda like a vacation, eh?"

Kalani took the bait. "Yeah, we bring da boards, right?"

Nodding enthusiastically, Crandall set the hook. "Absolutely. Wouldn't go without them. Imagine if we found a nice spot." Sketching with both hands, a bottle in his right, Crandall continued. "Can you see it? Six-foot right. Glassy. Nobody out. We anchor outside the break. Paddle out, surf for a couple of hours. Come back in. Break for lunch. Maybe a nap. Go back out." Kalani's glazed eyes stared into the distance, his mind focused on a virgin, pristine line of breakers beckoning somewhere in the South Pacific. Crandall reeled him in with one last temptation.

"I don't expect you to crew for free. You'll come back with three thousand dollars in your pocket."

"Three thousand?"

"You heard me right, Kalani. Three thousand for making the trip."

"Hey, okay, Skipper. No need to think about it. Count me in."

Crandall raised yet another bottle. "If you're sure, then we're good to go. We find ourselves some crew and I'll start plotting routes first thing tomorrow."

Kalani let out a whoop. Crandall added his voice and a chorus of laughter, then opened a another beer to finish the evening.

....

Chapter 24

County Road 9, southeast of Upsala

Punctuality, according to Darryl, was highly over-rated, which was why Becky, bundled against the cold, sat in her idling Honda on the side of a deserted county road, her patience eroding by the minute. They were well into their third week of jogging and today she had planned something different. Becky had insisted Darryl's brother pick him up for another training session. David, the more dependable of the two, could be counted on to make sure Darryl showed.

Another glance at her watch told her the siblings were twenty minutes late. Brooding gray clouds sailed leisurely across frozen fields, screening the sun, reducing it to an out-of-focus white blemish. Light snow had fallen during the night, blanketing unplowed back roads with an inch of powder. Only one driver had passed, a pale elderly woman with a death grip on the wheel who ignored the solitary car and its occupant by the roadside.

Stomping her booted feet to get her blood moving, Becky

shot another hopeful look at her rearview mirror. Relieved to spot two heads in a familiar maroon SUV heading her way, her irritation evaporated. It was David, with brother Darryl in custody. She got out of the Honda, pumping her arms, as much to warm herself as to attract attention. The SUV turned left at a T-junction and barreled down the highway, trailing a corkscrew cloud of snow. The blood-red car rolled to a stop behind the little Honda and David got out, waving. True to character, Darryl, half-awake and sullen, stayed behind, huddling in front of the blasting heater. Trotting to David, Becky gave him a hug, then knocked angrily on the SUV's windshield, rousting Darryl from his cocoon. Grudgingly, he cut the engine and joined them, his face obscured by a hood. "Morning, sunshine," teased Becky.

David cuffed his brother's ears. "Darryl's pissed because I wouldn't let him bring a favorite stuffed animal. "

"Fuck both of you. Do you have any idea what the wind chill is?"

Ignoring Darryl's complaint, Becky said, "Doesn't matter. Let's get down to business. We've got some walking to do. You ready?" She got a non-committal shrug from Darryl, a grin from David.

"I have something for you," said Becky, leading them to the Honda. Unlocking the trunk, she hefted two bulging, sleeveless jackets resembling safety bibs worn by highway workers. Made of canvas, each was hemmed and lined with rows of small pockets, sewn front and back. Thick padding lined the inside where the shoulders met the neck. "Try these on."

Holding the garment at arm's length, David turned the vest in his hands. "What the hell you up to, Becky?"

"These," she said handing a vest to Darryl, "are how we get the gold out."

"This thing weighs a ton," whined Darryl. "Whadaya got in it, lead?"

"Sand. I filled yours with fifty pounds, thirty in mine." Lifting a third vest from the trunk, Becky slipped it over her head, fastening Velcro tabs on both sides of her waist for a snug fit. Pirouetting, she modeled her vest for the two. "Well, what do you think? Go ahead, put 'em on." She helped Darryl, guiding his head through the hole in the yoke-styled vest, securing it with tabs at his sides.

Donning the bulky garment, David blew out his cheeks. "I think I got the wrong one. I want yours, it's twenty pounds lighter."

Shifting the weighted vest to get comfortable, Darryl chimed in, "Yeah, why fifty pounds? I thought me and David was only humping thirty-five each."

"You are. I'm just trying to get us in shape for the trip. If we can get used to hauling this much weight I figure we'll have no problem when it's for real."

Darryl snorted ragged clouds of breath in the frigid air. "What, you been running my ass around those roads back home. Ain't that enough for you? Now you hafta drag us out here in the middle of nowhere and load us up with this shit? Damn, Becky, have a heart."

"She's right," scolded David. "We need to get used to this weight. What did you have in mind, Becky?"

Gesturing at the snow-covered route running straight through white-blanketed fields, she announced, "Today we do a mile up and back just to see how we handle the load. Make sense?"

"That's it?" smirked Darryl. "You get me all the way out here in the middle of nowhere to walk two lousy frickin' miles? Hell, I could do that in my sleep."

"That's just for starters. Every three days we add another mile. Walk one day, take one day to recover, and jog the next day. Then, a day of rest and back to the vests. We add another mile each time we go out. That's our routine until we leave."

Curious, David asked, "How'd you come up with this plan? And how far we gonna walk once we get to Papua New Guinea? And have you figured out how we get the gold out of the country?"

"I got the idea for the vest from some cable show about a guy training for one of those Iron Man races. He used a backpack filled with sand. It gave me an idea.

I figured this would be an easy way to get the feel for the weight. And no, I don't know how far we'll have to go once we get there. But I think I have a solution about bringing the gold out. I'll lay it out for you when we finish our workout."

David smiled. "Very cool, very smart. Well, what're we waiting for? Let's get moving. I'm freezing my ass off out here as it is. Lead the way, girl."

"From where we're parked I make it a mile to that rise where the cell phone tower is. Up and back, two miles." Stabbing a gloved hand north toward the horizon, she said, "Our cars will be okay, plows won't be through here for a couple of hours." Without waiting for an answer, she stepped off, the brothers single file behind her, boots scuffing in snow.

Gusts of wind buffeted the trio, scouring the county road, driving loose streams of snow across the frozen gravel. Becky leaned into the biting wind, the heavy, unfamiliar pack digging into her shoulders. Matching her step for step, the Lindquists constantly made small adjustments to get comfortable with the load on their backs. The only sounds for the first mile were wind and crunching boots on snow. On the return, Darryl's earlier boast of "doing this in my sleep" gave way to a mix of profanity and tortured whining in a losing competition with the wind.

. . . .

Chapter 25

Ala Wai Marina, February 22

"We need sailors, Kalani, not sumo wrestlers."

Crandall stared at two hulking ebony men squatting placidly on the pier next to the *Sunshine*. Kalani Souza stood at the sailboat's open hatch, nervously glancing back and forth between Crandall, halfway up the teak ladder, and the pair on the dock. "You said to ask around, brah. These guys looking for a ride. They're strong. They know sailing. They're willing."

Crandall pinched his eyes shut in frustration and ran a hand through his unruly hair. When he looked up the pair still sat patiently where Kalani had told them to wait. "Look at them," he sighed. "They'd go through our entire food supply in a week. We'd have to tow a barge just to feed them. What the hell were you thinking?"

Kalani struck a pleading pose at the hatch. "At least talk to them, Skipper. Mebbe you change your mind, huh?"

"Yeah, yeah. Okay, what's the story with these guys? Who are they?"

"Twin brothers from Fiji. Family name is Lauofo. Big one is Joseph..."

Interrupting, Crandall arched a disbelieving eyebrow. "And which one would that be...the big one, I mean."

Kalani, missing the sarcasm, glanced over his shoulder at the Lauofos. "Joseph, on the right in the football jersey. The smaller one is Benjamin."

"Geez, Kalani, you need glasses or what? Do you even know what the word big means? Try huge. Try enormous. Either of those descriptions ring a bell? These guys look like starting linebackers for the U of H. What do you know about them?"

"They in school, but not the U. They stay over Laie. Brigham Young University. Both work at the Polynesian Cultural Center. Man, they homesick so bad. Just wanna go back to Fiji, brah."

More sarcasm from Crandall. "Oh, great, now I've got Mormons. They ever hear of airplanes, Kalani? Get 'em home a helluva lot faster than a sailboat."

"They got no money, brah."

"They trying to stay one step ahead of the sheriff?"

"No way," an indignant Kalani shot back, "not like that at all. They just want to go back home. Just talk to them. Please, Skipper."

Crandall made the mistake of making eye contact with the large youths. He got a wide, hopeful smile from both. He nodded politely and got friendly waves in return. "Okay, no harm in talking to them." Kalani broke into a wide grin but got a caution from Crandall. "But I'm not rolling over for these guys. I still think they're way too big for a boat this size and a trip as long as the one we're looking at."

"But hey, they're only going as far as Fiji. Can I ask them over, Skipper?"

Shrugging, an unconvinced Crandall sent Kalani ashore to fetch the brothers.

....

Chapter 26

Oahu, February 27

Crandall roamed *Sunshine*'s deck, seemingly everywhere in preparation for the departure for Kona. The trip to the Big Island—a shakedown cruise to test the Lauofos in open water—would give him an idea of how well his makeshift crew functioned as a team. A few daily milk runs off Oahu with both neophytes had gone well. The mid-morning sun climbed in a flawless sky, baking the harbor. Behind the marina, the Ko'olau, its lower slopes crowded with clinging houses, rose in steep waves of mottled greens and browns. Billowing clouds cast purple shadows as they drifted across the rugged peaks overlooking Honolulu. Burrowing in the engine hold, Crandall checked the restored Mercedes for the fourth time. Transmission fluid and oil were topped off. *Sunshine*'s 53-gallon fuel tanks were full. Ten extra five-gallon cans of diesel were lashed down below.

To Crandall's critical eye everything looked good. Time to put Chun's skills to the test. He switched on the glow plugs, counted to ten, switched them off, pushed the starter button, and was rewarded with the diesel's comforting rumble. Kalani eyed the gauges and gave a thumbs-up, grinning. Crandall's eyes and hands roamed over the 75 hp engine, looking for spurting oil, loose belts, or leaking hoses.

No surprises. Chun had done his work. He shouted over the throbbing four-cylinder motor. "Looking good, Kalani!"

While the engine warmed, Crandall wiggled from the engine compartment, bellowed to the Lauofos. He ordered the big Fijian youths to strip and stow sail covers. Standing at the wheel, he next sent Joseph forward to stand by the bowline,

Benjamin at the spring line. Kalani climbed to the dock to handle the stern line. Once *Sunshine* began moving he would take the line in hand, leaping on board as the boat abandoned its slip.

Crandall went below, emerging a moment later wearing an ironed Tahitian-print aloha shirt and pressed khaki shorts. Signaling for the lines to be taken on board, he eased into gear. Kalani nimbly stepped aboard as *Sunshine* slowly slipped from the dock that had been its home for the last eighteen months. Crandall spun the wheel to port, clearing the pier. His crew stood by with boat hooks—a precaution to save Crandall the embarrassment of his bowsprit snagging a neighbor's mast or piling on the way to the channel. He goosed the throttle forward and the Mercedes responded, purring perfectly. A rubber dinghy passed to port, motoring in the opposite direction. Its pilot, a fellow marina tenant, raised a hand in farewell.

Mamo and a girlfriend, leis over their arms, arrived a minute too late. The women rode to the end of the pier, tossed leis into the water, and blew kisses at the *Sunshine*'s crew. Yelling and giggling, both women waved at the departing sailboat, their voices growing faint. Crandall signaled to other boat owners who came topside to watch *Sunshine* motor gracefully toward the Ala Wai channel. Ahead of them, a five-man outrigger shot across *Sunshine*'s bow toward the canal, the canoe's steersman flashing his paddle in salute, shouting, "Pomaika `i!" Crandall waved thanks and turned his attention to clearing the harbor. The sluggish green water of the marina gave way to the channel's dark, ruler-straight outlines. To port, a dozen surfers scrapped over sloppy knee-high breakers hardly worth paddling for. To starboard, Ala Moana's man-made Magic Island echoed with childish voices from the park's enclosed lagoon.

Trade winds, a farewell gift from the Ko'olau, sent ripples across the channel. The ultramarine horizon beckoned. Kalani hustled, connecting halyards, readying the sails. *Sunshine*'s bow dipped in gentle incoming swells. As they cleared the channel mouth, Crandall ordered the mainsail raised. He observed its set and barked minor adjustments to Kalani. The Fijians shadowed him, studying his every move. *Sunshine* turned into the wind and Crandall had his crew set the foresail. Liking what he saw, he commanded the jib be set as well. Once the sails filled, he killed the engine, trading its hammering noise for wind power and blessed silence.

Stacked white hotel blocks lining Waikiki raced by, growing smaller as they approached Diamond Head. As *Sunshine* rounded the iconic landmark a few miles offshore, Kalani took over the helm. Crandall disappeared below, reemerging moments later in a sleeveless rash-guard shirt, tattered jeans shorts, and reef shoes. Crandall broke the silence with a wild, triumphant yell, startling the Fijians. Kalani grinned. He knew the signs. Each time Crandall hit the ocean, he changed from slothful laid-back harbor regular to energized open-water sailor. The winds stiffened, snapping at the sails. Spray peppered the foredeck like buckshot.

Crandall took over the wheel. "Prepare to get wet, gentlemen!"

The Lauofos exchanged apprehensive glances. Kalani slapped Joseph's broad back and told the brothers to follow him below deck to don more suitable clothing while there was still time. As the Lauofos changed clothes, Kalani secured all hatches, double-checked the main cabin for anything that might fly loose, then coaxed the siblings topside. With the trio back on deck and cinched tight in their safety harnesses, *Sunshine* was already racing toward the edge of the Kaiwi Channel between Oahu and neighboring Molokai. Crandall knew from experience the twenty-six mile crossing would be a challenge—a good test of the Fijians' resolve.

It took most of the remaining day to best the channel. When the sun finally died in a burst of flame, the winds slackened off Molokai. *Sunshine* slowed to three knots. Crandall called the twins to the cockpit for turns at the wheel, tutoring them in basic navigation. The west's glowing horizon was replaced with a black night sky painted with constellations close enough to touch. The night passed uneventfully.

Morning exploded in a wild palette. Heading southeast, they neared Maui's coast. Lahaina's lights sparkled in the dawn. They coaxed what wind they could most of the day along Maui's leeward coast. A new heading sent them south toward the Big Island. Wind filled the sails. Crandall felt the change and came topside with a mug of coffee to relieve Kalani and Benjamin. He sent the two below to sleep and gave Joseph the tiller for the next hour. When evening arrived, the schooner was riding long green swells due south toward Kailua-Kona.

On the morning of the third day, *Sunshine* reached landfall on the northwest tip of Hawaii. Mauna Loa's muscular slopes appeared, rising majestically to a snow-dusted summit. Flying fish arched ahead of them, silver flashes rocketing from the cobalt waves off the bow. High above them, a lone ìwa—a frigate bird—glided effortlessly on its ninety-inch wingspan, the big bird easily outdistancing the sailboat in minutes. At noon, Crandall changed course, heading south to parallel the Big Island's rugged coast. "All we're missing is a rainbow!" he shouted.

"Yeah, good signs, Skipper," added Kalani. The Lauofos sat facing the bow, one on each side of the cockpit, their huge arms draped over the cabin roof. Of the four aboard, Joseph had suffered the most during the battering in the Kaiwi Channel off Molokai. Bruised and broken by the end of the roller coaster passage, he acted like a man who had gone fifteen rounds only to lose the decision. Crandall cranked up the engine and had

Kalani and the Fijians drop sail just off a crescent of beach where wave action was negligible. With *Sunshine*'s bow into the wind, they set two anchors in fifteen feet over a sandy bottom with few rocks. "Little housekeeping, gentlemen," announced Kalani, handing out fins, masks, and snorkels.

Leading by example, Crandall, wire brush and putty knife in hand, was the first over the side. The anchorage was perfect, the water warm. The Lauofos were given stiff green scouring pads and tutored by Kalani in the finer points of cleaning a boat's hull. As barnacles and algae were scraped and scrubbed from the sailboat, small fish appeared, eagerly hunting edible morsels. Little fish inevitably attract larger fish. Surrounded by darting rainbow-hued fish, the four men were soon laboring in what became a crowded tropical aquarium. Each man had been given an assignment. Kalani erased a slimy green beard the length of the waterline. Diving repeatedly, Crandall chipped away at a keel encrusted with marine freeloaders.

Lolling alongside the boat like ebony elephant seals, the Lauofos attacked *Sunshine*'s bottom with enthusiasm, happy to be off the boat and in the water. After an hour spent cleaning, the four men came back on board for a break. Kalani and Crandall cracked open two cold beers. The Fijians, good Mormons, contented themselves with juice. The task finished, Crandall fired the Mercedes, hoisted anchor, and set the foresail and jib to take them toward the ancient fishpond of Kaloko, and beyond that, Honokohau Bay.

Reaching the rock-lined harbor mouth of Gentry's Kona Marina, Crandall ordered sail taken in. Trailing in the wake of two power cruisers, *Sunshine* motored into the refuge. Food, fuel, and a chance to dry out would be a welcome break.

Crandall had arranged for *Sunshine*'s hull to be hoisted from the water and power-washed. Whatever marine life remained on the hull would be stripped clean. Full-service boatyard facilities were few and far between where they were headed. Overnights in Kona were a needed respite, but first, Crandall had one more surprise in store for his green crewmen. Kalani, privy to what was about to happen, fought to keep his best poker face in place.

Crandall aimed for two concrete piers where a boatlift waited. The marina's grapevine lured a handful of dockworkers for the show. Crandall made a wide sweep, reversed, and backed stern first underneath a blue steel hoist straddling the piers. He killed the motor. Kalani and the Fijians threw mooring lines to shore. Two stoic Hawaiians stood on opposite stone piers, each one lowering a heavy nylon lift strap into the water, pulling the eighteen-inch-wide belt under *Sunshine*'s bow and securing it to the hydraulic lift.

"Joseph, Benjamin, you guys go over the side and pass the second strap forward of the stern." Winking at Crandall, Kalani tossed swim masks to the puzzled brothers. "Benjamin, you hold one end of the strap while Joseph takes the other end and swims under the hull. He gives that to the crew. They'll take it from there." Joseph was baffled. "Hey, Kalani, why we gotta do this?"

Shrugging, Kalani busied himself by coiling lines on the deck. "Just the way it works, brah. Soon's you get us hooked up, the sooner they get da job done, eh?"

Joseph hesitantly peered at the turquoise water. "Get sharks?"

"No mo sharks, brah."

"Get eels?"

"Nevah seen em yet, brah."

Objections exhausted, the compliant Fijians resigned themselves to the task. They peeled off shirts and donned masks. More laborers drifted to the pier to watch. The Lauofos timidly backed down the stern ladder into the water and dog-paddled next to pilings where two workers wearing hard hats lowered the second broad strap to Benjamin. Bobbing like a large black buoy, he treaded water just forward of *Sunshine*'s cockpit. Joseph took one end of the three-quarter-inch-thick strap from his brother, sucked in a lungful of air, and dove under the hull, pulling the belt with him. Surfacing on the other side, he handed the strap to a crouching worker who hooked it to the lift. The Lauofos swam toward the stern ladder, their faces in the water, scanning the shallow sandy bottom.

A huge dark shape glided underneath them.

Surfacing, Joseph screamed. Benjamin panicked as well, thrashing his way to the stern. Both men fought their way up the ladder, their combined weight tilting the *Sunshine* to starboard. Five hundred pounds of shrieking Fijian flesh flopped in the sunlight like a pair of mortally wounded walrus. Roars of laughter erupted from the dock. Howling laborers, lift operators, and bystanders hooted and clapped at the bewildered men. Crandall and Kalani joined in the cruel chorus.

"Just a ray, bruddah!" bellowed a burly mechanic.

"Ain't gonna eat you, brah!" yelled another yard worker. "Just curious!"

When laughter died, the embarrassed brothers toweled, dressed, and stepped ashore where Crandall and Kalani waited. Joseph steamed. Benjamin shyly grinned. "You got us good, Skipper. Next time we gonna get you fo sure."

"Don't be too upset," consoled Crandall. "My first time here, same thing happened to me. I walked on water to get back on board. Didn't seem funny at the time." Scowling, Joseph grumbled. "Still ain't funny."

Kalani laughed. "Happens to everybody who comes in here to use the lift."

"Yeah, but only once," said Crandall. "Mostly haoles if that makes you guys feel any better."

Rumbling into action, the marina's crane easily hoisted its eleven-ton burden as though it was a toy boat. The steel frame wheeled to a spot in the yard where it gently deposited the lead keel on scarred four-foot-square blocks of wood. Two teams of hardhats wrestled jack stands against both sides of the hull, fixing *Sunshine* solidly in place. A quick fresh water rinse with pressure hoses completed the job. A ladder was extended and lashed to the boat. *Sunshine*'s crew would sleep on board during the marina stay. His cradled schooner silhouetted against the early afternoon sun, Crandall gave Kalani a list of additional needed supplies to order and sent his crew to dinner. He stayed to scrape away a few stubborn scraps of marine life still clinging to the hull. In a few hours the bottom's old skin would be bone-dry, ready for one last cleaning and a fresh coat of anti-fouling paint. Then the crane's ballet would be reversed, returning *Sunshine* to the harbor. Crandall shot a last, loving look at his boat and went to dinner.

....

Chapter 27

Gentry's Kona Marina, next day

Sunshine, its newly painted hull gleaming in the noon sunshine, was returned to the harbor without mishap. After a leisurely lunch, Kalani took the boat to the fuel dock, topped off the tank, and added another half dozen five-gallon cans of diesel Crandall wanted as insurance. The rest of the afternoon was spent stocking lockers with blocks of ice, fresh vegetables, fruit, butter, and eggs.

Noticeably absent was Joseph Lauofo, the first casualty on

this leg of the trip. Crandall, not surprised, was still disappointed at the way in which the big Fijian had chosen to abandon the journey. According to Kalani, after apologizing, Joseph had disappeared, too ashamed to face Crandall. Benjamin offered no excuses for his brother's decision. Instead, he affirmed his commitment to stay on board *Sunshine* until they reached Fiji. Taking Benjamin aside, Crandall gave him three hundred dollars and the rest of the day to find his brother. "Tell him, no hard feelings. He'll need the money to get back to Oahu. Maybe he can return to campus without being missed. Take your time. Just remember, we shove off at first light."

"Thanks, Captain. I'll be back tonight for sure."

"I hope so, Benjamin. A third set of hands would make me feel a lot better."

"You got my word." The big man climbed to the dock, crossed the boatyard to Kealakehe Parkway, and flagged down a pickup loaded with a Hawaiian family.

Sitting on the cabin roof, Crandall and Kalani watched the Fijian climb into the truck. "Think he'll be back?"

"Easy, brah. Benjamin's cool. Gave his word. Good as gold, brah."

"Dunno. Hope you're right, Kalani. We got a lot of ocean ahead of us."

That night Crandall and Kalani dined ashore one last time. They ran through the menu, finished with dessert, and strolled back to the marina in the dying sun.

Waiting for them on the pier alongside *Sunshine* was Benjamin, wearing a determined look. Pleased at having a third crewmember, Crandall hid his delight, opting instead for a stoic handshake and slap on the man's broad back. Laughing, a visibly relieved Kalani wrapped the big man in a hug. In the morning, the three would cast off on a life-altering voyage. Tonight however, they settled for tamer pursuits. In the main cabin, Crandall slipped Vivaldi in the CD player. Strains of *Four Seasons* wafted through the cabin, drawing pained looks from his fellow sailors. He sat at one end of the folding table, studying charts. An hour later, he stowed the maps, shuffled a deck, and started slapping down rows of solitaire. Kalani and the Fijian, brows knitted in concentration, hunched sphinx-like over a game of chess. Crandall eventually put away the cards and crawled into his berth with an unfinished Patrick O'Brian paperback. When he snapped off his reading light an hour later, his crewmates were still locked in cerebral combat over the chessboard. Crandall drifted off to sleep, his mind replaying images of Becky embracing him in Florida surf.

Dawn came with coppery streaks setting clouds alight. Rising behind Mauna Loa, the sun's fiery disk outlined the volcanic mountain's purple profile. Cocooned in his berth, Crandall stirred. Synchronized long ago, his sailor's body clock was as punctual as the sun. Squinting in the early morning light pouring through the cabin's portholes, he sat upright, chucked his sleeping bag aside, and planted bare feet on the deck. Arching his back, Crandall stretched, yawning like an aged lion whose bones needed prompting. Dropping to the deck, he easily cranked out a dozen hurried push-ups followed by knee bends. Crandall tugged at the bundled figures sprawled in the cabin berths and heard muffled protests in response.

"Good morning, gentlemen! Rise and shine!" Grabbing a sweatshirt, Crandall opened the hatch to let in morning's cool air. He climbed on deck to check the mooring lines and dawn sky. Scanning the harbor, he silently recited the mariner's mantra, *Red sky at night, sailor's delight. Red sky in the morning...*Grinning, Crandall found nothing but pale blue sky showing behind gilt-edged clouds.

When he went below again his two-man crew was upright and alert. "Who won the chess game?" he asked.

"A draw," mumbled Kalani.

Wearing sweatshirts to ward off dawn's chill, the three ate a quick breakfast in silence, as though hesitant to leave the cabin's comfort. At Crandall's order, Kalani reluctantly climbed the teak steps and started the engine, letting it warm. Chatting on the radio with the harbormaster, Crandall poked his head from the hatch, comparing what he was being told about last-minute weather with what he saw. Benjamin finished breakfast and spent a few quiet last moments in his berth reading scripture. Ending the call, Crandall refilled his mug with fresh coffee, calling topside, "Okay, Kalani, let's shove off. "

Benjamin rolled out of bed, joining the other two stripping sail covers, connecting halyards, handling mooring lines, and pulling in bumpers. Easing from the pier, Kalani—Crandall at his elbow serenely sipping coffee—took *Sunshine* at low wake speed along a line of sailboats snug in their slips. A few early risers were already about, doing what sailors always do while in port: puttering, polishing, and painting. A few waved as *Sunshine* glided past. Kalani left the crowded marina behind, made a ninety-degree turn to starboard at the rock-lined entrance, then hard to port to clear the harbor mouth. Crandall took over the helm. Working as a team, Kalani and Benjamin raised the mainsail and set the foresail. A mile offshore, up went the jib after a knowing nod from Crandall who set course southwest, bellowing in the wind, "Next stop, Fiji!"

. . . .

Chapter 28

Anoka, Minnesota, February 28

Wet snow driving horizontally across Highway 10, combined with tailgating idiots, put Dale Morris in a foul mood. Arriving at the restaurant late—a failing he detested in others—didn't help his disposition. He was there to meet both Lindquist brothers and engage them in a question-and-answer session. The dinner was Becky's plan to get Morris' stamp of approval.

Sitting in a booth across from the brothers, Becky at his side, Morris fired off questions about World War Two, New Guinea, and the world beyond Minnesota. Only David held his own. As Becky instructed, he had done some reading about both subjects and his answers showed it. Time in the service had also obviously broadened his horizons. David, a Gulf War veteran, projected self-confidence and, though his taste of combat was short-lived, he and Morris at least had that in common. "It was your basic hundred-hour war," said David.

"That's the way to run them," replied Morris, studying the man. A few more answers and he decided he liked David, thought he could probably handle the trip.

The younger Lindquist was another story. The answers Morris pried from Darryl were not reassuring—not enough to disqualify him on the spot—but enough to give Morris pause about his readiness. Slouching in a sweat suit, the younger brother's attitude surfaced during the prodding from Morris.

"You know anything about the war, Darryl?"

"I seen stuff on the Military Channel. I know enough to hate the Japs, if that's what you mean."

"Not exactly what I'm looking for. Did Becky make it clear

we're going to one of war's toughest battlegrounds? Lot of men died there. I'm not sure if you appreciate what those guys faced. There may not be anyone shooting at us but we may find ourselves in some serious shit at some point."

"She spelled it out for us. We get it. It ain't no picnic."

"You ready for all the walking?"

"Becky told us all about it. We been working out. Busting our asses."

Morris gave up on Darryl, turned to Becky. "Hope you didn't sugarcoat this."

"I told them it was gonna be hard work. They both know that."

He pressed the men. "We'll be flying for twenty hours straight, you know."

"Can't say I'd like sitting that long in one place," groused Darryl, looking at the floor. "Won't like it, but I can handle it."

"We'll have to tough it out. No other way to get there," added David.

Morris was having serious second thoughts. Had he been given the final say, he would have tossed Darryl. But there was his promise to Becky to consider. Sitting in the restaurant, Morris thought David could take care of himself, but Darryl's readiness and stability seemed doubtful. *Maybe his intelligence, too*, Morris told himself. Hoping Darryl would bail, he gave it one more shot.

"Any second thoughts, gentlemen? Now is the time to speak up."

"Count me in," said David calmly.

"I'm okay with it, man," Darryl crowed. "Becky can depend on me."

Dismissing the immature bravado, Morris made a mental note. *David is going to be okay. Darryl? Punk*, he thought. *Problem with authority. Not a good sign. What the hell does 'I'm okay with it' mean?* wondered Morris. *Cryptic shorthand for yes? Are you on board or not, jerk?* Scribbling in a small leather notebook, Morris spoke without looking up. "I take it your answers mean you guys are throwing in with Becky and are willing to make this journey."

"Count me in," repeated David.

"Me too," echoed his brother.

When their food was served, the four ate while Morris tossed out anecdotes about previous trips to Papua New Guinea. Between mouthfuls, he embellished his stories with colorful descriptions of the natives, their customs, and the jungle. His tales, thinly disguised cautions to get them to change their minds, did nothing to change Darryl's defiant decision to tag along.

"S'not like we don't think this might be dangerous, you know. We wouldn't be going into some place we don't know nothing about without thinking about it. I didn't hear you say anyone's died on these trips."

"Correct."

"Well hell, there you go, dude. We follow the rules and no one gets hurt."

"That's the key, Darryl. Following rules." Morris glanced at him, then Becky, and David. "We're going into rugged territory inhabited by people who aren't used to seeing white folks…or outsiders, for that matter. We'll be on our own out there. Two days up, three days on site, and two days back. One day to spare."

Becky broke into the conversation. "But we'll have that missionary along."

"Sure, he'll be with us. We'll take our cues from him. I just want to make sure we all agree on this. He leads us in. He tells us how to act. My job is to make sure we get back in one piece." Morris surveyed the three. "Questions?"

No one took up his offer.

"Okay, I guess that's settled," he said without enthusiasm.

"Becky has a list of what you need. Get on it as soon as possible. May will show up before you know it." Becky signaled their server for the bill and paid.

Pushing away his plate, Morris slipped out of the booth, shook the brothers' hands, and put an arm around Becky. "Thanks for the meal. Your boys have a lot of work to do and so do I." Morris grabbed his coat. "Walk me out, will you?"

In the restaurant's foyer, Morris pulled her aside. "Okay, what's on your mind?" she asked.

"Your friend Darryl, actually."

"What about him?"

"Why do I just meet a guy and already have the definite impression he's not a happy camper?" Avoiding his eyes, she nodded in agreement. "He's gonna be a problem, Becky. Why do you have to bring him along?"

You don't know what you're asking. There's no way I can do this without these two, she told herself. *These guys are my ticket to success. Live with it.*

"I promised he could come. I gave him my word. Look, he'll be fine. When Darryl bitches about things, I've learned it's best to just ignore him." Shrugging, she explained. "Darryl's just being Darryl. He is what he is. Can't change that. He's never even been out of the country. David will keep an eye on him, I promise. He won't let him get out of line."

Sighing in frustration, Morris became stern. "I hope so. We've got a serious trek ahead of us. It's up to you to whip his attitude into shape by May."

"I'll stay on him. We'll do our best to keep him focused. He'll do okay. You'll see. We'll talk soon." After hugging Morris goodbye, Becky returned to the booth.

Darryl was smirking when she came back. "Well, for sure we got ourselves a real first-class asshole in charge there."

"Ah, he's all right," replied his brother. "A little controlling, maybe."

"Ya think?" snorted Darryl.

Becky wagged a scolding finger. "You guys better get used to it. Dale's been there, you know. The guy has his shit together. With him in charge, things will go smoothly. So try and get along. We need to work with him to find the wreck, okay?" Staring across the table, she scowled at Darryl. "Don't do anything to piss this guy off. The best thing to do is just keep your mouth shut when you're around him."

Pouting, his arms folded, the younger Lindquist pulled the wool cap over his ears as if to block the reprimand. He sat staring at the cluttered table without replying. When the awkwardness passed, David cocked an eyebrow at Becky. "Noticed how Morris sure liked putting his arm around you, girl."

Darryl stirred. "Yeah, better watch that old man. You know how they can be."

Bristling, she scorched them both. "Dale's old enough to be my father, assholes. He's looking out for me because he's worried about the guys I insisted on bringing along on the expedition. I gotta say he's right to be suspicious. He liked you, David, but you didn't seem very excited about the prospect of finding a couple million dollars."

He waved away her rebuke. "Chill, Becky. He was just scoping us out to see if we were for real about this trip. We're good on this, Becky. You got nothing to worry about."

Unconvinced, she threw a handful of singles on the table for the tip and stood. "You both need to get moving on your passports and shots. I've budgeted for that. Make sure you get started this week. I've already got mine."

Both men followed her from the restaurant. In the parking lot, David leaned against the driver's door while Becky warmed the old Honda. "What about the clothing, equipment, stuff Morris said we needed?"

"Next Saturday we'll go shopping. I'll pick Darryl up and come by your place at ten. We'll go down to the cities and look at a couple of outfitters, have lunch."

"Okay, see you then."

Yanking open the Honda's passenger door, Darryl scrambled in, crowing. "Guess who's going to give me a ride home, big brother!" Shaking his head, David hustled to his own car thinking, *I'm not rescuing you, babe. He's your problem tonight.* Wheeling from the lot, Becky headed northwest toward St. Cloud. Darryl, wearing his stupid lecher's grin, pawed at her all the way to Upsala.

....

Chapter 29

Lae, Papua New Guinea, April 22

Pushing away his plate, Crandall leaned back in his chair, his eyes scanning moored boats lining the piers in the harbor near the yacht club's restaurant. *Sunshine* rode between two ugly trawlers. Aside from a few tables filled with Aussie ex-pats quietly nursing beers, he and Kalani were the only other guests.

Crandall finished his iced tea and glanced at his watch. "It's almost noon. I'm heading to the airport to check on our chopper. Stay with the boat until I get back."

Crandall asked the club manager to arrange for a car to Nadzab Airport. Over-hearing Crandall's request, a portly bearded Brit named Cecil offered him a lift in his van. "I'm heading to the airport to pick up a friend and would enjoy the company." Five minutes into the ride, Crandall wondered if he had made a mistake.

The limey was a talker, a bore. Feigning interest, Crandall suffered a non-stop monologue as they jockeyed in sluggish traffic. A sea of wandering people in no particular hurry flooded the streets. Lae's entire population seemed to be on the move, shopping, engaging in conversation, or peppering the ground with streams of beetlenut juice. Though people on foot were friendly, returning Crandall's waves and offering shy smiles, the constant sight of businesses and homes fenced and wrapped in barbed wire depressed him. Endless mounds of decaying refuse lining the streets darkened his mood even more. Potholes made the ride uncomfortable.

The city and its streaming traffic gave way to shantytowns tumbling down the hills to the road where listless vendors offered pathetic pyramids of vegetables or fruit for sale. With the outskirts of Lae behind them, Crandall's self-appointed tour guide suddenly fell silent, his face grim as he accelerated along the pitted, serpentine Highlands Highway. "Too dangerous to stop, Yank. Got robbed here a year ago trying to be helpful. Bloody thieves. Not about to suffer that indignity again!" The chubby Brit drove through the hills at a white-knuckle, pothole dodging pace, testing Crandall's nerves.

The van flew past stoic barefooted pedestrians toting infants, burlap sacks of beetlenut, even lumber balanced on the carrier's shoulders. When they reached the airport, the van's rotund driver obligingly bypassed the main terminal to follow Crandall's sketchy directions along a muddy side road. On the airfield's fringe, the Brit dropped his passenger in front of a huge Quonset hut surrounded by rusting concertina wire. After profuse thanks, Crandall ambled through a gate propped open by charred tires. Just past the gate a mud-splattered motorcycle nestled against a wounded pickup truck with bald tires and missing windshield. A faded hand-lettered wooden sign—Buzz Dawson's PNG Charters—poked above banana trees sprouting at a corner of the structure's corroded ribs.

The isolated building seemed an unlikely spot for a helicopter service. *Not exactly what I saw on the website*, mused Crandall. He followed a muddy gravel footpath to a large concrete apron fronting the open end of the Quonset-style hangar. In the distance an Air Niugini Dash 8 roared down Nadzab's runway and lifted into the sky with a muscular rumble.

Surveying the hangar's cavernous ribbed bay, Crandall warmed to the familiar sight of a Bell 205 at rest on its skids. A barefoot, shirtless black man in khaki shorts balanced on a tall wheeled stepladder drawn up next to the chopper's rotor housing. Painfully loud PNG reggae pumped from a boom box sitting on the oil-spotted concrete floor. Crandall walked over to the CD player and hit the power button, killing the music.

Turning abruptly, the black mechanic on the ladder jerked his head toward the bearded intruder. "Hey! What yu doin'?!"

"Looking for Buzz Dawson," said Crandall.

Nodding toward a small wooden shack in one corner of the hangar the man on the ladder glowered at Crandall, pointing to a door. "Em slip."

"Thanks." Crandall hit the play button. The raucous tune erupted at full blast, restoring the mechanic's smile. The man resumed working.

Making his way past an untidy workbench groaning under a mound of tools, Crandall poked his head in the shack's doorway. A barrel-chested white man with a week's growth of whiskers reclined in a broken armchair, his ragged snoring competing with the music echoing in the hangar. The chair's occupant, grease-stained knuckles dragging on the linoleum, had propped his stubby legs on a desk overflowing with papers. Rapping loudly on the door, Crandall kept at it until the dozing man showed signs of life. Opening one bloodshot eye, the man shot his visitor an irritated look.

"You Buzz Dawson, the owner, the pilot?" Crandall asked.

"Who wants to know?"

"I'm Rick Crandall."

"Do I know you?" said the man without moving.

Crossing his arms, Crandall leaned against the office door. "I talked to you a couple of months ago about a charter flight over Popondetta way."

Shifting himself into a sitting position, Dawson blinked, yawned, running an oil-stained hand through a bristling crew cut. "Oh, yeah. I remember…sort of. Refresh my memory, Mister…"

"Crandall, but I'll answer to Rick."

"Right. Crandall. Call me Buzz if ya like."

Shifting a stack of dog-eared engine manuals from a folding chair to the desk, Crandall sat opposite Dawson. "Okay, Buzz it is. I called you about flying a pickup mission in Oro Province. Trekkers. In the hills southwest of Popondetta. Ring any bells?"

"Yeah. Bit of a stretch if I remember your description." Now fully upright, if not completely awake, Dawson reached behind him, cracking open a small refrigerator. "Care for lunch, Crandall? My private stock." He held up two sweating Heinekens. "Sure, why not?" Crandall took the offered bottle, twisted off the cap, and took a long pull of icy beer. "Thanks."

Dawson tapped their bottles together in a toast. "Don't mention it," he said, rubbing his bristles as if the gesture would prod his memory. "Long, long way that. Getting to Popondetta and thereabouts…and back, I mean."

Crandall leaned back. "About 190 miles one way. 380 miles round trip. It's possible."

"Know the route, do you?"

Crandall didn't answer. Instead, he planted his bottle on a filing cabinet, produced a map from his back pocket, and cleared the desk, pushing mounds of paperwork aside. Tracing his finger from Lae to Popondetta, he tapped a spot southwest of the town. "Here, in the hills. I don't have the exact spot yet but I expect to have it pinned down within two weeks. What do you think?"

Intrigued, Dawson wiped his hands on a rag and leaned over the chart. "I told you it's a bit of a stretch. I'm a tad leery, what with the distance and no fixed point."

"Trust me, I'll have it for you soon. And distance shouldn't be a problem."

Straightening, Dawson arched his back, his huge hands nearly touching the ceiling's yellowed panels. "Wouldn't be cheap. Mind you, I'm not signing onto it right off." He finished his beer, tossed the bottle into a soggy cardboard box full of empties, and ushered Crandall outside. "Let's take a look at my ship, talk some more. The air will do me good."

Crandall followed the pilot out the door. "Who's your mechanic?"

"Solomon. Good man. Found him in Goroka. He's got a wife and family there." Dawson winked at his visitor. "One in Lae as well. Works out to be a nice fit for both of us. Can't speak for the wives. He's got good skills, hard worker." Bellowing at the black man, Dawson introduced the American in fractured pidgin. "Solomon, name belong dispela, Crandall." The mechanic raised a wrench in response and Crandall waved.

The two men climbed into the Huey, Dawson taking the pilot's right-hand seat. Crandall caressed the instrument panels as Dawson ran through his reservations about the proposed mission. Crandall patiently answered each objection. "Your range is about 254 nautical miles, correct?"

"Give or take. But that's on paper. What you're talking about is a 612 kilometer round trip. See my problem, mate?"

Crandall ignored the comment. "This baby does about 100 knots, depending on the wind."

"Correct."

"You carry 200 gallons of fuel. Am I right?"

"You seem to know your stuff, Mr. Crandall."

"Always liked choppers. But I flew F-18s for the navy until my accident."

Dawson was intrigued. "Had an accident, did you? What happened?"

"Ah, a bad night. Two of us were ready to launch when an S-3 Viking came in hard and turned the flight deck into a pyre. I got away with a broken leg and burns. My wingman and the Viking crew didn't make it."

Dawson shook his head. "Bloody bad luck for those lads, eh?"

"Yeah, I was fortunate. Got out with a gold watch and a disability rating. You never know, do you? So, Buzz. Fill me in on your ship."

"Okay. Let's start with the load we're going to backhaul."

"I'll be flying with you and we'll pick up three for the trip back."

"Okay, that's five. What kind of landing zone am I going to find out there?"

Crandall smiled at Dawson. "Probably a piece of cake for a skilled pilot like yourself. Shouldn't be a problem. My people know they have to find a spot with plenty of room going in and plenty of room coming out."

"I always worry when someone says, 'piece of cake.' Weather's a bloody problem in PNG, Crandall."

"Right. Can't do much about it. But my party will have GPS, strobe lights, and flares if needed. And they'll be sure to be in the open."

"You been there before?"

"Nope. But they also have a satellite phone. I'll be in touch."

"At my maximum range I can get down there. But there's the rub, mate."

"What's the problem?"

Frowning, Dawson toyed with the control stick between his knees. "I won't have enough fuel to get back to Lae."

"I think I've got a solution to your problem, Buzz. Let's go back into your office. I want to show you something." Crandall led Dawson back inside the tiny office. Smoothing his map on the desk, he ran a finger along the coastline toward a spot north of Popondetta. "We've got Gona Beach right here, outside of town. That's close to where I'll be waiting."

"Why the beach? Won't you be flying from here with me?"

"Not part of my plan. I'll leave a couple of days earlier and be waiting for you somewhere on the coast near Gona. Pick a spot. You can land along the shore and refuel. I assume you know the coastline well enough to find a place to set down."

"Yeah, I know a dozen spots to pull that off. But where do we get the fuel?"

Grinning, Crandall slapped the pilot on the back. "We bring it with us."

Dawson shook his head, not understanding what the American was saying.

"You can carry what, 5,000 pounds on your cargo hook, right? Five gallons of fuel weighs about thirty-one pounds. That means..." Scribbling on the margins of the map, Crandall did the math. "We could carry 161 jugs of extra fuel with us if need be. Hell, we won't even need that many. Your ship's tank only holds 200 gallons. With your range of 254 nautical miles, fifty or sixty of those jugs would do it. That's way under your max load." Crandall's words tumbled out. "Just drop it west of Gona, make the pickup, and stop on the way back to refuel. Whadaya think?"

"Ah, I see your point. Ingenious. Hadn't thought of it that way."

"See," said Crandall triumphantly. "We can sling a cargo net with plastic five-gallon jugs of fuel, run down the coast..."

"Land, drop it or top off..." interrupted Dawson, "make the pickup, stop on the way back, top off again, and bring back the empties in the net."

"So, what do you think, Buzz? Can you do it?"

"Brilliant, mate!" Screwing his face into a scowl, Dawson whined. "Wait. If I drop off that much fuel there won't be anything left on my return. You don't know the locals. Bloody jugs will walk off by themselves the moment I'm gone."

"Bring Solomon. He can babysit them while we do the pickup," said Crandall.

"Right, that would make sense. Ah, one more thing."

"What?"

"I don't have that many five-gallon jugs."

"C'mon, Buzz," pleaded Crandall. "Work with me here. You must know someone who has them. Don't tell me you can't find fifty jugs in all of Lae."

Frowning in concentration, Dawson tugged on his beard, mumbling to himself for a few minutes before smiling. "Yeah, there's a bloke I know in town. I think I could round them up if I had to." He paused. "Your plan is good in theory but I think I see a flaw in it."

"Which is?"

Dawson studied the map and the margin notes. "If I sling that load I'll have a problem."

"How so?"

"An external load really cuts down on speed. That changes your range. And then you've got the bloody problem of motion. The whole kit starts swinging and pretty soon the tail is wagging the dog. Could get out of control. Bloody dangerous balance thing."

"I hadn't thought of that."

"Course not, mate. You're a fixed-wing bloke. All is not lost, however. I have a solution."

Crandall leaned forward. "I'm all ears."

Picking at his stubble, Dawson stared past Crandall at the helicopter on the pad. "Right. We'll take out the back row of seats and put in three 55-gallon drums of fuel. Strap them on a pallet and take along an electric pump. That puts us well within our load limit and no swinging net to slow me down or get out of hand. See my point?" Grinning, Crandall slapped the desk hard. "I like it! It's perfect. I say we're good to go then."

"Ah, one thing, Rick. My fee."

"Right. The fee. What's your cost per hour?"

"Three thousand."

"Your website quoted fifteen hundred for sightseeing tours."

A frown. "That's the old schedule. Outdated."

Glaring, Crandall ran a hand through his unruly hair. "Since when?"

"Since this morning. Besides, this isn't exactly sightseeing, is it?"

Crandall fell silent, doodling on his map again. "I don't see your ship making any money just sitting there, Buzz. And I don't see any lines of tourists waiting to tour the bush. Two thousand."

"You're a hard man, Rick. Two thousand. Satisfied?"

"That works for me."

Stroking his sparse whiskers, Dawson tried again. "In advance."

"You're a bloody pirate, Buzz."

"Not including fuel," added Dawson.

"Not including fuel," groused Crandall. "Fix a price."

"I'll toss you a quote the day before we fly. Best I can do, mate."

"Why am I not surprised? Okay, done." Pulling a roll of cash from his jeans, Crandall counted out three thousand dollars and handed it to Dawson. "Down payment. The balance when I see you on the beach."

The pilot pocketed the money. "Huh? So you won't be coming back to Lae then?" Crandall shook his head. "You Yanks are so trusting," said Dawson. "What's to keep me from taking your money and not showing?"

Crandall lost his smile. "In that case I WILL be coming back to Lae."

Dawson's laughter filled the office. "Right answer. Woulda said the same thing myself. Well done then."

"I want to see how she handles," said Crandall. "You know, a short run."

"Don't you trust me, mate?"

"Absolutely, Buzz. But humor me."

Shrugging, the pilot poked his head from the doorway, yelled to his mechanic. "Button it up, Solomon. Our friend here wants to see if she'll hold together."

The shirtless man gathered his tools, gave the rotor shaft a last look, and came down the ladder. The three rolled the Huey clear of the hanger. After unhooking the blade tips, Solomon handed Crandall a headset. The American climbed aboard, buckling in next to Dawson, who went through a preflight check and called Nadzab's tower to alert them to his test run. As the rotor turned the familiar whine of the Lycoming T53 turbine engine filled the air, echoing in the hangar.

In minutes, the blade was an angry, buzzing blur. Lifting from the pad, the ship lightly danced sideways as Dawson increased power. The ship's nose dipped as the Huey picked up speed. Racing along the grassy strip adjacent to the runway, the chopper rose smoothly, climbing over the palms and brush just beyond the airport perimeter. Making a slow circuit over the nearby hills and silver ribbon of the Markham River, Dawson banked, turning southeast before bringing the ship in for a graceful landing on the concrete. He shut down the engine, did a post-flight check, and stripped off his headset. Turning to Crandall in the co-pilot's seat, Dawson grinned. "Well, satisfied?" Flashing thumbs-up, Crandall disconnected his headset and exited the Huey, crouching under the slowing blades. He waited for the pilot.

"Thanks, Solomon," said Dawson. "Let's put her to bed."

The mechanic waited for the blades to stop, then tied them down. The three men pushed the helicopter back into the hangar bay. Dawson went into his office, rolled up Crandall's map, and handed it to him. "That one was on the house."

"Thanks. She handles well. I look forward to flying with you."

Dawson said, "You'll let me know when you get a reading on the pickup, right?" Crandall nodded. "I'll have Solomon run you back into town," said Dawson. He's heading that way. You shouldn't be out here on your own."

"Appreciate it."

"No problem, mate. All part of the service. I'll write up a flight plan, map out some spots along the coast."

Crandall paused. "Don't commit anything to paper…if you don't mind, Buzz."

Dawson's eyebrows rose. "Oh? Now what's that all about?"

"I prefer to do this on an informal basis if it's all the same to you."

A moment passed in silence. "Your call, mate. Better make it worth it."

"Thousand-dollar bonus when you drop us on the beach. I appreciate your understanding. I want this to be discreet."

"I don't haul drugs, Rick," bristled Dawson.

"No drugs involved."

"Or weapons."

"I wouldn't think of asking you to do that."

A shrug and a handshake. "Okay, you're on, mate. If we run over on time this might get expensive."

"I understand. I'll take care of it."

Barking over his shoulder at his helper without looking, the pilot locked eyes with Crandall. "Solomon! On your way home would you be so kind as to drop our guest wherever he'd like?"

The mechanic stowed his tools and held a set of keys aloft. Crandall followed him to the hobbled truck. To his dismay, Solomon instead straddled the muddied bike and kicked the Yamaha into life. Crandall reluctantly climbed aboard. After negotiating mud holes dotting the rutted frontage road, Solomon wheeled onto the main road's crumbling blacktop. He accelerated down the highway, weaving around the first of many pothole gauntlets. Crandall—second-guessing his sanity for accepting the ride—hung on for dear life, completely at the mercy of his driver for the next forty minutes.

....

Chapter 30

Pine Lake, May 4

One week before abandoning Upsala, when lake ice began to break up and open water grew along the shore, when what snow remained in the shadows of pines began shrinking in sunlight and farm fields softened in the melting runoff, Becky began to disappear. She permanently deleted her Facebook account, then logged in to Twitter and erased herself. An unexpected feeling of freedom came over her. Searching the computer, she hunted all files for personal information and scrubbed them clean. To be sure, she removed the hard drive and shattered it on the patio with a hammer. She was vanishing in degrees. Sweeping through the house like a whirlwind, Becky explored every room for traces of herself. Every photo she found ended up in the fireplace along with birthday cards, notes, and long-forgotten notebooks, their pages filled in her girlish hand.

Next came her clothes. She loaded her car at night to avoid questions from her neighbors. In the morning, she drove to St. Cloud to donate two closets worth of coats, shoes, and sweaters to the local diocese. While in town, she cleaned out her mail drop, returned the key, and used her cell phone to cancel the cable TV, stop the mail, and quit the telephone service.

Becky met David at a fast food place for a quick lunch. She wanted to hear him outline their final day. With the exception of a change of clothes and toiletries in a carry-on bag, the basic plan was for Becky to walk away from the lake house empty-handed that last morning.

"I've been thinking about our exit strategy," said David, notebook in hand.

"I didn't know we needed a strategy. I thought we'd just get on the plane and go."

"Not that simple, Becky. We have loose ends to tie up before we leave."

"Okay, run it by me. If I hear something I don't like, I'll tell you."

He smiled. "Fair enough. I see it like this. Ten o'clock this Friday, you lock up the lake house and drive to Darryl's. He'll have the tent and clothing you left at his trailer packed with his things in the pickup. He follows you to St. Cloud. The two of you stop at my apartment. I throw my stuff in his truck. I've left my bike and car with friends."

"So far, so good. Continue."

"Next stop is that mall parking lot close to I-94. We drop your Honda with the keys inside. Make sure there's no paper in the glove compartment to ID you. If we're lucky, some kid comes along and takes it. He does the job for us."

Becky frowned. "What if it just sits there?"

"No sweat. Eventually, mall security would call a tow truck. Hopefully, that will delay the discovery of the owner for days, maybe weeks. The three of us take Darryl's truck, drive to the airport, and check our baggage curbside. You and Darryl stay behind while I drive his truck to the Mall of America and drop it in one of the ramps. I catch the light-rail back to the airport. We rendezvous and go through security separately. We get something to eat and head for our gate where Morris meets us. What do you think?"

"I like it. It's simple. It works. But that leaves me with Darryl."

"Only until I get back from the mall. Think about it. My brother's a nut when it comes to you and me, always has been. He's jealous and naturally paranoid. If he stays with you while I get rid of the truck he won't make a fuss. It would be just like him to screw up a detail like this before we leave, so one of us has to do this to make sure it's done right. Take one for the team, girl. You can handle it."

Sighing, she gave in. "I'll do it. You're probably right. He'd mess up given the chance. Just make sure you make it back. I'm not getting on that plane without you."

"Okay, we're done," he said. "See you Friday morning. Where you going next?"

She grabbed her purse, rose from the booth, saying, "I'm stopping to see Barbara one more time. She's doing well, should be home at the end of next month."

He rose and followed her to the parking lot. "It's been a long comeback for her. Who's going to look after her while you're gone?"

Shrugging, Becky said, "My neighbors will figure something out."

The pair embraced and went their separate ways.

Becky drove to Albany and spent two hours in a sun-filled room with Barbara. They chatted, played cards, and did two exhausting laps in the corridor outside her room. By the time Becky returned to the lake house, it was late afternoon.

Buddy met her in the entry hall, eager to get outdoors. "Okay, boy, I'll change and we'll hit the woods." She scratched behind his ears. "Would you like that?" The dog's tail swept back and forth in anticipation. She let the Lab outside. Bounding down the steps, the dog galloped in ever-widening circles as Becky trailed him down the gravel road leading to the pine windbreaks lining the cornfields.

"Let's take a look over there," she said, hurling a stick toward a copse of birch and Norway pine. Leaping across old furrows bristling with stubble, Buddy left the familiar path and headed into a tangled grove, Becky twenty paces behind. Ducking beneath low branches, she found herself weaving between closely spaced trunks. The ground was carpeted with pine needles and brittle cones crunching beneath her boots. Spotting a huge fallen oak, Becky sat to catch her breath. Buddy was joyfully rooting, sniffing, and nosing among the trees that screened the road from view. Becky whistled. She heard Buddy bark once, saw him pawing at the pine needles. Buddy finally emerged from a wall of young saplings and loped to Becky's side. He sat contentedly, licking her hands as she rubbed his neck. She removed his collar and pocketed it. "There, doesn't that feel better, old boy?" As if the dog understood, it nuzzled its head against her knee.

"Isn't it a beautiful day, Buddy? Don't you love the thought of summer?"

The Lab stiffened, as if hearing something in the brush beyond the nave of pines. Sitting upright, Buddy looked back at Becky and then stared at the surrounding forest. Becky put her hand in a pocket, withdrew the loaded .22 pistol, and held it inches from the back of the dog's head.

She squeezed the trigger. The loud "pop" startled her.

Without a whimper, the big Lab slumped forward on a bed of pine needles.

Becky pocketed the handgun and stood over the dog's body. "Sorry, Buddy, couldn't leave you behind. I hope you understand, old boy."

She knew forest predators would fulfill their roles. By midsummer, the Lab's remains would be reduced to a few scattered bones and a rug of golden fur. Anyone who discovered the matted pelt while tramping through this stand of pine would likely think they had found the remains of a deer. If her neighbors asked after Buddy during her goodbye, she would tell them the Lab had wandered away and not returned. It happened enough to be an accepted tale. Becky took a new route through the forest to the lake. Pausing at water's edge, she hurled the gun as far as she could toward the middle of the lake. There was still packing to be done.

PART THREE

Chapter 31

33,000 feet above the South Pacific, May 10

Straight-jacketed despite a cushioned seat, Morris finished a Jessie Stone paperback and tucked it inside the seat pocket in front of him. He snapped off the reading light, tried to get comfortable but eventually gave up. Across the aisle, Becky, her neck fitted with an inflatable pillow, slept between the Lindquist brothers, her head lolling against David's shoulder to her right. Eyes half-closed, David sat in a catatonic state, fixated on a tiny animated jet symbol crawling across a blue screen on the seatback in front of him. On Becky's left, Darryl dozed, mouth agape like a corpse, iPod buds buried in his ears, heavy metal hammering his brain.

Morris glanced at his watch. They were eight hours into their thirteen-hour flight aboard a 747-400 heading to Auckland. After a short layover, they still faced an early morning three-hour-plus run to Cairns, Australia. Even for an experienced traveler like Morris, the Pacific leg was a grueling interminable transit. He could only imagine what was going through the minds of his three neophytes. He knew a day and night in Cairns would go a long way to restore the body and soul.

Releasing the seat belt, Morris unfolded himself, stretched, and ambled to the rear of the plane to join a silent queue at the bathrooms. The Air New Zealand flight was packed, the cabin lights dimmed, most passengers reading or napping. Morris took his turn in the bathroom, splashed cold water on his face to stay awake, then did knee-bends in the galley to get his blood moving—anything to delay a return to the confines of steerage. He finally went back to his seat and surrendered to sleep for the remainder of the flight.

When they reached Auckland, Morris and his team shuffled zombie-like to a tiny cafe in the international terminal and took a break for coffee. The quartet clustered around a small table across from a duty-free shop. Stupefied fellow passengers wandered past in glassy-eyed fatigue. Darryl finished his coffee, drifted to a nearby magazine rack, and eventually made himself at home in a bar. David and Becky sat chatting and laughing with an easy intimacy Morris envied. The pair finished their beverages and deserted the table, leaving Morris alone. Slinging his backpack over his shoulder, Morris joined a crowd heading for the boarding area where three lines became one for a last security check. He went down a hallway, rode an escalator to a lower-level waiting area with soft lighting and etched glass panels. The carpeted lounge filled rapidly.

Becky and David sat in self-imposed isolation, each with earphones. Darryl finally showed, smelling of liquor. Morris stood off by himself, giving Becky and the Lindquists plenty of privacy. When their flight was announced, passengers, their voices subdued with the exception of a few whimpering infants, boarded an Air New Zealand Airbus A-320 in pre-dawn darkness. Becky and the brothers were at the front of the line. Morris followed the other sheep aboard. After stowing his carry-on he sank into a comfortable leather seat and watched a never-ending parade of travelers shuffle past. Cheery, efficient flight attendants in trim gray blazers bustled through crowded aisles, settling passengers, soothing toddlers, and rearranging luggage in cavernous overhead bins. With the plane filled, everyone seated, and lead attendants taking head counts, screens came to life with a safety video as Morris felt the engines throb with power. Easing from the jetway, the big plane turned toward the taxiway. "Good morning, ladies and gents, boys and girls," announced a calm male Kiwi voice. The usual banter from the speakers continued until the jet took its place at the end of the runway. "Flight attendants, please be seated." In minutes, they were airborne, winging over the Coral Sea, racing the sunrise northwest to Queensland.

As Morris predicted, Cairns was a refreshing stop for the exhausted travelers. Meeting them after they cleared customs and immigration was a lanky, bespectacled gray-haired man holding a pasteboard sign to his chest with "Morris Party" printed in two-inch-high black letters. "Farrel's the name," their greeter said, bobbing and smiling at the Americans. "Call me Billy, if ya like." He led them to a small white bus with a trailer hitched behind it. After stowing their luggage in the trailer, Farrel got behind the wheel, counted heads, and headed into an ugly crowded freeway reminiscent of Los Angles traffic sans smog. Twenty minutes later, he deposited his fares on a curb by the Hotel Cairns. Morris asked the brothers to unload while he registered their party. The hotel, a white, two-story layout with two wings of rooms, was hidden in lush foliage at the busy intersection of Abbott and Florence streets across from a towering Holiday Inn.

"Very nice," said Becky approvingly. "Good pick, Dale."

"Your dime. Thought our crew would enjoy it."

"We could be in southern California for all I know," joked David, piling luggage at the entrance. "I can feel the humidity already. No haze, though."

"It is tropical," agreed Morris. "Cairns's a resort town. You can hit the Great Barrier Reef from here with one of a hundred different tours. It's a local industry."

"You been to the reef before?" asked Becky.

"Never had the privilege. Only seen it from the air. Seems I'm always coming or going. Like to do some diving sometime in the future."

Distributing room keys, Morris announced he was going to take advantage of the hotel's secluded pool, then nap until dinner. "Let's meet in the entrance at six and walk to the restaurant."

"It better be close by," whined Darryl.

"Next door," said Morris, nodding at a peaked-roof building, blindingly white like the hotel. "Beautiful setting. High ceilings, outdoor garden dining under a big Teflon canopy and live music. Food's outstanding. Try the kangaroo steak cooked on a hot stone."

"I'll pass," scowled Darryl. "I'll give the Aussie beer a try, though."

"Suit yourself," said Morris, shouldering his duffel bag. "I'm heading to my room and then the pool. See you folks at six."

....

Chapter 32

Cairns, Australia, the next morning

Rising in darkness, Morris stepped under a cold shower, shaved, dressed quickly, and repacked his bag. He went down the hallway, knocking on each of his companion's doors until he got a muffled reply. He checked out and lugged his baggage to a trailer tethered to a waiting van. Becky and David shuffled sleepily down the stairs, deposited their bags in the trailer, and followed Morris to the rear of the van. No one spoke. Darryl showed and climbed aboard. A Chinese couple, sleeping toddler in the mother's arms, joined them in the little bus. Their driver took them down darkened neighborhood streets and through two roundabouts before stopping twice at hotels for more fares—Brits, Americans, and Germans.

By the time they left for the airport, the van was filled with sleepy-eyed passengers.

Herding his companions through the airport ritual of ticket counter, baggage check, and security, Morris kept everyone moving, only relaxing when he led the way upstairs to the departure lounge where dawn peeked from Cairns's hills.

A single deli bar, open at one end of the terminal, lured Becky and the Lindquists for over-priced bottled water and snacks. The trio wandered toward their gate, Morris in the lead. Early risers, scattered among the couches, read day-old tabloids discarded on the seats. A flock of female flight attendants in bright red Quantas plumage blew through the lounge, chattering, giggling, gossiping. The babbling covey, much too loud given the hour, claimed couches for themselves.

A brilliant blood-colored sun broke through the clouds, bathing the terminal in light. When their flight to Port Moresby was called, Morris and the others queued at the gate. The passenger list was an eye-opening cultural mix for Becky. A few diminutive Asians, Aussie business types in ties, natives in colorful tropical shirts, shorts and sandals, unkempt eco-tourists with backpacks, plus a trio of East Indians. Morris and his crew fell somewhere in the middle of the mix. After boarding, they taxied in a blinding sunrise and were soon airborne over the forested hills, crowded marinas, clustered buildings, and sprawling homes that was Cairns.

Queensland's coast dropped behind them as the Air Niugini turboprop turned north over the Coral Sea. Flight attendants served a modest breakfast. Ravished, Morris attacked his food while staring out a window at the vast sea below. Coral beds shaped like jade scimitars appeared—the Great Barrier Reef. Within the hour, boats would be anchoring above underwater gardens, their divers busy exploring one of earth's jewels. Morris envied them. Coral playgrounds gave way to gray-green water dotted with the shadows of puffy cumulus floating like barrage balloons, each anchored above its assigned sector of ocean. Morris nodded off. When he awoke, a hazy outline of humped shoreline appeared and the plane dropped toward Port Moresby.

Immigration and customs was a casual affair. A cacophony of Pidgin English, a few words of welcome, and a relaxed sense of duty passed for official entry to Papua New Guinea. Uniformed officers asked a few desultory questions. Morris, along with the others, accepted a cursory pat down of his luggage and a low-key lecture about bringing in snacks containing nuts and fruit. With waves and gold-toothed smiles from the inspectors, the four visitors were free to go.

Morris directed Becky and the Lindquists to a currency exchange where they traded 150 dollars for PNG kina. Morris phoned for a van while his team gawked at an endless stream of natives wandering aimlessly along the airport's sidewalks.

Port Moresby's humidity hit the newcomers hard. Thick, moist air, unlike anything they had encountered up to now, hit them like a wall. The early flight had pushed the limit for the Americans. Morris too, began to feel the effects of jet lag combined with Papua New Guinea's suffocating air. In minutes, their clothes were soaked with sweat, their bodies flirting with exhaustion.

"We'll get you to the hotel and you can sack out in some air conditioning. That should refresh you," said Morris. "Our flight from Cairns put us in Port Moresby too late to catch the morning run to Popondetta. We'll catch tomorrow morning's first flight."

Becky's face registered relief. "I don't care. One more flight today and you could've carried me in a bag. I need a shower and sleep."

"The Airways Hotel is a class act, Becky. You'll like it. They have a great restaurant and rooftop pool. You'll bounce back."

Darryl asked, "They got a bar?"

"Yeah, Darryl, they have a bar. Right by the pool. Great view."

When the van arrived, their driver threw the group's luggage in back and shot back up the hill to the hotel's barred iron gate manned by two security guards in white shirts, ties, and baseball hats. The men saluted the visitors, drawing chuckles from Becky. At the entrance, two white-coated doormen hustled the luggage into a soaring two-story marble and stone lobby. Polished pieces of aluminum floated in a large mobile dominating the reception desk, itself a long wooden counter covered in shiny, riveted metal mimicking an airplane wing.

Once registered, the newcomers followed eager bellhops through a set of glass doors, across a driveway, and down a flight of steps leading to a wing of rooms on the ground floor. The air was stifling. A trough, paved to carry away rainwater, ran the length of the outside hallway. Just inside the front door was a tiled bathroom with shower, sink, and toilet. Each room had two queen-sized beds, a desk, chairs, a TV, and teak closet. The Lindquists were sharing a room. Morris and Becky had quarters to themselves.

"Hallelujah!" cried Becky spotting an AC unit high in the wall. She hit the power button, cranking the cooling dial to max. After tipping her porter, she locked her door, laid out fresh clothes on one bed, and stripped for a shower. By the time she emerged dripping wet, the AC was delivering cool air. Falling onto her bed wrapped only in a towel, she slept until roused by Morris for dinner.

She awoke refreshed, dressed, and rode with him in the elevator to the hotel's seventh level. They strolled along a footbridge overlooking a mounted, full-sized Air Niugini DC-3 fuselage bolted to the hillside as if in mid-flight. Pausing on the walkway above the outrageous eye-catching display, she asked, "Where are David and Darryl?"

"Couldn't roust 'em. They're dead to the world."

"How hard did you try?"

"I knocked a couple of times," he said unconvincingly. "They're big boys.

I told them we were eating at seven. They don't know what they're missing."

"I almost believe you."

"Honest. I did my best, Becky." Morris ushered her to a linen-covered table on an open, sheltered balcony overlooking the city. A gentle breeze stirred palms on the steep hillside, offering relief from what was left of the day's heat. Low chatter from other diners floated around them from candlelit tables. After ordering wine and dinner for both, Morris relaxed, staring at flickering lights in Port Moresby. Hazy bluish smoke hovered over the rooftops far below. "For a city of two hundred thousand, you'd think you would see more light."

Becky followed his gaze down the hill. "Not exactly the Big Apple, is it?"

"Nope. Doesn't come close to the Twin Cities, either. It's not really on the same planet." Blue strobe lights from police vehicles converged at some distant point in the darkened town. "Probably raskols getting it on with the cops."

"Raskols?"

"Criminals. Pidgin for rascals, thieves," explained Morris. "Probably won't be the last time you hear that word."

Laughing, Becky scolded him gently. "Okay, raskols I can

understand. But getting it on? I haven't heard that expression in a million years."

"Well, I don't know what you youngsters say these days. And I guess I am a million years old. I felt like it today. Forgot what it was like to make this trek." Looking across the table, he gently asked, "What about you? You doing okay?"

Tossing back some wine, she grimaced. "It was harder than I thought it would be. I just figured once I got on that plane in Minneapolis there was no turning back."

"How about your boyfriends?"

"Ugh. They're not my boyfriends, Dale. They're…guys I know. That's all."

"No attraction there?"

"What are you, my dad?" she huffed. "Don't spoil a romantic evening, okay?"

"Romantic? Why Ms. Peterson, I had no idea."

A groan. "You know what I mean." Waving her hand at the candles, lights winking below in the hills, and the sky, she said, "It's beautiful tonight. I'm enjoying the company, okay? 'Live in the moment,' as they say."

"I'm enjoying your company as well, Becky."

Twisting her hand in limp blonde curls, she growled. "Good. Then don't spoil the mood for once."

Morris backed off immediately. "Point, set, match."

Their food arrived along with more wine. Lifting his glass, Morris proposed a toast. "To the success of our trip. May we find your grandfather's plane."

Raising her glass, Becky lightly bumped Morris' goblet. "I'll drink to that."

They ate. Engaged in small talk. He told a few war stories. She told him what she knew about Lt. Peterson. Having listened to family stories, she knew some details about the missing pilot. And there had been the diary, of course. Morris recited more details about his wife's betrayal. Becky told tales about school in St. Cloud and how she had met the Lindquists. Their words filled the evening. By the time they shared dessert and more wine, she was certain she had told him everything without saying anything. Point, set, match.

....

Chapter 33

Girua Airport, Oro Province, next morning

Slipping into a steep left-hand turn, the Air Niugini commuter flight dropped over an endless sea of palm oil groves and lined up with a distant asphalt runway. Morris stared from his window at Mount Lamington, a dormant volcano with shattered slopes resembling a malignant blossom frozen in mid-opening. Crowned with early morning clouds, the sleeping cone still seemed capable of repeating its 1951 eruption that had killed 3,000 inhabitants and wiped out the town of Higaturu in the process. Morris's attention shifted to eroded emerald horseshoe shapes—outlines of aircraft revetments from the war. The berms, evidence of the huge American airbase that had been Dobodura, passed under the plane's belly as they neared Popondetta's airport. Grinding noises announced landing gear being lowered, and moments later the Dash 8 turboprop touched down, wheels squealing on rough pavement. Running the length of the blacktop, the white-hulled plane taxied to an apron fronting the terminal. As the engines died, the flight attendant opened the forward hatch, lowering narrow stairs. Morris unbuckled, rose, and retrieved his carry-on bag from the overhead.

Following a line of passengers, he led his team into stifling morning humidity. Passing through a gate, they headed toward an ugly, squat cinder-block building surrounded by a barbed wire–topped fence. A handful of locals loitered, staring blankly at outbound passengers waiting for their flight to be called. Airport workers in dark blue coveralls, and in no particular hurry, bantered among themselves at the check-in counter in the building's spartan interior.

Morris and the others waited patiently for their luggage in the shade of an overhanging porch. Clumps of sodden insulation dangled from a crumbling ceiling.

"We're definitely not in Kansas anymore," whispered Becky to Morris.

He smiled, remembering his own introduction to the airport four years ago. At the parked airplane, workers quickly emptied the cargo hold. "Did all our stuff make the flight?" she asked hopefully.

Surveying the growing mountain of luggage, he nodded. "I see everything belonging to us. Haven't always been this lucky." Morris dropped his bag at her feet. "Keep an eye on this for me. I'll see if our ride is here."

With Morris gone, Darryl, wearing baggy cargo shorts, an olive drab T-shirt, and an attitude, sidled up next to Becky. "What an absolute shit hole. Even the bathroom's locked," he complained. "This has got to be the poorest fucking excuse for an airport I've ever seen."

She silenced him. "And just how many airports have you really been in, Darryl?" Irritated at her rebuke, he stared across the tarmac.

Morris returned, a short black man in a white shirt and shorts at his side. "Guys, this is John Two. We nicknamed him that because we had another guy named John on my last trip.

Made it easier to keep them separate. Course the other guy was white." The two laughed. "Van's out front," announced Morris. "He'll take us into town."

Smiling broadly, the round-faced man shook hands with the others. "Yeah, you call me John Two. More easy for remember, okay?" He followed the quartet to the luggage cart and helped ferry their bags to his vehicle.

At the van's rear doors, a mesmerized David Lindquist stood gaping at the skeletal fuselage of a bomber parked in grass near the terminal's fence. The plane's tired gull-like wings were propped up with supports.

"Is that what I think it is?" he asked.

"A B-25, Mitchell bomber," said Morris. "Like Doolittle flew over Tokyo."

"Give me a minute, will ya? I gotta get a couple of pictures." Circling the relic, David beamed like a kid, snapping a half-dozen shots before jumping in the van. "That," he said pointing at the plane, "was pretty cool."

From the front seat, where Becky sat sandwiched between the driver and himself, Morris grinned at David. "You'll get a chance to take a lot more pictures once we get to the wreck site. By the way, did you notice that some enterprising soul dropped a couple of P-47 engines under the wings to make it look authentic?"

"You're kidding, right?"

Raising his right hand, Morris laughed. "So they say, David. For tourists. You have to admit a bomber looks better with engines…even if they're the wrong ones." Everyone but Darryl laughed. Brooding, he glared at the back of Becky's head, then stared out the window at the passing countryside.

After ten minutes of decent paved highway came rutted, iron-hard roadbed rattling the van's frame. John Two dropped his speed to lessen the pounding the vehicle was taking. Shaking his head, he shot a disapproving look at Morris. "Ah, this road not the best."

Grimacing, then laughing, Morris steadied himself with one hand against the ceiling. "You said that two years ago. Yeah, I forgot how bad the roads are."

Between them, Becky braced both hands against the dashboard as the van hit yet another gaping pothole. In the back with the luggage, Darryl held on to the padded bench seat with a death grip. Opposite him, his brother jammed both legs against the piled suitcases to keep his place on the seat. The van skittered across ribs of stone poking through the packed dirt and accelerated along through a head-high corridor of kunai grass hemming both sides of their route. Their progress was short-lived. Slowing for a file of locals, John Two shifted left, giving berth to walkers hugging the side of the road. A bearded father in shorts and T-shirt, machete in one hand, infant cradled against a hip, led a family of six along the track. All were barefoot, gaunt. Two skinny children at the rear of the group broke into broad smiles, dancing and waving as the van passed them in a cloud of dust.

On the outskirts of town the road mercifully turned into pavement again and John Two raced along, his passengers gulping air streaming through the windows. At a street junction, the van turned into a short driveway strewn with trash and came to a stop at a gate with a small guard shack. Above the gate hung a crude hand-painted sign welcoming the newcomers to Popondetta's Comfort Inn Motel. Beyond a wire fence topped with ugly barbed wire, several rows of rooms sat surrounded by flowers and banana palms—an oasis in the scruffy grass and dust. Watching from the shade of a sheltering tree, milling men and women gazed passively, indifferent to the Americans in the idling van at the locked gate.

A blast on the horn shocked the guard into life. Emerging from the hut, a man in dark trousers and threadbare polo shirt spit a stream of beetlenut juice into the dirt and wordlessly opened the gate, allowing the van to pass. They skidded to a stop on a gravel patch in front of the motel and Morris went inside to register his party.

Becky and the Lindquists tumbled from the vehicle to restore circulation in their limbs. John Two stayed with the vehicle and its luggage. The three surveyed their surroundings. "That was one of the worst rides I've ever experienced," groaned David, arching his back.

"And I thought the airport was bad," snorted his brother. "Geez, how much worse can this get, Becky?"

"Morris said this wasn't going to be easy," she replied, stretching. "And this was probably the easiest part of the trip."

"All I gotta say is this damn well better be worth it," huffed Darryl.

Morris emerged from the motel's main building followed by two white men. Holding room keys aloft, he announced. "Got us signed in. John Two will drive our luggage around back." Tossing a set of keys to David, he said, "You're bunking with Darryl. Becky, you're next to them and I'm one door down."

Turning to the two men at his side, Morris introduced the pair. "Your television crew arrived yesterday. This is Sean Gallagher." A freckled, grinning, muscled man with wild red hair, in a riotous floral shirt, shorts, and sandals, stepped forward to shake hands with Becky and the Lindquists. Morris motioned to a taller, unshaven, morose man in a mesh T-shirt and shorts. "Hugh Nelson. They'll accompany us to shoot video. Seems we're going to have our fifteen minutes of fame after all." The group laughed and each shook Nelson's hand.

"At least in Australia," piped Gallagher, grinning. "Can't guarantee this will make you stars stateside."

"We'll all meet for lunch in half an hour," added Morris. "Does that work for you fellows?" Both men shrugged in acceptance. "Lunch it is," said Gallagher.

Introductions done, Morris ushered Becky and the Lindquists through the main entrance, showed them the motel's spartan dining room and the bar with its concrete patio and picnic tables, then herded them down a covered walkway to their rooms. "At least you've got air conditioning and a TV, plus bathrooms. Might as well enjoy it while we can. This is good living compared to where we're going for the next few days." His remarks drew another groan from Darryl.

Each of them explored their rooms, simple affairs with two beds, refrigerator, TV, coffee maker, and tiled bathroom with stool, sink, and shower.

"Man, I need a shower," announced Darryl, snapping on an air conditioner set high in the wall. "Yes, you do," teased his brother collapsing on a bed, arms behind his head. John Two followed close behind, depositing luggage on each threshold. Morris palmed a few kina in the driver's hand, thanked him, and retreated to his room. Reappearing twenty minutes later, after a shower and a change of clothes, he set his AC on high, locked the door, and headed to the dining room. The inn's manager intercepted him outside the motel's office with a note. Morris thanked him, scanned the slip of paper, and pocketed it for sharing with the others later.

In the dining room, Becky sat at a long table with the Australians, sipping a canned soft drink. The trio's chatter died when Morris entered. Two lazy ceiling fans barely stirred the muggy air. An air conditioner was laboring hard.

"Your rooms okay?" he asked, taking a seat at the head of the table.

"Luxury, mate," grinned Gallagher hoisting a beer bottle. Nelson, sucking on a bottle, signaled his approval with a raised eyebrow.

Becky put down her drink. "Can't complain. Well, I guess I could. Wouldn't do any good, would it?"

"Nope. It's not as fancy as the hotel in Port Moresby, but it's decent, considering." Morris signaled to a silent waitress who entered the room. Making a tippling motion he asked, "Another SP?" A half-smile passed across the brown face and the woman padded into the kitchen.

Cocking her head, Becky asked, "What's an SP?"

"South Pacific. Beer," answered Gallagher raising his bottle. "Not bad. Beats water. Actually, water's good. Bottled water. Better than beer. But…beer will do for now, eh, mate? Alcohol's a cleanser of sorts to my way of thinking."

Reappearing with a single sweating bottle on a tray and two menus, the slim woman set the beer in front of Morris. "You like glass?" she said softly.

Shaking his head, he held up two fingers. "Two more coming for lunch." Flashing an enigmatic smile, the woman returned with additional menus and resumed her place at a small desk in the corner of the room.

"What do you suggest?" Becky whispered across the table. "I mean, is the food here safe to eat?" Across from her, Gallagher giggled.

Sipping his beer, Morris smiled. "Never been sick once on my previous trips. Stayed here both times. Yeah, you should be okay. I prefer the curry myself. It probably kills whatever could harm you."

Pointing to Becky's soda can, Gallagher dropped his voice. "Wouldn't hurt to wipe the top of your can with a moist towelette next time, miss."

Glancing down at her open can, Becky blanched.

Nodding at two tall urns on a serving table, Morris lowered his voice. "He's right. I usually pass my silverware and cups under the hot water they boil for tea. Just a precaution."

"And don't brush your teeth with tap water or swallow while you're taking a shower," Gallagher added.

"I take it you've done this kind of thing before," said Morris.

"Yeah, we've banged around a bit. Picked up our share of bugs in our day, mate. Nothing like a little PNG revenge to humble ya. Not really a pleasant thought, is it, miss?" Becky blushed, the result Gallagher wanted.

The Lindquists entered and pulled up chairs. "Please tell me that's a beer," said Darryl inspecting the beverages Morris and the Australians held. Pointing at the bottle, he told the hovering server, "I want one of those."

"Make it two," added David.

"Three," ordered Morris, finishing his beer.

"Five, luv," barked Nelson, emptying his bottle.

The waitress came back with the drinks, wrote down lunch selections, and returned in fifteen minutes with plates filled with steaming rice, chicken, and fruit.

While they ate, Morris read aloud the note given him earlier. "Seems our missionary is delayed. He'll be down from the hills the day after tomorrow. Can't be helped, but that puts us off by one extra day." The others ate without comment.

Morris continued. "We built a couple of days into our outbound flight schedule so it won't hurt us. Actually, it might work out better. We need to shop for water and supplies before he gets here. When he shows, we'll probably have a few more things to pick up. You can do some daytime sightseeing in the meantime."

At the comment, Darryl, his mouth full of chicken, locked eyes with Morris. "You've got to be kidding. What the hell would be worth seeing here?"

Morris let the comment slide. "Or hang out. Watch TV. Catch up on your rest. It's been a long journey for everyone."

"I'm content to stick around here," interjected David. "I brought along a couple of paperbacks. I'll kick back in my room. Maybe I'll visit this fine establishment's bar."

Stabbing the air with his fork, Darryl seconded the idea. "That's exactly what I'm going to do. What I've seen of the town is enough to make me stay in my room until we hit the jungle or wherever the hell it is we're going."

"What about you fellows?" Morris asked the cameramen.

"We'll shoot some footage round town," volunteered Gallagher. "Get a little local color in the can, as they say. Better to have too much film than not, eh?"

"Suit yourselves, people," replied Morris. "There's an Aussie war memorial in town. Couple of blocks from the motel. Easy walk. Well-kept. Has a good chronology of the battles fought not far from here. Worth a visit if you're interested."

"Maybe I'll do that," answered Becky. "We could go later, guys."

Shoveling more food into his mouth, Darryl mumbled, "And sunburn my ass? I don't think so."

"Well, anyway," offered Morris, "think about it. I'm stopping by the bank later and changing more currency for us. I'll pick up a couple of cartons of water. We're just waiting for Wood to show up. He knows we're here."

Glancing at his watch as their server began removing dishes, Morris announced, "I'd like to catch some rack time myself. I suggest we meet at the bar before dinner. We can go over some of the details about our little adventure. Okay with you folks?" The five agreed.

"Good, he said rising. "See you this evening." Stepping up to the small corner desk, he signed the group's restaurant chit and headed to his room.

....

Chapter 34

Popondetta, evening

Intercepting Becky outside her room, Morris asked, "Can we take a walk before we join the others for dinner?"

"Sure. What's on your mind?"

"Our friend, Darryl."

Pointing across the lawn to a thatched roof gazebo surrounded by flowers, Morris suggested they talk out of earshot. They strolled to a pair of stone benches and sat facing each other across a concrete table. Morris glanced across the garden to the bar's patio where the Lindquist brothers sat with the two Australians and a half dozen locals, drinking beer and playing cards. Loud South Pacific hybrid-reggae music pumped from the bar's CD player. "Darryl's attitude hasn't changed for the better has it?"

Shrugging, she sighed. "No. But I told you we wouldn't let him get out of line."

"I know," he said sternly. "I was hoping being here would humble him a bit."

"He's putting up a brave front. He's worried. Can't say I blame him."

"You'll do fine, Becky. I'm not worried about you. But once we leave here we can't just send someone back to his room because he's unhappy, you know." His tone softened. "By the way, how are you holding up so far, really?"

Becky stared up at Morris, her face and neck glistening with perspiration. "I'm okay," she said, brushing away strands of limp blonde hair plastered to her forehead. "This heat and humidity just takes some getting used to."

"Do what I do."

"What? Some tropical trick?"

"Nah, nothing that exotic. Just think of the absolute worst August you ever experienced in Minnesota," said Morris. "Then triple it and you'll feel right at home." She smiled despite her obvious discomfort. "I really don't feel like talking about Darryl right now, okay?"

"Sure. I just wanted to let you know I'm still keeping an eye on him. Let's get some chow," he suggested. "And this time try the chicken curry."

They collared the team members from the bar and headed for the dining room where they were the only customers. Conversation was as spare as the table settings. After the meal everyone retired to their rooms.

Rain, which had begun falling during dinner, continued all night. Pools appeared in low spots along the motel's cement walks. The downpour pummeled flowerbeds and palms bent under the deluge. Morris lay awake, listening to raindrops rattle like pebbles against the horizontal glass panes in his windows. The room's air conditioner's on-off humming eventually lulled him to sleep.

Three hours before dawn, he was awakened by muffled voices. Straining to hear, Morris propped himself on his elbows and cocked his head to one side, unsure if he was really hearing things. Curious, he slipped from bed, walked barefoot across the tiled floor, and pressed his ear against the shared wall of Becky's room.

Muted, indecipherable words and occasional soft giggles came through the cinder blocks. Morris went to his door, quietly opened it, and scanned the concrete walkway. Empty. Despite constant dripping rain, the voices were clearer, one of them obviously Becky's, the other male and familiar. Reaching above him, Morris gave the bulb above his door a few quick twists, plunging the length of sidewalk outside his room into darkness. An invisible voyeur, he leaned against the wall, listening, most of his body hidden by the doorframe.

Just as he was about to trade his vigil for bed, the door to Becky's room slowly opened. Morris remained undetected in the shadows. Shirtless and shoeless, David backed from the doorway and looked both ways. Becky reached out, caressed David's face and kissed him passionately before sending him away. Fascinated, Morris watched David tiptoe stealthily along the walk like a guilty lover returning home not knowing he had been discovered. His door closed without a sound, leaving Morris in the dark.

He left the light untouched, went inside, and locked his door. For the next few hours Morris lay awake, staring at the ceiling, listening to the rain's soothing rhythm. An odd sense of betrayal descended. *Why does this bother me? She has a right to do what she wants, doesn't she? Is it jealousy? She's an adult. Do I care? Should I care?* The nagging thoughts kept him awake until dawn.

. . . .

Chapter 35

In morning's gray light, with her body clock still off-kilter, Becky dragged herself from bed and took a cold shower. She threw on a T-shirt and shorts. Opening her door, she timidly stepped barefooted on the sidewalk's cool, damp cement. The air tasted thick with moisture from the evening's rain. Fat drops glistened on the sodden lawn. A steady trickle from rusting gutters dripped into overflowing buckets placed at each building's corners. A thin blanket of fog hugged the grounds.

To her left, a bathroom light meant Morris was stirring. The other members of the team had yet to rise. Their rooms were dark, air conditioners sweating in the humid air. Her watch showed 5:30. Becky went back inside, quietly closed and locked the door. She lay down on her bed and in minutes, was fast asleep. An hour passed before she awoke to the sound of steady knocking.

Groggy, she propped herself on her elbows, mumbling, "Who is it?"

"Morris. How about some breakfast?"

"Ugh, I'll meet you in the dining room." Putting her ear against the door, she heard him shuffle down the walkway. Stumbling into the bathroom, Becky threw water on her face to wake and ran a brush through her hair. She followed Morris moments later, rapping on the Lindquists' door in passing. The Australians were left to fend for themselves.

Becky, eyes puffy from lack of sleep, slumped in a chair next to Morris. "I'm not a morning person." He shrugged in feigned sympathy. Coffee and tea water perked in silver urns on a side table. Chilled carafes of orange juice and a plate piled with sugared buns sat next to a basket of different teas. Morris got up, poured a cup of coffee, and placed it on the table in front of Becky. Inhaling the fresh aroma brought her to life.

"Didn't get much sleep, eh?"

She shook her head slowly from side to side. "The rain."

"Among other things," he replied cryptically. She dodged his dart.

"Good thing we have a day of idle time," said Morris. "I suspect the rest of the team could use the break too."

Slipping into the room from the kitchen, a diminutive dark woman wrapped in a colorful sarong handed them fly-specked menus. Morris ordered without looking. "Eggs, scrambled, and toast, please,"

"Same," whispered Becky, sipping coffee.

Beyond the floor to ceiling windows of the dining room, Popondetta awakened. A steady stream of people passed along a path worn in the grass outside the motel's wire fence. Trucks, fitted with benches, their beds roofed with blue tarps, drove by, crammed with passengers heading into town. School children, some in uniforms, and others accompanied by women, strolled unhurriedly toward the heart of town. Singly, and in groups of twos and threes, natives tramped along the roadside. Without exception, each person carried a bilum bag slung diagonally over one shoulder. Occasionally, someone sauntered by carrying a small wooden bench or plastic lawn chair, a prized possession not to be left behind. A rare motorcycle trailed the packed trucks. Becky stared, fascinated at the constant movement outside the windows. It seemed as though the entire town was afoot.

"G'day! Lovely day, ain't it?" Gallagher, shadowed by Nelson, burst through the door shattering the morning's silence. After helping themselves to juice and making tea, the men claimed seats at the table. "How'dya sleep, miss?" barked Gallagher. Becky arched an eyebrow at the loud man, sending him into a fit of laughter at her pained expression. Nelson, the frowning one, ignored his partner and went to work on a frosted roll. When the server delivered breakfast to Morris and Becky, the two newcomers asked for the same.

"Shooting in town today?" asked Morris.

"Sure, we'll hit a few of the spots," replied Gallagher without raising his face from his cup. "Get a bit of local color and all."

"What was your last project?"

Nelson paused, his fork in mid-air. He glanced at Gallagher, who answered.

"*Day of the Croc.* A little ninety-minute film on those nasty buggers."

"We call 'em salties," deadpanned Nelson.

Gallagher put an arm around his friend. "Biggest reptiles in the world. Shot most of it in the Northern Territories. Almost lost me mate on that shoot, didn't I? Hugh here has a habit of finding his way into the worst spots on occasion, don't you, mate?" Pointing at an ugly whitish scar along Nelson's right forearm, Gallagher crowed, "A monster female that took a liking to him in a billabong. Oh, she was in love, she was." Nelson shrugged, kept eating, as if bored by the tale's telling.

Becky stirred. "What's a billabong?"

Gallagher put down his teacup. "It's a pool of water, a branch off a river or stream that forms in high water. Might be left behind when the water drops. Crocs like it." Winking, he added, "Good for mating and nesting. Easy to get into, hard to get out if you're carrying a camera, right, Hugh?" Nelson said nothing.

"In the states we'd call that a slough or an ox-bow," explained Morris.

"Exactly, mate," agreed Gallagher, wagging a finger at the American.

Enter the Lindquist brothers, sleepy-eyed and hungry. Ignoring the others, they immediately headed for the serving table and scooped up the remaining rolls.

"Morning," said Morris, rising to refresh his coffee. He got a muffled hello from both men, filled his cup, and turned his attention to the Aussies. "You two been freelancing long?" he asked Gallagher.

"Long enough to pay the bills, mate."

"Do any TV work?"

Pushing away his plate, Nelson growled, "You ask a lot of questions."

Gallagher smiled benevolently, his hand on his partner's shoulder. "Man's just curious, laddie." Sipping his tea, he eyed Morris. "Done our fair share at Seven Melbourne, Channel Seven that is. Didn't really take to regular hours, though. We're more the free spirits, ya might say."

"Ya might say," echoed Nelson, standing. "I'm off to check our gear."

"Mind you make sure it hasn't walked off anywhere, mate."

Nelson excused himself and went out. Gallagher followed soon after.

Nibbling on a piece of toast, Becky blinked to stay awake.

"Try some of this," said Morris, bringing her more coffee. "How about you guys," he said to the brothers. "Any plans this morning?" Both shook their heads and continued eating. "If Mr. Wood arrives as scheduled, we head out tomorrow," Morris reminded them. "Last chance to get a good look at Popondetta."

Grunting and chuckles greeted Morris's last remark. He grinned at Becky, finished his coffee, and signed for the meals. Pocketing a banana from a fruit basket, Morris nodded to his companions and went to his room. Trips to the bank, postal station, and hardware store were on his agenda—as was packing and a long afternoon nap in anticipation of the coming trek.

Returning to her room, Becky rummaged in a canvas duffel bag for the hard plastic case housing a satellite phone. She slipped outside. Behind one wing of rooms, she found a secluded spot of lawn open to the sky. Floating lazily overhead, great white clouds drifted from the mountains, across a china-blue sky framed by palms. Holding the black phone, she pushed a button, tapping the iridium battery's power, and entered the requested pin code. In minutes, the phone's tiny screen lit up with several bars, indicating ample power. She typed in a number and pressed the green OK button on the right of the keypad. Becky pressed the phone to her ear, the device's six-inch antenna pointing heavenward. She waited for what seemed an eternity. A buzz, a clicking sound, and then a male voice, clear and strong, came through the receiver. "Yes?"

Beaming, she turned her face to the sky, phone gripped tight with both hands. "It's me, Becky. Can you hear me okay? We're here. Where are you?" Swaying in delight, she nodded at the sound of the voice on the other end. "Yes, I'll be there. Perfect timing. Can you believe this is actually happening?"

Another series of rapturous smiles, a rapid nodding of her head, and then a reluctant goodbye as she ended the call. Clutching the instrument to her breast, Becky lingered for several minutes, eyes closed. She returned to her room and packed away the phone in its black foam padding. She locked the orange case and stuffed it back inside her bag. A glance at her watch read seven-fifty. Calculating the distance from town, Becky figured she had a six-hour window of time before she would be missed. She tossed two bottles of water in a small backpack, along with sunscreen and a handful of snack bars. After scribbling a note to Morris, she poked her head out the door. Two chattering maids distributing fresh towels were the only signs of life. Sounds of a TV kung fu movie next door reassured her the Lindquists were likely back in their room. Morris, she thought, would soon be walking the few blocks into town to do chores once the stores opened. The Australians were nowhere to be seen. The motel's bar was closed.

Crossing the patio unobserved, Becky stopped at the office to ask for John Two. "Most likely in the car park out front, miss," answered the manager. She gave the smiling man a note for Morris and went outside to the white van parked in the shade of a large tree. The car's hood was raised. Fighting her excitement, she strolled to the vehicle. John Two's torso was squeezed under the yawning hood.

"Hello, John Two. Will you take me somewhere?" she asked.

Backing from under the hood, the driver peered around the side and broke into a wide grin. "Sure. Where you wanna go? Town?"

"I want to see Gona. Where the Japanese came. Can you take me to the sea?"

"Gona? Yeah. Mebbe one hour. You sure you wanna go there?"

"Yes. Is the van okay?"

Wiping his hands on an oily rag, John Two slammed the hood shut. "Sure. When you wanna go?"

"Now."

"You say 'now'?"

"Yes, now," she replied, taking the front passenger seat.

"I take you there, no problem. Mr. Morris, he coming too?"

"No, just me. I will pay of course." She handed him one hundred kina. Pocketing the money, John Two climbed behind the wheel, started the engine, and drove from the lot, waving to the guard as they passed through the motel's gate. They went one block and picked up a chipped asphalt highway heading north.

No sign of Morris, she thought. *Good. He'll get my note and I'll be back before anyone's the wiser.*

On the outskirts of town the pavement ran out, replaced by familiar bone-jarring ruts. They passed the town's humming power plant, then huts on stilts filled with clusters of waving children. A depressing-looking camp, surrounded by guard towers and a high fence topped with coils of concertina wire, interrupted the monotony of kunai grass and scrub brush. Small groups of men sat on the ground idly picking at grass or staring passively in the distance.

The scene to her right chilled Becky. "A jail? Why here?" she asked.

Shaking his head, John Two frowned. "Buri Prison. Plenty raskols there."

"Raskols?"

"Bad men. No gut."

"You mean, no good?"

"Yeah. No gut."

The stockade fell behind them, replaced by more walls of grass and palm oil groves. People on the move, most of them heading toward Popondetta, wore the same smiling, patient faces she had seen on the way into town from the airport. To a person, they returned her wave. Trucks turned into makeshift buses tottered past, each one packed to its blue tarp roof with passengers who could afford the fare. Everyone else was on foot. The road worsened the farther they went from town.

Sporadically, manicured lawns and school buildings came into view. Groups of young people sat on well-kept grounds in semi-circles, obviously classes.

A soccer field with a fringe of cheering people suddenly materialized to her left along the road. Rows of classrooms on stilts lined up next to a huge open-air church wearing a thatched roof and a skirt of low coral walls.

"Government school?" she wondered.

"Mission school," he explained as he slowed to negotiate a yawning pothole filled with chocolate-colored rainwater. An overloaded truck slowed as it slid past. Waving, John Two exchanged rapid-fire phrases in Motu with the other driver. Both men laughed. The swaying truck's riders whistled, waving and crowing as the white van worked its way around the watery obstacle. They drove for fifty minutes.

"We almost there?" she asked.

"Not far," he answered, eyes focused on the scarred, muddy track.

More tended lawns and tidy houses appeared on both sides of the road and then, abruptly, palms framing a beach. John Two slowed, then braked to a stop at the beginning of a stone jetty washed by a gentle shorebreak.

"Gona," he announced calmly, killing the engine.

To their front, the sky dropped down to meet a horizon of dark blue ocean. Becky surveyed the scene from the parked van. On her right, under a huge spreading tree, a large crowd of locals sat on blankets or driftwood logs in shade. Men and women continuously spit beetlenut in the sand. Youngsters wandered through a chattering impromptu market doing a rapid trade under the branches. Mothers, children in hand, wandered the shore, umbrellas protecting them from the sun. Twenty-foot open boats, their outboard motors tilted out of harm's way, were drawn up on the dark gritty sand. Small overloaded boats puttered offshore, heading east to Buna or west toward Lae. Nosed up next to the stone jetty, a huge inter-island ferry had dropped its bow ramp into shallow water. Porters hauled bulging burlap bags of beetlenut from a row of parked trucks to the boat's ramp in a constantly moving column.

Becky's eyes swept the horizon until she found what she was looking for. She got out of the vehicle, went to the driver's window, and handed John Two more kina. "Can you come back here for me at four o'clock?"

"Mebbe you don't stay here by yourself, miss. Not so gut, you know."

"I think is gonna be gut," she said in imitation. "You come back, John Two?"

He took the money, smiling, gold tooth flashing. "Okay. I come back for you, four o'clock."

Showing her watch to him, she tapped the numeral. "Four o'clock, yeah?"

Flashing his wristwatch at her, John Two grinned, pointed to the glass face and the number. "Okay, four o'clock, I come back."

"John Two, will you promise me something else?"

Grinning conspiratorially from behind the wheel, he nodded. Lacing her fingers together in a prayerful pose, Becky said, "If Mr. Morris or anyone else asks, tell them I went to see where the armies fought. The Americans, the Australians, and the Japanese, yeah?" She placed her hand on his arm. "Promise me, John Two?"

"Yeah, yeah," he shrugged. "I understand. You want see where they make big fight. Okay, see you at four o'clock."

"Thank you, John Two." Becky waited, watching until he had backed the white van from the rock causeway and turned back for Popondetta. Only when she was satisfied he had gone did she cross to the west side of the jetty where the large stones ended and beach began. Shielding her eyes with her hand, she stood, entranced by the sight of a two-masted sailboat riding at anchor on the glassy sea. An inflatable dinghy left the moored schooner and rapidly made its way to shore where children waded. When the inflatable nosed into the beach, she spotted a tanned, bearded man in T-shirt and shorts step from the craft at the water's edge. With the children's help he dragged the boat ashore. Stepping onto the gray sand, Becky began walking toward the stranger. When the man raised his arm and waved to her, she broke into a run.

....

Chapter 36

Popondetta, May 16

Arriving mid-morning the following day, missionary Brad Wood had his driver drop him at the motel, then sent him into town to refuel the station's Land Rover. The ugly, balding tires and patched spare needed air. After rousting Morris from a nap and introducing himself, Wood and the Minnesotan headed to the dining room for an early lunch.

"Might as well take advantage of your hospitality while I can," said Wood.

Over rice and chicken, Morris ran through the names and personal history of those making the trek. As Wood finished his meal, Becky and the brothers arrived, taking a nearby table. Morris introduced them. When Gallagher and Nelson showed, they shook hands with Wood. More food arrived. "Won't get a decent restaurant meal like this for a while, folks," Wood told the team. "Enjoy it while you can. Go ahead and eat. I'll brief you about where we're going."

Unfolding a large dog-eared map, Wood sketched their route

while the others ate. Smiling paternally at Becky, the missionary added a warning. "Since I first made contact about the wreck site some things have changed. There's a different slant on what we're going to encounter up there…the village where we're going."

"Change in plans?" asked Morris.

"Not exactly. Just a bit awkward up-country right now. What I mean is…it's just that you ought to know we might find ourselves in the middle of something of a family feud."

"A feud?" asked Becky. "Violence?"

Wood shook his head. "Sorry, poor choice of words on my part." Smiling to ease the sudden tension, Wood explained. "Sort of a generational dispute going on in the village right now."

"Is this where my grandfather's plane is located?"

"Yes, Ms. Peterson."

"Call me Becky."

"Okay. Becky. Yes, the village's old guard is having a hard time with some of the younger set. It's my sense some sort of power struggle is going on up there."

"Enough to queer the mission, mate?" asked Gallagher.

"Not at that point yet, friend. Just wanted to make you aware of it."

Morris was concerned. "If you think there's any danger involved, Padre, say the word. I won't risk taking these folks into the middle of something."

Wood finished a cola and asked the hovering server for another. "Understood. I wouldn't expect you to put your people at risk. At the same time, I wouldn't throw away two years of work up there if I didn't think we had a decent chance at making the trip. You want to see an airplane; I want to do some soul winning. Besides, my contact in the village doesn't seem to think this family squabble is going to be a real problem. Hopefully it'll be ironed out before we get there."

"Locals hereabouts tend to iron out their differences with machetes," said Gallagher.

"They do indeed. I hope we're not at that stage yet."

"We came a long way, Mr. Wood," pleaded Becky. "It was very expensive."

"Oh, how I know. I appreciate your investment, Becky. I'm still determined to make sure you get to see your grandfather's airplane."

Folding his map, Wood rose, telling Morris and the others to meet him in the motel's car lot in half an hour. "Thanks for the lunch. I'll go see what's taking my driver so long. Morris and Becky will ride with me. The rest of you will follow us in your hired van. We're going to be packed to the gills with supplies for the mission, plus your gear. It's a five-hour trip to my station."

"Put all your spare baggage in my room," ordered Morris. "We're running a tab while we're gone. You'll get new rooms when we return. Questions?"

The five team members remained silent. "Okay, people, let's pack it up," barked Morris. "We leave in twenty minutes." The group broke up to return to their rooms for their belongings. Gallagher followed the missionary out the door.

A few minutes later, a grinning Gallagher shambled toward Morris who stood outside his room adjusting straps on his stuffed backpack. "Got another mouth to feed, mate."

"What does that mean?"

"Hope you don't mind. Me and Hugh hired a bloke to help with our gear."

Yes, I do mind, thought Morris. Frowning at the latest last-minute change, he stopped what he was doing, eyes narrowing at the Aussie. "It's up to Mr. Wood. He's running the show now. You'll need to talk to him about hauling another body. Might not have the room, Gallagher. You thought of that?"

Clapping a hand on the American's shoulder, Gallagher did his best to soothe Morris. "Not to worry. I took the liberty of speaking to the reverend after lunch. I explained our situation. Me and Hugh's that is. Said we needed this Noah fella to share the burden of carrying our equipment. That way he won't have to use his own blokes for the task. He's agreeable. It's all settled."

Sighing in exasperation, Morris fiddled with his backpack, speaking without looking at the Aussie. "We're not paying him."

"Don't expect you to, mate. Our hire. We'll take care of him."

"You gonna feed him too?"

"We've got his rations covered. Doesn't look like he eats much. Probably could carry me and our camera if I get tired, to tell you the truth."

Morris disguised his irritation. "I'll talk to the padre about where to put him."

Gallagher beamed. "He can squeeze between the Lindquist boys if need be. Or ride on top for all I care." Gallagher squinted at Morris. "Might have him run alongside the van all the way to the mission station if he has to."

"Where is he now?"

"Out front. Packed and ready to go. Name's Noah Vujari, from the southern highlands. Care to meet our lad?" Feigning nonchalance, Morris tightened his pack's nylon straps again. "You can introduce him when we load up. You and Nelson packed?"

"Been ready since yesterday, mate. Having Noah will take a load off us, eh?"

"S'pose so. Do me a favor. Tell the others to get stuff they're leaving behind to me. I'm ready to lock my room."

"Righto, mate." Gallagher disappeared down the outside walkway.

After loading his gear, Morris glanced at Gallagher's hire.

Corkscrew dreads crowned a large head framed by mutton-chops and set on muscular shoulders. Gallagher's description of his man's ability was obvious. Noah looked as if his body had been forged from cast iron. Barefooted, wearing the uniform of rural natives—T-shirt, ragged shorts, a packed bilum over one shoulder, and a long, razor sharp machete cradled in the crook of his arm—the new man was deep in conversation with Gallagher. The native projected menacing strength.

Shrugging, Morris nodded at the newcomer when introduced by Gallagher and took his place in the front seat next to Wood's chauffeur. Becky and the missionary pressed in next to him. Wood said he and his driver would change seats periodically. Steeling themselves for a long and uncomfortable journey, the passengers in the back of the vans pushed and pounded the cargo to create small niches for their backs, knees, and elbows. Promised stops every two hours to restore circulation to cramped limbs would be their only relief.

Gallagher's new man somehow made himself smaller to fit alongside the Lindquists in the second vehicle. Tents, five-gallon jugs of fuel, food, and packed bags were jammed to the ceiling of both vans. The motorcade turned southeast from Popondetta making good time along the main paved road until it ended.

The familiar torture began anew.

Ten minutes out of Popondetta, the two-car caravan left good highway behind and began the expected bone-loosening, kidney-damaging travel on what passed for roads. After two punishing hours, Wood had his driver pull over and park at a swift-flowing river's edge. "Stretch your legs. We'll wait our turn to cross." Rushing rapids upstream swirled around naked, abandoned concrete piers that marched across the river minus their decking. Widening, the stream slowed slightly at a ford where the crossing was marked by clear, knee-deep water flowing over a riverbed of smooth round stones. Four massive dump trucks packed with mounds of oil palm nuts—the reason for their stop at the river—slowly made their way down an incline on the opposite shore. A cluster of women, several topless, pounded laundry on rocks in the sunlight, interrupting their chore briefly to stare at the Americans spilling from the vans. Morris and Becky waved, sending the women into shy giggles. Children bathing in pools by the rocks squealed in delight at the visitors' attention.

Lumbering through the shallow water like huge snorting beasts, the company trucks entered the current. Driving slowly without stopping, the lead vehicle emerged on the far shore, its engine laboring in low gear as it ground up the hill, exhaust stacks belching gritty black clouds. Queued at the ford, the other behemoths followed in turn. When the last truck cleared the ford, Wood ordered everyone back into their vehicles and his driver led the way into the river. Rushing water backed up against the car's tires, unnerving Becky. She huddled against Morris in the front seat, her eyes clinging to the far shore. Once they gained the other side, she breathed a long sigh of relief. Anxiously looking over her shoulder, she glimpsed John Two's white van muscling its way through whitewater. Only when the van reached dry land did she relax.

"Piece of cake," Morris reassured her.

"I'd prefer bridges."

"Normally, so do I," replied Wood. "Did you see those concrete piers back there? Just upstream from where we crossed?"

She nodded.

"Got wiped out in 2007," he said grimly. "All of Oro Province got hit. Roads washed out, bridges collapsed, everything under water. Not a good time for the people."

"Why doesn't the government rebuild them?"

A deep laugh. "Good question. I've asked myself that many times."

"Priorities," said Morris, his face glum.

"Right. Priorities. Money. Will. The people just go on, though. They endure."

"And the company trucks keep running regardless," said Morris.

"Keeps the economy going. You'll appreciate the next bridge we come to. It'll put things in perspective for you."

Ten minutes later, a detour routed them away from another destroyed bridge, sending them to a riverbank where angry, snarling whitewater swirled around boulders midstream. Upstream of the ruined bridge, abandoned piers, useless and shorn of their trestles, poked above the jungle. To provide a crossing, huge logs had been felled end to end over rocks in the rapids. The makeshift arrangement proved a precarious crossing for hardy souls on foot. Shaky sapling handrails provided scant security along one side of the old logs. In place of the destroyed bridge, palm oil company engineers had created pyramids made from steel shipping containers piled on opposite banks. The giant metal boxes were packed with loose rock from the riverbed. On top of the temporary footings, workers had laid a Bailey bridge—sturdy steel trusses with metal planking to carry the corporation's heavy trucks. The link was a godsend for local vehicles.

"Pretty ingenious," marveled Morris. "Gotta love those engineers."

"Have to keep those trucks rolling. Didn't I tell you?"

"Whatever works." Morris leaned out his window, admiring the structure as they headed for the opposite shore, their tires rattling on gratings fifteen feet above boiling rapids. Once safely across the improvised bridge, another hour of pounding passed before Wood's driver abruptly left the rocky route for a set of weedy tracks running south. He drove between dark walls of jungle that swallowed both vans.

....

Chapter 37

Wood's Mission Station, Oro Province

Four hours later, the caravan slowed when the road ended at a wall of oil palms and an adjacent village of thatched huts on stilts. A small herd of children whooped in joy as the vans passed. A crowd of people suddenly appeared along one side of the road, waving and smiling at the visitors. Swarming, the children sprinted in the motorcade's wake, following Wood's caravan into a grassy compound framed by hedges of colorful blossoms. Circling, the vehicles parked next to a large clapboard structure sitting on thick poles. The riders spilled from the vans, stiff-legged but grateful the trip had ended.

An elegant woman with porcelain features, her white-blonde hair tied in a ponytail, posed at the top of the steps in khaki pants and shirt. Wood swept his arm at Morris and the others gathered behind him. "Folks, may I introduce my wife and mission partner, Dorothy." Bowing slightly, the woman smiled sympathetically at the weary faces. Descending the stairs, she embraced her husband and gestured to the clipped lawn next to the stilt house. "Please make yourselves at home as best you can. We've prepared dinner for you. You must be hungry."

Wood, arm around his wife, introduced each member of the group. His driver was already unloading both vehicles with the help of a small army of curious, willing villagers. "Set up your tents there," ordered Wood, indicating an open space between the house and two outbuildings.

Approaching Becky, Wood's wife took the visitor's arm, steering her toward the steps of the missionary's home. "You'll stay in our guest room of course, my dear."

"That's very kind of you but I can manage…"

"Nonsense," interrupted the woman. "As the expedition's only female, you can have a cot in our home for one night at least. Believe me, you'll get more than enough of the jungle where you're going. I insist."

"That's very kind of you, Ms. Wood."

"Call me Dorothy, dear."

Linking arms with Becky, the blonde woman winked conspiratorially. "We've rigged up a shower at the back of the house. Very private," she said. "The sun's been heating the water in a drum on the roof all day. You must enjoy it before supper." Arm in arm, the two women marched up the steps into the house.

Tents were going up in the yard. An old man started a fire in a shallow rock pit circled by tents. Somewhere in the nearby brush a generator came to life, purring in the growing dusk. A large blue tarp was raised on poles sunk into the ground near the tents. Mission volunteers set up a table, covered it with oilcloth, and hung two lanterns on the posts. Wooden pew-like benches were arranged in a square beneath the awning.

"Let's wash up before we eat, brothers." Wood, in shorts and shod with sandals, appeared at the tents, towel draped over one arm, bar of soap in hand. "The Lord has provided running water close by. Great way to cool off. Who's game?"

Gallagher stripped to khaki shorts, his pale body luminous against dark brush. "I'm with you, mate. Lead on." His partner, Nelson, demurred with a shake of his head. "Gonna smell a little rank, Hugh," bellowed Gallagher in a parting shot. Morris and the Lindquists fished towels from their tents and, wearing only hiking shorts, followed the missionary in single file along a narrow path to the river. Noah and Wood's driver brought up the rear. The sight of white men heading to the river attracted a giggling audience of kids from the village who tagged along behind. Crossing a small, slow moving tributary, Wood warned his guests to "watch out for the poisonous frogs."

"Is he kidding?" asked Darryl, worried.

His brother wasn't reassuring. "Maybe, maybe not."

"And mind the bloody rocks," added Gallagher, stumbling.

On the riverbank, the bathers were told to find a large boulder in thigh-deep water. "Anchor yourselves against the upstream side to avoid being caught in the current!" instructed Wood. Braced with large rocks between their knees, each man let cooling water bubble around them as they lathered themselves with the shared bar of soap. Crouching, Morris, his eye on a big boulder near Wood, crept across the streambed. His foot plunged into an unseen hole, throwing him forward. He went down. Flailing uselessly, Morris was swept away.

"DALE!" screamed Wood, lunging too late for a pale outstretched arm.

Powerless in the river's grip, Morris, struggling on his back, washed over stones toward the middle of the river. At the last second, a strong hand grasped his waving arm.

Noah pulled Morris to his feet with a single powerful tug. Both men stood knee deep in the rapids, Morris gasping for breath. Reaching for the black man's muscular shoulders, he nodded silent thanks. Both bathers stumbled toward the bank where calmer water pooled placidly between large flat rocks. Coughing, Morris steadied himself on his rescuer's arm. "I owe you one." A solemn nod and a trace of smile crossed the native's somber face.

Hoots, hearty laughs, and a smattering of applause greeted Morris when he returned to his starting place. "You were on your way to the sea for sure, mate!" crowed a soapy Gallagher.

"You okay?" asked Wood, concerned.

"Yeah," murmured a humbled Morris. "Thanks to Noah here."

"Gotta watch that current," scolded David. "Can't lose our guide!"

"Man, you were all ass and elbows!" gloated Darryl.

"Seems to me I remember being on my back," shot back Morris. He sat in the shallows, chastened by his experience, taking the ribbing without complaint. After washing, he joined the others toweling themselves on the pebbled shore. Thanking his stoic savior again, Morris took his place at the tail end of the line heading back to the mission station where supper waited. He expected the story of his unexpected baptism to be recited more than once around that evening's campfire at his expense.

....

Chapter 38

The Trek, Day One

Embers, coaxed into life by a village crone, set a pile of kindling ablaze in predawn blackness. Soon, coffee and breakfast tea boiled in enameled coffee pots hung over the flames. Muted voices and clinking sounds of metal plates being set on the picnic table woke Morris and the others. Wood's voice rousted a reluctant Darryl from his tent. The sleepy American, wearing a headband with a small camping light, scuttled to the nearby latrine. Gallagher and Nelson stood at the yard's fringe of tall grass, brushing their teeth and spitting into tall weeds. Morris ran through a series of exercises to loosen his bones. From the mission house, Becky emerged dressed in hiking clothes and carrying a cup of hot tea.

"Sleep well?" asked Wood, standing by the fire.

"Yes, thank you. After all day in the van, a bed felt wonderful."

"Good. We'll be on the ground tonight."

Morris wandered to the fire pit, helped himself to coffee, and warmed himself in the cool morning air. "Breakfast, everyone," announced Wood. After saying a short blessing, he invited the team to eat. The cook, named Anna, arranged her pots along the edge of the fire. As each person passed in line she slopped oatmeal, scrambled eggs, a scrap of what looked like meat, and a slice of toasted bread smeared with jam on each tin plate. Leftovers were dished out to a dozen men acting as the expedition's porters. The carriers squatted around the fire, savoring their portion. Morris and his companions sat on wooden benches under a sagging blue tarp, eating in silence. Anna, armed with enameled pots, went round to each, offering coffee or tea. Breakfast done, the cook and a young girl helper gathered the dishes, pots, and utensils and washed the lot in a small stream running through the mission grounds.

Morning announced itself with pink brushstrokes on clouds drifting from the mountains. Tents were dismantled and packed. Each team member's pack was hurriedly stuffed with clothing, extra socks, basic toiletries, cameras, lights, bug lotion, and other personal items. Morris had lectured Becky and the brothers to follow his example by traveling light. For the most part they had followed his advice.

Food, nylon tarpaulins, ropes, and—most importantly—a daily ration of two-liter bottles of water would be humped by the locals from the mission village. The twelve men, "my apostles," Wood called them, stood in a ragged line, barefoot, machetes in hand, each villager saddled with a full pack. From this point on there were no roads, only trails. They would be carrying everything needed.

Pulling her hair into a short ponytail, Becky wound a towel around her neck and adjusted the balance of her backpack until she was comfortable. She carried one dozen plastic Frisbees and soft foam baseballs as gifts for the villages they would visit. "Befriend the children and the mothers will follow," Morris had told her. Digging in David's pack, Becky checked to make sure their lifeline—a satellite phone—was sealed in its plastic case and wrapped in a change of clothing. It was safe, packed with packs of colored glow rings and sticks she had also insisted on bringing. "You'll see, kids will love them," she promised.

"We leave in ten minutes," Wood barked. "Use the latrine if you have to. We'll take ten-minute breaks every two hours on the trail. Don't want to leave you behind by mistake. Stay with the group. Got it?"

"Yes, daddy," mumbled Darryl under his breath, drawing a frown from Becky. Impatient to be off, the bored Aussies sat on the mission house steps in jungle fatigues, packs shouldered and ready. Their man Noah leaned against a palm tree, an aluminum camera case mounted on his back, machete in hand. Barefooted like the porters, he wore a ball cap, T-shirt, and shorts.

Wood's wife, white-blonde hair loose about her shoulders, came out to stand on the porch, smiling at her husband—off again after his beloved airplanes. Waving an arm toward the palm oil grove behind him, the missionary finished his briefing. "We need to make eight hours on the trail today. I sent a crew ahead of us yesterday. They'll be waiting for us in a small village. We'll be tired, but we'll have a few hours of daylight left by the time we reach them, God willing. We must get there before dark. They took plenty of supplies with them to lighten our load going out. Water in particular. They'll also have a couple of large tarps set up for us and hopefully a fire going when we get there." Worming into his pack harness with the help of his point man, Wood shifted its weight, continuing, "My guess is we might have to dry out a bit anyway." The seasoned Aussies chuckled, drawing a knowing smile from Wood. He bowed his head and asked God's blessing on the trip they were about to undertake. After quoting Bible passages, Wood ended his prayer and moved to the head of the queue.

"Rubbish," scoffed Nelson under his breath. He left the steps to take his place in line. "Can't hurt, mate," replied Gallagher. "Might need all the help we can get."

Wood's lead man set the pace as hikers and porters wound their way through the mission grounds, across the road and into the village's palm oil grove. A gaggle of children shadowed the group for a hundred yards among the towering trunks until shooed away by the last man in line.

Like soaring columns of a mysterious Egyptian temple ruin, mature palm oil trees dwarfed the travelers. Interlocking fronds blocked sunlight from reaching the floor of the grove. Birds called to each other, their nervous cries the only sound among the dark rows. Despite deep shade created by endless ranks of palms, the muggy air tasted of heavy humidity. After twenty minutes spent walking half the length of the grove, the column took an abrupt turn, emerging in burning sunlight. The heat instantly made Becky yearn for the shade of the palms. Before she had gone fifty steps, sweat drenched her shirt. Tying a bandana around her head lessened salt stinging her eyes but did nothing to stop perspiration from soaking her clothes. Ahead of her, the Lindquists suffered as well. Darryl had already finished the first of his two water bottles. An hour into the walk, Wood became aware of the toll the morning pace was taking on his charges. He wasn't worried about the Aussies but the Americans were obviously lagging.

Wood asked one of the villagers to cut walking sticks. Two quick strokes from the native's machete produced shoulder-high poles from young trees. Morris and the others took the offered staffs. The trimmed saplings made walking easier. Gallagher and Nelson had Noah cut them each a pole as well. Following a narrow, hard-packed footpath just twelve inches wide in spots, the line of marchers wound steadily upwards through head-high kunai grass covering a slope. Morris wore gloves to protect his hands against the serrated blades. Becky and the brothers followed suit as they plodded up the incline. They followed in the footsteps of the previous day's hikers. Directly ahead, impenetrable-looking jungle loomed where the grassy foothill ended.

The forest masked a series of intimidating ridges beyond which rose the azure silhouette of the Owen Stanley Range wreathed in cloud. Wielding a machete, the column's point man slashed an arch-shaped opening, widening the gap where the trail entered a wall of thick jungle. Guides cut away vines and branches, allowing enough room for everyone to avoid the sun's rays. Just steps inside the tree line, Wood called his first halt in the canopy's shade. "Not quite two hours yet, people. Thought we should break and see how you're faring so far." Wiping his brow with his sweat-stained bush hat, Wood eyed Darryl, who was panting heavily. "You okay?" Leaning on his staff, the midwesterner's only answer was a glassy-eyed robotic nod. Water bottles were passed among the hikers. To a man, porters from the mission station politely declined the water. Despite faces painted with a sheen of sweat, the carriers had yet to show any adverse effects from the march. Even Anna the cook and her helper stood like uncomplaining hunchbacks, their bulging netted bags of pots and utensils held in place by broad straps across their foreheads. Amazed at their stoicism, a hurting Becky determined to hide her own exhaustion.

After the promised ten-minute respite, Wood gave a signal to continue. Stretching accordion-like, the file proceeded in fits and starts as Morris and his team—constantly chivvied up and down the line by Wood—struggled to keep pace. The Aussies held their own, bringing up the tail without slowing. Two hours passed before the hikers broke the march again. To add insult to injury, the heavens opened, drenching everyone. The sound of fat raindrops pelting leaves was deafening.

They spent their next ten-minute break huddled under scant cover as water soaked every square inch of clothing. Wood ordered them back on the trail despite the unrelenting rain. In a losing effort, a pair of natives hurriedly cut branches and brush to corduroy the waterlogged trail. Calling a halt, Wood sent scouts ahead on higher ground. Donning ponchos, Morris and his crew waited out the deluge on the side of a footpath turned quagmire. Both Lindquists fell into a soaked, sullen silence, their angry eyes blaming Morris for the pelting rain. When his point men returned to the column, Wood's face darkened with worry. Shouting into Morris's ear above the din, he sketched a change in plans. "The trail up ahead has deteriorated! We need to detour across the stream below us before it becomes impassible. We'll gain the ridge above where it's drier," he explained. "One of my guys has gone ahead to pick up the trail!" Gallagher, in shiny poncho and sodden Digger hat, sloshed up the muddy path behind Wood to kibitz. "You're absolutely bloody sure we can't continue on this track, mate?"

"Getting harder to follow with each step!"

Shrugging, Gallagher backed off, wiping water from his eyes, waiting.

"Okay. I get it!" yelled Morris to Wood. "We cross here. Then what?!"

As water poured from his hat brim, the missionary gestured to a steep, leaf-covered hillside dotted with saplings. "We'll go down this hill and work our way across to high ground," he bellowed. "We'll pick up our point man somewhere in the jungle over there. He'll get us back on the trail. It'll be easier to follow. We have to move fast before the water gets too high!"

Using hand gestures, Wood shooed the main column to the edge of the trail. At the bottom of the incline, a trough of muddy water shot through a rapidly deepening v-shaped cut. One by one, carriers descended, left hand steadying supplies on their shoulders, right hand gripping young trees rooted in the saturated earth. Wood followed his villagers, mimicking their movements, using the thin trees to steady himself. At the bottom of the hillside, Wood spanned the rushing stream and clawed his way up the opposite slope. On the hill's crest he tied a rope to a sturdy tree and threw the line to the remainder of the party.

Morris ushered Becky to the top of the hill and handed her off to one of the natives who stood planted ankle-deep in mud. Her feet went out from under her and she slid into another man stationed halfway down the incline. Helping her to her feet, the porter held her hand until she regained her balance. She stumbled, pitched forward in a wild slide until she reached the stream, which she spanned in a single leap. Despite the ordeal, a giddy smile crossed her face. She immediately grasped the rope and scrambled after Wood. David slipped at the top, flailing in the muck as he shot down the slope in a shower of mud and debris. Ending up on all fours in the stream, he was helped to his feet by a native and attacked the hill, using the rope to climb hand over hand without once stopping. Waving Darryl forward, Morris held his breath as the younger brother, out of control from the start, sailed down the hill, spinning from tree to tree as the villagers jumped out of his way. Somehow he made it down, regained his feet and jumped the muddy cataract without losing his pack. Morris let himself down the hill, stumbling past trees, arriving at the swollen stream splattered head to toe with mud and plastered with dead leaves. After the Aussies and their man Noah crossed, the last porter worked his way down the scarred hill and leaped the roaring flume.

To Wood's relief, the high ground along the jungle ridge was wider and drier than the just-abandoned trail. Reforming into a column with Wood and a guide at the head, the expedition pushed forward. Every few yards, the point man hollered into the jungle, waiting for an answering call. Eventually, the rain cooperated, slackening into a light drizzle. The two voices grew stronger until Wood's party reached the source of the calls. Perched on the gnarled roots of an enormous hardwood giant, a placid guide waited, one cheek ballooned with a wad of beetlenut. Retracing his steps, he led them unerringly to the trail.

Muddy, miserable, and morose, Morris and his team staggered along behind Wood and the carriers. To make up for lost time, they pushed on without stopping. No one seemed to notice the missed breaks. Americans and Aussies plodded along the footpath, soaked to the bone, hungry and yet remarkably beyond exhaustion, or perhaps beyond caring.

Two hours before dusk, the waterlogged party of hikers reached the bivouac—a relatively level open space of matted grass walled in by jungle on all sides. A village consisting of four dilapidated huts on stilts was inhabited by emaciated, hollow-eyed natives befuddled by the new arrivals. A few pigs wandered about, rooting for something to eat. Gardens, fenced with saplings and bamboo, were scattered among the houses. Brush and immature trees at the edge of the tiny village had been hacked down to make room for tents. A pyramid of firewood sat stacked to one side, a poncho thrown over the branches to keep them dry. Wood's advance party sat contentedly under two enormous blue tarps, their corners lashed to sturdy poles. Rain dripped along the shelter's edges. Smoke from a fire curled from under the tarpaulins.

Shouts of welcome and bantering pidgin rang through the jungle as the last of the porters brought up the rear of the line. Disheveled and muddied, the Americans and the Aussies stood gaping at the campsite and its inviting fire. There was just enough room in the clearing to erect shelters for the night. At Wood's command, villagers began unpacking the group's tents. Dropping her burden, Anna the cook claimed a corner under the tarp and began sorting pots and pans needed for the evening meal. In moments, tents were up and staked, rain covers in place, gear stowed inside. Driving sharpened branches into the ground around the fire, Morris hung each hiker's soggy footwear on wooden stakes to dry.

The rain finally ceased, lightening the mood. Screeching birds serenaded from the canopy, adding a surreal touch to the setting. Kindling crackled in flames. Pans banged against each other in a primitive kitchen. Laughter, echoing in the clearing, mixed with an indecipherable dialect. Stripping off his soaked shirt, Gallagher, to the amusement of the locals, broke into an Aussie drinking song at the top of his voice. Nelson stomped off in rubber sandals, searching for the crude latrine dug at the edge of the clearing. Wood, with Morris at his elbow, hunkered with trackers to plan for the next day. Two guides from the distant village were expected by noon. They would shepherd the last leg. Anna served a heavenly feast of tinned beef, canned peaches, and bread. There were no leftovers.

....

Chapter 39

The Trek, Day Two

Fog bathed the bivouac. Distant treetops poked above a haze clinging to hillsides.

A mission worker breathed life into the previous night's ashes. In minutes, a small tongue of flame rose from a bundle of dry sticks as the native fed more wood to the fire. The camp awakened. Sleeping forms wrapped in blankets stirred beneath blue tarps sagging with rainwater. Wood and Morris collected the prized runoff in empty two-liter plastic bottles. Excess water was boiled for coffee and tea. Boots ringing the fire pit had dried during the night and Morris delivered each owner's footwear to their respective tents.

Wood told everyone he expected to break camp and leave once his escort from the village arrived to take them the last few kilometers.

Breakfast was a simple affair—bread slathered in peanut butter and jam and canned pineapple. Famished, Becky wolfed down her food and returned to her tent. After packing her belongings for the day's hike, she emerged with towel and soap, intent on bathing. She headed for a waterfall fed by a small stream spilling over a series of rock ledges just beyond the campsite. The previous night the cook and her girl had scrubbed pots by the boulders below the waterfall. Becky passed by the fire where

Morris and others sat drinking coffee. "Remember to hang on to the rocks like I did," he chided, cup in hand. Yawning, Darryl scratched himself, leering. "Need me to come down there as a lifeguard? I'll wash your back if you want." Ignoring the comments, Becky followed Anna and her helper to the waterfall where they separated.

Kneeling by a pool upstream, Becky waved to the women. Stripping off her damp shirt and pants, she wiggled out of her sports bra, draping the clothes over bushes to dry. Wearing only minuscule white bikini briefs, Becky slipped out of her sandals and stepped into the cool water, soap in hand. She settled in the current, letting it rinse away the previous day's sweat and grime. Rising to her feet, she peeled off her panties, dipped them in the pool and wrung water from them, then spread them on a flat rock to dry behind a screen of ferns. Lathering her body in knee-deep water, Becky spotted Anna's helper staring at her. Smiling, Becky waved. The girl broke into embarrassed giggles at being discovered. Glancing over her shoulder, the cook shook her head, breaking into a wide grin before returning to her pots. Laughing, Becky slid back in the rock basin, languidly washing soap from her naked body. She stood, reached for her towel, then froze.

A long, mottled green serpent slid sinuously across a rock and paused, its head raised as if studying her. Momentarily mesmerized, Becky watched the snake enter the pool. With powerful undulations of its body the reptile, its small head above the surface, swam toward her.

"Don't move!" ordered a male voice behind her. Petrified, Becky obeyed.

Morris stepped into the water in front of her, machete in his right hand, long forked sapling in his left. Speaking softly, Morris fastened his eyes on the swimming snake. "Back up. Slowly. Get out of the water. Now."

The serpent circled to Morris's left. He shifted between Becky and the creature. Prodding the snake with the forked stick, he pushed it to the far side of the pool, pining the viper's head against a rock. Becky stood perfectly still on a shelf of sunlit rock, Morris in front of her. Twisting, the snake wriggled against the pole as Morris pushed it from the water. Once the snake gained dry ground, its writhing body coiled tightly around the stick. Momentarily disorienting the creature by lifting the pole free of the ground, Morris set it down on the opposite shore. Shaking itself free, the snake fled, slithering into a fissure in the rocks, suddenly gone.

"I think you're safe now," said Morris.

Covering only her breasts with the towel, Becky, stammered tearfully,

"I couldn't move. I was terrified. You…saved…my life."

Facing her, his gaze locked on her eyes, Morris allowed a faint smile. "Probably a good thing you didn't make any quick moves. It might have been tempted to strike…or offer you an apple. You'd better get dressed."

"Morris…"

"Yeah?"

"How long have you been watching me?"

"Long enough. You might want to think twice about bathing around all these men. If I could spot you, so could the rest of the gang. No one's gonna give the cook or her helper a second look, but you certainly will get a different reaction." She avoided his eyes. "One more thing," he said. "You can never be sure what else lives in the water here. Lots of nasty things you can't see somehow end up inside you. Keep that in mind."

Nodding at a pair of hiking boots and socks by the pool's edge, he added,

"I brought those. Wood expects his village contacts to show

soon. When they arrive, he'll be anxious to move out." Brushing past her without looking back, he added, "Nice butterfly though. Hadn't noticed it before."

Becky reddened, her left hand covering a tiny winged tattoo on her bare buttock. She dressed quickly, her wary eyes on the rocks ringing the pool.

Within the hour Simeon, Wood's friend and guide from the distant village, arrived with another native. With the addition of these latest two, plus the scouting group sent ahead the day before, Wood's troupe had grown to two dozen, counting Aussies and Americans. After breaking camp, they followed their new guides for two hours, stopping briefly once, and then resuming their trek.

At three in the afternoon, Wood called another halt in a copse of towering hardwoods. Sailing free from a distant peak, a slow-moving rain cloud passed overhead, pelting the column for an hour before moving on. Draped in rain-slicked ponchos, the troupe finally broke free of the clinging forest at the edge of a wide grassy plateau dotted with isolated thickets of stunted brush. Wood's column plunged ahead, the cloud-crowned Owen Stanley Range filling the horizon to their front. They crossed an endless sea of grass crisscrossed with silt-choked river channels. Reaching the first flowing stream, Wood called another halt and sent his point man to test depth and current.

Becky took the opportunity to remind David to take a GPS reading. He was one step ahead of her. Surveying the wide expanse of grass around them, he whispered, "This looks like a perfect spot for a helicopter pickup. No trees, and the river makes a good landmark. The ground's firm enough," he said. "Plus, we'd be right out in the open. Be hard to miss us. I'm taking compass readings too. Might come in handy." Her brow furrowed in concentration. "We have to be able to get back here.

Plot our progress just in case we can't find a better spot closer to the village." Shouts interrupted their discussion. Wood's man was across the river.

Signaling from a long sandbar hugging the opposite shore, the native waved to Wood. Stationing porters at six-foot intervals in the rapids, he sent the rest of the party sloshing across the wide, thigh-deep river. In the relatively level plateau multiple tributaries had cut wide swaths, scouring the soil, exposing long pebbled shoals on their way to joining the river. "You should see this place in the rainy season," shouted Wood, sloshing across. "Turns into a raging lake."

"And you call this the dry season?" scoffed David.

Another hour of following the deepening, roaring river on their right ended at a jungle curtain where the water abruptly took a ninety-degree turn left across their path. The column halted at the foot of a makeshift bridge of saplings lashed together in a primitive arch. Each end of the bridge was anchored in crude piers made from piles of rock—resourceful but hardly reassuring to the visitors. Thirty feet below, a wild cataract of boiling rapids thundered past. The point man confidently worked his way across, balancing between two skinny handrails of bamboo running the length of the dubious-looking span.

"We're supposed to trust that?" gasped Becky, the Lindquists flanking her.

Wood nodded to the doubters. "It's stronger than it looks. Those bundled trees tied together have give to them. Lot of flexibility. Trust me, it's quite safe. Besides, we've got no choice if we want to reach the village."

"You go first then," challenged Darryl.

Wood took his place in line and began crossing as soon as the man ahead of him reached the opposite shore and waved him ahead. Putting one foot in front of the other, Wood took his time, reaching the far bank without a problem. Six of the carriers crossed without stopping, followed by Morris feigning nonchalance, though the swaying bridge gave him pause. The group's cook went next, all clanging pots and halting steps, her helper following. It was suddenly Becky's turn. Summoning her courage, she stepped out on the shaky structure. It took every ounce of self-discipline to keep moving.

"One foot in front of the other! Keep your hands on the rails and don't look down!" bellowed Gallagher waiting his turn behind her. The deafening rapids unnerved her, causing her to halt midway. With Morris encouraging her, Becky took deep breaths and resumed moving in timid steps on rubbery legs until she reached the safety of the far shore. Shaking with fear, she stepped onto solid ground, collapsing in Morris's arms. He tried to lighten the moment. "We have to stop meeting like this." Relieved, she laughed, exhilarated by what she had just done.

The rest of the expedition made the crossing without incident, resuming their trek along a beaten path that led them along the bank of the rushing river now on their left. Another two hundred yards and a final pass through a screen of jungle, the group was at the mouth of a narrow valley. Steep hills rose like ramparts on each side. Morris pointed to scarred hillsides above them to their right. "Slash and burn farming. Not the best way to do it." Becky shadowed him, her eyes following his stare. "What do you mean?"

"Farmers cut down trees, burn the brush off the hillsides, and plant crops. When it rains they get mudslides. Big problem in a lot of the third world."

"Like California, huh?"

Morris laughed. "Yeah, you could say that. Only in California that hillside would be covered with million-dollar homes and crawling with insurance agents. Same result either way you slice it."

"People gotta farm to eat." David had come up behind them.

"That they do," agreed Wood. He halted the column, sent his point man ahead with Simeon and the other villager, then came back down the line. "This is it, folks. We're finally here. Just want to give the headman some time to compose himself before we enter the village."

"They obviously know we're here," said Morris.

"Oh, yeah. They've been following us since the bridge."

Becky and the Lindquists scanned the woodline and hillsides as if expecting tribesmen to pour from the jungle, spears poised. "You knew they were following us?" Darryl fumed. "You shoulda told us."

Wood took a pull on his water bottle and shrugged. "To what end? Didn't want to panic you. They're just curious. They knew we were coming."

"I didn't see a thing," mused David. "Kinda like something out of a National Geographic cable show."

"Creepy if you ask me," hissed Darryl, loud enough for Wood to hear.

"You'll get used to it," said the missionary. "Remember, they're not accustomed to seeing outsiders either…especially white folks."

Becky eyed Wood. "But you've come up here before, right?"

"This makes my third visit. A word to the wise: I'd like to come again, so be on your best behavior while we're here. Don't do anything stupid. We're their guests after all."

"You talking to me?" spat Darryl, his fists balled at his sides.

Wood ignored the challenge and shuffled to the head of the column, leaving others behind. Darryl stood at the side of the trail, fuming. Catching Becky's eye, Morris arched a weary eyebrow at her. Acknowledging his signal, she shrugged and stayed behind to soothe the moody brother with attention. She had her own reasons for keeping him focused on what they had come to do.

....

Chapter 40

Simeon's Village, late afternoon

"Okay, people, let's move out!" Wood urged them forward. The Aussies lagged at the rear of the troupe. Coiling smoke rising from trees at the far end of the valley marked their goal. Rough grass gave way to cultivated yam fields on both sides of the well-traveled track along the journey's last quarter mile. Women working plots divided by bamboo fences halted their gardening to stare at the straggling line of strangers. The column entered the outskirts of the village. Men erecting a skeletal timber frame for a new house paused in amazement. Children fell in behind the visitors as they passed a line of huts on stilts. Forming a chattering rear guard, youngsters gazed in wonder at outsiders suddenly in their midst.

Wood and his group were ushered into the village center where a welcoming committee of elders waited. At the far end of a row of huts, a crew of women unrolled woven mats under a raised thatched platform with no walls. More women appeared, carrying small stools and low benches, which they arranged in two parallel lines facing each other. There was to be a formal meeting between elders and visitors according to Wood. "Village protocol," he said. Three precious pigs were to be slaughtered and buried in an underground oven for an evening celebration marking the team's arrival.

The missionary signaled Morris and his team to join him in the village square. After briefing them about the upcoming banquet, he told them of a forthcoming meeting with the chief's deputy. Rules for exploring the aircraft wrecks would be discussed. To Becky, Wood was apologetic but firm. "No offense," he said, but as a woman, she would be sidelined during the parley with the elders.

"I hope you understand," Wood said. "The old boy wouldn't think of dealing with a woman in council."

"No need to apologize for the old chauvinist pig," she scoffed, "I understand." After extracting a solemn promise from Wood and Morris to share what they learned, Becky opted to wander the village with her camera. Each time she shot pictures, she shared results with her subjects. Curious children and their timorous mothers were equally awed by the instant digital images. She snapped wandering pigs, bashful youngsters, flowers, birds, and mountains. A brief shower drove her under cover in a cooking hut with split bamboo walls where she sat with the cook Anna and her helper. Squatting on a log in front of the smoldering fire, Becky listened to the patter of rain and village gossip shared by matriarchs in their singsong dialect. Instinct told her she was the subject of conversation.

A barefoot elfin girl with reddish hair, in a too-big ragged T-shirt drooping to her ankles, approached her. Drawing the child to her knee, she let the inquisitive youth touch her white skin and play with her blonde curls. Becky's mind was elsewhere—on the downed planes somewhere close by. With daylight still remaining, it was agonizing to be this close without being able to explore the wrecks. From the hut's doorway, Becky stared at the animated silhouettes of Wood, Morris, and the Lindquists meeting with the headman. Sporting an incongruous mix of checkered shirt, ragged shorts, and a pair of wingtips sans socks, the chief's head counselor talked for two hours. To Becky, negotiations for permission to search the crash sites looked to be a vigorous discussion. Gallagher and Nelson had begged off in favor of filming their surroundings. *Lucky Aussies*, she thought. They were nowhere to be seen, off with their man Noah somewhere.

How many thatched huts on stilts and cooking fires do they need to film?

Their real mission ran through her mind, making her anxious. *They'd better not be sneaking around looking for planes before we get permission. Last thing we need is to have someone screw up our chance to explore.* She heard the women's droning voices, but her mind drifted back to the broad river bed with the wide-open skies. *Perfect spot for a helicopter. All we have to do is make sure we can get back there. The key is to follow the river back to the bridge of saplings. Then what? This is crazy. What am I doing here?* She set the child aside and calmed herself. *Tomorrow we'll find the planes. One thing at a time. I've come too far to turn back empty-handed. I know it's here somewhere. I can do this. I have to do this.*

....

Chapter 41

That evening, the valley's entire population turned out to celebrate, transforming their village into the center of the world. Moving in a ragged chorus line, colorful costumed natives swayed to a symphony of voice, percussion, and horn. Flames accentuated village choreography as dancers circled several large fires. Accompanying the shrill, oddly melodic choir, men with long tubular wood drums pounded out the beat. Wearing feathers, woven straw breastplates, loincloths, and boar tusk necklaces, muscular bearded men with spears stamped the packed earth with precision, their faces and bodies decorated with ash and clay.

Topless women in woven grass skirts, beaded headbands, and chokers formed two chanting rows. Older women, sagging bosoms swinging at their waists like deflated brown sacks, danced alongside pubescent maidens with small, firm breasts. Darryl pushed his way to the front of the audience to ogle the women, embarrassing Becky. Morris kept a wary eye on warriors in the front row who stared at their guests with suspicion. Aussies Gallagher and Nelson set up on the edge of the crowd to film. Ushered by Simeon, Wood made his way to a large house dominating the village center. An ebony gnome, with a head too large for his thin, wrinkled body, perched on a low wood stool. Obviously the paramount chief, the old man sat in the middle of a half-dozen fierce-looking young men. The six bodyguards wore scowling faces daubed in rainbow colors and framed in priceless feathers. The village headman who orchestrated the earlier negotiating session sat next to the chief. Wood produced a shiny wristwatch, held it to his ear, and presented it to the chief. The old man flashed a toothless smile as he slipped it on his wrist. He wore the new watch next to several others with batteries that had given up the ghost.

Chief and missionary shook hands.

"Holy shit! Will you look at that," whispered Morris, stunned. He stared at the chief surrounded by his ring of bare-chested warriors. "Can you believe it?"

Craning her neck, Becky pushed next to him. "What are you talking about?"

"The chief, Becky! Check him out. Look at what the old boy's wearing!"

She studied the wizened figure seated next to Wood. Underneath the feathers and boar's tusks, the wrinkled man wore a pectoral of faded yellow rubber around his neck. A worn leather strap looped under his left arm, revealing the unmistakable pistol grip of a .38 cal. revolver snug in a vintage holster. Becky, unsure what had excited Morris, looked from the chief to Morris and back again. "I don't get it."

Taking her arm, he steered her toward the edge of the dancing crowd to get a better view of the leader. Morris nudged her. "That thing around his neck. Recognize it?" Bewildered, she stared at the flattened yellow yoke, shaking her head. "It's a Mae West!" he exclaimed. "A life jacket! Pilots wore them!"

"Is that…" she left the question unfinished.

"And the holster he's wearing on his left shoulder," he added. "See it?"

She nodded, agreeing with Morris at what he was seeing.

"That's a pilot's personal sidearm," he said, lowering his voice. "A .38 cal. revolver. Can you make out the letters 'US' stamped in the leather? Your grandfather would have carried a gun like that just in case."

"In case what?"

Morris leaned over her, whispering. "In case they were shot down." She fixed her gaze on the chief. "Stay here," cautioned Morris. "I want to get closer."

"Maybe you shouldn't do that…not yet."

"Gotta take a better look while everyone's attention is on the dancing. Wait here," he commanded, slipping away.

The drumming took on a more frenzied tempo. A half-naked dancer, his face covered in a tall bark mask with holes cut for eyes, leaped athletically, thrusting a long spear in exaggerated lunges at invisible enemies. As the crowd cheered, chanting its approval, Morris worked his way toward the chief's perch. He waved, smiled at Wood and the chief's bodyguards as he leaned forward for a better look. The old man, his head bobbing in time with the drumming, turned, grinning at Morris with a knowing look. The American bowed slightly in deference, found what he was looking for, and nonchalantly backpedaled into the crowd where Becky waited.

"Well, did you find what you wanted?"

He shook his head. "Yes and no. The Mae West didn't have a name on it. Might be your grandfather's or belong to one of the pilots of the other plane Wood says is nearby. Guess we won't know until we do some digging."

"But it's a clue, isn't it? I mean, it could be from that other plane."

"There are a lot of them in these hills. But it's an eye-opener just the same. Maybe the chief thinks the life vest has magical power. Or he might wear it for ceremonies. To our way of thinking they believe a lot of strange things."

Becky was disappointed. "When you got so excited, I was hoping you'd find my grandfather's name on the vest or something. Weird, huh?"

"Not at all. It sure as hell got my blood going. Still, it's a pretty good clue we're on to something. You have to figure that gun and vest are seventy years old."

"You're sure they're genuine?"

"Oh, yeah. They're the real deal, all right. Maybe the old boy himself will tell us where he got them."

"Sorry I'm not more excited, Dale…I just feel like sleeping. I'm beat."

Putting his arm around Becky, Morris gave her an encouraging hug.

Chanting tapered off, then ended with a chorus of yelling. The chief conferred with Wood then signaled for the feast to begin. A group of men excavated the smoking underground oven, hoisted the baked pig carcass, and set it on a bed of banana leaves. Costumed males stood in small clusters, chatting or staring at the visitors. Bare-breasted girls, chaperoned by a crone with blackened teeth, appeared bearing coconuts with severed tops for their guests. Accepting the treat from the nubile adolescents, the visitors sipped from the hairy brown shells. The sweet, refreshing milk restored the team's energy. Bottled beer magically appeared from somewhere along with canned soft drinks. Once the visitors were served, villagers took their share of the pig with much good-natured shouting and laughter.

Wood sat with the chief and his headman, Morris, and the rest of the male team members flanking them. Becky, pointedly ignored by the village's male elders, remained a curiosity to the women and children. She sat with a group of older females, eating greasy pork and yams served on banana leaves. Heedful of Morris's warning, she drank only bottled water mixed with flavored energy powder.

The chorus line and drummers returned, fired with new enthusiasm for a night of feasting and singing to honor their guests. Dancers and drummers paraded past, filling the night with hypnotic rhythms. Voices rang across the village square. "It's a sing-sing," explained Morris as he joined Becky and her legion of native admirers. "And all for our benefit."

"When do we get to see the wreck site?" she asked.

"Tomorrow morning. The chief's agreed to let us spend two days there." "Finally we're getting somewhere. Is he going to be looking over our shoulders the entire time?"

"I doubt it," said Morris shaking his head. "Oh, he'll send his spies along to make sure we're not doing anything improper. But we'll pack a lunch and make a day of it. It's what you came for, isn't it?"

Chin in hand, Becky sighed. "Seems like we agreed to this one hundred years ago. I just hope it doesn't rain on us while we're there."

"Funny you should say that. The chief says every time someone goes near the wreck site, it rains."

"I hope you're pulling my leg," she groaned.

"He swears it's true. Says the pilot's spirit cast some sort of spell."

"Oh, great. More superstitious bullshit."

"We'll see." Morris got up from the log where Becky sat. "I'm going to make myself scarce, wander off and get some shut-eye. Hopefully I won't be missed."

"That's a great idea. I'm going with you. This party looks like it could go on for hours." Morris helped Becky to her feet. Smiling and using sign language, she excused herself as best she could and slipped away from the circle of women and children. Several young girls seemed determined to follow her until she gently shooed them back to their mothers.

Morris and Becky passed a cluster of young men sitting around one of the fires. In the midst of the gathering sat the Lindquists and Gallagher. Darryl, his cheek bulging, his eyes glassy, hailed the couple. "Hey, dude. Becky, baby. What's happenin'?" A villager seated next to Darryl took a deep drag on a hand-rolled joint and passed it to him. Aiming a stream of beetlenut juice into the flames, the younger Lindquist, his chin stained with reddish spittle, grinned. "These guys are alright. They got some really great shit. Kinda like chew, only tons better." Offering her the smoldering cigarette, Darryl attempted to stand, only to collapse backward over a log in a giggling heap. The circle of men broke into laughter.

Grabbing a fistful of shirt, Gallagher pulled the American back into a sitting position, telling Morris, "The bloody fool's taken a liking to buai and some of the other local herbs."

Shaking his head in disgust, Morris said, "We're going to the wreck sites in the morning, Gallagher. Maybe you ought to get him back to his tent. He won't be worth much tomorrow if he doesn't get some sleep."

"Ah, he'll be okay, mate. I'm calling it quits myself after another round."

"Suit yourself. Just make sure he doesn't end up in the wrong tent."

Saluting with a drunken wave, the Australian flashed a lopsided grin at Becky. She and Morris left the fire, disappearing between rows of thatched huts. When they reached their camp, they parted. Morris burrowed inside his one-man tent. Becky followed her flashlight's beam to a newly dug latrine villagers had prepared. When she came back to the little colony of staked tents, she stood for a long time, gazing at a million stars through a hole in the canopy.

A steady cadence call from frogs in a nearby marsh echoed in the surrounding jungle. Morris's backlit silhouette fluttered briefly before his tent went dark. Dying fires cast odd shadows along the ground. A chorus of native voices filled the night. Unzipping the mosquito netting of her tent's door, an exhausted Becky crawled into her refuge, resealed the opening, and removed her boots. She immediately fell into a deep sleep, fatigue rendering her oblivious to the music and chanting, neither of which showed signs of fading.

....

Chapter 42

The Trek, Day Three

Morning arrived along with fog creeping across the ground. Every bone in Becky's body protested her leaving the primitive comfort of her tent. Crouching, her limbs stiff, she wriggled from the shelter's opening, toothbrush in hand.

Morris was waiting. "Morning. How'd you sleep?"

A groan escaped her lips. "Ugh, can't you tell? Like a princess."

"Did you find the pea I put under your mattress?"

Squinting at him through puffy eyes, she grumbled, "What mattress?"

"Good question. You look like a laundry basket turned upside down."

Becky quipped, "Have you looked in a mirror this morning? You're no prize yourself, Morris." Laughing, he stretched. "I'm going next door to grab some breakfast. We have a big day ahead."

In a neighboring hut a fire was being fed wood scraps by Anna, the cook. She and her young helper nestled several pots on stones amid flames on the earthen hearth. A crude table of split bamboo, draped with a blue tarp, had been set for breakfast with plates and cups. Gallagher, wearing four days of thick stubble and trademark floral shirt, showed no signs of the previous night's partying. He leaned back against a wooden rail, drinking his morning tea. "G'day," he sang, lifting his metal cup in salute. Nodding in reply, Morris ducked under the overhanging thatch, greeted the cooks, and poured himself a steaming cup of coffee. He sat next to the Aussie. "I would never have guessed you'd be up this early."

"Maybe I haven't been to bed yet. Naw, you can't keep a good man down, eh? Last night was child's play, mate. Can't vouch for your boy Darryl, though." Gallagher chuckled, sipped his tea. "He must live a repressed life back home. Seen it before. Lads come out here and cut loose at the first opportunity. Mind you, it doesn't always end up without someone getting hurt." Nelson meandered by, offered a cursory greeting, took a cup of tea, and wandered out as quickly as he had come. Gallagher looked after him. "Strange bloke, Hugh. Take no offense, Morris. He's in his own world, he is. Has a good eye for the camera, though."

Shrugging, Morris watched Wood and the villager Simeon heading his way.

At the same time, Becky and David arrived as Anna lifted a pot of porridge from the fire. "Just in time for breakfast," announced Gallagher. Setting aside his tea, he spooned some of the boiled cereal in a bowl, the others following suit.

Wood arrived, helped himself to breakfast, and cornered David. "Looks like we're missing your brother. Better go roust him. We're leaving after breakfast."

"I'll do it," volunteered Becky. She headed for Darryl's tent, poked her head inside the flap, and pinched a naked foot. Darryl jerked awake, his bleary eyes trying to focus. "What the hell! Becky."

"We're leaving for the wreck. If you want to eat you'd better get it now."

"Ahhhh, I'm in no shape to do anything. I feel like shit."

"You look like shit. Get up anyway. You've got a job to do, remember?"

Mumbling, he threw aside his poncho liner. "Yeah, I know. I'm awake."

Becky snarled at him. "I'm not leaving until I know you're moving. Get up, Darryl! Haul your ass out of bed!" Curling into a fetal position, he moaned, began to gag. "Can't make it, Becky. I'm sick. Haven't eaten."

"Ask Anna for something. The rest of us are gonna be out all day."

"All day?" he whined. "Ahhhh, forget it."

Becky backed from the tent, leaving the disheveled man to himself. Morris shook his head in disgust. Gallagher, backpack over one shoulder, strolled to Darryl's sagging tent. He knelt, took one look at Darryl's sprawled body, and pronounced him unfit for duty. "Next time try not to swallow the beetlenut, mate." The Aussie's attempt at humor prompted another round of gagging sounds. Darryl raised himself on one elbow, eyes closed; then rolled on his back, obviously spent. Gallagher returned to the group, chuckling. "The lad's hors d' combat, gentlemen."

Wood hesitated. Becky and David remained silent. "We're wasting time," volunteered Morris. "I say we head out, Padre."

"Anyone have a problem with that?" asked Wood. No objections. "Right then," he said. "We're off. Simeon will lead us to the site." Smiling conspiratorially, Wood turned to the team members, his voice lower. "Mind your manners, we'll have eyes and ears with us today." Four barefooted men wearing T-shirts, shorts, and impassive faces stood off to one side, oiled machetes cradled in sinewy arms. "So let's be careful, folks," he added. "No souvenir filching, agreed?" Wood waved Simeon ahead. The trekkers moved through the village, two chaperons behind Wood's point man, another pair at the tail end.

. . . .

Chapter 43

Fifteen minutes into the hike, the column reached a rectangular clearing—thirty meters by one hundred meters—hemmed in by jungle on all four sides. A rickety-looking watchtower, complete with bamboo ladder and thatched roof, stood at the north side of the cleared field. Wood called a halt under the shade of an enormous tree. "Tell me what you see," he asked the group. Gallagher, shaggy head cocked to one side, spoke without looking at the missionary. "It's a bloody landing strip! Your missionary pilots fly in and out of here, don't they? And to think we had to walk in here!"

Amused, Wood turned to the Aussie. "You're right, it's an airstrip. But our pilots have never stopped here." Morris joined the pair. "But it's definitely a jungle strip, Padre."

"Yes it is," said Wood, hands on hips. "I found it the second time I came up here." Planting himself in front of the others, he said, "Ever hear of cargo cults?"

Gallagher laughed. "Aw, c'mon, a bit of ancient history isn't it, mate?"

A light went on in Morris's eyes. "Yeah, he's right. Kind of a pseudo-religious movement during the war. Islanders all across the Pacific thought their gods had something to do with all those goods the allies brought when they built bases."

Wood smiled. "Very good, Mr. Morris. You nailed it. The locals had never seen so much material in their lives. Food, clothing, housing, runways, airplanes, roads, machines, and Coca-Cola. Americans piled up so much stuff the locals were mystified. They actually thought those goods were meant for them and white men had stolen them."

"So what's the connection?" David asked.

"This," said Wood gesturing to the clearing, "is their version of an airstrip."

"If you build it, they will come, huh?" said Morris.

Wood opened a bottle of water and took a drink. "Exactly. Cargo cults thought if they built an airstrip, planes full of cargo would show up. Just like it happened at all those airfields our boys built."

"You can't be serious," scoffed Becky. "People can't really believe that."

"But they do," replied Wood. "At least the older ones. The thought has a lot of appeal to these people. That's why someone is keeping this place in reasonable shape." Pointing down the shorn field, Wood explained. "Actually, a skilled pilot could land a helicopter or a small plane here without too much trouble." Gallagher and Nelson exchanged quick, knowing looks.

Morris spoke for the group. "Why make a point of showing us this?"

"So you'll know what we're dealing with here. It's part of that generational dispute I told you about. The villagers are split in two factions. The chief and his elders like the way things are. Younger folks like Simeon want to change things.

It's not a closed book yet. I'm not sure how we play into this but I think we're part of it somehow."

Morris shouldered his backpack. "Well, we can't solve it today, can we?"

"No, we can't. Just wanted you to be aware of the dynamics of the dispute."

"Can we keep going?" pleaded Becky. "Are we close?"

"Very close," said Wood, waving at the jungle. "Just beyond those trees and across a stream we'll find two airplanes. One is the P-38 I found on my first trip."

"My grandfather's plane?" said Becky, gazing toward the trees.

"Yes, it's definitely his fighter. On that first trip I also spotted a larger plane. Thought it might be a bomber or a cargo plane."

"Which was it?" interrupted Gallagher.

"Got a chance to see it on my last visit. It's a C-47."

Gallagher's eyes lit up. "You're positive?"

"Yes. I know my aircraft. Did a walk around but couldn't get a longer look. For some reason, the chief and his cronies didn't like me nosing around too much. After some haggling, I left after getting them to promise I could come back."

"What changed their minds, a little kina grease?" asked Morris smiling.

Putting a hand on Becky's shoulder, Wood looked into her eyes as he answered Morris. "Yes, that, plus I told them a family member from one of the plane's crews wanted to come here to see where their warrior died. They respect that. They agreed." Coughing discreetly, Simeon shuffled up to Wood. "Pasta, we must go now." Aware of their four escorts squatting impatiently in the shade, Wood shooed everyone back to the trail. "Simeon's right. Let's see what we've come for."

Filing back on the path, they followed a serpentine dirt track winding through a crowded stand of immature saplings and wild banana. In a copse of towering brush, Wood called a halt. He organized his team in a line, each person five meters apart and abreast of the others. Nelson, camera mounted on his shoulder, tagged behind Gallagher at the rear of the formation. "We're right on top of the wreck site," said Wood. "Just keep an eye out. Give a shout if you spot something." He waved them forward. It was slow going.

Becky, in the middle, was the first to find the Lightning. She froze. "I found it!" Squealing in excitement, she fastened her eyes on a partly buried wing tip, as if afraid it would vanish if she looked away. Wood and Morris hurried to her side. David high-stepped through brush to stare at the slab of weathered aluminum. Kneeling, Simeon and the other villagers wielded machetes to scrape leaves and dirt from the wing. Traces of a faded white star on a blue field emerged, barely visible after seventy years. The Aussies circled, filming the discovery.

"That's part of it," crowed the missionary. "The fuselage should be ahead to our right. I figure this wing might have come off when he first hit." The escorts chopped a path through another thirty meters of clinging brush before more scraps appeared, some half-buried in the soil. Shredded aluminum twisted into metal pretzels was embedded in the limbs of mature trees all around the searchers.

"There!" bellowed Wood coming upon a jutting prop. The Lightning's outline suddenly appeared, buried under a net of matted vines. In the months since Wood's last visit the jungle had reclaimed the fighter. In a frenzy of slashing machetes, the P-38 emerged. Morris, together with David and Gallagher, clawed at the tangled vegetation, freeing the airplane. In two hours, they cleared the entire wreck. Becky stood in the shade, at a loss as how to react to what she was witnessing.

Taking her by the hand, Wood led her to the cockpit. Reverently brushing away the last of the leaves, he revealed a row of seven faded rising sun symbols. "Your grandfather was an ace, Becky. You should be proud of him."

"I am," she whispered, touching the weathered metal skin. "This is so unreal. Standing here next to his airplane is like being in a dream. It gives me goose bumps. But his body…his skeleton…shouldn't there be some trace of him? What did you find on your first visit?"

"I didn't turn up anything that proved to be human. It didn't seem prudent at the time to ask the chief about it. But now that you're here I'm certainly going to find out if they know anything about his remains. Hopefully we can sit down with the chief and the elders and get some answers." Morris stepped forward. "I saw enough evidence at the welcoming feast to convince me they know something."

Wood put an arm around Becky, drawing her to him. "We'll find out what happened. We'll bring him home. That's a promise." A soft rain began falling. Wood smiled. "Remember what the chief said?"

"About the rain?"

"Right. Whenever someone comes near the wreck site, it rains."

She smiled sheepishly. "I thought it was just some stupid superstition."

Tossing back his head, Wood lapped at raindrops, laughing. "Well, I've seen a lot of strange things out here. I'm tempted to just call it weather but I have to admit this is one for the books."

Gallagher stomped through the piled vines to the Lightning, his wild floral shirt soaked with sweat. "What about the other plane you said you spotted?"

"Right. The C-47. Let's have a look, shall we?"

"Lead on, mate. We got some great shots here with Becky and her grandpa's plane. I personally guarantee it'll make great television. This next wreck site ought to put even more icing on the cake for us."

"Want me to stay with you?" Morris asked Becky. She waved him ahead. "No. Go on with the others. David and I will catch up. I want to spend a few moments here. Take shots of my grandpa's plane."

"Take your time, Becky," said Wood. "I understand. Join us when you can. We'll leave two of our babysitters with you. They'll show you the way."

Morris followed the Australian camera crew and Wood toward a towering grove of trees a hundred meters distant. Simeon and two of the chief's men led the way, cutting a fresh trail to the bigger plane. Becky and David, shepherded by the two remaining scouts, gathered at the Lightning's cockpit to talk.

"Okay, what now, Becky?" asked David.

"We check this new site out before deciding what to do." Leaning against the fighter's nose, Becky fell silent. David put a hand on her shoulder. "Look, even if the gold's there we can't do a thing with everyone crawling all over the wreck." Pausing, he said, "Besides, my guess is that it's probably not there."

"You don't know that!" she said angrily, fists clenched. "It HAS to be there!"

"You have to prepare yourself, Becky," he said sympathetically. Taking her by the elbow, David ushered her toward the trail where their two minders waited in the shade of a hedge. Pointing machetes in the direction Wood had taken, the natives set off single file at a leisurely pace. Deliberately lagging behind, Becky and David continued their conversation in low tones. He said, "I'm not saying the gold never existed. What I am saying is, don't be disappointed if we don't find it today."

"Just what the hell is that supposed to mean?" she grumbled.

"You heard what Wood said about cargo cults, didn't you?"

"Yeah, but he said that was during the war."

"He also said it was alive and well after the war, even today. Becky, the only people close enough to keep that make-believe airstrip cleared live in the village."

"Your point being…?"

David tarried, letting the guides continue without them. He

repeated himself, his face inches from Becky's. "My point being that if we find this next plane empty—and I think we will—we have to take a close look around the village. That's a lot of gold to move, Becky. I'd be surprised if they've managed to spend it all. My guess is a lot of it's here somewhere…just not in the plane."

"It's been almost seventy years, David." Her eyes teared. "Maybe it IS gone."

"Wait a minute! You're the one who sold us on the dream that it was here. We came a helluva long way to find it. So don't give up. Not yet. Promise me you won't bail on me." She didn't answer.

....

Chapter 44

Darryl struggled into a shirt, hastily buttoned his pants, and laced up his boots. Emerging from his nylon cocoon on hands and knees, he crawled several feet, vomited, and passed out. From her perch under a thatched roof, the cook witnessed Darryl's struggles. She sat tending a small fire, feeding it twigs to boil water in a dented copper teapot set on two stones in the flames.

A sudden shower shook Darryl out of his stupor. Raindrops the size of large pearls pelted him as he lay spread-eagled in the grass. Still groggy from the previous night, he rolled on his side, pushing himself into a kneeling position. In seconds, Darryl was soaked, his clothing plastered to his skin. Scrambling on all fours, he groped blindly in his tent for a towel. Darryl's head ached. His back ached. His entire body ached and his wet boots felt like sodden weights.

A gaggle of village children sprinted across the clearing, skipping like small brown gazelles in the downpour. Laughing, they waved at the befuddled American who stood in the deluge, staring at them with bleary eyes. The children vanished between two huts. Squinting in the rain, Darryl waved to Anna. Contented and dry, she signaled him to join her. He stumbled toward shelter, a towel wrapped around his neck. Once under cover, he shook himself like a wet dog, peeled off his T-shirt, and hung it on a nail to dry. He rubbed his face and hair with the towel. Anna looked at him with a maternal mix of concern and judgment. She pointed to a tiny wooden stool near the fire. He sat like an obedient child, knees under his chin. Rain dripped from the overhang, splattering the hut's outside walls with a skirt of mud. Smoke from the fire stung Darryl's reddened eyes.

"Tea? You like some tea? Gut for you."

Darryl nodded. A hot drink sounded good. Easy on an empty stomach. The cook poured a bit of boiling water into a ceramic mug, emptied it on the ground, and refilled the cup. She dropped a shriveled tea bag in the steaming water, spooned sugar into the mug, and handed it to him. Settling her bulk opposite him, she broke into a gap-toothed smile, her round weathered face a collection of wrinkles. "Too much buai. Not so gut for you, eh?"

He recognized the word for beetlenut and accepted her verdict without arguing. The rain lessened. She watched him sip his hot tea and when she judged him ready to eat, handed him a thick slice of plain bread. He devoured it. She offered him another slice. He kept the food down. After thirty minutes, his head began to clear. He sat staring into dying embers surrounding the copper kettle.

"Those people go see plane, you know," said the cook.

"Yeah, I know." He patted his belly. "Too sick to go."

The rain eventually stopped. Darryl stood, shook off his stupor, donned his damp shirt, and announced, "I'm going for a walk, Anna. Thanks for the tea and bread." Her disapproving look failed to register with him.

Following a beaten path, Darryl strolled through the center of the village.

He dodged an angry sow defending her piglets, watched a crew patching holes in a thatch roof, and showed some kids how to toss the Frisbees Becky had given as gifts. Skirting a line of huts on the edge of the village where jungle had begun to creep back in, he paused to relieve himself in the brush.

He went on, passing a solitary man shouldering a load of freshly cut bamboo, machete in hand, a naked toddler tagging behind. Nodding in greeting as he passed. Darryl backpedaled, waving to the curious child. Continuing along the path brought him to a fork where hard-packed spidery tracks intersected. Distant voices and laughter drifted from tangled foliage to his left—the village over there, somewhere beyond the thick jungle. Darryl opted for a heavily traveled path snaking into a long shadowy corridor of trees wrapped with strangler vines. The voices faded.

Huge butterflies flitted overhead. Towering fig trees blocked sunlight, their branches heavy with flying fox—furry, repulsive rust-colored bats wrapped in leathery wings. The forest grew still, its fetid air even more oppressive, heavy with the scent of rot. Wary, but too curious to turn back, Darryl kept on. Eventually narrowing between waist-high ferns, the footpath lured him to a claustrophobic clearing hemmed in by ancient gnarled trees standing like elderly bowed sentinels. Not a leaf in the surrounding jungle stirred to disturb the ghostly setting.

Like some abandoned ark, a long, thatched-roofed lodge built of wooden planks perched on a dozen carved tree trunks sunk deep in the soil. The aged poles, each six feet tall with a twenty-four-inch girth, supported an elaborate windowless house. Curved fore and aft like a boat, the sagging palm roof rose twice as high as any Darryl had seen in the village.

A rickety bamboo ladder teetered against the thatch, fresh fronds stacked next to it as if someone had interrupted their task of repairing the roof. At one end of the deserted hut, elaborate grotesque carvings bearded with moss framed a single door made of weathered boards. The entry beckoned from the top of stairs fashioned from split logs. The steps climbed to a porch under an arching overhang. Darryl, fearful but oddly fascinated, surveyed the scene, awed by the mysterious building. "Hello," he yelled. "Anyone here? Hello! Hello!"

Clinging to a branch high in the leafy canopy, a spectacular long-plumed bird of paradise screamed at the intruder. The bird's alarm call ignited a raucous avian chorus that took minutes to die. Darryl timidly circled the strange building before returning to the log steps. After a few calming breaths, he climbed, pushed open the door, and peered into a funereal interior. "Hello," he called in a hesitant, childish voice. No response. *Creepy. What the hell is this place?* he asked himself. *Some kind of special club? You're not scared are you? Yes. Maybe. Hell no. Might as well see what it's all about. This will make a great story to tell the others.* After carefully testing the bamboo floor with his foot, Darryl timidly stepped inside and let his eyes adjust to the tomb-like darkness.

. . . .

Chapter 45

The C-47 site

Becky and David resumed walking, the path taking them through a stand of soaring brambles. Voices drifted to them from a dense thicket straight ahead. They were close enough to see people moving beyond a lattice of vines.

Wood yelled at them from beyond the trees. “Becky, David! Over here!” Taking a deep breath, David plunged ahead through a tangled fringe of forest, Becky on his heels. Emerging into a narrow sunlit corridor, the two found themselves next to Wood and Morris. The hatless missionary, his clothes soaked with sweat, was giving orders to Simeon and the other villagers. “We clear all the trees, yeah? We want to look inside, savvy?”

Nodding, Simeon and the quartet of locals attacked the C-47’s burial shroud of foliage. After twenty minutes of labor, first the fuselage, then a row of windows, appeared. Morris waved David to his side. “If we can free this door, we’ll gain access to the interior.” The pair yanked vines and dead branches away from the plane’s rear cargo door. Forcing the opening seemed impossible. The aircraft had obviously bellied in, plowing a deep furrow in the soil. Decades in the open had sealed the exits like a tomb. Frustrated by the unyielding door, Morris and Wood crabbed their way toward the plane’s nose. Wood, boots on Morris’s shoulders, wriggled headfirst through a shattered cockpit window. Morris followed with help from Gallagher. Nelson and his man Noah found a vantage point at the plane’s tail from which to film the discovery. In ten minutes, Wood’s face appeared in a gaping window near the jammed door. “Keep at it. We’ll give you a hand from inside.”

At the rear of the plane, David, Simeon, and machete-armed villagers furiously chopped chunks from packed soil blocking the lower half of the C-47's cargo door. With Wood and Morris shoving together from inside, the exit was eventually freed. Wood's hands waved triumphantly from the partially opened door. Turning his body sideways, the missionary wormed through the exit. Becky tossed him a bottle of water. He drank half of it and passed it to an exhausted Morris who had squeezed through behind him.

"What did you find?" asked Gallagher.

Arching his back against the big plane, Wood laughed. "Nothing. But I now know how old Jonah must have felt in the whale's belly."

Becky drew in a sharp breath. David caught her distraught look and sidled up to her, whispering, "Okay, we'll try Plan B." She heard him but continued to stare at the hulk, her eyes brimming with tears. David motioned for Becky to join him in exploring the C-47's interior. Concealing her frustration, she made her way to the hatch. Gallagher hovered over Nelson as he poked his lens through a gaping window. David muscled his way inside the fuselage. Becky followed, careful to avoid jagged aluminum peeling around the doorframe.

Inside, the two surveyed the sepulchral interior. Bare curved ribs running the length of the aircraft braced the plane's skin. The C-47's sloping floor was choked with dry leaves, tree limbs, and seedlings poking from cracks in the ruined deck. Light streamed in through bullet holes and tears in the metal skin. Rooted in the plane's belly, a twisted sapling the thickness of a man's thigh grew through wide cracks in the overhead, exploding in a leafy umbrella shading the fuselage.

David sidestepped the trunk and stopped, his eyes glued to something on the floor. He put a finger to his lips. Reaching down with gloved hand, he pried loose what looked like large blackened scissors. Becky leaned over him. "What the hell is that?" Raising fused iron shapes pitted with rust, David said softly, "Machetes." Lifting another blackened blade, its wooden handle long since rotted, he whispered, "This has to be part of the…"

"Cargo," she interrupted. "Part of the cargo mentioned in the diary." Kicking at a corroded ammo can missing its top, Becky peered inside the metal box. A small lizard scurried away, drawing a shriek from her.

Outside, Gallagher heard the cry. "You okay?"

"We're fine. Just one of the residents."

Bellying up to the hull the burly Aussie barked rapid-fire questions through an opaque window. "What do you see? Anything worth filming? What are we missing?" Dropping the corroded blades, David climbed across the tilted deck, poking his head from a window framed with jagged teeth of fogged plastic. "Like the pastor said, Gallagher. It's empty. Weeds and lizards as far as we can tell. You're welcome to waste your time in here if you want. I'm going to check out the cockpit. Then we're coming out." Creeping forward through the cargo bay, the two passed what would have been the radio operator's cramped station, now overgrown with grassy stalks. The flight deck was a mess. Rotted wires, indistinguishable from dangling vines, hung from the overhead. The main instrument panel, pried loose and stripped of dials, resembled a dozen empty eye sockets. Tree branches grew through the crumpled windshield. Stepping between the pilots' seats, David sent a small green snake slithering to safety in a hole beneath the pedal controls. Becky pressed in behind him, shards of broken glass crunching underfoot.

"Seen enough?" he asked.

"Yeah," she said forlornly. "It's been picked pretty clean,

hasn't it? Where are the bodies? Shouldn't there be bones or something?"

"Yeah. Kinda odd, isn't it? Wood said he's going to look into that. Kick some ass and take names." David backed from the cockpit into the narrow passage leading to the rear of the plane. He followed Becky, steadying himself against the metal ribs. Pushing through the partially open door, they emerged in a gentle drizzle.

Compared to the plane's stifling air, the light rain was a blessing. Simeon and other natives stood on the port wing, tersely awaiting Wood's order to abandon the site. Morris circled the cargo plane again, tramping down weeds, shooting pictures, and double-checking his notes about the faded hull markings. Wood took a third GPS reading. "Well, we've had quite the day," he exulted. "Let's head back."

....

Chapter 46

Retracing his steps, a panicked but exhilarated Darryl sprinted along the jungle trail. Angry rumbles shook the mountains with salvoes of thunder, each more ominous than the last. Menacing clouds drifted closer, promising an afternoon deluge. Darryl knew from experience that being caught on a dirt path during a violent storm could be disorienting. A downpour in the jungle would slash through the trees, washing away traces of a footpath in minutes. When the rains finally came he planned to be back with Anna, sharing a pot of tea, watching her prepare dinner. The oncoming clouds spurred Darryl on. The few first drops hit leaves high above him. Somewhere just beyond a bend in the trail would be the edge of the village.

He reached a fork in the path. *Left or right? Which one did I take coming this way earlier? The left? No, the right. To go back, I take the left. Yeah, go left.* As Darryl dithered, a wraith-like figure in ragged shorts and a grimy Chicago Cubs sweatshirt stepped from the shadows, planting himself in the trail.

Darryl panicked, his heart drumming. Sweat poured from his body. He tried to speak but his mouth filled with cotton. The muscular bearded native shouldered a bamboo pole, its ends weighted down with fronds like the ones being used to repair the mysterious building's roof. The man was obviously returning to complete his task. What caught Darryl's eye was a long curving knife the size of a sword the laborer carried. The menacing villager with the machete stepped closer. "Hey, Darro, yuorait?"

Recognizing his name despite its mangling, a panicked Darryl smothered his fear, eagerly offering his hand and a shaky greeting. "Hey, Micah!" The villager facing him on the footpath had shared his cache of beer, buai, and marijuana the night before. Tucking the big knife under an arm, Micah, his bearded jaw bulging with beetlenut, pumped hands.

"Hey, yeah, I'm okay," said Darryl, his voice breaking. Pointing in the direction of the village, he nervously announced he was headed that way. "Going back. You know? Pastor Wood, okay?"

"Ren kam, Darro," declared Micah, calmly glancing up, silvery machete thrust heavenward as if to cut holes in the clouds.

"Yeah, rain," said Darryl catching the word. "We go, yeah?"

If Micah understood, he gave no indication. Instead, mimicking a smoker, the native hung his bundled sago palms between two saplings and offered the American a fresh joint. Rubbing his stomach and affecting a pained look, Darryl politely declined.

Micah shrugged, tucked away the newly rolled cheroot in his bilum, and signaled with his knife for Darryl to follow him. The two backtracked toward huts huddling on the village's outskirts. After a hundred paces, Micah paused, arced a stream of beetle-nut juice into the brush, and again produced his handmade cigarette, which he lighted. Darryl kept going, unsure if the man understood he wanted to avoid the rain. Wearing a wide, mellow grin, Micah took deep drags on his cigarette, hailed Darryl, and offered it. To placate him, Darryl drew a long hit on the potent joint. His nausea lessened, and after several puffs he reluctantly surrendered the cigarette.

A huge cloud shaped like a monstrous dirigible passed over them, aiming for the valley. At first the gentle rain was a welcome shower cutting the heat, but its tempo increased. "Hariap!" urged Micah, shooing the American ahead. "Ren kam. Yu go!" Sprinting through pouring rain, Darryl reached Anna's refuge just as the heavens opened. The imperturbable woman, poised over the flames as she had been earlier, tended the fire, calmly feeding it from her magical pile of inexhaustible kindling. Two blackened copper pots, balanced on sooty stones, simmered in the flames. Darryl greeted her and helped himself to a bottle of water from a plastic cooler. Leaning against a pole, he listened to rain punish the thatch above. Micah had disappeared somewhere in the curtain of rain. Darryl smiled, imagining his friend hunkered down, a banana leaf held overhead, smoking his hand-rolled cigarette as he waited out the deluge.

"Where is everybody, Anna?"

Answering without taking her eyes from the fire, she said, "Coming soon."

Darryl shifted his gaze beyond the team's buffeted blue and yellow tents. An hour later, a line of soaked figures emerged from the jungle and sloshed its way through a flow of mud running between huts. Villagers accompanying the team broke off, each man continuing to his family's lodgings. A frowning Morris led the column to a picnic table set under a sagging blue awning. The shelter was in danger of collapse from pooling rainwater. Morris and Wood, with Gallagher's help, tipped the tarp, spilling water that had collected. Becky and David staggered to benches under the nylon top to shuck wet boots and gear. Simeon started a fire in a sheltered corner under the tarp, attracting the team members. Nelson straggled in, scowling and wet but seemingly none the worse for wear. His porter, Noah, set the camera case on the table, out of the rain.

Spotting Darryl, Gallagher strolled over to talk. "Ah, feeling better, eh?"

"Yeah, thanks. How'd it go today?"

"Dry hole. Found the planes though."

Darryl nodded at the aluminum box. "Get good footage?"

Gallagher snorted. "Of what? Your little lady making eyes at her grandpa's plane? Bit of a letdown if you ask me." The Australian peeled off his wet shirt, wrung it, and toweled himself. "Damned rain. How was your day? You still rotten?"

"What?"

"Rotten. Drunk. Hung over."

"Oh. Nah, I slept it off. Took a tour of the village. Wandered about."

Becky tossed a comment their way. "Manage to stay out of trouble?"

"As a matter of fact, yeah, I did."

"That's a first."

Gallagher propped his sodden boots next to the fire where Wood and Morris, stripped to the waist, were drying out. David took off his shirt, draped it on a tent pole, then joined Becky and his brother. "You finally rolled out of the rack, huh?"

"Yeah. I got going around noon."

"Geez, your highness, I would have liked to have slept in myself."

"Well, you won't be seeing the Lightning," Becky sniffed. "Or the C-47. You missed your chance. No remains. Dale says we're probably not going back."

Darryl shrugged. "So what. Gallagher says you came up empty anyway. I was doing my thing, remember? Besides, Gallagher says they got plenty of footage of you hugging the plane. That oughta be worth something."

"It's not worth shit. I came all this way for nothing. What a waste."

"David told me he didn't think we'd find anything. Like I needed reminding."

Brightening, Darryl, an imbecilic grin pasted on his face, folded his arms in triumph. "I wouldn't say it was a wasted trip, Becky. We have to talk."

"I don't feel like talking."

"Trust me on this, babe. We need to talk, after dinner."

A snarl appeared, mixed with defeat. "Don't call me babe. I'm not in the mood. And I'm not eating more beans and rice. I never want to see them again."

David stepped between Becky and his brother. "Easy, Darryl. She had a rough day. We all did. She's wet. She's tired. She's pissed. Hell, we're all wet and tired. We walked our asses off and came away empty-handed. The less said, the better."

Both men stared at Becky slumped on a bench beneath the blue tarp, her blonde hair matted, muddy clothing plastered to her, eyes filled with either tears or rain—or both. Every inch screamed, "Leave me alone!"

The downpour slowed then stopped abruptly. The maternal Anna brought Becky a steaming mug of hot sweetened tea, getting a mumbled thank you in return. Turning to his brother, David tried to lessen the sting of Becky's words. "Leave her alone for a while, she'll be her old self in no time."

"You mean the lovable, loud-mouthed bitch we all know and love?"

"Yeah, something like that. Got anything to tell us?"

"Tonight. My tent. After everyone's asleep," he said tersely.

"We'll be there."

Pointedly ignored by Wood and Morris, Darryl sat watching Anna and her helper lay out dishes and utensils for the evening meal. Becky got up from the bench, abandoning the mug of tea for her tent. Darryl strolled to the fire, lingering in the smoke to discourage mosquitoes. He tried without success to make small talk with a weary, indifferent Morris. The Australians and Wood filled the awkward gaps by replaying the day's events for their AWOL team member. David, wearing dry clothes, returned, telling the others Becky would not join them at dinner. "Too tired," he said. The men took to the table, eating in silence, stuffing themselves with the predictable beans, rice, and tinned beef.

After dinner, Anna's helper scrubbed cooking pots by the light of a kerosene light dangling from a tree branch overhead. Before retiring to a nearby hut, Simeon fed a pair of logs to the fire and left it to Wood's party. The Lindquists faded early, followed by the Aussies, who begged off. The missionary and Morris sat, bathed in wood smoke, batting at insects and drifting sparks. The two traded stories in the fire's glow. Wood wove tales of searching for war birds in the mountains; Morris about close calls in Vietnam's skies and previous trips to Lae and the Sepik River.

. . . .

Chapter 47

Well past midnight, with flames dying and huts dark, Becky emerged from her tent and stood motionless, listening to night sounds. From the far side of the clearing, Gallagher's ragged snoring competed with Wood's whistling and Morris's nasal rumblings. From the jungle, frogs added a rhythmic congregational call like bamboo xylophones being hammered by ten thousand mallets. Mountains and millions of stars disappeared, screened again by ragged, humid mists drifting into the valley. A spooked dog barked, got a stone in reply, and yelped. A dreaming sow grunted beneath a nearby hut. Lights flickered in the huts like fireflies and then went out one by one. Silence settled over the village.

Satisfied no one stirred, Becky crept stealthily to Darryl's tent, which was staked farthest from the others. Running a fingernail down the nylon to announce herself, she knelt by the zippered screen. David's face floated in front of her. She crawled inside, curling near Darryl, shelving her discomfort at his sulfurous breath and the closeness of his sweaty body.

Across from her, David put a finger to his lips, purring, "Speak verrrry softly."

"Do you think anyone saw through your act today, Darryl?" Becky whispered.

"Nah. Morris was pretty pissed at me for not going out but I don't think he caught on. No, we're good. But you guys owe me. I got really shit-faced last night."

David chuckled. "You loved every minute of it, didn't you? Hey, it was for the cause. We appreciate it. So, you looked around the village? What did you find?"

Nodding, Darryl repeated his story about discovering the

odd house in the jungle. Becky and David listened in rapt attention as he recited his find in an agonizingly slow telling. A beam of light bounced across the nylon dome above them. Voices headed their way. Paralyzed, the trio held a collective breath as footfalls passed, then faded. In minutes, the footsteps returned, pounding toward their hiding place. Lights flashed against the taut yellow shell, flickered, then went out. Silence. Only the sound of breathing filled the tent.

"Just somebody using the shitter," hissed Darryl.

"Okay, tell us what you found," urged David softly.

Darryl smiled. "Better yet, I'll show you." He clicked on a penlight, shielding its pinpoint of light over a folded crimson bandana in his hand. Becky leaned forward, her forehead almost touching Darryl's brow as he carefully unfolded the red cloth.

Becky gasped. In the narrow cone of light glittered a tiny gold strip. "Is this…?" She couldn't finish the question.

"It is," whispered David triumphantly.

Becky reached out, reverently running a finger along the small bar, caressing the metal. "Are there more?" she breathed.

Darryl grinned. "A lot more."

"How many?"

"Shhhh," said Darryl, clamping a hand over the light. "Ammo cans full of 'em. We just have to figure out how to get them out of there."

Becky, euphoric, fought to control her excitement. "We have a down day tomorrow. As far as I know, there are no plans to visit the wreck site again. Another feast, a farewell thing. We pack and start our return to the mission the next day. We have to go tomorrow to make this work."

"I only took one so nobody would get suspicious," said Darryl. "There's no way I could have carried the rest without getting caught. Too risky."

"You did the right thing," cooed Becky. "But we only have one more night."

"Will that be enough time?" asked David.

"No way," cautioned Darryl. "We gotta have a better plan."

"Maybe if we somehow got the others to go back to the wreck that would give us a couple of hours. Darryl could get the rest of the gold. What do you think?" asked David. "Could you do that?"

"Daylight's no good. They have someone watching the place. I ran into one guy on my way back from there. He was working on the roof. Scared the shit outta me. They catch us there and they'll cut us into pieces so little no one could tell who was who. They'd feed what was left of us to the pigs or," he giggled, "eat us."

Silence filled the tent. David broke the spell. "It has to be done at night. Maybe during our big goodbye dinner."

"No, we'd be missed," she cautioned. "We're better off waiting until everyone's asleep."

"That's better," said David. "Darryl and me hit the place at midnight. Get the stuff and get the hell out. That would give us, uh…about five hours' head start."

"In the jungle, at night," sputtered Darryl. "You crazy?"

Becky felt for his arm. "We HAVE to go then. We'll have a sat phone, GPS, flashlights, and David's compass points. I'll make a call tomorrow to set up our pickup. All we have to do is backtrack. Follow the river to the bridge. By then it will be getting light. We get to the big river and the sandbank and I'll make another call on the sat phone. The chopper shows and picks us up. Sure, it's crazy, but if we're gonna do this, we do it that way. Are you with me on this?" she asked. "Otherwise, we go home empty-handed. If we follow our original plan we'll be okay. Speak up if you disagree." Neither brother challenged her.

"Okay, that's enough excitement for tonight," cautioned

David. "Back to your tents. Get some sleep if you can." Wiggling to the opening, he waited for Becky.

Darryl tapped Becky's arm, handed her the folded bandana. "Take this. There's more where this came from." Stunned by his gesture, she reached for the small cloth bundle, clutching it to her heart. Becky whispered, "I won't forget this." Waving away her thanks, Darryl, pleased with his spontaneous gift, grinned unseen.

"Okay, let's break it up," breathed David. "We'll talk after breakfast."

Becky knelt to follow. Darryl grabbed her arm. "You stay."

David thrust his head and shoulders back inside the darkened tent. "Are you nuts? What the hell are you doing?"

"Becky stays."

Spitting words through clenched teeth, David hissed. "Sonofabitch! What are you trying to pull, Darryl?"

A knife-edged minute passed, their plan about to rip apart.

"It's okay," soothed Becky, her arm on David's shoulder.

"No, it's not okay!" raged David, his voice rising.

Becky, resigned, her voice composed, said, "No, really, it's okay, David."

"See," crowed Darryl in the dark. "She wants to stay."

"Bullshit!" challenged David.

Becky was trying to hold her dream together. "Please, David, I'll be fine."

Her pleading disarmed him. David backed from the tent, anger eating him from within. The thought of his brother with Becky consumed him. Impotent, he stood at the entrance of Darryl's shelter, fists clenched, hating them both. Dazed, he stomped to what was left of the fire and knelt, hurling a fistful of brittle sticks at the glowing embers. Burying his head in his hands, David stared, numbed by what had just happened. At home, he would have taken Darryl down without hesitation, beating him senseless for the affront. In this bizarre world, thousands of miles from home, surrounded by strangers, trapped in a fantasy designed by a woman he loved, David was completely helpless. Whatever loyalty to Becky he had begun the trip with evaporated when she agreed to his brother's demand to stay behind. It was Cain and Abel. Ishmael and Isaac. David was on his own.

In the pitch-black tent, Darryl reached for Becky and slowly unbuttoned her shirt. "Take it off." His heavy breathing was the only sound besides the rustle of fabric. "Come closer." Reaching out to caress her bare shoulder, Darryl ran his fingers down her arm. He rolled toward her, letting his hand drop to cup a breast, lingering there, then shifting to fondle the other one. Recoiling slightly, Becky tensed, waiting for his next move. Suddenly, Darryl pulled back, snapping, "That's it. Get dressed."

"What? But I thought..."

"Well, you thought wrong. I just wanted to see how far you'd let this go. Girl, you've got it bad. You're a real piece of work. Get out. I gotta sleep."

Stunned, she groped in the dark for her shirt. "You...you really are an asshole, Darryl. You know that? A real asshole!"

"Shhh. You might wake Morris—your favorite dirty old man."

"Fuck you, Darryl."

"Well, not tonight, babe. But thanks for asking just the same." Laughing, he turned his back to her.

Humiliated, Becky hurriedly dressed and scrambled from the tent in shock. The thought of Darryl's rough hands on her body burned inside. *All these years without letting him touch me once and now he has me crawling on my knees.* Her eyes filled with hot tears. Shame mixed with fury mixed with renewed hatred for him. *Darryl, you bastard! I can just imagine what David thinks of me now,* she thought. *That's it! I have to talk with David. Make things right between us...if I can. If it's not too late. We can't lose our focus. Not yet. Not now.*

....

Chapter 48

The Trek, Day Four

The next evening, their last in the village, the team attended a farewell dinner in their honor. The feast went on for hours, accompanied by the usual dancing, chanting, and singing. With daylight fading—and without being noticed by the diners—Becky gathered a small crowd of children and slipped away from the village with them. Leading her charges away from the clustered huts, Becky played Papuan pied piper—marching at the head of a straggling line of giggling, curious children. Past yam gardens, through a grove of banana trees and palms, into a thick stand of fig trees and finally down to the river trooped her little band. When she reached the bound, arched saplings spanning the rapids, Becky stopped. Opening her pack, she spilled a handful of lifeless plastic sticks and tubes at her feet. Anticipating magic, the inquisitive adolescents surrounded their white visitor. She did not disappoint. Bending several fluid-filled sticks in her hands, Becky vigorously shook the slender plastic tubes until they burst into light.

Awed by the miracle, youngsters stood gaping at mysterious lime-green luminescent wands. Laughing, she twisted tubes into circles, lowering them over her head. Becky created another ring—one of vivid blue—easily winning the audience with her wizardry. She handed a luminous necklace to the tallest child who bravely placed it around her neck. A bright yellow halo was bestowed on a laughing boy, and red and purple bracelets around outstretched arms. As fast as she created them, Becky gave away colorful prizes until each awed child wore several. With her giggling admirers adorned in rainbow neon, Becky set to work fastening glow sticks along the trail. Working backwards from the bridge—which she marked with a pair of 22-inch lime-green hoops—Becky hung tubular lights every fifteen feet, nearly exhausting her supply by the time she reached the edge of the farmed plots. Shooing her laughing, glowing, multi-colored tribe ahead of her, she returned to the huts and gave away the remaining glow sticks to little ones who had stayed behind in the village with their mothers. She waved goodbye to the excited, delighted children.

Avoiding the farewell celebration, Becky headed for the trees surrounding the team's tents. With everyone attending the send-off she was confident no one would miss her. She scrambled far enough into the jungle to remain unseen and yet close enough to find her way back. Becky found a hole in the canopy where stars glittered between passing clouds. She dug in her pack, pulled out the satellite phone, and made a call.

"Been expecting you. Any last-minute changes?"

"None."

"Your status?"

"Ready. We'll leave at midnight tonight and be there by first light."

"Right. Call from the LZ."

"I can't wait."

"I know. But stay focused. Stay safe."

"Trying my best. I love you."

"Same here. See you tomorrow. Get some rest."

"I'll try. Wait for my call."

"I'll be there. Don't be late."

Becky shut down the phone and doubled back to the campsite. She slipped inside her tent, packed her backpack sparingly, and slept with boots on. An hour passed before she heard voices. Morris and the others had returned from the farewell celebration. Before long, ragged snores were competing with the jungle's nightly frog chorus. After several hours of chasing sleep without success, Becky sat up and held her watch's luminous dial inches from her face. It was time to leave.

Dark gathering clouds obscured heaven's vault above the peaks. Cooler air sent a thin layer of fog across the sweet potato fields where it settled like a blanket. Becky crept from her nylon shelter. She carried a backpack stuffed with flares, satellite phone, three bottles of water, and a handful of energy bars, along with passport and bib-styled vest. Standing like a statue in the shadows, she listened for sounds from the other tents. To a man they were asleep. Following a beaten path along the edge of the clearing, she gained a row of banana and knelt in the shadows, waiting. Two crouching shadows made their way across the open field toward the wall of trees. Becky stepped from her hiding place, tapping each brother on the shoulder.

"Ready?" whispered David. The other two nodded.

"Follow me," hissed Darryl, tiny penlight in hand. He set off along the footpath leading to the sacred house. Becky followed close behind, tethered to him by two feet of knotted cord. Behind her came David, his hand grasping a similar length of rope she held. Occasionally Darryl paused, flashed the tiny light to get his bearings, and then continued, his heart hammering against his chest. Entering the cramped clearing, the three moved quickly to the log steps of the deserted longhouse.

David took Becky aside. "Under the stairs out of sight," he ordered. "Knock twice if you see anyone coming. Got it?" Obeying, she handed over her pocketed vest and took up her station behind a carved pillar. Both men slipped out of their backpacks, threw the sleeveless jackets over their arms, climbed the stairs, and pushed open the plank door. Despite moving stealthily, the floor groaned beneath them. Kneeling, Darryl snapped on his headlamp, fixed the beam on a row of grinning human skulls lining a woven palm carpet. One by one, he moved the remains aside. That done, he pushed away the mat, revealing a row of rusting metal ammo boxes set in a niche in the floor. David spread a sheet of plastic on the floor.

As Darryl lifted boxes from the vault, David emptied their contents on the plastic, creating a mound of rotting sawdust turned mostly to dust. The brothers sifted each pile in the headlight's beam. Flashes of dull yellow appeared in the bobbing light. Darryl dug through the sawdust while David plucked small gold bars and stuffed three of them in each of the stitched pockets lining the front and back of his vest. He worked until the rows were filled. Running his hand over each small pocket to make sure it contained three gold bars, he pressed Velcro flaps in place. That done, he began slipping ingots into Darryl's vest. The two-ounce bars kept coming. More boxes, more gold. When Darryl's jacket was filled, they stuffed Becky's tiny pockets with more gold, and then closed the Velcro tabs, their looting complete. A sizable scattering of ingots still shone among the litter. Darryl locked eyes with his brother. "Let's take it all."

"No. The plan was to get ninety pounds."

"Are you crazy, bro? It's right here in front of us for the taking."

"We gotta walk this out of here, Darryl. Ninety pounds is plenty."

"That's fucked up and you know it. It's a chance of a lifetime."

"Stick to the plan," rasped David. "Use your head. We've got to get the hell out of here before they figure out what we're doing."

"Shit. I can't believe we're letting this get away."

Reluctantly, Darryl scooped gold and dust with cupped hands, dumping the mix into empty cans. He returned the containers to the primitive safe and shoved the palm mat back into place. David shook dirt from the plastic sheet through floor slats, removing any obvious traces of their theft.

The brothers stood, immediately feeling the burden of their packed vests. Each of them carried an extra thirty-five pounds on their lean frames. They shuffled to the doorway, David leading, Becky's packed vest in his hands. At the top of the log stairs, he scanned the clearing for signs of movement. Satisfied they had not been discovered, he carefully descended, his brother close behind. A misstep or injury now would be a death sentence putting them all at risk.

Pausing at the bottom of the steps, David offered Becky her loaded jacket, commanding, "Take this." She squirmed into the twenty-pound jacket, fastened the Velcro straps at her waist, shouldering her pack without complaint. The brothers helped each other into their backpacks and picked up their walking sticks.

As the only one of the three who had studied the route during daylight, Darryl took the lead. Grasping the taut rope, Becky, second in line, held a cord in each hand, David on her heels. Avoiding their original route as a precaution, Darryl made one wrong turn, lost the trail, but quickly corrected himself, painstakingly feeling his way along the village perimeter.

Finally reaching the community's vast yam gardens without raising an alarm, the three, out of breath, halted where cultivated fields ended and jungle began. Scraps of cloud played tag, floating aimlessly across the sky. Mist seeped from the hills, spilling from ridges, rising from hidden gorges, gliding across the valley floor, seeking the river. Within the hour, well-traveled trails would be blanketed with disorienting fog. They had to move. Tension and their extra burdens had already extracted a price. They were an hour behind schedule. Precious time lost packing the gold and skirting the village by a different trail had put them at risk. On the beaten path, David exchanged places with Darryl to take over the lead to the river.

Becky's idea of hanging fluorescent glow sticks in trees to mark a path to the river came into play. The rainbow beacons gained them precious minutes. As they passed each shimmering tube she collected them, leaving the path behind devoured by darkness. Her glowing colored markers took them unerringly toward the ominous sound of roaring water. Timidly descending along a fern-covered bluff, David led Becky and his brother to the primitive span they had crossed days before. A pair of lime-green neon necklaces dangled from the bridge's skinny handrail. Becky gathered the last of her neon lights and tossed them into the rapids below, creating a surreal underwater lightshow. Whitewater thundered underneath the rickety structure, making conversation difficult.

....

Chapter 49

The village, 2:00 a.m.

"We got big problems, mate."

Gallagher woke with a start. Nelson's unshaven face inches away, his breath hot, sour. "What?"

"It's the girl and her boyfriends. Shonky business, that."

"Becky? The Lindquists?"

Dropping to one knee, an agitated Nelson rattled on about the trio's betrayal. "Noah heard the three of them talking in

Darryl's tent after everyone went to sleep. Seems they've been cooking up their little plan ever since we got here. He followed them to the old meeting house."

"Did they see him?"

"Nah, they're amateurs, mate. Anyway, Noah says the brothers left Becky as a lookout while they went inside and cleaned out the place."

Fully awake now, Gallagher didn't like what he was hearing. "The gold?"

"Bloody whackers," snorted Nelson, "they took most of it."

"Not all of it? What the hell?"

"They took enough."

"Where are they now?"

"Noah says they're headed for the river crossing."

Gallaher got to his knees. "We've got to stop them. They can't go far in the dark. We've got a chance to catch 'em."

"What about the gold they left behind?"

Gallagher ran a hand across the stubble on his chin. "Right. Might as well scoop up what's left, then catch up with those three before the sun's up."

"Time to get down to business, mate," growled Nelson. "I'm going armed."

"No other way to do it," agreed Gallagher. He pulled the aluminum case to him, snapped it open, and plucked the camera from its foam packing. Nelson began ripping it apart while Gallagher stripped the soft lining from the metal shell. He pried loose two 9mm magazines, each loaded with seventeen rounds. The camera lay in pieces on the tent floor. Nelson worked quietly, quickly assembling a pair of Glock 17s from components concealed in the dummy camera's body. He handed a completed weapon to Gallagher, who slapped a magazine in the butt of the pistol's handgrip and chambered a round. Nelson did the same. Both men, now armed, emerged from the tent. Noah stood by quietly, gripping a razor-sharp machete, backpack on his shoulders.

Gallagher led his team away from the clustered nylon shelters where Wood and Morris slept. "We're not coming back once this hits the fan, mate," he whispered.

"Fine with me. What do you have in mind…besides running down these bloody whackers?" asked Nelson.

"Find them. Take them out. Get the gold. Once it's ours we keep moving."

"Works for me, mate."

"Take Noah with you. Go to the longhouse. Pick up what's left of the gold, then head for the bridge. Don't come back here for any reason."

"And you?"

Gallagher, his face grim, spat out the words. "I'll catch up to Little Miss Becky and her boys, mark my words. Follow my trail. We'll keep going from there. I'll take the satellite phone. Don't worry, she'll be alright, mate. If we get in trouble we'll call Baxter to bring the chopper in early."

"Right," whispered Nelson. "Noah, come with me." The two trotted along the hard dirt path toward the longhouse. Gallagher shouldered his backpack and headed for the river, pistol in hand.

....

Chapter 50

David adjusted his headlamp, tapped the others, pantomiming crossing. Getting nods in agreement, he set off, nimbly negotiating the bundled saplings to the far side. Becky was next. Thrown off balance by her extra twenty pounds, she stumbled under the weight. Impatient to put the bridge behind him, Darryl started crossing before Becky gained the opposite shore. The slender span—designed as a one-person walkway—sagged dangerously under their combined weight. Becky, her voice lost in booming rapids, screamed profanities at Darryl. Ignoring her, he pushed from behind, sending her tumbling into a stand of high grass on the far side. Becky scrambled to her feet, fists clenched, ready to battle. "SONOFABITCH! I almost ended up in the river!"

"Whadya expect? You were taking too fucking long!"

Dousing his headlight, David stepped between the two, his arms holding them apart. "Shut up, both of you!"

To Darryl: "That was stupid. She might have gone in, and then what?" Not waiting for a response, he turned to Becky, hissing, "You weren't moving fast enough. Keep up. We can't afford to slow down." Dropping to his knees, David slipped out of his backpack and vest. He unsheathed a machete. "I've got an idea."

Becky knelt beside him. "What are you doing? We can't stop!"

"Change of plans."

"Are you crazy?" she pleaded. "We've got to keep going."

Ignoring her, David turned to his brother. "We have to drop this bridge. We take it out and they can't come after us. At least not right away. Let's get to work."

David tied three guide ropes into a line and knotted it around his waist. "Hold onto me, little brother." Big knife in hand, he crept on hands and knees until he felt the rope go taut a third of the way across. Snapping on his headlight, he focused on twisted vines tying saplings together and began hacking furiously at the woven bindings. After a half-dozen strokes, several poles loosened. Two more cuts, and they shot into the angry torrent thirty feet below. A second set of timbers was cut free of fibers holding them. The crippled bridge swayed precariously, held by only a final handful of scrawny saplings. Again and again, David brought his machete slashing down on stubborn knotted bindings holding the middle of the arch together.

One final cut, and the bridgeway tottered for a few seconds, then gave way. Scrambling to avoid following the splintered bridge into the roaring cataract, David dropped his machete. Falling backwards, he kicked frantically until he felt solid ground beneath him. Exhausted, he let himself be dragged to safety among ferns on the far shore. Darryl untied the ropes, passed one each to Becky and David, keeping one for himself. "We gotta move."

David gasped, sucking air. "Gimme a minute, will ya?" Donning his weighted vest and backpack, he sat, head resting on his knees. David pulled a crumpled note card from his shirt pocket. Using a small penlight, he sat studying scribbled compass headings and a crude map. "We head one-five-zero degrees for the next thousand meters. We keep the river on our left. Hold on to the rope in front of you. I'll flick my flashlight every few seconds to make sure we're on track. No talking. Becky in the middle. Stay connected. Stay close. Got it?"

Taking their silence as approval, David staggered to his feet, handed a knotted line to Becky, giving it a tug to make sure she was with him. She in turn similarly signaled Darryl behind her.

One quick flash of light to pick up the trail and David asked, "Ready?"

"Ready," they whispered back up the line. The trio took one step in the fog.

Two shots split the night.

"GET DOWN!" David's frantic voice.

"What the hell was that?!" screamed Darryl. "David, you okay?"

In front of Darryl, a bewildered Becky gave a weak pull on

the rope. "He's okay. Says to low crawl for a few meters, then run when he says to."

"Hell, yes! Tell him anytime!"

From across the rapids, somewhere along the ragged jungle edge, a savage voice roared above the river's thunder. Loud. Unintelligible. Gallagher.

....

Chapter 51

In the longhouse, Nelson flinched at the sound of gunshots. "There goes our cover." Dumping a handful of tiny gold ingots into a bulging canvas bag, the Aussie dropped to his knees, feeling for bars he had missed in the dust spread before him.

One dozen rusting ammo cans lay on their sides, emptied of treasure. Nelson stood, adjusted the bag's straps on Noah's muscled back. The man was a mule, unaffected by the heavy load he shouldered.

"Let's go!" ordered Nelson, kicking aside skulls, scattering them across the sagging floor. Noah followed the Aussie out the door. Nelson paused at the top of the stairs and snapped a lighter at the drooping sago palm roof. Flames licked at the drier bottom layer of thatch. Thick gray smoke slowly billowed from the shaggy roof, spreading to the opposite eave. Noah, horrified at Nelson's arson, scrambled to the bottom of the log stairs, the gold burden digging into his back.

Bounding down the steps, Nelson joined Noah in the trees ringing the clearing. "That oughta keep 'em busy. We're not staying around to make sure it burns. We're off! Lead on!" The pair followed a trail through the brush to the river where Gallagher waited. Nelson glanced back once to check his efforts. In the distance, a blossoming yellow glow outlined lacey tree silhouettes. The fire had taken. He and Noah emerged on the far side of farm plots and jogged to the booming rapids. Gallagher stepped from the shadowed roots of a mammoth fig tree.

Nelson stared at the gap where the arch of saplings had been. “What the hell happened?” Pacing nervously, Gallagher pointed the Glock at the opposite shore. “What does it look like? Cheeky bastards cut the bridge just as I got here.”

“We heard shots,” said Nelson.

“Gave it a try, mate, think I nicked one of ’em,” he said hopefully.

Shrill voices drifted from the waking village. The three looked back at the waking hamlet, a disturbed, angry anthill filling with milling figures. Gallagher waved his weapon in Noah’s face. “Can you find us a ford?” Shaking his head, the native stared through the Aussie at the bridge’s splintered remnants.

“We’ll be missed,” said Nelson, his eyes fixed on coiling smoke and flames from the longhouse. “No way to go back now. Morris and Wood will figure this out before long. Aye, we’re fucked both ways, mate.”

Gesturing at the jungle lining the rapids, Gallagher remained calm. “Maybe not. Good on ya for firing that old hut. Perfect diversion. It’ll buy us time. We have to go downstream now! Take our chances. Find a shallow place to cross. Catch up with them. Call for a pickup. Make a stand. The way I see things, it’s our only option.”

“You’re right. Can’t stay here.”

“Cheer up, mate. We’ve been in tighter spots.”

Not that I can remember, thought Nelson.

With the burning house buying them precious time, Noah

and his machete led the Aussies into claustrophobic jungle lining the south bank of the boiling current.

....

Chapter 52

Awakening to chaos and acrid smoke, Wood scrambled from his tent to find Morris surrounded by a hysterical knot of babbling villagers. Bulling his way into the crowd, the missionary stepped between Morris and two angry men waving machetes above the Minnesotan's head. Ignoring the threatening pair, Wood linked arms with Morris, yelling, "What happened? Where is everyone? Talk to me! We in some kind of danger?"

"I don't know what the hell is going on! I thought I heard gunshots."

"Gunshots?"

"Yeah. The next thing I know I'm being dragged out of my sleeping bag. Then you show up. They're not making a hell of a lot of sense."

Morris craned his neck toward the jungle. "Maybe that has something to do with all this." Both men, their profiles bathed in flickering yellow light, stared at flames feeding on a thatch roof beyond a screen of trees. Flames sputtered at the base of a column of thick, drifting smoke.

"What is it?" asked Wood.

"Your guess is as good as mine."

Distracted momentarily by the fire, Wood and Morris found themselves in the middle of a tug-of-war. Wood linked arms with Morris as the mass of villagers surged back and forth.

A crescendo of accusatory shouts grew, then died as the throng suddenly parted. The chief, his aura of authority intact despite a disheveled appearance in ragged shorts, angrily stomped to the center of the ring. Two bodyguards pushed back a sea of shaking fists, forcing the Americans' release. The headman fired questions at Simeon, Wood's liaison. The missionary was relieved to see a friendly face at the old man's side. Stepping close to Wood, Simeon translated. "He wants to know where the rest of your group has gone. When did they leave? Why did they run away in the night?"

"Tell him I didn't realize they were gone."

Sweeping an arm at the natives pressing in, Simeon added, "These people, they say all your friends have disappeared after setting the sacred house on fire."

"We know nothing about that. Ask the chief to let us look in the tents. Morris, check after the Aussies. I'll look for Becky and the others."

Without waiting for permission, the two men pushed to the campground escorted by a posse of bellicose villagers. The people closed in around the nylon shelters, wide-eyed children peeking through a forest of legs. Morris crawled halfway into Becky's tent, emerged with a handful of clothing, and ducked into both Lindquists' tents. A flashlight, a pair of sandals, and sodden clothing was all he found. Wood's search of the Australians' quarters turned up pieces of black plastic that had once been a camera. Wood showed Morris the evidence. "What's this supposed to mean? You find anything in Becky's tent?"

"Not much. She and the brothers seem to have left in a hurry."

"Willingly?"

"Good question. No signs of a struggle that I can see. Now what?"

A pair of runners approached, hailing the chief. More news. For a moment, Wood and Morris were forgotten. Whatever message the old man heard sent him into an apoplectic rage. Focusing on the two Americans, the chief screeched a string of obvious curses, further agitating the crowd. The villagers closed in again, their anger mimicking their chief's.

"This ain't looking good, Brad. Might go south any minute. Do something!"

"Like what?"

"I dunno. Talk to Simeon."

Another cry went up when a trio of men seeking the chief's attention delivered more bad news. Simeon, his eyes locked on the new arrivals, passed the report to Wood and Morris without looking. "The bridge across the river has been cut."

"Of course! That's it! I'm going after them!"

"You crazy, Morris? You don't know where to start. Or where they're headed."

"That's where you're wrong. It's obvious what they're doing. The Aussies, or Becky and friends…or both…are backtracking. That's why they took out the bridge. So we couldn't follow."

"Simeon also said villagers heard shots," reasoned Wood. "That means one or more of them is armed. Maybe they kidnapped Becky and the Lindquists. Forced them to go along as hostages."

Morris was incredulous. "Hostages? For what? Why the hell would they pick up in the middle of the night and run? There's something else going on here. We just don't see it. Sure as hell don't have time to figure it out now."

Smoke from smoldering sago palm drifted through the restive crowd. A group of soot-covered men staggered to the chief to announce the fire at the longhouse had finally been quenched, though the hut would need rebuilding.

"The chief has a pistol I could use," whispered Morris. "Maybe they have other guns we don't know about. It's worth a try. I don't like the odds of staying here doing nothing."

"You could be right. But I say we stay put. Let the village take care of this."

"We're wasting valuable time. Ask the chief for his pistol."

"It's a bad idea," pleaded Wood.

Stepping toward the chief, Morris held out his arms, booming, "Simeon, tell him we had nothing to do with this. Ask him if he will give me his pistol and let me go after them!" Simeon did as Morris asked. The request was followed by a huddle of the old man and his advisers. A runner was dispatched while the haggling continued. Morris turned to the interpreter. "What are they saying, Simeon?"

"Some agree you should be given a chance to go after these people. Others say, they go, you stay."

"What does the chief say?"

"I think pretty soon he gives you a chance."

"He won't be sorry."

The runner returned with a cloth bundle and gave it to the chief who held it in his gnarled hands. Solemnly unwrapping the fabric, the diminutive village father revealed the .38 caliber handgun Morris had spotted at the sing-sing the first night. Holding the weapon aloft, the old man recited a short incantation and delivered the pistol to Morris's keeping. He handed four questionable-looking rounds to the American. Morris popped open the gun's cylinder to check for more ammo. The chambers were empty, giving him pause. "I'm supposed to go after these guys with four rounds? I must be nuts."

Wood stepped up. "Not too late to back out. Let them run the chase."

"Not on your life. Ask Simeon. I bet I couldn't back out now if I wanted to."

Nodding, the interpreter confirmed Morris's comment. "They are sending two parties to search for these bad people. One group will fell trees to make the bridge strong enough to cross."

Finished loading, Morris asked, "And the other group?"

"You will go with them. They will follow the river downstream until they find a place to cross. You must be careful, Mr. Morris. They will move fast. They will not stop until they find them. You may be left behind."

"Not likely, Simeon."

"I'll go with you, " volunteered Wood. "I know the woods well."

Putting a hand on the missionary's arm, Simeon cautioned, "No. The chief says you must stay, Pastor Wood. Only one may go. Mr. Morris is the one chosen."

Despite the gravity of the situation, Morris winked at Wood. "Maybe the old boy thinks I won't come back. Besides, these people need you more than me, Brad. Try to find out what the excitement's all about while I'm gone."

"Will do." Wood tossed a backpack to Morris. "There's extra water and power bars in there. You may need them before this is over. Remember, don't do anything stupid. Don't try to be a hero."

Slipping into the backpack, Morris hefted the service pistol in his right hand. "I'll try to keep a handle on these guys. Don't wait up, dad."

"God be with you, Morris."

"Him and this," brayed Morris holding the pistol aloft. "I'm ready."

Two-dozen bare-footed natives, draped with bilums and

armed with machetes, axes, bows, or spears with sharp, fire-blackened tips, stood in clusters. Animating his words with a bony finger, their bellicose chief fired instructions at them. The villager Micah, bandoleer and woven bilum roped diagonally across his scarred chest, sidled up next to Morris, an ancient double-barreled shotgun cradled in his arm. The armed man grinned mischievously, his cheek bulging with buai.

"I assume he's with me, not as my chaperon," quipped Morris nervously.

Wood suppressed a smile. "Probably coming along to make sure the chief gets his pistol back. Seriously, Morris, take care of yourself. Promise me you'll let these guys get out front, okay?"

Morris couldn't respond. The deputized warriors were already moving at a hurried gait, heading to the bridge to take up the chase. In the midst of the armed phalanx, Morris kept pace, flanked by the shotgun-toting Micah and a grim ax-wielding accomplice.

At the ruined bridge the vigilantes split into two bodies. One group began hacking at trees to make a temporary repair to the crossing. They would continue the chase once the span could support a man's weight.

The second group, with Morris, probed the riverbank, their practiced eyes studying the undergrowth for tracking signs. Within minutes, the men signaled one another to begin the hunt. Moving rapidly over moss-covered boulders and twisted roots flanking rapids, the file of warriors followed a sloppy trail left by Gallagher's party. The lead man, one of the village's most proficient archers, stayed in front of the pursuers, leaping from boulder to fallen tree trunks, arrows and bow in hand.

Morris labored hard to stay with his escorts. His shadow, Micah, whom he christened "Shotgun," negotiated the obstacles with ease, his long-barreled gun always at the ready. Occasionally lead trackers paused, kibitzing among themselves, deciding strategy. The column would halt, the men silent, patient. In the overarching canopy, birds screeched in protest at the invaders below. A ten-foot python clung like a pale green noose on an overhanging branch, waiting for a meal.

Dawn's leaden sky opened up, briefly soaking the pursuers. Clouds drifted away, allowing morning sun to climb in a clearing sky. In the rain's wake, rising humidity sucked energy from Morris but left his companions unaffected. Pushed near his limits by the constant task of climbing over rocks and upended trees, Morris entertained second thoughts about having volunteered for the pursuit. Grateful for the short respites while point men debated the fugitives' track, he drank water sparingly and was content to nibble on snack bars as the river roared past a rock shelf he shared with "Shotgun" Micah.

....

Chapter 53

5:30 a.m.

Silhouettes of emergent hardwoods loomed above the jungle canopy. Traces of the beaten path David had lost and found a dozen times became easier to spot in thinning, knee-high fog. David's pace slackened, then slowed. He stopped without speaking, consulting his note card of compass headings. *We should be seeing grass soon.* Closing his eyes, he oriented his position by listening for rushing water. *Good. The river is where it should be—on our left. Keep it on our left.* Shuffling slowly forward, he blinked back tears, trying to focus on the sodden footpath. Stabbing pain returned, twisting like a serrated blade in his side with each step. Grimacing, David gathered the loose hem of his shirt into a ball, pressing the bloody fabric against his side to put out the fire.

Behind him, Becky plodded on, head down in exhaustion, oblivious to David unraveling in front of her. Darryl, trailing two feet in her wake, gripped the rope she held, the loaded vest digging into his shoulders. He was past complaining. Light rain fell, breaking up the ground fog but adding to their misery.

Ten minutes crept by, and finally the brush thinned, giving way to grass. David smiled. He halted, swaying unsteadily. The guide rope, slick with blood, fell from his hand. Slowly folding like a rag doll, David crumpled to his knees, pitching forward in the rough grass without a sound. Becky felt the rope go slack. Raising her eyes, she saw David curled at the side of the path. Kneeling beside him, she nudged his shoulder. No response. "Darryl! Help me!"

Darryl dropped beside his brother, tried to shake life into him. They rolled David on his back, revealing the blood-soaked shirt wadded in a gaping wound. Sobbing, Becky rocked back on her haunches, head in her hands. Dazed, drained of energy, Darryl stared blankly at his surroundings, his voice a stuttering monotone. "He, he…never said…he was hurt. Can you… believe it? A hole in him like that…and he…never said a word."

Rain swept across the trail, shocking Becky into action. Crawling to David's body, she struggled to strip the sleeveless jacket from his bloodied torso. "No time to lose, Darryl. Give me a hand. We can't stop now!"

Passive, immobilized by fatigue and his brother's death, Darryl huddled in the downpour. Gazing with dull, defeated eyes, he watched Becky fight to free the packed bib-like vest from its wearer's lifeless arms. She cried, "I can't do this…without your help!" She pulled half the vest from David's limp form, tried rolling him on his back. No good. Crouching over the corpse, Becky slapped Darryl, hard.

He recoiled from the blow. "What the hell…?"

"Get a grip, Darryl! We HAVE to get his vest and keep moving!"

"What's the point, Becky? This whole thing is fucked now."

"Because they're coming for us! Think what will happen if they find us!"

Wailing, his head bowed, Darryl bawled, "David's dead because of us! He's dead and we're fucked! WE'RE ALREADY DEAD!"

"No we're not. And you are NOT quitting!" she snapped. "David would want us to keep going! Stay if you want, you sorry piece of shit, but I'm not quitting."

Her brutal scolding worked. With Darryl's help, Becky wrenched the weighted jacket from the body. Slipping out of her own vest, she donned the heavier, crimson-stained one. Rifling David's pocket gave her the card with handwritten notes about azimuths, GPS settings, and terrain. Darryl fished in his brother's pockets, found a military compass, wallet, and passport which he passed to Becky. From her backpack she took the orange plastic satellite phone case and powered up the device. She punched in her code and a number. She waited, GPS in one hand, the phone against her ear. The familiar voice in the receiver made her smile in relief despite her tears. She read their position, gave an estimate of their time to the landing zone, and recited a compass heading. The call was quick, reassuring. She put away the phone and got back to the business of flight in a hostile land. Being pursued with one less partner to share the load was going to be challenging. Even if Darryl was unaware how much Becky needed him—how close they were to losing everything, including their lives—she was acutely aware there was no turning back. *I'm walking out of here with every ounce, nothing less. And you're coming with me.*

"Carry my vest for a while," she ordered. "We can trade off if it gets to be too much." Mechanically, a subdued Darryl picked up Becky's jacket with its twenty pounds of gold and shrugged it over his own without complaint. The increased payload made him lean forward to ease the strain on his back. Becky struggled with her new burden. The weeks of walking rural county roads with a sand-filled vest had prepared her, but she groaned as she donned David's bloodstained pack.

Gazing at his brother's pale shell washed by falling rain, Darryl leaned on his walking stick, his voice resigned. "We just gonna leave him here like that?" Sweeping his arm at the grass and jungle walling them in, he sobbed, choking on his words. "It's not right to abandon him…you know…like this."

"I know," she cooed sympathetically. "I know. I feel the same way. We'll come back for him when the chopper picks us up."

"Promise?"

She put an arm on Darryl's stooped shoulder, her face somber and her lie silky, convincing. "I promise."

With the open compass in one hand, Becky consulted David's notes jotted days before on their in-bound leg. Her voice changed to flint. "We're heading due north. We'll hit the river soon. Should see the ford. Our pickup zone is on the opposite bank. We're practically there, Darryl. Ready?"

Getting the affirmative nod she wanted, Becky took a reference sighting on an isolated clump of acacia in the distance. She put away the compass, picked up her walking stick, planting her feet on the soggy trail. Immediately, she felt the increase in weight digging into her shoulders with each step. Bowing against pelting rain, Becky turned every few minutes to make sure Darryl was following. She saw him laboring under the combined load of two packs—fifty-five pounds. There was no need for the guide ropes looped at her waist.

Bathed in dawn's gray light, the terrain seemed familiar, but no less threatening. Somewhere ahead of them the river would curve northeast, widening. They would cross where sandbars on both banks formed in the bend—where a shallow rocky bottom chopped the current into riffles before splitting into two meandering channels.

Cocking her head to one side, Becky heard the comforting sound of rushing water and quickened her pace. Toiling in her wake, Darryl stayed with her, his eyes fastened on the bobbing figure in front of him. Five hundred steps in pouring rain took them through clinging chest-high kunai grass to the river. Arriving at a sloping bank covered with smooth round stones, they stood staring at rushing slate-colored water. Both of them broke into radiant smiles. Sheer luck, or David's dying gift of scribbled compass headings, had delivered them to the very spot where they had crossed a lifetime ago.

Sinking to her knees in the stones, Becky unzipped her backpack and pulled out the satellite phone. Her first call didn't go through. Concerned, but not panicked, she waited five minutes before trying again. She connected on the sixth ring, announcing, "We're at the pickup point. How much time do you need?" She read out a GPS setting. "Got it? Good. When I have you in sight I'll throw out lights to mark our position. Hurry, we're in some trouble. We'll talk about it later."

As Becky talked to their rescuer, Darryl busied himself by kicking rocks aside to create a place to sit. She put away the phone and uncoiled six feet of nylon rope. Handing him one end, she said, "We have to cross. It'll be safer if we stay tied together."

"Can't we rest for a few minutes? Geez, I'm dying here."

Like a mother speaking to a reluctant child, Becky bored in. "No time to take it easy yet. Have to reach the other bank to be picked up. Follow me."

"Ahhh, my back's killing me."

"So is mine. You don't hear me whining. C'mon, we need to move."

"You're not carrying twenty extra pounds."

Turning on him, Becky snarled, challenging Darryl. "Poor baby. You wanna trade packs? I can carry it if you don't think you can." Glowering at her insult, Darryl summoned enough energy to rise to his feet, both vests layered over his shoulders. "Bitch," he snorted under his breath.

Becky heard the slight but pretended otherwise. *Call me anything you like, just get those vests across that river, Darryl.*

Roped to her balky accomplice, Becky stepped into the current, probing the treacherous bottom with her staff. Water swept past her knees, then her thighs as she tested each step before planting her feet. Staggering behind her, Darryl held the taut line with a death grip, his other hand grasping a walking stick. In the middle of the river, Becky stepped into an unseen hole, lunging face first in the rushing river. Surfacing, she gasped for air. Caught in the powerful surge, she flailed against its pull. Only being tethered to Darryl saved her.

"HANG ON!" he screamed, dragging her upright to regain her balance. Becky leaned against the current, fighting step by cautious step to break free of the turbulence. Gaining the other bank, she crawled through sand and rocks on her knees, pulling the taut rope behind her. Dazed from the battle, she lay on her side, retching, one hand gripping the line.

An arm's length from safety, Darryl tripped on a submerged rock and went down, the heavy vests dragging him under. A rooster tail of whitewater erupted around him as he fought for his life. Panicking, Darryl stabbed his pole at the rocky bottom to anchor himself. The river snapped the staff, tearing it from his hand. Clawing at the safety line with both hands, he kicked violently to right himself. Becky anchored the safety line around her, trying to pull him to the riverbank. Her body toppled backwards, the rope suddenly slack.

Snatched by the raging torrent, Darryl twisted in the river's grip. Out of control, he rolled, gasping for air, fighting to keep his head above the surface.

Struggling to her feet, Becky, hands to her mouth in horror, spotted a waving arm, clenched fist, and a booted foot, then nothing. Darryl had been swept away as easily as a leaf.

Looking upriver, Becky was stunned to discover how far downstream she and Darryl had been carried from where they had first entered the water. Shedding her backpack and vest in an overgrown pile of brush, she unsheathed a machete from its waterlogged scabbard and immediately headed downstream. Stumbling over rocks and slashing a path through brush along the river's edge, Becky pushed ahead on rubbery legs, her boots filled with water. *Make the effort. You owe him that much.*

At a wide bend in the river, where the current slowed, eddying between humped sandbars ringed with smooth stones, she found him.

His pale body lay pinned against a partially submerged logjam of bleached hardwood giants. The bulky sleeveless jackets had been Darryl's undoing, snagging him in the tangled branches. Once he was trapped, the powerful current had impaled him on a dagger-shaped branch, piercing his lower back, holding him in place.

A bloodstained spike poked from a gruesome puncture in

his abdomen. As if the wound was not enough, his shattered right arm twisted grotesquely behind his head. One bare foot bobbed in the angry current.

Becky, heart pounding wildly, gazed intently at the macabre scene. Both vests, though twisted like nooses around Darryl's neck, were intact. Becky battled treacherous waist-high water to reach him. Freeing the canvas bibs proved awkward. She groped underwater to free the Velcro tabs around his waist and fought to pry loose the twenty-pound vest from his shoulders. It took fifteen minutes to free it.

After dragging the vest to shore, she battled her way back to the jumbled driftwood. Becky jostled Darryl's body to separate the final strap from his mangled arm. Easing the second heavy pack over his head, she was startled by a barely audible cry. Panicked, she stumbled, off-balance in the swirling whitewater, almost losing the vest. Darryl's eyelids fluttered. His mouth opened, lips drawn back in pain. He called to her.

Unnerved, Becky, wide-eyed in shock, backpedaled to the safety of the shallows, pulling the treasure with her. Retreating to a muddy shoal, she sat with knees drawn up, head resting on her arms. When she exhausted her tears, Becky stood, her face grim, her mind fixed on what she needed to do. Wading to his side, she yelled above the boiling rapids to rouse him from semi-consciousness. Her pleading voice prompted a moan of recognition. "Good...Becky...you..."

"What happened?"

"Rocks...hit some rocks...can't...feel my legs..."

"We don't have much time, Darryl. I'm going to try and free you. It'll be painful. Forgive me, okay?" Working his shattered arm from the forked branch behind his head set off animal-like shrieks, startling her. Wrapping his useless arms around her neck, Becky strained against the rushing water, lifting his body off the bloodied spike. Darryl fainted from the effort. It took every ounce of strength to drag him from the logs without becoming trapped herself. Gently turning him on his back, she gripped his collar, towing him clear of the rapids into deeper water, away from the twisted tree limbs. His eyes opened, trying to focus. Soft groans escaped from his lips. "Ahh, Becky…hurt…tried."

"Shhh, don't talk, Darryl. Save your strength."

This is not going to work. Even if I get you to shore, I can't carry you much beyond that. You're too badly injured, Darryl. You can't come with me. Sorry. Am I sorry? No… maybe. Sort that out later. Becky pushed Darryl well beyond the sunken trees—to where the current was strong—and let the river claim him again.

....

Chapter 54

South bank, 6:00 a.m.

For two hours, luck favored the Australian fugitives and Noah. Halfway through the third hour, fate intervened. Misjudging his footing, Nelson fell from a massive boulder, plummeting fifteen feet to rocks below a waterfall, breaking both bones in his lower right leg. Writhing in agony, he blamed the mossy stone for his injury. Gallagher faulted the man's carelessness but did not say it aloud. Noah silently blamed Nelson's scattering of ancestral skulls with his boot while pillaging the sacred longhouse. While Gallagher hovered over his crippled friend, Noah rifled the canvas bag, pocketing a fistful of gold bars unseen.

"How much pain you in, mate?" asked Gallagher.

"Whadaya think? Hurts like bloody hell, it does."

Squatting next to Nelson, Gallagher ran over their options. "Your choice, mate. We can leave you here and you can hold 'em off, buy us more time..."

Interrupting, Nelson sneered. "Not bloody likely."

"Or...we rig you a splint and you hobble along as best you can." Scratching at his beard, Gallagher squelched his own suggestion. "Course that means we probably lose our chance at getting little missy and the rest of the gold."

"Noah could carry me," said Nelson hopefully, staring at the native.

Gallagher twisted on his haunches, eyeing their companion. "What about it, Noah? Think you can carry our friend here?"

"Tu slo. No gut."

Barking profanity, Gallagher waved his pistol. "Carrying him is no good?"

Propping himself on his elbows, Nelson calmed the fuming Gallagher. "He's right. How about we rig a stretcher, mate. Use my shirt. Button up, tuck in the sleeves, and run two poles through 'em to make a seat. That's what I'd do if it was you, Gallagher."

"Hell you would, mate. You'd leave me a couple of biscuits, some water, and a pistol, and then be on your way. Okay, your call. We'll try the stretcher idea."

Tucking his weapon into his waistband, Gallagher relieved Noah of the heavy canvas bag filled with gold bars and huddled next to Nelson, speaking softly. "I'd say we've got about an hour, maybe ninety minutes if we're lucky, mate."

Scowling to mask his pain, Nelson nodded in agreement. "Ain't gonna be a waltz when those blokes show."

Gallagher took a pull on a water bottle, offered it to Nelson. "Like bloody hell. We can take care of 'em. They'll find out soon enough." Using a pocket knife, he began cutting strips of cloth from his hobbled partner's trousers. Next, he halved a fallen branch, trimmed the sticks, fashioning a simple splint for Nelson's ruined leg. "That'll hold you for a while." With his eyes fixed upstream, Gallagher thought out loud. "What if we left the river, got into cover, found us a clear spot, and called Baxter on the sat phone? We could hold out until he picked us up in the chopper."

Patting his swelling leg, Nelson mused, "Nah, I'd only slow ya up. There might be another way."

"I'm all ears, mate."

Nodding at the river, Nelson sketched an idea. "Noah lashes a bamboo raft together and the three of us float our way out of here."

Brightening, Gallagher sat up, faced the rapids, his back to the jungle, the bag of gold between his knees. "It just might work. Don't know what's between here and the crossing we used coming up here, though."

"Don't matter, does it? Better than what's behind us."

"Righto, it's settled then. We're taking to the water. Quickest way out of here." Spreading his arms to show what he wanted, Gallagher called to the native. "Noah, cut plenti poles, kwik, kwik! Strong ones, eh?"

The native obediently trotted to a nearby grove of thick bamboo along the bank and began chopping. He felled a dozen twelve-foot lengths, making two trips to the waiting Australians. On his second trip Noah dumped the last six poles, the bamboo clattering like pieces of a wind chime. "Make a little noise, why don't you?" carped Nelson, irritated.

"No matter," said Gallagher. "They know we're here, mate."

Noah picked up his machete, went back for more bamboo

without being asked. Gallagher fished in his backpack for coils of nylon rope. "Remember your asking me why I was bringing this along? You never know, do you?"

"Shit, Gallagher, not now," rebuked Nelson without looking, his attention drawn to the surrounding jungle. Working quickly, efficiently, Gallagher lashed a dozen lengths of bamboo together into a semblance of a crude raft. For stability, he added rope around the middle. "Wish I had more time to fashion a proper one."

Increasingly anxious, Nelson's temper sparked. "Any time, your grace."

"Ungrateful Philistine," retorted Gallagher, finishing his task.

Pistol in hand, Nelson dragged himself over rocks to the water. Inspecting Gallagher's design with a wary eye, he voiced approval. "It just might work."

"Might work? It's a piece of art."

"Just launch the fucking thing, will ya!"

"You're right there, mate. Desperate times call for…" His busy eyebrows shot up in puzzlement. "What the hell. Where's Noah got to?" Hollow chopping sounds had ceased, replaced by the river's powerful voice, Noah nowhere in sight.

Pulling a Glock from his backpack, Gallagher burrowed behind a rock, scanning the menacing trees, muttering, "Did the buggers get him?"

"Dunno. But I'm certainly not going quietly, mate." Boosting himself into a sitting position with his muscular arms, Nelson wedged his body between two boulders wet with spray, sighting his weapon upstream. Save for the river's roar, the humid jungle bower filled with unnerving, expectant silence. A flock of startled birds exploded from canopy upriver. Dark shapes broke from cover, leaping across rock ledges, climbing the forested banks, and closing in.

"They're here," hissed Gallagher, wiggling into his backpack's harness. "Cover me while I ready the raft."

A small avalanche of soil and stones, disturbed by an unseen foot, spilled down an eroded bank to Nelson's right. Spooked, he fired twice at shadows without effect. A cane arrow ricocheted off the rocks, narrowly missing him. An unseen archer high in a tree shot a second arrow that buried itself in Nelson's thigh.

Screaming in pain, he snapped the shaft and pulled out the blackened tip. Scuttling sideways to his companion, Gallagher fired into the canopy to buy time. He tore a piece of cloth from his shirt, tying it over Nelson's wound to staunch the bleeding.

Another arrow flew past their heads. Pointing the makeshift vessel downstream, Gallagher shouted, "GET ON!" Ignoring his pain, Nelson threw himself face down on the lashed bamboo. Gallagher handed the canvas bag to him.

"Hang on to this, mate!" Taking careful aim at two darting shapes, he fired, dropping one silhouette. Easing the primitive craft into the raging current, one hand gripping a rope leash, Gallagher pointed his 9mm upriver, spraying shots to intimidate their pursuers. Pushing off, he flung half of his body on top of Nelson, his trailing legs serving as rudder. Immediately sucked into the rapids, the fleeing Australians were swept beyond their would-be captors' reach.

Morris sat on a large flat rock bathed in sunlight, his left shoulder bloodied and throbbing, the river raging behind him. His part in the pursuit was finished. By pushing the lead tracker out of harm's way at the last second, Morris had paid for his selflessness. Gallagher had tagged him with a lucky shot. Micah fashioned a poultice from leaves to staunch the wound and tied it around Morris's arm with plaited vines. The American had earned the natives' respect for saving one of their party. After a hurried consultation, it was decided two men would guide him back to the village. The story of his action would be carried back to the chief along with the old man's prized firearm and its suspect bullets.

"I'm good enough to go on," Morris protested to deaf ears. The rest of the pursuers broke into two groups. Six natives, Micah among them, were dispatched immediately to take up the trail along the west bank of the river. They slipped silently into the jungle, intent on intercepting the fleeing men at some point.

The remaining dozen built and launched two bamboo rafts to chase the Aussies down a river they knew better than their prey. Watching with envy, Morris stood as the men poled their craft through the rapids. *My money's on these guys, not Gallagher and Nelson,* he thought with satisfaction. *The Aussies turned out to be tougher than I thought but still, I wouldn't want these guys on my ass. Wish I could be there to see how this is going to end.* The rafts rounded a bend in the river, disappearing in a sudden shower. Morris turned reluctantly, following his two guides—his minders as disappointed as he was to miss the end of the hunt.

....

Chapter 55

Downstream, 8:15 a.m.

Sobbing loudly, Becky sloshed ashore, struggled into the two soaked canvas vests taken off Darryl, and walked west along the riverbank in a near-catatonic state. The combined burden of both vests pressed down on her. High in a blue sky scrubbed clean of rain clouds, the sun scorched the landscape. For forty punishing minutes, she trudged on rubbery legs, her goal the upstream ford she and Darryl had crossed two hours before.

Reaching the spot where she had cached her belongings, Becky fell to her knees, toppling on her side. Too exhausted to remove the yoked bibs filled with bullion, she slept as dead.

Only the skittering movements of a tiny lizard across her outstretched arm roused Becky from bone-numbing fatigue. Recoiling from the reptile's alien touch, she bolted awake, flinging the startled creature into the grass, doing the inquisitive lizard an injustice. Its curiosity had awakened her in time to hear the steady, unmistakable thumping sounds of a helicopter. The chopper circled, searching. *Quick, the light sticks!* Wiggling from under the weighted vests, Becky crawled to her backpack, fumbling for the remaining glow sticks. Grasping them, she stood unsteadily, holding the six-inch plastic tubes to her chest. With what seemed her last burst of strength, Becky snapped the flexible rods, shaking them to produce blinding light. Each stick was designed to burn its usual twelve hours of low-level light in just five intense minutes as a rescue flare.

In desperation, she said a quick prayer, tossed a tube high in the air in a fiery, eye-catching arc, and held her breath. Slowly, the helicopter banked, turning in her direction. She threw another. The chopper came in low, making another pass over the sea of grass. Holding the last two glow sticks aloft, she waved them frantically to get the pilot's attention. The tactic worked. Dropping toward the dazzling signal, the Huey hovered directly overhead in a cloud of stinging sand.

Shrieking uncontrollably, Becky, burning her final reserves of adrenaline, did jumping jacks on wooden legs, glow sticks in her hands. The helicopter's blades made muscular slapping sounds in the humid air, the rotor downwash flattening a large circle of yellow-green grass. Buffeted by the turbulence, a mesmerized Becky dropped the light sticks at her feet.

Settling on its skids, the chopper's big turbine shattered

the air with its deafening whine. In the left seat, a bearded man removed his headset, said something to the pilot. Spotting a familiar face framed in the windshield, Becky sprinted in a crouch to the co-pilot's door. Rick Crandall dropped to the ground, immediately engulfed by a weeping Becky hysterical with joy.

"Where are the others?!" he yelled.

"Gone!"

"You're it?!"

Bawling in his arms, she nodded.

"You said you were in trouble."

"It's a long story."

The two ran hand-in-hand to her piled belongings. She slid the twenty-pound bib over her head. Slinging the two heavier vests over his shoulders like saddlebags, Crandall snagged her backpack with one hand, pocketed the glow sticks, and pushed her toward the chopper. Sliding open the Huey's starboard side door, he tossed the bulky sleeveless jackets on the cabin floor next to the fuel drums, then lifted Becky into one of the jump seats. Ordering her to buckle in, Crandall slammed shut the door and ran to take his place as co-pilot. Once strapped in, he donned headphones, gave Buzz Dawson a wide grin and thumbs-up. The Aussie increased power, rising ten feet before running along the river to gain speed. The Huey leveled out at 200 feet, then banked toward the coast.

To Becky, the thirty-minute trip to the coast seemed to last forever. Dawson took the Huey north. He flew just above the shaggy palisade of jungle lining the shimmering river that had swallowed Darryl and nearly killed her. Leaning back against the ship's bulkhead, she stared listlessly at green carpet rushing by below. Exhausted from her ordeal and lulled by the rotor's vibration, Becky fell into a troubled sleep. Occasionally, Crandall turned in the co-pilot's seat to check on her.

He needn't have bothered. She was out cold, mouth open, eyes closed, hands gripping one of the heavy vests at her feet. Threatening clouds filled the valley behind the Huey, shadowing the chopper all the way to the coast.

Dawson hit the beach southeast of Buna and headed out over the turquoise sea for a quarter mile before paralleling the coarse sand shore west to Gona. Once there, he turned south, circling Crandall's boat, anchored two hundred yards beyond the shore break, then aimed straight for the beach. Coming in low, the Huey banked right toward a narrow strip of shoreline crowded by palms and settled in a cloud of grit. Shielding himself from the swirling sand, Dawson's faithful mechanic waited by the black inflatable where he had been dropped at dawn. The Australian kept the turbine at idle to run the electric pump. Crouching, Solomon ran to the Huey, hooked up a two-inch hose, and began transferring Jet A fuel from the drums to the main tanks.

In the cockpit, Crandall handed Dawson a thick manila envelope, shouting, "We're square, Buzz! Nice working with you!"

Dawson hefted the envelope. "Been a pleasure, Yank!"

Crandall dismounted, scrambled to the passenger seats, and shook Becky awake. "We're here! Gotta move quick!" Groggy with fatigue, she slipped from the chopper without a word. Crandall pulled the vests from under the seat and piled one on her shoulders. He sent her stumbling under the load toward the rubber boat at the water's edge. "Love to give you a hand, Buzz, but..." Crandall left the thought unfinished. From his perch in the pilot's seat, a grinning Dawson waved him away. As eager as Crandall to put the coast behind him, Dawson was equally impatient to get back in the air. Solomon was already at work topping off the Huey's tanks for the return trip. In thirty minutes, they would be airborne.

At the shore, Crandall tossed two vests across seats in the rubber boat and told Becky to get in. Running on empty, her eyes dull, she did as ordered without complaint. Dragging the rubber dinghy behind him through the shore break, Crandall muscled the Zodiac into waist-deep water, pointing the blunt bow seaward. Hoisting himself aboard, he flopped over the gunwale and fired the little boat's outboard motor. After punching through the waves, Crandall aimed the dinghy at the horizon where *Sunshine* waited. Following Crandall's earlier instructions, Kalani had already begun raising sail.

From her perch in the bow, Becky managed a wan smile for Crandall. The most difficult stage of the plan was behind her. She thought, *How difficult could fleeing in a sailboat be after what I've just been through?*

Slowing as he approached *Sunshine*, Crandall motored alongside the hull's starboard side and threw a line to Kalani. Becky felt feather light as he passed her to the Hawaiian. "Show her below," he barked. "Put her in the middle berth. Tell her I'll be there as soon as we stow the dinghy and get underway." Shuffling on the crewman's arm, a bewildered Becky allowed herself to be led below. Heaving the loaded vests onto the boat, Crandall climbed aboard, dragging the sodden packs across the deck. He passed Kalani who had come back on deck. "Gee, brah, she don't look so good, you know."

"Yeah, she's had a rough time of it. She'll be okay after she's had a chance to eat and get some sleep."

Kalani reached for a vest. "Need help?"

"Leave it! I'll take care of it. Just get the motor off the inflatable. I'll be back to help you get it on board." Crandall heaved the vests over his shoulder and went down the ladder into the main cabin.

Shrugging, Kalani lowered himself into the rubber boat and wrestled with the outboard. Back topside, Crandall took the small engine from Kalani and propped it by the hatch. The two of them heaved the inflatable aboard and flipped it over, fastening it over surfboards strapped to the cabin. Leaving Kalani to finish the job, Crandall muscled the outboard below, stowed it in the bow compartment, and went into the main cabin to check on his passenger.

Becky sat on the edge of a bunk, head in hands. Crandall paused to fix a cup of hot chocolate in the galley. While it heated, he knelt in front of her to remove her soaked boots and socks. "Stand up," he commanded. She did as told. Working quickly, he unbuttoned the wet, grimy shirt, peeling it from her. Next, he took off her trousers. Too numbed to cover herself, Becky stood there, naked, overcome with exhaustion. Crandall wrapped a soft, white terrycloth robe around her and lowered her gently to a berth spread with an open sleeping bag. "Don't go anywhere," he said, propping a pillow behind her head. Returning with a cup of steaming cocoa, Crandall sat on the edge of berth, steadying her hands as she grasped the heavy mug.

"Drink this. Once we're underway I'll get some soup in you." Leaning over, Crandall gently kissed her forehead.

"I thought..." she began, her eyes brimming.

"Shhh, not now. There's plenty of time to talk about it later. You need food and rest." Pointing over his shoulder, Crandall said, "Head's there. Sorry, that's the bathroom." Grinning, he took her limp hand, kissing it gently. "It's good to see you again. You look wonderful."

"Liar. I look like shit."

"Nah, you might feel that way but you sure as hell don't look it."

"I stink, too. I need a bath."

"A shower will have to do…but later. I brought the clothes you wanted. I'll lay them out for you when you're ready." Crandall eased from the bunk. "I've got to give Kalani a hand. We've got a decent offshore wind building. Be a shame to waste it. Besides, I don't want to hang around. I want to clear the reefs in daylight, get us into deeper water. Don't worry, I'll be back to check on you. Finish your hot chocolate, then get some sleep. You look like you're about to hit the wall. It'll be okay, Becky, you're safe now."

"I love you, Rick."

"And I love you, Becky. Always have."

"Where did you put the…"

Knowing she was asking about the treasure, Crandall tapped a foot against a storage locker below the berth. "You're sleeping on top of it. It's right where you want it to be." One last kiss and he went through the cabin, bounding topside where Kalani was already raising the mainsail for their escape.

....

Chapter 56

South riverbank, 9:45 a.m.

Gallagher's raft and Nelson came apart at the same time. Having floated for an hour under a brutal sun, the two hit a series of rapids that splintered the bamboo craft into useless sticks. Nelson, bag of gold looped around his neck, screamed in agony as he was dragged over submerged rocks, his injured leg banging against unseen obstacles. Had it not been for Gallagher holding his head above water, Nelson would have been pulled under by the weight of the gold. Using the current to guide them both into shallow water, Gallagher dragged his partner to the north side of the river, collapsing on a stony beach. Marooned, but momentarily safe, they lay on their backs, panting. Rolling on his side, an exhausted Gallagher pressed his face to the rocks and slept.

It was Nelson's moaning, suffered in the river mauling, that stirred Gallagher. Or perhaps it was the sense of being watched that made him open his eyes. A pair of calloused, splayed feet, planted inches from his face, shocked Gallagher awake. Squinting, he slowly raised his head, seeing only a man's ebony torso silhouetted against the sun.

Carefully, Gallagher cautiously elbowed Nelson.

"Wha…what?" His hobbled companion was semi-conscious.

"We've got company, mate," Gallagher warned, shielding his eyes.

Stepping back, the owner of the gnarled feet squatted a prudent arm's length from Gallagher, who raised himself on his elbows. Sunlight blinded the Australian. Pinching his eyes shut, Gallagher instinctively knew the man was armed with a machete. He dropped his head, thought better of the move, and raised himself as though doing a pushup. Feeling for his pistol, Gallagher slowly patted his soaked trousers for the weapon. Not there. Running his hands over Nelson was equally fruitless. Their boots were gone as well, deliberately stripped while they slept.

Not a good sign. Couldn't get far on bare feet.

The silhouette spoke in a familiar voice. "Ah, yu lukim for gan, eh?"

Noah! Alive! Gallagher breathed easier. "Noah, how the bloody hell did you end up here, mate? We're glad to see you, aren't we, Nelson?" A mumbled reply. "What happened? We thought you were dead. How did you get away, Noah?"

"Mi swim. Long swim. Mi holam bamboo."

"You held on to bamboo logs? Like us, eh? Plenty smart, Noah."

On hands and knees, Gallagher played his cards cautiously, his eyes drifting to the bulky canvas bag behind Noah. *Must have stripped it from me, along with our guns and boots. Bit of a sticky situation. Think fast.* Sitting back on his heels, Gallagher acted confidently, though he suspected Noah might not buy it. "Nelson's hurt, Noah. Hurt bad. We have to move him before they find us, right?"

"Lek bruk. Nogut."

There was brevity, a dismissal, in Noah's voice that chilled Gallagher. Gesturing to Nelson, he tried again, using his most charming smile. "Yeah, bad break with his leg. Has a wound too. But we can fix him up. You, me, we carry Nelson, yeah? We go kwik, kwik, yeah?"

"No." The answer was flat, emotionless, and final. Hoisting the heavy bag to his shoulders, Noah backed up, machete held defensively. "Mi go long ples."

Propping Nelson into a sitting position, Gallagher took a step toward Noah, his arms out, pleading. "We'll split the gold, mate. Equal shares. The three of us."

Seconds passed, both men trying to read the other's motive.

A suddenly aware Nelson staggered upright on his good leg, staring at the retreating native with hatred. "He's leaving, Gallagher. Just like that. The bloody bastard's abandoning us. Noah, you sorry sonofabitch! After all we've done for you!" Gripping a large stone in each hand, Nelson called to his friend. "Help me. We'll have a go at him yet." Gallagher offered an arm to Nelson, steadying him.

Unmoved by Gallagher's transparent appeal and ignoring Nelson's threat, Noah edged from the riverbank, bush knife at the ready. "Gutbai, Gallagher."

As the black man turned, Nelson loosed a rock at the native's head. The first missile missed but was followed by a second stone that struck a glancing blow at the native's back. Enraged, Noah pivoted to face the pair, machete raised. He checked himself, his attention caught by something in the distance.

Gallagher, arm cocked to hurl a rock, saw the fear in Noah's eyes and turned toward the river. Glancing over a shoulder, Nelson followed his friend's gaze across the rapids. A group of armed men stood on a sandbar, witnessing the trio's brawl.

"We're dead, truly fucked, mate," rasped Gallagher, dropping his stone.

"Tell Noah to give us back our guns," barked Nelson, holding out his hand, eyes locked on the opposite shore. "It's our only chance."

"He's gone," answered a resigned Gallagher glancing at a fresh furrow in the wall of waving kunai grass where Noah had been. "We're out of time."

Propping his broken leg on a boulder, Nelson slumped in resignation. "You might have a chance if you run. 'Qui audet adipiscitur.'"

"Who dares wins." Sighing, Gallagher dismissed the suggestion. "Noble sentiment, that. But with no boots, no weapon, no water, I'm done as well, mate."

Nelson snorted at his companion's bravado. "We're both fixed. It's not as if you'd have a chance dragging me along, is it?"

"What, leave me mate to face these lads alone? Not bloody likely."

Both men leaned against the rocks, calmly awaiting their pursuers who were fording the river, weapons at the ready. A dozen warriors gained the shore and warily circled their quarry. Squinting at a native he took to be the group's leader, Gallagher opened with his most charming smile. "Gentlemen, hello.

Believe it or not, we're glad to see you." Gesturing to Nelson's bruised and swollen leg, Gallagher explained the obvious. "Leg broken. Can't walk. We must carry him, okay? You savvy? You understand?"

A tall, well-muscled man, gap-toothed mouth framed in a luxuriant beard, stepped forward, smooth club in hand. Grasping Nelson's swollen foot to examine the broken limb, he casually moved it back and forth, drawing howls of pain from the Aussie.

Gallagher stepped in front of the man, protesting in a flat voice. "Hey, my friend, can't you see the man is hurt? Leg broke. No good. No walk. You savvy?"

Dropping the Australian's swollen foot, the native's shaggy brow furrowed at the white man in front of him. "Mi save. Dispela raskol. Yu raskol." Angry murmurs of agreement swept the ranks surrounding them.

"Whoa now. No, no. Mi no raskol." Gallagher pointed at the fresh tracks leading away from the shore. "Noah raskol." As if the Aussie has signaled for it, a shot boomed in the distance. All heads turned toward the sea of grass.

"Raifol!" a voice cried.

"Rifle? What the hell?" said Gallagher.

"It's Noah," replied Nelson, raising himself. "Didn't sound like your Glock."

Barking orders at his party, the tall man ordered three natives into the wall of vegetation to investigate. He sent another pair armed with axes to fell trees. Pointing at Nelson with his cudgel, he announced the obvious: "Em no wokabaut."

"That's right. He can't walk. Good," brightened Gallagher, "maybe we're finally getting through to these blokes. They'll make a stretcher for you."

Nelson remained glum. "You know they'll take us back to the village."

"So what? Cheer up. At least you won't be walking. Besides, we'll talk our way out of this. You'll see."

"How are you gonna explain firing at the chief's men?"

Arms folded, Gallagher winked. "Self defense. We didn't know who they were. Mark my word, I'll dazzle them with my bullshit, mate."

The group of natives parted. One of the three trackers who had gone into the brush arrived, Gallagher's backpack slung over his shoulder. Gallagher made a show of reaching for it but was stopped by the leader who poked his club in the Aussie's chest. The scowling man snatched the pack and searched it, first tossing a half-filled bottle of water to Gallagher, then holding aloft the Australian's Glock for his hooting audience. Shoving the handgun in his waistband, the posse's leader continued fishing in the waterlogged backpack.

"What I wouldn't give to get my hands on the Glock," whispered a subdued Gallagher, passing the water to Nelson.

With a triumphant yell, the head of the trackers held three small gold ingots overhead for everyone to see. Glowering, he turned on Gallagher and Nelson, waving the small yellow bars in the Australians' faces. "Ol raskol i go stil gol belong mipela ples!"

"A little something for your rainy day fund?" said Nelson.

Blushing, Gallagher threw out a half-hearted excuse. "Noah's doing, mate."

"Cheeky bugger. Can't say I blame you under the circumstances."

An ominous hush descended on the knot of clansmen guarding the Australians. The warriors parted to make room for four men carrying Noah's body. Behind them strolled six more villagers, one of them armed with a vintage shotgun cradled in his left arm, a bulky canvas bag looped around his neck. He surrendered the bag to the headman. Angry martial whoops rippled through the growing crowd. Noah's body was dumped unceremoniously in the middle of the crowding circle. He had been shot in the chest at close range. *Likely with the shotgun*, thought Gallagher. Any hope he and Nelson had of escaping now vanished. Not only had the native party doubled in size, but Noah's being run to ground while holding the cache of gold implicated the Australians.

"Gonna take some fast talking," groused Nelson. Gallagher didn't respond.

A rapid-fire exchange in a dialect the Aussies couldn't decipher ignited between the shotgun-wielding tracker and the tall man with the polished club.

While the arguing continued, two axmen returned with trimmed twelve-foot tree limbs balanced on their shoulders. After dumping the two logs they were sent to fetch a third one.

Whatever discussion preoccupied the two alpha males of the tracking parties ended in agreement. Leaving Gallagher and Nelson in the open to bake in the sun, the natives found what little shade they could by squatting underneath stunted brush. A cloud of flies, drawn by the scent of death, found Noah's corpse and crawled across bloodied flesh. Ignoring the swarming insects, a pair of villagers tied the dead man's ankles and wrists with cords. They thrust a tree branch under the dead man's bound limbs and shouldered the log. With Noah's trussed corpse swaying like a prize, the two marched triumphantly to the river.

Nelson stared at the two remaining poles, horrified. "Oh, sweet mother, you don't think…" His words were cut off midsentence. Four men leaped on him, pinning the Australian against the large rock.

Gallagher too was jumped by a quartet of muscular natives and forced to his knees in front of his friend, arms stretched painfully behind him. Anticipating what was about to happen,

Gallagher roared out a string of curses, struggling against his captors, battling to the end like the soldier he once was.

Shocked, Nelson watched the tall man approach Gallagher. The heavy club flashed in the sunlight against a perfect blue sky. The knobbed mallet smashed against the back of the Australian's skull, killing him instantly. Gallagher collapsed on the ground, a broken, discarded doll.

Another pair of trackers scurried to Gallagher's limp body, quickly lashing his ankles and wrists to a tree branch. They bore the dead man to the riverbank where he was laid beside Noah's corpse.

Petrified, Nelson stifled his sobs, replacing them with anger, not resignation. His jaw scraped against the rock as he stiffened against steel-like hands restraining him. Sweat poured from his body. His broken leg throbbed with pain. Gnarled feet appeared in front of his eyes. The last thing he saw was the club's shadow lifting; then he heard a grunting effort and felt a shock of incredible searing pain as his head exploded.

....

Chapter 57

Straggling into the village center on the arm of one of his escorts, Morris was delivered to Wood. The missionary eased him onto a bamboo platform in the cooking hut. A liter of bottled water and a can of peaches restored the exhausted American. "I need to take a look at that wound," scolded Wood. "Didn't I tell you to let others get out in front of you?"

"I did. Guess they just weren't out far enough. It's just a flesh wound." Wood gingerly unwrapped the makeshift bandage. "In this environment there's no such thing as a flesh wound. Looks like it hit muscle, though. You'll need a stitch or two. We need to get you back to our clinic, clean the wound and pump some antibiotics in you just to be sure. Still, you're lucky, I guess."

"I thought you padres didn't believe in luck."

Wood laughed. "Touché. The Lord was watching over you. Aside from this, how did it go out there?"

Swinging his legs to the edge of the makeshift cot, Morris grimaced as Wood cleaned the ragged wound. "Rough. I had a hard time keeping up with the posse."

"Shoulda listened to me. I told you to let them handle it."

"You were right. But I felt obligated. Know what I mean?"

"I do indeed. Difference is, I'm aware of my limits. You should be happy to know the whole village is buzzing about your taking a bullet for one of their own."

Flinching as the missionary daubed his wound with antiseptic, Morris huffed. "Pure instinct. If I had been thinking clearly I might not have done it."

"Still, your act impressed the chief when he heard about it. He'll be obligated to do something for you."

"Please tell him I don't need a wife."

Chuckling, Wood pressed a sterile gauze pad against the ugly gash, which had begun to bleed again under his probing. He finished by wrapping surgical tape around Morris's bicep and put away his first-aid kit. "Think you'll need a sling?"

"Thanks, doc, I can manage."

"You're welcome. Let's take a walk where we can talk privately, okay?"

"Sure. What's on your mind? Got state secrets to share?"

"Something like that. What I'm going to tell you is off the record."

"Fine. I have no problem with that."

The pair strolled to where the tents were staked and settled on two small canvas folding chairs belonging to the missing Australians. Holding his bandaged arm against his chest, Morris smiled as Wood scanned for eavesdroppers.

"Okay, what's with the hush-hush drama?"

"Simeon risked his life to tell me what's going on."

Morris leaned forward. "With the Aussies, Becky, the brothers?"

"That's part of it. Fact is the village has been sitting on a gold mine all these years and Gallagher and Nelson apparently came here to take it."

"A gold mine?"

"Not actually a gold mine. A gold cache. The C-47 that crashed was carrying a lot of things...but gold was its most important cargo."

....

Chapter 58

In a hidden clearing three hundred meters from the village, the chief and his retinue waited patiently for the hunting party. A runner sent ahead of the main body had arrived an hour before to deliver a message that they had been successful. Trackers were due momentarily with their trophies. Shrill whistles from the jungle announced the warriors' arrival and the chief stood to receive his returning men.

The first of four sets of bearers entered the clearing with a trussed black corpse hanging by its hands and feet from a pole. They passed by the headman and lowered their burden to the ground in front of him. Three more teams followed, each bearing a dead white man. As the diminutive village leader inspected the row of bodies, a tall, brooding man walked beside him, gesturing with a bloodstained club as he recited details of the pursuit and killings. Nodding sagely, the old man listened intently to the tale.

Finished with his initial questioning, the chief sat cross-legged on the jungle floor, his men gathered in a circle around him. He thought for a long time without speaking before finally unburdening himself. Though lavish with praise for the party's success, the old man was nonetheless troubled. With others listening respectfully, the chief presented the village's dilemma as he saw it. *Killing a white man would bring trouble. It has always been thus. The deaths of three white men would surely bring the government to the village, something he wished to avoid.* He tossed out his questions and listened to terse responses from the scouting party.

What had become of the woman?

She has not been found. Perhaps she is still alive, though that is doubtful since she, like the other visitors, is a stranger to the jungle.

Who had killed her companion, the one called David?

The man had been shot, but not by our warriors. He had been found along the trail not far from the river crossing and brought here with the others.

Where was the fourth white man, the one known as Darryl?

Missing. Perhaps he is with the woman. We will look for them again.

Which of the dead Australians had shot Morris, the American?

Both of the dead Australians had fired their guns. Samuel, our best archer, wounded the one with the broken leg. It is believed the other man shot the American named Morris, but it was difficult to tell with any certainty.

You have returned the gold taken from our longhouse. But some of it is still missing. What has happened to the rest of it? Who took it?

We found some with the man Noah, who the Australians brought with them. Perhaps the rest of the gold is lost to us. Or perhaps the missing American woman and the other man have it with them. We heard a helicopter today but it was far away and did not stay long. The Australians carried a telephone with them. Maybe they called for the helicopter to help them.

....

Chapter 59

Incredulous at Wood's revelation, Morris asked, "Just how much gold was on that C-47?" Wood shrugged. "Simeon doesn't know. It was seventy years ago. His great grandfather was village headman when the planes went down. Simeon's father was just a kid then. There were no survivors from the crashes. The villagers pulled the bodies from the planes and buried them. When they emptied the Dakota, they came across the gold and hid it. They covered up the aircraft, even planted trees to hide them from searchers. You know how fast things grow here."

"In this climate? One month and you'd never find those planes from the air."

"That's exactly what happened. The village went from a hand-to-mouth stone-age existence to overnight wealth."

"Rags to riches, eh?"

"Right. They suddenly had timber, canvas, tents, rope, crates of kerosene lamps, drums of diesel, food, weapons, ammo, and..."

"The gold," interrupted Morris.

"And the gold," echoed Wood.

"What about the search the army did?"

Gesturing at the surrounding peaks, Wood asked, "How hard do you think it would be to lose a plane in here? It's possible they didn't even know where to begin looking."

"So that's the end of the story? But how did the Aussies know? When did Becky and the Lindquists find out?"

"I'm not sure Becky knew. Remember, she met Gallagher and Nelson the same time as we did."

"She told me a relative arranged for them to film the trip. Was she lying?"

Wood shrugged. "Not sure. She seemed genuinely surprised to meet them. Guess you'll have to do some digging back home to find out."

"I hate to think of her on her own out there. She could be hurt. Maybe dead. You know, I've made three trips here. This is the first time I've ever seen as many things go wrong at one time." He looked away, brooding. "Hell…sorry…I've never seen anything worse than a sprained ankle or a case of PNG revenge and now…this."

"There's more to Simeon's story. The village got hooked into the whole 'cargo cult' thing as a result of their good fortune."

"That explains the makeshift airstrip we saw."

"Correct. But that one C-47 was the only gift from the sky the villagers got."

"It was enough."

"True. Simeon's grandfather eventually became chief and followed the old man's rules about spending the gold. It was to be used for the village's needs, not hoarded. Simeon's grandfather had been afraid such sudden wealth would lead to quarrels. When the chief died, Simeon's father honored the tradition of using the gold for the good of the village. They bought only what they needed to survive. It's been a well-kept secret all these years."

"Someone had to notice this isolated village suddenly showing up with gold."

"Not necessarily. Gold's been mined commercially in PNG since the thirties. When the war started, the mining industry collapsed. It eventually came back, but gold's not unknown among the tribes. The village limited its use so they wouldn't attract attention. It's worked well for them ever since the war."

"So explain to me how all of this changed?" Morris asked while keeping a wary eye on clouds moving their way. "What happens all of a sudden? Somebody get greedy? Spread too much gold around town on one of their buying trips?"

Pausing as if ordering his thoughts, Wood said, "Remember, Simeon was just a kid when his father died. An uncle assumed the role and when he died, his son, the current chief, took over. That's when problems began."

Wood continued. "It's obvious the chief's in his dotage. His sons want to use the gold to purchase more weapons. And they've also been buying pigs to pay bride prices for more wives."

"Don't know about the wives," mused Morris, "but they're well on their way with the guns. It was surreal to see some of my posse carrying M16s alongside guys with spears and bows. Lucky me, I was supposed to make do with four bullets and a pistol from the war."

"It's a big problem," said Wood. "There are too many guns showing up in the hills these days. Australians sell them or they're brought across Indonesia's border."

"So what does Simeon want, Brad? Hard to keep him down on the farm once he's seen the city, is that it?"

"Close enough. He'd like to eventually reclaim the chief's title and build a school, church, and clinic here. And he thinks they can capitalize on the wreckage like other villages have done."

"Bring in visitor's groups like ours?"

"Hopefully without the same outcome," Wood said ruefully. "But, yeah, a little bush tourism. And if that doesn't work they could always salvage aircraft parts for sale. Willing collectors for that kind of thing, you know."

"True. But once you sell it, it's gone."

"Hard choice. But it's got to be their decision. I don't know how much gold they had left, but what they did have was hijacked. They may not get it back."

Cradling his arm to ease his pain, Morris smiled. "My money's on the posse. They were off to the races after I got hit. Did you know the Aussies got away on a raft they made?"

"Clever. Must have been their man Noah's idea. We won't see them again."

"Don't count on it. There's still a lot of green between them and safety."

A wooden spoon beating against a metal pot interrupted their discussion. Anna was calling them to dinner. Both men stood, folded the campstools, and continued talking as they strolled to the cooking hut. "Any way you look at it the gold is bound to run out some day," said Wood. "Then what happens?"

"That's when you think Simeon's dream comes into play, huh?" Morris was skeptical. "It means more outsiders discovering this valley. It would bring income, but that carries its own complications. There goes your seclusion. No turning back at that point. Welcome to the big bad world, people."

"I agree it's a risk," said Wood. "I don't think Simeon and the others realize all that it entails. But he has a vision for his people. My wife and I would like to be part of that, if asked."

"To keep things honest and win a few souls while you're at it, eh?"

"Something like that I suppose. But only if they want us to be involved."

Tea water bubbled in a blackened kettle set over flames on a scrap of steel planking from a wartime runway. Smoke rose from the cooking fire, curling under the sago thatch. Clucking sympathetically, Anna ushered them to a table set for two, hovering over the bandaged Morris like a mother hen. Though neither man felt much like eating they were reluctant to hurt her feelings. They dined in silence, aware of one hundred pairs of suspicious eyes trained on them from the huts.

As a subdued Morris and Wood ate, the village chief, with the support of his elders, made decisions that were unanimously endorsed. The longhouse was to be rebuilt immediately. Tomorrow, villagers would begin felling and hauling logs for the new sacred house. The heads of the four dead enemies would be severed and placed in holes dug for the supporting posts. The bodies were to be buried in the clearing, with all present sworn to secrecy. What remained of the gold was to be returned to its rightful place and the visitors told nothing. Government police would not come if there were no corpses to find.

When the discussion ended, the men rose and broke into a victory song.

A villager with an ax went about his assignment with grim efficiency. Collected in woven baskets, the grisly trophies were delivered to the longhouse site that night. In keeping with the old customs the heads were placed in deep pits beneath corner posts as ordered. In one week's time, the new structure would rise near the old location. Only the palm roof would take longer than planned due to heavy rains heralding a premature end to the dry season.

. . . .

Chapter 60

Wood knelt next to Morris, his voice low. "The chief wants to talk."

Morris propped himself on his good elbow, asking, "Please tell me he's in a good mood, Padre."

"Hard to read. I told him we've got a chopper coming in the morning."

"That for real?"

"Yes."

"How'd you arrange that?"

"Used my satellite phone to call the boys at NTM—New Tribes Mission. I'm on good terms with them. We've done each other favors over the years. They've got helicopters and you're my mercy mission. Got to get you out of here, the sooner the better."

"I can walk out, you know." Frowning, Wood shook his head. "Not in your condition, iron man. You may feel able, but we're two days of hard walking to the mission. This way we'll be there in under an hour."

"Lot of trouble for a dinged shoulder."

"I told you, it's not that simple. But my wife will put you right in no time. There's a small strip near our mission station. Once she's done with you it's still a rough five hours in the van to Popondetta."

Simeon timidly approached, hailing Wood. "Pastor, you come with me, please."

"The chief? He wants to see us?" The native tilted his head in response. "Yah, you too, Mr. Morris." Declining Wood's offer of help, Morris struggled to his feet. "Lead on, gentlemen."

Simeon steered them past a crowd of the curious to the open-sided, tin-roofed hut in the center of the village where a row of stony-faced elders and scowling chief waited. Morris recognized two of the tracking party squatting in shade, their oiled M16s leaning against a palm's curving trunk. The Americans ducked under the rusting eaves and sat cross-legged on a mat opposite the row of elders. Simeon settled next to them to act as interpreter. Tilting his head slightly to the chief, Wood smiled at the old man but got no sign of recognition in return. "Not the best way to start," he whispered to Morris. "That and the automatic weapons."

"Tok English?" Wood asked. The chief nodded. Wood pointed to Morris's bandaged wound. "I must take my friend to my place. Fix him with medicine." Waving his arm in the air he added, "We must go to Popondetta. Helicopter comes to take us away tomorrow."

"Mebbe yu bring police," scolded a wrinkled senior, his challenge stirring murmurs of agreement among the assembly.

"No police," shot back Wood. "I will go away with my friend."

Calling Simeon to his side, the chief engaged him in urgent whispered conversation. Wood and Morris studied the pair's body language without success. After dismissing Simeon, the chief summoned two villagers behind him. The men bent low to hear instructions from the village leader, then turned on their heels and disappeared in the ring of tribesmen watching the parley.

"What's going on, Simeon?" asked Morris, leaning across Wood. "Is the old boy okay with us leaving?"

"Yes, I think he will send you on your way."

"We're free to go?"

"Not yet. He wants to give you something to take with you. You must wait."

"Do we have a choice?" Morris asked Wood.

"Not really. It would be bad form to walk out before he sends us on our way. Just be patient."

Coconuts, tops sliced off, were passed among the group as refreshment. Morris and Wood shared one while they waited. After ten minutes, the two villagers returned carrying three large, bulging woven baskets. The pair set the containers in front of the chief and retreated. Simeon crawled on hands and knees to the chief for another whispered conversation. That done, he sat back on his haunches and waved Wood forward. The missionary peered into both baskets for several minutes before returning to his seat next to Morris, who asked, "What's going on?"

Struggling to keep his composure, Wood spoke softly. "Mystery solved. You're not gonna believe this."

"Try me," hissed Morris.

"Bones."

"Bones? Do you mean…from the wrecks?"

Before Wood could answer, a slight, hatchet-faced elder in faded Nike T-shirt passed five sets of metal chains down the line of village leaders. At the end of the necklaces dangled familiar shapes—U.S. dog tags. The Americans struggled to hide their shock. Taking possession of the military IDs, the chief draped the dog tags over a shriveled arm, solemnly pretending to decipher each one in turn. His charade complete, the headman passed the relics to Simeon while nodding to Wood and Morris. The two held out their hands to receive the unexpected gift with due reverence.

"Why these. Why the bones? Why now?" marveled Wood, fingering the metal chains, scanning the oval disks. "Why not?" grinned Morris, taking the tags. "Now is not the time to look a gift horse in the mouth."

Wood pulled Morris to his feet and beckoned their interpreter. "Simeon, please tell the chief I wish to talk with my friend,

Mr. Morris." Stepping out of earshot, the two ran through their options. Wood spoke first. "The old boy's up to something. Don't get me wrong, I'm glad he's giving us these but…"

"But what? Look at the names," said Morris, reading the tags. "Goggin… Hills…Stickler…Groteluschen. My guess is these belong to the C-47 crew. Their serial numbers will be easy to verify." Exhaling slowly, a grinning Morris offered the last tag to Wood as if awarding a trophy. "And this, my friend, is…"

Squinting, Wood plucked the ID from Morris's hand. "Lloyd Peterson."

"It's him, Brad. The name and address below his name and number might be his mother or wife. Some dog tags had a next of kin notice stamped on them."

"Huh, Betty Peterson," whispered Wood. "Becky's grandmother? Rural Route One, Upsala, Minnesota." He turned to Morris. "Do you know it?"

"Nope. Probably outstate. But it should be easy enough to find."

"That was almost seventy years ago."

"My guess is the town's probably still there. There might be people there who would have known the Petersons. I'll get around to it eventually. Right now, I'm mainly curious about the old boy's change of heart." Glancing at the relics, Morris asked, "What's the chief doing? All of a sudden he gives us all this stuff. Why?"

A nervous Simeon approached to interrupt the two. "Ah, one thing, Pastor," he said in a low voice. "The chief…wants your promise that no police come here." Rubbing his brow, Wood waited a moment, then put on his best diplomatic face. Passing a hand over the baskets and displaying the five dog tags, he said, "This will go a long way to settling questions of what happened to these men. I will do my best to make sure you are not disturbed. But tell him I cannot guarantee that more Americans will not visit again." Wood swept an arm toward the jungle. "Perhaps they will want to see the airplanes for themselves."

When Simeon relayed Wood's words, a low rumble passed through the line of elders. Clutching his wounded arm, Morris leaned toward Wood. "Not exactly what they wanted to hear."

"I'm not going to lie to them. I told you I want to return here myself."

"Well, that's your problem, Brad. You can tell them for me my lips are sealed. I'm going home."

"Someone will certainly be asking questions about Becky and the Lindquists…and the Aussies."

"I'll root around a bit when I get back, see if I can turn up anything. There's your contact in California who talked to Becky. He might know something. I can talk to him and the law back home. If Becky or the Lindquists have family, I'll contact them. Right now I don't see any reason for me…or you…to stay out here indefinitely, hoping to get answers. Besides, finding out what happened to Gallagher and Nelson is not high on my agenda. Remember, it was me they took a shot at, so I'm kinda prejudiced about their fate. I say good riddance. They've all vanished into thin air as far as I can tell. If these old boys in the village know something, they're not talking. I wouldn't hold my breath waiting to find out what they're hiding."

"You might be right," mused Wood. "The police are definitely going to be interested in what happened to five visitors who just disappeared. You and I could stay around to see how this comes out. Put this thing to rest."

"Padre, the last thing I want to do is hang around answering questions in some PNG police station. They'd never let me leave. You know that. Hell…sorry…let's be realistic. I might end up staying anyway. My airline tickets are probably shot."

Wood grinned. "Oh, sorry, I forgot about that. I've good news. Dorothy's been on the radio working it out for you. Took some doing, but you are to leave Popondetta in three days on the morning flight to Port Moresby, using your existing tickets."

"And then?"

"From there, it's on to Cairns and eventually Brisbane. The hotel you booked there has been notified. They'll honor your original reservation."

Morris sighed. "Wow! That's humbling. This puts a different light on things. I don't know how to thank you."

"Thank Dorothy when you see her. She's done all the heavy lifting on this. I don't blame you for wanting to leave. If you're determined to go, the best I can do is give you time to clear the country before I report what's happened. News travels slow from the bush, you know."

"That's no small thing. I appreciate the risk you're taking."

The two returned to the council and sat down. With eyes locked on the chief huddling with his advisers, Wood called to the interpreter. "Simeon, tell him we're grateful for these things. We accept them. We will take them with us. The bones and identification tags will be very helpful to our people. The families of these warriors will be pleased that their men are finally coming home." Waiting for his words to be translated, Wood confided to Morris, "We've got what we came for. Let's just make sure we get to take everything with us when we leave." Holding aloft the ID tags, Morris flashed an ingratiating smile at the stoic choir of old men.

Across from them, elders continued jabbering at one another. At one point, the chief pulled Simeon into the discussion. Sitting quietly, Morris fanned away insects with a banana leaf as Wood gingerly inspected the jumbled bones.

Having gambled on winning the visitors' silence with the

gift of the pilots' relics, the chief and his men found themselves in an awkward position of sending the Americans on their way with evidence from the nearby wrecks. The valley's isolation, which had served the village so well, had been compromised, perhaps forever, and they knew it. They would have to trust in the pastor's God and their familiar spirits to make things right. After a thinly veiled plea for secrecy, the two were dismissed by the council with smiles and handshakes all around. Simeon was delegated to escort the pair to their tents.

Wood and Morris spent a restless night, replaying the past two days in their minds, not quite sure what was going to happen in the morning. They needn't have worried. The next morning, true to his word, the chief sent them on their way with his blessing. Morris and Wood, plus a nervous Anna and helper, led a small army of chattering natives to the crude airstrip not far from the village. Two men had been assigned to carry the bundled remains to the landing zone. Equipment and clothing, abandoned by the expedition, was distributed among the villagers once the chief's cronies had taken what they wanted. Solemn adult faces in the crowd reminded Wood and Morris of the village's risk in sending the secrets of the dead aviators with them. That morning, the clouds cooperated, parting an hour before the helicopter was due.

Long before it arrived, the rescue bird announced its presence with the familiar chopping sound. Following the river, a white Bell Jet Ranger swooped above the trees like a giant metallic dragonfly. It circled the clearing, amazing villagers, scattering delighted, shrieking children in all directions. When the ship touched down, the crowd backed away, shielding their faces against the rotor's downblast. The co-pilot unloaded sacks of rice, tins of kerosene, and eight crated piglets Wood had requested as a parting gift to the village. A few last hurried handshakes and the team members climbed aboard. Between Morris and Wood, prized cooking pots clenched between shaking knees, Anna closed her eyes in fright, her arms wrapped around her equally terrified assistant. Wood waved goodbye to the transfixed crowd. The bird increased power, lifting from the jungle clearing in a scouring whirlwind of dirt and leaves, then soared toward the river in the humid morning.

At the Woods' mission station, Morris was treated like a king. After a week in the jungle, two hot showers—courtesy of a five-gallon water jug left in the sun each day—went a long way in restoring his soul. Despite his protests, Wood gave Morris a spare set of clean clothes. Tending to his bullet wound, Dorothy Wood was as good as her husband's word. She cleaned the gash, put in three stitches, and pumped him full of antibiotics to stave off infection. At night, he slept in an iron frame bed with a real mattress and mosquito netting. He listened to rain drum on the tin roof like gravel and—for the moment—forgot about his ordeal. For two days, he healed.

The night before Morris left, he and Wood sat in a screened porch walking each other through the previous week.

"How long before the police show up here and start asking you questions?"

Wood shook his head. "I don't know. If it were a tribal feud or some clans going after each other, the government would ignore it as long as it didn't get out of hand. But foreigners? That's something else. I expect the police to at least make an effort to come as far as my mission station. My guess is our embassy might want to get involved once the word gets out. As far as the wreck site…I'll turn over the remains along with dog tags, maps and photos. Hopefully the embassy will get that material to Hickam's lab in Hawaii. They'll start the process of identification for the families. As for the rest of it…I think the embassy will certainly be curious about what happened to three American citizens. They'll ask me for names and what I know. I'll have to be up front with them."

"Knowing you, I wouldn't expect otherwise."

"Even after you get back, somebody from Washington might want to talk to you at some point."

"What would you advise me to say?"

"Tell the truth."

"Great. So there I am—a witness who just happened to have left PNG without alerting the authorities. How do you think that's going to play?"

"You'll find out when the time comes. It's the best I can do at this point. At least you'll have access to legal resources if you need them. We still don't know what really happened. Becky and the others disappeared without a trace."

Morris brooded. "I have my suspicions, but that's all they are without proof, without three bodies…or four…or five. If Gallagher and Nelson are still alive, they're the only ones who can shed light on this."

"And they're on the run."

"Exactly."

"I don't think we'll ever find them," said Wood.

After a final breakfast and blessing from the couple, Morris, along with Anna and her faithful helper, was sent on his way in the station's battered van. The entire village turned out to see them off. Morris took a seat next to the vehicle's taciturn driver and waved farewell to the Woods and their congregation.

Followed by the same noisy gaggle of children who had welcomed him days before, the van headed down a shady corridor bordering the village's oil palms. Five torturous hours on rough roads lay ahead of him, but Morris didn't care. There would be one last night in Popondetta, an early morning Air Niugini shuttle to Port Moresby, and a noon flight—first to Cairns, then Brisbane for a final overnight in Australia. From there, it was three hours to Auckland and another twelve to Los Angeles. By the time Wood talked with PNG authorities, Morris would be well on his way to the states. The missionary had bought him valuable time at no small risk to himself—Morris intended to repay the favor by spending not one minute more than needed.

PART FOUR

Chapter 61

The Solomon Sea

Raising herself on an elbow, Becky studied her surroundings. A polished brass lamp above her tilted with the ceiling's motion, adding to her disorientation. Light poured through small, sealed rectangular windows, bathing the room in pale yellow. Swinging her legs over the bunk's wooden railing, she tightened the robe's belt and ran a hand through her hair.

A gentle rocking sensation and voices brought her back to reality. *I remember the river, the jungle, and a beach. But how did I get here? Rick! I'm on his boat.*

I'm actually on Sunshine. I made it! I'm alive! Burying her face in her hands, Becky sobbed, the weight of the last two weeks overwhelming her. When her tears ended, she felt cleansed, relieved, free. Planting her bare feet on the deck, she rose shakily, hugging the thick, varnished column in the passageway that was the mainmast. Steadying herself against the pitching deck, Becky braced her hands against the bulkheads, slowly groping her way to the teak ladder and the voices. Kalani, manning the tiller, spotted her. He yelled to Crandall. "Skipper! Lady coming up!"

In seconds, Crandall's head and shoulders filled the hatchway's frame. Smiling, he extended a hand. "Good morning, sleepyhead, care to come on deck?"

Grabbing the offered hand as if her life depended on it,

Becky scrambled up the ladder. Fresh air, heavy with a taste of salt, hit her in the face, snapping her fully awake. Crandall linked arms to hold her upright as *Sunshine* pounded through a wave trough. Beyond the bowsprit, the horizon blazed yellow-orange against dark turquoise water. Crandall led Becky to the cockpit, arm draped protectively around her shoulders. The air's chilly edge made her burrow into him.

"Becky," he boomed, "meet Kalani!" Their eyes met. She vaguely remembered the youth helping her aboard. The Hawaiian brusquely nodded and focused on the horizon. Becky shifted her gaze to Crandall. He beamed at her, drawing her closer.

"Is that the sunset?" she asked.

Crandall laughed, white teeth flashing in an auburn beard. "That's the sunrise. East. We're heading east, sweetheart."

"I remember it being daylight when we left the beach."

"It was," bellowed Crandall above the wind. "You've been sleeping for two days. Don't worry about it. You were exhausted."

She shook her head in disbelief. Ten minutes passed. "I'm cold," she said, pulling the robe tighter. "I should change."

"Go below. I laid out clothes on the bunk across from yours. Put away what you don't use in the waterproof locker beneath the berth. All your gear is there. Your new passport and money are in the safe. I stowed those other things you wanted in the fo'c'sle. You can pull them out later and get to work once you get your sea legs. Now go get dressed."

She rose in a crouch, unsteady. Holding onto railings, she reached for the open hatch. Becky turned at the top of the ladder, smiled at Crandall. "Thanks for everything."

"Hey, it was mostly your money that got us here. You paid for *Sunshine*'s refit. And by the way, thanks for the new set of sails you bought. I ordered them from Lee's Sails in Hong Kong in February. They were waiting for us in Lae."

"I'm glad it worked out. Okay, I won't be long. Don't go anywhere."

Crandall roared with laughter. "No worry about that happening. We're gonna see a lot of each other for the next few months." The corner of her eyes caught Kalani watching them. He abruptly shot a glance at the telltails in the billowing mainsail. When he looked again, Becky was gone.

Crouching at the open hatch, Crandall shouted after her. "Might want to slip into a windbreaker, too. You're gonna get wet up here. Can't avoid it. That's a downside to sailing. Wet things never dry out. You'll have to get used to it." Returning to the cockpit, he gestured to Kalani at the helm. "Want me to spell you for a while?"

Waving away the offer, Kalani grinned. "Having too much fun, brah. You go take care of the lady, eh?"

"Okay, man. You got it. I'm cooking tonight, don't forget. You'll love it."

"As long as it ain't noodles again."

Crandall feigned hurt. "We have a half-ton of those to go through yet, Kalani. And I can't promise you dinner won't have Spam in it."

"You know Spam's always okay with me, Skipper."

Heading for the hatchway, Crandall paused, looked back at his helmsman. "Gonna be something special for our guest's first meal on board, you know."

"Surprise me."

"Oh, I will. You sure you're okay for now?"

"Easy. Go do what you gotta do. I'm good."

That evening after dinner, when Crandall had cleaned the galley and put away the dishes, he poured two glasses of red wine. Kalani was at the helm. With mainsail and jib set, *Sunshine* was practically steering herself on a moonlit sea.

The lovers sat across from each other at the polished mahogany table in the cabin, melodious slack-key music wafting up the companionway to the deck. The overhead lights were dimmed. After sipping from his goblet, Crandall lowered the glass, stroked Becky's hand. "In the next few weeks it's going to seem like I'm pounding a lot of sailing stuff into your head for my own amusement. Not so."

"I know that, Rick. You want me to know what to do."

"True. But you don't realize that we're in a bit of a bind here. Sailing a boat this size with just three of us is not the safest way to do it. I know some people who do this all the time, couples I mean. But it's not prudent. We've been blessed with good weather so far. But one of these days or nights we're going to run into foul weather. I thought we were going to have five of us to handle the boat..."

Interrupting, her expression pained, Becky said, "I'm sorry about what happened..."

"I'm not blaming you. I'm just telling you we're going to have to rely on you more in the coming weeks. I think you'll do well, considering."

"Considering what...?"

"That you've never been on open water."

"I'm a survivor. I can be tough if I have to be."

"Yeah, I know. You don't have to prove anything to me, Becky. That's a quality that I love about you. But we're going to have to step up your duties."

"Which means what?"

Crandall took a long swallow of wine. "It means we've got to get you to do real sailing. It's one thing to have you take day watches when the seas cooperate. I'm right there if you get into trouble. But handling sails and making quick, correct decisions automatically so they become second nature, that's the goal. Even getting to the point where you could sail alone if you had to…that's what we'll shoot for."

"I wouldn't want to keep going without you."

Taking her hands in his, Crandall gazed into Becky's eyes. "I know. But realistically you'd have to be able to do it. That has to be your target, okay?"

Finishing her wine, Becky eyed him over the rim of her glass. "So when do we have to do this…training?"

"We'll start tomorrow morning. Couple more weeks like this and we'll make landfall at Port Vila, Vanuatu's capital. We'll take turns with Kalani, decompressing on shore. He needs a break, too." Pointing at some imaginary point across the cabin, Crandall finished with, "After Vanuatu we'll hit Fiji, then Samoa. From there it'll be a long slog across a lot of green to get to South America. Lot of water in between. Anything could happen. You have to be prepared."

Becky stared at the table. Reaching for her hands again, Crandall tried to soften the weight of his words. "Didn't mean to scare you with all this heavy talk…"

"Well, you sure did a good job of it."

"I just want to make sure you know what we're facing."

"Thanks. But seriously, could we change the subject?"

"Sure. You wanna play chess? Cribbage? Watch a DVD?"

"No. Besides, you should sleep. You have to relieve Kalani in two hours."

"Won't be able to sleep now. I'll be thinking of the look on your face when I finished my 'scare the new crew member' talk."

She laughed. "Maybe I'll turn in early," she said. "That way I could keep you company when you take your turn on watch later tonight." Easing from behind the table, Crandall leaned down and kissed Becky. He took the wine glasses to the sink, washed them, put them away, and went up on deck to chat with Kalani.

Returning below, Crandall killed the lights, leaving only red bulbs burning in the galley, head, and navigation station. He made preparations for bed. He found Becky in his berth, a sheet gathered to her chin, naked shoulders showing.

Grinning mischievously, she held a finger to her lips, nodding at the ladder to the deck. "Perhaps," she cooed softly, "the captain would like some company before he takes over the helm."

Stripping off his T-shirt and shorts, Crandall turned up the CD player's volume and wiggled under the coverlet, whispering, "Perhaps the captain would."

....

Chapter 62

8° 59′ S, 150° 29′ E

In dawn's dim light, Becky came bearing gifts. Holding two mugs of honeyed tea spiced with lemon wedges, she made her way topside to join Crandall in the cool morning. Becky offered him a kiss and one of the teas. He took both. She put a hand on the tiller. "Morning, Captain, sleep well last night?"

Sitting back, Crandall took the mug. "I dreamed there was a woman in my bunk who looked a lot like you."

"Really? Is that a good sign?"

"Yep. Hard to separate fantasy from reality though."

Sipping their tea, the two huddled together at the stern. Under full sail, with a steady twenty-knot wind off the starboard beam, *Sunshine* knifed easily through blue-green chop. In the pale light, Becky used binoculars to spot several islands dotting the northern horizon. Unlike the rugged hills of New Guinea, these were low-lying silhouettes trimmed with palms.

Following her gaze, Crandall said, "Those are the Trobiands. Look south and you might be able to see Goodenough Island, part of the D'entrecasteaux group."

"Will we be stopping there?"

"No. They're in PNG territorial waters. As long as we're making progress, we'll stay the course. We've only made 200 nautical miles. I aim to get us as far as Vanuatu, another two weeks at the most. It's a tropical paradise. You'll love it, I promise. We'll all be due a little rest and relaxation by then."

"I'll be up for that. I already feel like I've been on *Sunshine* for months."

Shaking his head, smiling, Crandall turned to Becky. "Bored? You still have a lot to learn about bluewater sailing, lady. You know, some sailors would be superstitious about having a woman on board."

"You're superstitious."

"I am?"

"Yeah. I've watched you. You whisper new compass headings and you don't talk out loud about the w…"

Interrupting, Crandall quickly put a finger to Becky's lips. "Shhh, I know what you were about to say…don't. Call it a sailor's habit, tradition, but not superstition. There's a difference as far as I'm concerned."

She gave his finger a playful nip. "What about having a woman on board. Kalani says it's bad luck."

"Aw, that's old school. Lots of women do deep-water cruising these days. We'll see our share before we're done. Hey, I'm captain and I'm not superstitious about having a woman on board

Sunshine. Matter of fact, I think it's a great idea. Makes the skipper happy and gives the crew something to talk about."

"And what if the crew gets jealous?"

"Ah, then we might have a problem."

"You think Kalani's jealous?" she said teasingly.

"About us? Are you serious?"

"Yes." Eyeing Crandall over the rim of her porcelain mug, Becky added, "I've seen him watching us. You're like most guys, oblivious to that sort of thing until it gets out of hand. But he's not happy about my being on *Sunshine*."

"Hey, it's much too early in the morning for serious conversation. Kalani usually keeps his emotions close to the vest, but don't go looking for a problem where none exists." Crandall handed his mug to Becky and made a minor adjustment to the mainsail's trim. Satisfied, he reached for his tea and resumed talking. "When one third of the crew is female there's bound to be some friction."

"Like 'three's a crowd' or 'three on a match'?"

"I promise to do my part to make sure public displays of affection don't get out of hand. Wouldn't want to disturb the rest of the crew."

"I wouldn't mind," she purred, curling next to him.

"You're pretty forward for someone so young."

Laughing, she tousled his hair. "And you haven't changed since Florida. You sailors are all alike."

"You keep saying that. Go below and make breakfast, woman."

"Sexist pig."

"Turnabout is fair play. I cooked dinner last night, remember?"

Sighing, Becky leaned over Crandall, her hands digging into his thighs. She threw him a wistful look. "Yes, and it was wonderful, Skipper Rick. Especially the dessert. I'd like to order that again, please…soon."

Blushing, Crandall threw up his hands. "You're incorrigible, girl."

"And you love it."

"Yeah, I do. I love it. Love you."

Pausing at the hatchway, Becky said, "I'll call you when it's ready."

"I'm not going anywhere. Wake Kalani for chow. He's got the next watch."

"Let him sleep. I'll take over for him." She disappeared below. Crandall heard her humming softly as she started breakfast. He smiled to himself. *Things were going smoothly. They had a good wind, the sky was favorable, the seas perfect.* He thought these things but did not say them aloud—his sailor's habit.

Stretching out on the cockpit's port side bench, Crandall listened to waves slap against the hull. He lay back, feeling the sun on his face. Kalani was sleeping below. *Sunshine* was set on a broad reach course to take advantage of a steady wind. After breakfast, Becky took the tiller, marveling at the sight of the main and foresail harnessing the wind's power.

In the following days, Crandall initiated her schooling in basic seamanship. He taught her to read charts and set compass headings. He got her to memorize a mariner's dictionary of nautical terms and patiently explained the power and capriciousness of the southeast trades. A fast learner, Becky got her sea legs in days, not weeks. She was soon taking turns at the helm in daylight hours under Crandall's watchful eyes, parroting words back to him in daily topside lessons. At the end of two weeks, she was able to run through her list flawlessly. "Clew, foot, tack, leech, luff, head, sheet, shroud."

"Good. Now I'll give you definitions, you give me the right word. Ready?" Rolling her eyes, Becky nodded and Crandall began. "Top corner of a sail, forward lower corner of a sail, trailing edge of a sail."

"Head, tack, and leech." Clapping his hands in delight, Crandall continued. "Lines used to hoist sails. Lines used to trim the mainsail."

"Halyards. Mainsheet."

"Terrific. I'll make a sailor out of you yet."

"My head hurts. Can we do recess now?" Laughing, Crandall put his arms around the novice, kissing her. "Recess it is." He nestled beside her in the shade of the boat's blue Bimini top. After several minutes he said, "Feel like talking about what happened back there in PNG?"

"I guess. What do you want to know?"

"What about the two who were with you, the brothers? The guys you said would sail with us?"

"Not much to tell, really. We all went into this whole thing not really knowing how dangerous it was. We were pretty naive. They kept telling me they didn't think we'd find anything, that this was some sort of fantasy I had. It was a gamble. We knew that going in."

"You weren't really sure yourself, were you?"

Glancing at Crandall, Becky sighed, remembering being plagued with doubts about the outcome. "I guess I convinced myself that it had to be true. My life was going nowhere. I wanted to get out of my rut so bad I believed we'd find the gold. I willed it to be there."

"Okay, you found your treasure. What went wrong?"

"The Australians with us turned out to be crooks. The backer who financed my trip told me they were there to protect his investment in the expedition. I thought they were there to scout

out the wrecks for possible salvage. Turns out they were there for the gold after all."

"Maybe. But the market for authentic WWII airplanes is hot these days."

"I know, but that was just a cover story. I should have figured out early on they weren't really serious about filming. Thinking back I can see they were just playing along with that whole phony camera thing to make us all less suspicious."

"You told me in your email you didn't know who hired them, who put up the money for your trip."

"That's right. I met someone who worked for him. He was kinda scary, actually. But I never found out who was really funding me. The guy wouldn't tell me the name of his boss."

"Any danger this mysterious money man will come looking for you? Maybe send his hired gun to get his investment back?"

"Why would he bother if he thinks I've disappeared?"

"He doesn't know that for sure. If those Aussies find a way out, they may get word to him that you outfoxed them. So far, he's out his seed money and the gold. A man with that kind of power is not likely to let you get away with it."

Bristling defiantly, Becky said, "He has to find me first. Nobody knows about you and me…or the *Sunshine*. No one knows I survived."

Crandall hugged her. "That's my girl." He shifted on the padded bench. "Let me take over for a while. Keep talking." Crandall eased Becky from the tiller. "Tell me what happened to the Lindquists. Why weren't they at the landing zone?"

A moment of silence passed. Becky's eyes watered. "I never thought it would end the way it did. I mean, we were doing fine. We got away okay. David even insisted we stop to cut down a bridge so we couldn't be trailed."

"Smart thing to do if you're being chased."

Shaking her head, Becky continued. "It wasn't part of the plan, but yeah, it made sense. Bought us some time. That's when the Aussies caught us. One of them shot David. We didn't know it right away, so we kept going. David got us to the river just before he died." She paused, wiped her eyes with the hem of her T-shirt, then continued. "We couldn't carry him with us. Had to leave him. We took his personal effects and the vest and kept going."

"You had no choice. It would have slowed you down," agreed Crandall.

"I know. But it seems so heartless now."

Crandall gave the helm to Becky. "Hold that thought." He went below for two bottles of water and came up on deck. "Kalani's dead to the world," he reported, handing her a chilled bottle. "Gonna let him sleep." Crandall took a long swallow of water. "Leaving David was tough but smart. I would've done the same."

"You're just trying to make me feel better."

"No, really, you did the right thing. So you were down to the two of you… this other guy…"

"David's brother, Darryl."

"So, you and Darryl got to the river. Is that when you called?"

"Yeah. We were going to cross first, then call, but I wanted to make sure you were coming. Halfway across the river I got pulled under. Darryl saved me. I got to shore but he got caught in the current."

"That was it?"

"No. I hiked downstream. Thought he might have come ashore. I found him but he was hurt bad…real bad." She paused again, searching for words. "I…took the vests…had to. He was in terrible shape. Couldn't walk. Tried to pull him to shore but he got caught in the current again. I never saw him after that. There's no way he could have survived in that river."

"Not without a raft or life jacket," Crandall said, downing half his water. "Then there are the crocodiles." Shuddering at the thought, Becky shook her head. Crandall asked, "What was your plan if these two guys had made it out? I planned for three of you. Extra rations, spare clothing. Would have been good to have more hands on board."

"I said I was sorry."

"Not your fault. On the plus side, we're loaded with extra food and water. We'll just have to get by without your friends. But I'm curious. How were you going to deal with them once we left PNG?"

"Didn't think that far ahead. Just thought beyond getting out and reconnecting with you. I figured they were just going to have to go their own way once we got to the states. Not much of a plan, huh?"

"Not when two of the guys you were counting on don't make it. I still can't believe you pulled it off." Nodding, she stared at the waves, avoiding his eyes.

"I find it hard to accept what's happened. Those two..."

"But you completed your mission, right, Becky? Against all odds, you succeeded. You survived."

"I guess."

Pulling her to him, Crandall kissed her forehead, cupped Becky's face in his hands. "I have to be honest with you, sweetheart. No one, myself included, would have given you a snowball's chance in hell to pull this off. I wasn't even sure if I was going to see you. The best scenario I hoped for was getting you back and nothing more. You've earned every penny of what you brought out. No one can take that away from you. You do understand that, don't you?"

Mustering a tearful nod, Becky closed her eyes, speaking softly. "Funny, I never thought I'd do this. Then, out of the blue,

I was given more than enough money to make this trip. When I was figuring out how to get the gold out, I thought of you and your sailboat. But what I really wanted was to find you again. I didn't have a clue if this was going to work, Rick. Didn't know where you were or if you'd be interested. All I really wanted was another chance with you. I would have given up every bit of that gold just to be with you again. That's what I dreamed of more than anything. I just didn't want it to happen under these circumstances…but it did. I can live with that if I know you're going to be part of my life."

Crandall, one hand on the tiller, drew her against his chest, absorbing her sobbing, his eyes moistening. "Well, you've got both of us in a helluva fix, Becky. In the middle of the South Pacific, a cargo of government gold, a short-handed crew, and no plan other than getting home. And when we do get there, we might end up with some mysterious, pissed-off Daddy Warbucks who wants his money back. Then what will we do?"

"I'm sorry, so sorry, Rick. Really, I am. I had no right to drag you into this."

"Well, sweet lady, not exactly. I went into this with eyes wide open. Let's make up our minds right now to finish this adventure of yours—ours—by getting your treasure back home. I'll be with you every minute of every hour, of every day. What more could a sailor want other than a good ship, a beautiful woman, and treasure?"

"How about a safe voyage?" sobbed Becky, smiling through tears.

"Absolutely. Definitely that. Look, we can do this together. I let you get away once. I'm not going to let that happen again. You can take that to the bank."

She kissed him. "Along with the gold."

Laughing, he wrapped both arms around her. "Yeah, along with the gold."

Exhausted by Becky's cathartic confession, they clung to each other for the better part of an hour without speaking. Crandall's gentle, curious probing had opened a floodgate of emotions neither of them anticipated. Their time alone drew them closer, something they would discover in the weeks ahead. They let Kalani sleep through his watch, reluctant to break whatever spell had taken hold of them.

....

Chapter 63

Cannon Falls, Minnesota, June 15

Morris crashed for a week when he got home. The following Monday, he began working the phones. One call was to his local clinic, arranging a visit to follow up Dorothy Wood's doctoring. The wound was tender but healing. Morris wanted to be sure he was on the mend.

A second call went to the cell phone number Becky had been using since their first meeting. He got what he expected—a canned response. "The person you are calling is unavailable. At the sound of the tone, please record your message. When you are finished recording…" Hanging up, he next dialed information to troll for St. Cloud listings belonging to the Lindquist brothers.

No Darryl in the book, but Morris found numbers for two David Lindquists and tried both. The first call connected with a beleaguered woman with infants wailing in the background. Her husband was a National Guard sergeant on assignment with the

Red Bulls. Apologizing, Morris moved on to the second number. After six rings, a familiar voice came on the line. "Hi, this is David. Not at home. Leave a message and I'll get back to you…maybe. Just kidding. Or, try me at work at…" Morris jotted down the number for calling later.

A final call to Terry, Brad Wood's California contact, bore fruit. The same day Morris cleared Australian airspace, the missionary had emailed an introduction to the aircraft researcher in the event Morris called. Without going into details, Morris identified himself and jotted down contact information for Becky Peterson. Running through a short version of the PNG expedition, Morris begged off the call with a promise of a future update. He looked at the address he had been given. *So, it's Upsala just like it said on Peterson's dog tag. Becky said she lived in St. Cloud,* he thought to himself.

Rifling through his desk's junk drawer, Morris pulled out a dog-eared Minnesota map, checked the list of towns, and discovered Upsala. *Huh, not that far from St. Cloud, after all. Close enough. Maybe she had told the truth about where she lived. Other than the new address, all he had was a post office box number in St. Cloud. Shouldn't be hard to run that down. I can try the Upsala phone number later.*

The phone rang. His clinic's nurse was calling. There had been a cancellation. If he could come within the hour his doctor would see him. Putting aside the hunt for Becky and the Lindquists, Morris agreed.

The next day, Morris awoke early and tried David Lindquist's work number after breakfast. A woman who answered said he was on an extended leave from the assistant manager's job. No one at the St. Cloud restaurant could tell him where Lindquist had gone or when he was due back. Morris tried David's home phone but hung up when the familiar recorded message started.

Since Becky's cell was a dead end, he tried the number the California source had given him. A robotic female voice answered after five rings, repeating the number called but giving no names.

Time to take a drive to Upsala, thought Morris. He drove north on Highway 52 toward St. Paul, crossed the Mississippi River into downtown, and picked up westbound Interstate 94. Approaching Minneapolis's glass-sheathed skyline, Morris recrossed the river's loop and headed northwest. He drove for an hour, stopped for gas in St. Cloud, and left the interstate at Albany, a sleepy town dominated by a massive brick church with soaring spire. His GPS ordered him due north on a two-lane road running through thirsty cornfields shimmering in a Grant Wood landscape.

Slowing as he entered Upsala, Morris counted one school, a silver water tower, and three churches—Covenant, Lutheran, and Catholic. Brutal summer heat baked the town, turning Upsala into a ghost town. On a deserted main street, an American flag hung limply at the post office. A dog napped in a patch of shade and a sweating bank sign lazily blinked ninety-two degrees at one o'clock. Morris drove through the heart of town without seeing another soul.

At the north end of Upsala, he finally spotted signs of life at a gas station and stopped for information. A pimply teen manning the counter proved worthless, but the attendant's lone groupie—a pale, long-haired Scandinavian beauty sucking on a cola—volunteered directions to the Peterson house on nearby Pine Lake. Back in his pickup, Morris scanned the GPS and drove northwest, following the animated arrow on the screen. Winding his way to the north end of the lake, Morris passed summer homes screened by dark woods to his right. As directed, he turned on a gravel road carved through leafy stands of hardwood and pine. Slowing the pickup, he crept up a long driveway shaded by towering oaks. A white van sat in the open mouth of a two-car garage. Morris killed the engine, got out, and was greeted by a galloping dog hurtling through the forest on his left. The mutt circled him, tail wagging. "Hey, boy," said Morris, "you my welcoming committee?"

"Hello! Can I help you?" The voice belonged to a lean man in khaki shorts and white T-shirt, who jogged down a gravel spur leading to a house next door. Morris stroked the panting dog's head and raised a hand. "Yeah, I'm looking for the Peterson place. Am I in the right spot?"

Nodding at the house behind Morris, the man motioned for his dog to heel. Wary, the new arrival thrust out his hand. "You got it. John Soderlund. My wife and I live next door. What can I do for you?"

"Dale Morris." The men shook hands. "I'm looking for Becky Peterson."

Tilting his head as if he had not heard correctly, the neighbor parroted, "Becky Peterson?"

"Yeah. Becky Peterson. You know her?"

Soderlund squinted at Morris. "Well, yeah. You sure you have the right Becky Peterson?"

Curious at the doubt in the voice, Morris rubbed his jaw, tried again. "Becky Peterson. I was told she lived in Upsala."

"Yes, she does…or rather, did. She's deceased."

Morris was taken aback. "Huh, that's news to me. You apparently know more than I do. I thought if she had family I might talk to them. Maybe share some information they may not have heard."

"John, what's going on? Is there a problem?" Behind the two, a door creaked open. Both men turned to face a stern middle-aged woman peering from the threshold.

Smiling, Soderlund waved. "No problem, Mrs. Larson." He

gestured to Morris. "This gentleman—Mr. Morris—is looking for Becky's family."

"Oh, yes. Well, what does he want?"

Morris took a step toward the porch. "I have some details about her disappearance the family may not know."

"Disappearance? You mean death, don't you? Oh well, I suppose you might as well come in. It's much too hot to be standing out there all day. Barbara's on the screened porch, finishing lunch. I'll tell her you're here. Mind you, don't tire her." She beckoned to them and went inside, the screen door slapping behind her.

Arching a bushy eyebrow, Soderlund whispered, "Amy Larson, Barbara's caregiver. The gatekeeper who eats visitors alive. Hard of hearing and a bit overbearing, but she means well. She's been a godsend to Barbara." Trailed by the dog, the two climbed the stairs together. "Would you have any objection to my sitting in, Mr. Morris? My wife and I were close to Becky and her mom." It was not a question.

"Fine with me. I wasn't aware her mother was alive."

"Barbara had a rough time with the news of Becky's death," cautioned Soderlund. "Her health is still quite fragile. It was touch and go for months after the accident. For a while we thought we'd lose her. She's only been home for two weeks, you know."

"What exactly are you referring to?" Morris asked.

"The automobile accident. The drunk driver who rear-ended them in Sauk Rapids. You said you had details."

Pausing just inside the doorway, Morris lowered his voice. "Maybe there's been a mistake. I'm not here about an accident. I'm here to talk about Lloyd Peterson, Becky's grandfather, the Army flier from WWII."

A light went on in Soderlund's eyes. "Oh, you mean Barbara's father, the pilot who disappeared in the Pacific during the war."

Seizing on the neighbor's remark, Morris offered one detail. "New Guinea actually. I was unaware he had a daughter. It was actually his granddaughter, Becky, who asked me to join the group who went there to find his plane."

"Well, now I'm the one who's confused, Mr. Morris. You aren't with an insurance company or some law firm?"

"No. I'm here to report on Becky's disappearance."

"You keep referring to her disappearance, not her death. No offense, but you're not making sense, Mr. Morris." The pair entered the front hall with its view of the lake and heard Mrs. Larson call from a screened porch, beyond the kitchen. Soderlund ordered his dog to curl at his feet. Before Morris had a chance to focus on what the man had said about not making sense, Mrs. Larson appeared, brusquely summoning them to the porch. "You mustn't keep Barbara waiting."

Soderlund obediently led the way to a pale figure in a wheelchair. He leaned down and gently kissed her cheek. "Afternoon, Barbara."

A nod and a reedy voice came from a seated woman who looked to be in her early seventies with short, thinning gray hair. "How nice of you to visit, John. Who is your friend? Not another doctor, I hope." Her comment drew a chuckle from Soderlund.

Morris's eyes were drawn to a wicked-looking pink scar wandering along the old woman's hairline from the top of her forehead to lower left jawbone. A plastic splint, molded to prevent fingers from curling into a claw, encased her left hand. Despite her condition, the wounded woman managed a wan smile when Mrs. Larson introduced their visitor. Waving Morris forward, she announced, "This is Mr. Morris, Barbara."

"Dale Morris," he said. "Thank you for agreeing to see me, Ms…Peterson?"

A flicker of a smile passed across the woman's colorless lips.

"Oh, I haven't been called Peterson in years, young man. My married name is Wickstrom, but please, Barbara will do just as well."

"Okay, Barbara it is."

Soderlund and Morris drew up two chairs across from their host. The older woman smoothed the silk gathered in her lap and cleared her throat. "Amy said you might have details of Becky's death. If you had come a month earlier I wouldn't have been able to listen to a word."

Plunging ahead, Morris started with, "I have to confess that in talking with your neighbor here, I find myself turned around a bit." Three pairs of curious eyes trained on Morris. "Am I correct that you are the daughter of Lieutenant Lloyd Peterson who disappeared in 1944 over New Guinea?"

"Yes, you are correct, Mr. Morris. Sadly, however, I never knew my father. He disappeared before I was born and my mother remarried after the war. I kept the name Peterson until I married Dean Wickstrom in 1977. He was a wonderful husband and father. It's been…how long since Dean's death, Amy?"

"Ten years," snapped the caregiver.

"About Lloyd Peterson's granddaughter " began Morris.

"My Becky," interrupted the figure in the wheelchair. "Lovely girl. So caring. The light of my life after Dean died. Amy said you had details of her…death. I remember nothing of the accident, you know."

Casting his eyes toward Soderlund for help, Morris found none there. Leaning forward expectantly, the crippled woman waited. Eyeing Morris suspiciously, Amy Larson, meaty arms folded across her chest, hovered protectively at Barbara's side.

"Perhaps you can help me out here," pleaded Morris. "I traveled to Papua New Guinea in May to confirm that your father's plane had been found."

An audible gasp escaped from the patient. "You were able

to find his aircraft after all these years? Amy, did you hear that? How wonderful. Did you by chance locate any…were there…"

"Remains?" blurted Morris. "Not exactly, Ma'am. I'll get to that. I brought photos of the plane as we found it. Serial numbers we were able to read on pieces of the airframe confirm it as your father's plane. There were faint traces of paint on the fuselage reading *Home Run*. Squadron records say that was the name of your father's aircraft. As far as remains…we did bring back a collection of bones local natives gave us. There's a strong possibility they may belong to your father. However, another plane had crashed in the same area and that crew's bones may be mixed with his. That happens in some of these cases. Those will be turned over to the U.S. government. At some point you may be contacted to volunteer a DNA sample to help confirm your father's identity."

A moan escaped the immobile woman. "Not another test. Mr. Morris. I've been probed, prodded, and bled enough in my lifetime for two people."

"I've heard it's quite harmless, Barbara," soothed her caretaker. "No more than a mouth swab probably."

"She's right," agreed Morris. "Really very simple if next of kin are available. The Joint POW/MIA Accounting Command—JPAC—runs a forensics lab in Hawaii that does amazing work with MIA and POW remains these days. They're the final word in a situation like this."

She softened. "Maybe that kind of a test would be okay."

Breaking into the conversation, Soderlund badgered Morris. "But what about Becky? You were asking about Becky Peterson. What's that all about?"

Morris stared at the lazy ceiling fan turning above him, carefully choosing his words. He focused on the wheelchair-bound woman. "Ma'am, I was contacted by Becky Peterson to accompany her to Papua New Guinea—PNG—to find her grandfather's airplane. She and two friends from St. Cloud flew with me to Australia and then New Guinea to locate the airplane."

Leaping to his feet, Soderlund sputtered, "Ridiculous!"

Stunned by the man's outburst, Morris shut down. Barbara Peterson stiffened.

Mrs. Larson's icy glare riveted Morris to his chair.

Crossing the room, Soderlund loomed over their visitor, his face beet red. "Why would you come here with a tale like that? You're way out of line!"

"Perhaps you've said enough, Mr. Morris!" bellowed the nurse. "You're upsetting Barbara unnecessarily."

Bounding into the room, the big Lab added its bark to the loud voices. Morris stood, hands raised, recoiling from Soderlund. By sheer will, Barbara brought the room under control, her shrill voice cutting through the din, her frail arms waving wildly for attention. Sanity temporarily restored, she motioned for everyone to sit. Calmly, she turned to Morris, asking haltingly, "When exactly did you…meet my daughter?"

"January of this year."

"Impossible!" barked Mrs. Larson. "Barbara, you don't have to listen to this."

Waving aside her nurse, the chair-bound woman pressed Morris to answer. "How did you meet?"

"She called me about going to PNG to find her grandfather's P-38 Lightning. A missionary had found the plane. Becky said she talked to a military researcher in California who put her in touch with a search group. That's how she got my name. I've made trips before with this group to specifically search for old wrecks from the war."

"And did you meet with her to plan this exploration?"

"I did, ma'am, several times. I was reluctant to make the

journey at first, but she was very persistent. Kept at it until I agreed to accompany her."

"You're absolutely certain this was in January?"

Morris went over the dates in his mind before speaking. "Yes, early January, then several follow-up meetings to keep things moving along. At one point, she introduced me to her two friends, the Lindquist brothers."

"That's it, Barbara!" boomed Soderlund. "The Lindquists! You know what he's saying don't you? It has to be…"

Ignoring the outburst, Barbara waved for silence, asking, "Can you describe my daughter, Mr. Morris?" He closed his eyes to conjure Becky's image. "About five-three, long dark hair, which she changed to a spiky blonde hairdo a month before we left. Striking blue eyes. Very attractive girl. I say girl, but she told me she was thirty-five. Certainly didn't look her age."

The frail woman raised her hand. "Please stop, Mr. Morris. I've heard enough." Signaling her helper to her side, the women whispered softly. Morris, perplexed, wary, watched Mrs. Larson waddle from the room and disappear down a hallway. On Morris's left, a seething John Soderlund rose, pacing nervously.

Returning with a thick photo album under her arm, the nursemaid marched onto the porch, glaring at Morris. She set the leather-bound volume on her charge's lap and took up position opposite Morris like a prison guard flanking a condemned man.

Gripping the book with her good hand, Barbara Wickstrom locked eyes with Morris. "You are no doubt surprised by my friends' tempers. You must forgive their outrage. They have my best interests at heart. They watch over me to make sure I continue healing." Glancing at her friends as if absolving each in turn, she returned her attention to the bewildered Morris.

"It is obvious to me, sir, that you are unaware that you could not possibly have met with my Becky in January as you have said. My daughter died the previous November in the same crash that has confined me to this chair. Becky has been in her grave these past eight months."

"I'm sorry, in no way did I..."

She held up her right hand, cutting him off. "Let me finish, please. I want to show you a picture, Mr. Morris. Take a very close look and tell me what you see."

Slowly, Morris got up from his chair and knelt to study the glossy pages held in front of him. After several minutes, he got to his feet, leaned over the thin woman, and pointed to a smiling young woman in the front row of a girl's volleyball team. "This," he said, "is Becky Peterson. As I told you, we first met in January."

"Are you sure?"

"Absolutely positive. It's the same woman who flew to Papua New Guinea with me in May."

Sighing, as though air was escaping from deep within her, the woman gently closed the leather book, her lined face squeezed in pain, her eyes moist. "That girl, Mr. Morris, is not my daughter."

....

Chapter 64

"I don't understand," sputtered Morris. "I know this woman. You don't travel together and endure the hardships we did without knowing the person. I'm telling you THAT is the Becky Peterson I know."

"Try again. This time take a good look at the girl in the back row, top right."

He drew his finger across the page to the first teenager he

had identified as Becky Peterson. "That's odd. This girl…here… they could be twins. It's uncanny. I'm not sure."

Barbara closed her eyes, a wan smile formed. "That girl in the back row IS my daughter, Mr. Morris. This is the only photo album I have left."

Returning to his chair without saying a word, Morris sank down, eyes on the floor, dumbfounded. It was finally Soderlund's turn. Speaking with icy calm he said, "Actually, you've done us a favor, Morris. You're due an apology. It's obvious what's happened here. You've been duped. Fooled. Scammed."

"Now wait a minute," bristled Morris. Retreating, Soderlund forced a smile. "Don't be offended. You're not the only one here who's been conned."

"What John is trying to say, Mr. Morris, is that the woman you picked out as my daughter is actually Rebecca Lund, Becky if you prefer. She answered to that as well. She has lived in my home for these past four years. She was a dear girl, a very close friend of my daughter's. When she was about five, her parents were killed in a house fire in Albany. She came to live here in Upsala with her grandmother, a friend of my mother's. When her grandmother died, Rebecca came to live with us. It was better than having her get caught up in that whole foster home system. You have to understand, the girls shared the same first name, were the same age, had attended the same schools since elementary school and went to the same high school. Have you ever had the kind of friend who sometimes finished your sentences, liked the same movies you did, the same books, played on the same teams in high school?"

"What exactly are you trying tell me, Ms. Wickstrom?"

"Those two girls were inseparable." Lowering her head, the

invalided woman wept. Her nurse moved to comfort her. "Barbara, you don't have to go on."

"No, no. We must clear up this misunderstanding for our guest, Amy. He deserves answers as much as we do. But I'm tiring. You and John tell him the rest."

The nursemaid gently laid a hand on her friend's shrunken shoulder. "Rebecca Lund was always just a bit wilder than our Becky. Came from a troubled family. She married Darryl Lindquist six years ago…"

"What!" Morris came out of his chair. "Are you saying she was married to Darryl Lindquist? The same Darryl who came on the trip to PNG?"

"I assume he is the same person. You mentioned his brother, David, correct?"

"Yes. Same last name. Look, they didn't hide the fact they were brothers. But none of them volunteered the fact that she was married to Darryl."

"Not married long," Soderlund interjected, "they divorced after one year. Rumor had it he was an alcoholic."

"He was certainly that," added Mrs. Larson venomously.

Despite obvious fatigue, Barbara took up the story again. "As John said, don't feel too badly, Mr. Morris. We were all taken in. My daughter and I opened our home to Rebecca when she divorced the Lindquist boy. She had nowhere else to go at the time. We loved having her with us again. She was good for my Becky and my daughter was good for Rebecca. We were a perfect trio. Those girls made this house a happy place."

Soderlund brought the story telling back to reality. "And then the accident."

"Yes," sighed Barbara, "the accident. Becky was killed and I was in the hospital for a long time. From there, I had to go to Sisters of Mercy to begin my recovery."

"It's a rehabilitation facility in Albany, south of here," Mrs. Larson explained. "You were in pretty bad shape, Barbara. More bad days than good until a month ago."

"Yes. If it hadn't been for Rebecca I wouldn't have made it. She took over the house, helped arrange the funeral, and visited me almost daily as I healed."

"So what happened?" Morris's question hung in the humid air.

Deferring to Soderlund, both women turned in his direction. "Rebecca had a visitor around the first of the year. Guy shows up one night in a black SUV. I saw him. Rebecca was at work. I called her to let her know about her caller. She said she would make sure everything was on the up and up. She checked him out and called me to say it was okay."

"Do you remember what she said about him?" asked Morris.

"According to her, the guy was kinda arrogant, pushy. I thought maybe he was FBI or some sort of cop. A Fed. Maybe ex-military. I figured it had something to do with Darryl, her ex. He was always screwing up. 'Wasn't that,' she said. They talked for two hours and then he left. She told me he was there to talk about family business."

"Huh, then shortly after that she calls me out of the blue," added Morris.

"She never said a word about you," snorted Soderlund. "I had no idea she had gone to New Guinea. Until you drove up, none of us had a clue that's where she'd gone."

Mrs. Larson put a protective arm around her friend. "She was so good about visiting Barbara all those months. Then, one day she announced she was going back east for two weeks to take care of some family business. What family? What business? She just disappeared. Left her job at the market."

"Here one day, gone the next," sighed Barbara.

Morris was sorting out the information. "How about you, Mr. Soderlund? What did she tell you?"

"Pretty much what Amy said. When time passed and she didn't return, we called the county sheriff's office. Talked with a deputy. He wasn't much help. Said it didn't sound like a missing persons report. Said she'd probably turn up eventually. His opinion was that stress made her run. What with Barbara needing all that care, and taking care of the property, it made sense."

"And there was Darryl, of course," growled Mrs. Larson.

"True," Soderlund continued. "Darryl is enough to make anyone want to disappear. Always phoning her at odd hours, leaving harassing messages…or drunken crybaby stuff. She played some of the calls for my wife and me. Actually, once we figured out she wasn't coming back, my wife and I made arrangements with Amy to take over Barbara's recovery. I mean, Judy and I helped out a lot at first, but without Amy being here it wouldn't have worked."

The invalid reached out to stroke her caretaker's hand. "I'm blessed, Mr. Morris. I'd still be in long-term rehab at the Sisters of Mercy campus in Albany if it hadn't been for the Soderlunds and Amy."

"Seems like we've been talking for hours," scolded Mrs. Larson. "How about some iced tea and snacks?" Getting to his feet, Morris stifled a yawn. "Sounds good. I'm pretty thirsty even though you folks have been doing most of the talking."

Thrusting hands in his pockets, Soderlund cocked his head at Morris. "I'd say we're due some enlightenment from you. Your turn on the hot seat. Tell us what you know, since you're the last one here to see Rebecca…Becky."

"Fair enough. Where would you like me to start?"

A voice from the wheelchair. "Tell us about finding my father's plane. What happened after that?" Appearing in the doorway with a tray of glasses, pitchers of iced tea and lemonade, and plates of fruit and cheese, Mrs. Larson made a show of pouring. "Go ahead with your story, Mr. Morris, don't mind me." Filling in the blanks took two hours with questions from the threesome. As dusk seeped through woods surrounding the screened porch, Morris answered as truthfully as he could, saving only a few details for himself. He concluded with the same question his interrogators were asking: What had happened to Becky-Rebecca Lund? Was she alive? Where could she have possibly gone on foot in such a hostile place? Whose responsibility was the missing woman? What about the Lindquist brothers? Who was the mysterious visitor Rebecca had met with?

Morris confessed his own bafflement at the fate of the person he had known as Becky Peterson. Despite the obvious frustration shared by everyone, the trip to Upsala had been an epiphany for Morris and a revelation to the others. He asked Soderlund for the name of the sheriff's deputy who had taken the original missing person report.

He promised to follow up with his own phone call. The group's mood had changed dramatically. They agreed to stay in touch should things change. Soderlund was to be the connection. Even Mrs. Larson—so set on killing the messenger just hours before—sent him away with a fresh loaf of bread and a jar of her coveted strawberry jam. He also carried some of the missing pieces of a puzzle he was determined to solve.

....

Chapter 65

In the morning, searching for more answers, Morris started with the Morrison County Sheriff's office in Little Falls. Making no headway with the duty deputy, he asked to speak to one of the department's investigators. Soderlund had warned Morris he'd find little help there and he was right. "Yeah, we've looked into that missing persons case already. You hafta understand, Mr. Morris, you got no body, no report of a crime…"

"Not completely true, officer. The woman disappeared overseas, along with two of your county's residents. They haven't showed up at work or their homes since late May. Doesn't that concern you?"

"I understand. But you have to realize everything you're telling me happened overseas in Australia…"

"Papua New Guinea," Morris corrected the cop.

"Whatever. We got nothing to go on here. You see our predicament? If they show up back home in Upsala at some point, we'll talk to them. But geez, I dunno what to tell you. Sorry." Morris wanted out of the conversation. "Yeah, yeah, okay. Thanks."

"You could try the feds. Seems like this might be their kinda thing."

"Yeah, goodbye." He didn't wait for the cop's reply.

Morris dialed the FBI's field office in Minneapolis. The agent who took his call seemed earnest, but the more questions he asked, the clearer it became to Morris nothing would happen. Terrorism wasn't involved. The fact that three Americans were missing was a serious matter, the agent reassured him, but there was no evidence a crime had been committed. The gun battle with the Australians was "a matter for their law enforcement people." Trying to sound positive, the agent droned on. "I'll forward this to my supervisor to get his angle on it, Mr. Morris. If you're correct about the missing woman passing herself as someone else with that person's passport, it might interest the state department. Using someone else's passport is serious business. It's likely our embassy in Port Moresby is doing some of their own investigating as we speak."

Not bloody likely, thought Morris.

"You might hear from someone in Washington, but I wouldn't sit by the phone if you know what I mean."

Sighing, Morris parroted the line, "I know exactly what you mean." He took the agent's number and hung up. With the exception of the startling confrontation in Upsala, everything else had been a rabbit trail. Two weeks later, Morris got an email from Brad Wood in Papua New Guinea adding more of the puzzle's missing pieces.

Hello, Dale, Hope you recovered from your wound. Things here as confused as when you left. I notified the local constabulary about our situation. As I write, they have yet to visit our station or go up country to Simeon's village. I suspected as much. Couple of things to note. The bones are not going anywhere soon. I still have them with me. I packed them in spare plastic bubble wrap. The police don't want to deal with them. I've emailed our embassy here to advise them of all that's happened. Things will move pretty slowly, if at all. We don't have anything to go on for Becky and the Lindquist problem. Some lower-level embassy paper pusher got the case dumped on him. He's said all the right things but I don't hold out much hope we'll solve this one. I'll keep after them but nothing seems to be working when it comes to finding them…or where they ended up. These mountains swallow people alive. They don't want the bones either at this point. Don't know when the next JPAC team will be here to look at sites. Embassy's military liaison officer told me JPAC won't even consider our bone collection since they were removed from the original site. I'm going to send some of my photos to them and see if that stirs their interest. For now, I'm keeping the remains. May have to give them a military funeral myself. Kinda sad to think of them staying here. If you have any contacts or pull stateside, please have at it. We'll see.

The next part of the letter made Morris sit upright, his eyes riveted to the computer screen. He read the entry twice to make sure he understood what Wood had written.

Now, for some good news/bad news about our Aussie friends. Seems they were not who we thought they were. Surprise, huh? Only their first names were real. Gallagher's real name is O'Hara and Nelson's is Norbert. They never worked for Melbourne's Channel Seven. Check out the station's website. I did. There was a Gallagher and Nelson film team who freelanced for the station. The real guys did shoot animal documentaries. "Day of the Croc" does exist. You'll find all this on the web if you're interested. The real Gallagher's deceased. A friend in the government helped me with this. He circulated my pictures and got several hits from law enforcement. Bad news: both those guys were ex-Australian SAS. They got booted for numerous infractions, if you can believe that. My source wouldn't give me all the details. He said they'd be interested in talking to those two. Wouldn't we all? Those guys certainly have the right skills to survive and if they got away they've obviously gone to ground. I'd say they are a lost cause at this state in the game. I just hope they don't turn up back here.

Don't get into Popondetta much, but next trip I'll take photos with me and visit cops and the local prison camp. For all we know those two could be sitting there eating bad food and asking for a lawyer. I'm going to let things cool a spell and then make another trip into the hills to visit Simeon's village. I've got unfinished business there. Got some public relations fence mending work to do if they'll have me. Any luck with your tracing Becky and the brothers? Dorothy sends her best. Trust her stitches held and that you are mending. Stay in touch. God bless, Brad

Morris saved the message, made a printout, and added it to a folder labeled "PNG."

....

Chapter 66

13° 2′ S, 160° 4′ E

Groping his way forward, Crandall hunched over to lock the anchor chain's hatch cover, which had worked loose. He stood, gripping the headstay with one hand, the other one raised high. Shouting, as if preaching to Becky from the bow pulpit, he bellowed at her. "Elijah told his servant, 'Go and look toward the sea. And he went up and looked. 'There is nothing there,' he said. Seven times Elijah said, 'Go back.' The seventh time the servant reported, 'A cloud as small as a man's hand is rising from the sea.'"

Baffled, Becky cocked her head at Crandall. "What in the world are you talking about?"

Working his way to the cockpit, he posed theatrically. Speaking without looking at her, eyes locked on the horizon astern, he said, "Old Testament passage. Had a sailing instructor at the Academy fond of quoting it when we were out on Chesapeake Bay. He taught us how to read weather."

"Are you reading the weather now?" Nodding, Crandall turned serious. "I am. And I'd bet we have an hour, maybe less before it hits us."

"It?" She sat up, following his eyes back along *Sunshine*'s wake. A spreading wall of dark cloud was growing from the sea, rising and spreading across the water. A ragged bolt of lightning pierced the cloud's heart, startling her.

"Shouldn't we take down sail to get ready?"

"That's where the wind is, Becky."

"But it looks pretty big."

"If we took down sail for every black cloud that appeared we'd never get anywhere. Scared?"

She grabbed his arm. "Should I be?"

Crandall reassured her. "Not really. *Sunshine*'s built for this. She'll do fine. So will you. We'll get a lot of good miles out of this if we're lucky." Grinning, he kissed her and sent her below. "Wake Kalani. Tell him Poseidon's in a bad mood. We're getting company. We'll need to break out the safety gear. I want you to shut all cabinets and forward hatches. Put away anything loose you find below. Then get your rain gear on and come back on deck. Go!"

Craning his neck to check the masthead's weather vane, Crandall crabbed forward, scanning the deck for anything out of place. When he got back to the cockpit Kalani was coming through the hatch, pulling a sleeveless wetsuit top over his head. "Get storm or what?"

"Coming faster than I thought," Crandall replied, pointing at the growing cloud. "I'll fire up the laptop."

"Already did. Shows weather heading northeast. Barometer's falling but it ain't exactly going crazy."

"Good thinking, Kalani. May be just a strong squall. Take over. I'm going below to suit up. I'll double check the cabin to make sure everything's secure."

In two minutes, he was back on deck, Becky in tow. He ordered her to the tiller, took Kalani forward, and reefed the foresail to half size. The pair scrambled aft and did the same to the mainsail. The wind increased steadily as minutes crept by. Feeling the wind, *Sunshine* picked up speed, slicing through building swells. Crandall sealed the main hatch, put on his safety harness and helped Becky into hers. Kalani took over the helm just as a wall of driving rain announced the squall's arrival. The trio felt *Sunshine* surge ahead, surfing long, unbroken waves.

With Becky back at the helm, Crandall clipped his harness to the safety lines running forward. He and Kalani took down the foresail to slow the boat. The squall played with them for the rest of the day, then moved on as if searching for bigger game. They were left with a gift of fifteen-knot winds until sunset.

Becky was shaken but energized by the encounter. Both Crandall and Kalani had seen worse, but they listened patiently as she excitedly replayed the squall. They reversed their routine with the sails. Up went the foresail, followed by raising the mainsail. Within the hour, the sky was scrubbed clean and the moon rose, escorted by a lethargic flock of silver-tinged cumulus.

....

Chapter 67

Vanuatu, June 23

Arriving in Port Vila late Saturday afternoon, Kalani and Becky stowed the sails while Crandall ran up a quarantine pennant. Motoring to the harbor's bobbing yellow quarantine buoy, he dropped anchor in thirty feet of water. Two other tardy boats, a well-worn Cherubini 44 and a hulking trimaran, were anchored near the buoy. The boats and crews would have to wait two days to clear customs and immigration. Crandall didn't mind. "We'll kick back until Monday. That'll give us time to catch up on sleep and do a little housekeeping. Gotta make *Sunshine* presentable for the authorities."

Port Vila's harbor was filled with sailboats and yachts of all sizes flying flags of a dozen countries along with courtesy pennants for Vanuatu. Chatter and music drifted across the anchorage. Rubber dinghies buzzed between moored yachts and the shore. Becky stared longingly at Efete Island's tree-covered hills, palm-lined quay, and houses—civilization in a jeweled tropical setting. Forty-eight hours until she would feel ground beneath her feet seemed a lifetime away. *I'm just happy to be here*, she thought to herself. Kalani and Crandall wrestled the rubber dinghy on deck, partially inflated it, and lashed it down on the cabin roof for use Monday. Every hatch on the boat was cranked open, allowing fresh, cleansing breezes throughout the cabin. Bedding was hung out to dry.

Crandall called Yachting World's radio to arrange clearance on Monday and asked the office to look for moderately priced lodging for two weeks. Once cleared to land, he and Becky would rotate with Kalani every three days. The cycle would leave someone onboard *Sunshine* at all times, a concern of Becky's. Along with agreeing to arrange for a room, the radio voice passed along a three-day forecast: clear skies, lots of sun, high humidity, and moderate seas.

Grateful for the calm waters in the anchorage, Becky went below to the galley and prepped for dinner. That night, they dined on the last of the mahi-mahi Kalani had landed four days prior.

Crandall drew up a list of minor repairs and cleaning to be done and all hands turned in early. Kalani made his bed topside under the stars by turning the plump, half-filled rubber boat into a mattress. Music from nearby resorts drifted across the harbor. Crandall and Becky fell asleep in separate bunks, their hands clasped across the narrow passageway.

Another four sailboats arrived late Sunday afternoon. At nine o'clock on Monday morning, a pair of Customs and Immigration agents approached to process the moored boats. They started with the trimaran. After signing off on the multi-hull and the Cherubini 44, the officials boarded *Sunshine*. Crandall introduced Kalani and Becky, then led the officials below. He politely offered the men iced tea and a folder with ship's papers and the crew's passports. Making themselves at home at the table in the main cabin, the officers sipped tea and shuffled through *Sunshine*'s paperwork. Scanning the forms, the customs man arched an eyebrow at the firearms declaration. "So, you keep a handgun on board, correct?"

"Yes. My permit is in proper order and I keep the pistol under lock and key at all times. Only my first mate and I know the combination."

Curious, the officer asked, "Perhaps you would show it to me."

"But of course. It's quite secure." Crandall lifted a small floral patterned curtain to reveal a small metal safe sunk in the bulkhead by the navigation station.

"Open it, please."

Dialing the safe's tumbler, Crandall opened the door, revealing a sealed plastic bag bulging with a .357 Smith & Wesson and a small plastic box of ammo. The handgun was fitted with a trigger lock in place. Crandall removed the pistol from the bag and offered it to the customs official butt first.

"Loaded?"

"No. I keep it unloaded and locked. It's purely for self-defense against sharks if one of us has to go in the water to check the prop or rudder."

Turning to his slouching partner, the customs man said,

"What you think?" He got a bored shrug in reply. Returning the pistol, the official said, "Very well.

I will make a note of this. You may put away the weapon. We don't see many of these. If you keep it secured for the duration of your visit we will have no problem."

"Of course. I understand completely."

"Good."

After a cursory walk through the boat, and perfunctory probes under mattresses and peeks in lockers, the men were satisfied. An order to remove floor panels for a look at the bilge alarmed Becky who peered down the open hatch. Holding her breath, she went forward, resigned to the inevitable discovery. Below deck, the Customs man ran his penlight's beam up and down the dank bilge. Finding nothing amiss, and after a few more questions, the two-man team was satisfied. They signed off on paperwork, returned the ship's papers and passports, plus visas good for thirty days. "Welcome to Port Vila, Mr. Crandall. You and your crew enjoy your stay in Vanuatu."

"Thank you. We are cleared to go ashore?"

"As you please," answered the officer as he and his partner climbed down to Yachting World's yellow skiff. Pushing off, the pair headed to the remaining quartet of quarantined sailboats anchored astern of *Sunshine*.

Shielding her face against the sun, Becky let out her breath. "Where did you stash it?" she asked, panicked. Crandall, who had come topside to see off their visitors, replied, "Tucked it out of sight in the engine compartment."

"That was clever of you." He shrugged. "Actually, no. That's one of the first places they usually look. Don't know how they missed it."

"Are you serious?" she said in disbelief.

"Not really." Laughing, Crandall backed away from a furious Becky who flashed a wicked grin of relief. Frowning, Kalani asked, "What you hiding, brah, the stuff she brought on board in PNG?"

"We'll talk about it later."

"Damn right we will. My ass on the line too, Skipper. I have a right to know what we carrying." Soothing the Hawaiian, Crandall raised his hands. "No drugs. I'll explain everything when we get ashore."

Becky studied Kalani's face for a reaction but saw only that first flash. Crandall's vague promise to explain their cargo troubled her more than the youth's thinly veiled anger.

After trading the yellow quarantine flag for a homemade Vanuatu courtesy pennant, Crandall finished inflating *Sunshine*'s dinghy and tethered it to the stern. Kalani raised the anchors and stowed them in the bow locker. Becky covered the sails. As instructed by Yachting World's staff over VHF radio, Crandall motored south to Vila Bay's deeper water.

Momentarily putting aside her misgivings about the way Crandall had handled Kalani, Becky marveled at the tropical panorama surrounding her—Port Vila's colorful, bustling waterfront to port and forested Iririki Island with its exclusive hotels to starboard. Among the resort's palms, rows of peaked huts lined up shoulder to shoulder on crescents of white sand dotted with kayaks and tanning visitors. Giddy with anticipation at walking on solid ground, she perched on the cabin roof, hugging the mainmast, mesmerized by the sight of people, buildings, and traffic in such an exotic locale. They passed the Grand Hotel and Casino, its white, curving seven-story facade complete with harbor-side pool. During the day, hotel guests sat under umbrellas in a broiling sun, sipping tall, cool drinks as if they were in Santa Barbara. Slowing for a skiff crossing his bow, Crandall pointed out the cone-shaped thatched roof of the

Waterfront Bar and Grill. He yelled to Becky and Kalani. "Over there! Lunch! Today! On me!"

Grinning, she threw him a kiss.

Beyond the restaurant—silhouetted above a forested slope crowded with large homes—rose the orange-tiled roof of Parliament House, Vanuatu's government seat.

Aiming as the VHF voice directed, Crandall maneuvered toward a string of vacant buoys just beyond a group of catamarans. Kalani, armed with boat hook, poised in the bow pulpit like a harpooner, ready to snag their assigned buoy. They tied up near two-dozen sailboats moored in deep cobalt water.

Kalani muscled the outboard from the foc'sle and came topside. He lowered the engine to Crandall who clamped it on the inflatable's transom, then scrambled on board. In the cockpit, Crandall outlined their schedule. "We'll change some money and have lunch. After that we'll stop by Yachting World's marina office and see about a hotel. Get your gear, Kalani. As number one mate you get first crack at shore duty. Three days and nights." His earlier outburst about the mysterious cargo forgotten, the Hawaiian nodded, loving the idea of sleeping in a bed.

"If we all agree on a hotel," continued Crandall, "Becky and I will stay on board *Sunshine*. Then we switch. Three days and nights on, three days off. Depending on weather, I figure on twelve days here to make minor repairs and give each of us two turns on shore. Fair enough? Any complaints, people? None? Good. Becky, bring a change of clothes, some towels, and shampoo. We'll use the marina's showers when we get back to town after dropping Kalani at his hotel."

They went below and emerged with small packed bags. After locking the companionway hatch boards in place, the three settled in the Zodiac and headed for the dock belonging to the Waterfront Bar and Grill.

As they motored to shore, Crandall told Kalani, "You're on your own for meals, brah. Think you can handle it for three days?"

"Just try me, Skipper. But just so you know, I'm short on cash."

"We'll fix that in town."

The trio tied up at the restaurant's dock and stepped on dry land for the first time since leaving Papua New Guinea. To Crandall's amusement, Becky battled the rolling sensation that follows sailors ashore after weeks on the water. Giggling at her own awkwardness, she wobbled off-balance, hanging onto Crandall's arm.

First stop was Goodies, next door to the restaurant. In addition to selling local handicrafts, the small shop ran a popular money exchange for visitors. Crandall traded six hundred dollars for vatu, the local currency. He walked away, pockets bulging with bills, and discreetly divided the money with the others. The three took a table set in sand under the bar's soaring thatched roof. Crandall ordered three sweating bottles of Tusker beer, a local brew. Congratulating each other, the trio toasted a successful first leg of the voyage, the cold beer quenching fires in their throats. Even at mid-morning, the place was quickly filling with expatriates and shore parties from moored boats. At the suggestion of their server who warned of a cruise ship with its thousands due momentarily, Becky and crew ordered and devoured lunch.

Crandall paid the bill and led the way to the yachting service's office where they ran through hotel options. As requested, a young staffer had culled names meeting their needs from a list. After a few minutes of reading Becky said, "This one looks nice. Price is certainly right."

Crandall read over her shoulder. "Trade Winds Resort?"

She nodded, passed the sheet to him. "I like it. Looks perfect. Only nine rooms plus a pool. Kalani, you good with this choice?" He flashed a thumbs-up.

After the receptionist called and booked the room, she walked them to the doorway. Pointing to the street behind the marina office, she said, "Go to the main road, flag down any van you see with a 'B' in the license plate. Tell them you want to go to Trade Winds Resort. Way cheaper than a taxi. All the drivers know it. Same thing when you want to come back to town, no problem."

In minutes, a van appeared as predicted and stopped. A burly ebony driver filled most of the front seat. Two friendly local women dressed in flowered mother hubbards took up the center seat, baskets balanced on their ample laps. The three new arrivals sat in back.

The van driver went south on Kumul Highway, left on Rue Picarde, and eventually took another left on Captain Cook Avenue. He dropped the women at a large, blue-roofed house and continued on Captain Cook until the next right, where Erakor Lagoon floated into view. Leaving pavement for a crushed coral road skirting the water, the driver stopped in a copse of large shade trees, booming, "Trade Winds." The fare was 1,500 vatu each, a bargain considering the distance from town. They paid and piled out. The van roared away in a cloud of coral dust.

Lush foliage, flowers, and palms surrounded the small resort, a cluster of yellow concrete villas with metal roofs, small patios, and a view of the lagoon.

There was a pool, crystal clear and fenced by hedge for privacy. After explaining their three-day rotation scheme at the front desk, Crandall registered, paying for the first three nights with cash. They were shown a large, airy corner studio with tiny kitchen, dining table, bathroom, and futon. The queen-sized bed sat under a lazy ceiling fan. Kalani dropped his bag and sprawled on the bed. "Three days, brah," Crandall reminded him. He and Becky said goodbye, strolled to Captain Cook, and flagged down a crowded van with one vacant seat. Becky sat in Crandall's lap all the way into town.

The couple showered at the marina's bathhouse, changed into fresh clothes, and had cold drinks at the bar. Crandall gazed at a glowing Becky toying with a fiery red hibiscus in her damp hair. "How'd it feel to finally take a real shower?" he asked. "Fantastic," she said. "Like I had died and gone to heaven. Do you realize that's the first fresh water shower and shampoo I've had since I came on board?

I'm squeaky clean for the first time in weeks. I love it."

"How time flies, huh? I usually go for a couple of weeks between showers."

She wrinkled her nose at the thought. "Boys will be boys, I guess." She put down her drink and locked eyes with Crandall. "What exactly do you figure on telling Kalani?" An awkward silence descended. Crandall stared into his drink, searching for words. "You could argue he has a right to know."

"That's bullshit, Rick. He's not part of the plan."

Crandall tried another tack. "I promised him three thousand to make the trip."

Becky seized on his comment. "Well, I didn't promise him anything. I didn't go through what I did back in PNG just to give it all away."

"Okay. Look, I don't want to get into an argument over this, Becky. Not now, not here, not us." Several minutes passed before she spoke. "Sorry." Softening, she reached for his hand. "I agree. Look, why not give him the money and a plane ticket back to Hawaii. Think he'd go for that?"

Shaking his head slowly, Crandall reasoned, "That leaves us even more short-handed. Still a lot of ocean to cover."

"But could we do it?"

Crandall propped his elbows on the table, head in hands. "Ahhh, I'd have to think long and hard about that."

"What if we send Kalani back and find someone else to take his place?" She swept her arm at the tanned, laughing, chattering sailing crowd filling the restaurant. "Look around. There's bound to be someone here who might want to hitch a ride."

Surveying the crowd, Crandall answered without looking at her. "Not that simple. If we found some willing soul, we'd still end up with the same problem. We'd have to deal with someone else who might eventually find out what we're carrying. Plus we'd be out the money for Kalani's ticket AND the three thousand I promised him."

"That's it? That's all you're going to say?" Frustrated, Becky sank in her chair, eyes fixed on the forest of masts in the harbor. "Dammit, I know what's going to happen. He'll want a share. You watch. That's where this is headed."

Crandall didn't want to admit that she was probably right. "Couple of things come to mind," he said. "We have three days to think about what Kalani's part in this is, we have to plan for the next leg of our trip, and…" He paused.

She waited for him to finish the thought. "And?" she finally asked.

He waved away their server and stood. "And right now we have a job to do."

She rose from the table. "And that would be…"

"Ready to turn yourself into a goldsmith for a couple of hours?"

"I'm not gonna let this thing with Kalani go."

He sighed. "I know. Something will come to me…us. But for now, let's concentrate on what needs to be done. I got the tools you wanted. Let's get everything set up and have at it for a couple of hours. You game?"

"Okay. Let's do it."

They walked to the bar's pier, tossed their towels and laundry in the inflatable, and motored to *Sunshine*. Below deck, Crandall set up a workbench of sorts in the foc'sle. First, he laid out a large scrap of carpet to protect the decking. Next came two rubber pads on which he positioned a twelve-inch square of thick oak. On top of the wood, he set a small anvil. Squeezing behind him, Becky sank to the deck, the anvil between her knees, cotton wadded in her ears, a pair of plastic safety goggles protecting her eyes.

After rummaging in the locker beneath her berth, Crandall squatted next to her, a single gold bar between thumb and forefinger. He handed Becky a heavy hammer and a slim ingot of the precious metal. "We have to completely obliterate the imprint of the eagle and the letters. Once that's done, pound until it doesn't resemble a bar anymore. People will be curious enough about where we got the gold. We don't need them alerting authorities about rumors of some mysterious government hoard."

"Got it." Positioning her first gold bar on the anvil, Becky struck the ingot, timidly at first. With the second bar, her hammer blows became heavier, faster, more efficient. The rubber pads absorbed the pounding. Crandall fed her tiny strips of gold, and when she tired, he took her place. After two hours, they had a sizeable pile of disfigured gold bars.

"Break time," he announced. They went topside with two bottles of water and sprawled in the cool shade of the bimini top. Becky laid back, her head in Crandall's lap, guzzling icy water. A cooling breeze swept through the harbor, turning halyards into wind chimes. *Sunshine* tugged gently at her buoy.

Gazing up at Crandall, Becky asked, "How many did we do so far?"

"I counted forty." Frowning, Becky silently calculated the total weight. "Ugh, that's a lot of work for only eighty ounces."

"Only six-hundred and forty bars to go, girl." A groan escaped her lips. "How are we supposed to get all this done before Kalani gets back?"

"We've got three days, remember?" She lay back, silent. "Can we do it?"

"Absolutely. Relax, we'll get it done. Let's work another couple hours, then break for dinner, okay?"

"Sure. I'm ready. You go first. My arm feels like lead but I'll give it one more hour when you're done. After that I'm not even sure I could lift a glass of wine."

Kissing her forehead, Crandall whispered, "Then I guess I'll just have to raise the glass to your lips for you." She smiled. "Is this a sailor's idea of foreplay?"

"Just trying to make points with the lady," he replied.

"Consider your points earned, mister. I'll see you below." He followed her down the teak stairs into the foc'sle and wrapped his knees around the anvil. Becky jammed cotton in their ears, handed him the hammer, and passed him ingots for the next three hours. When Crandall finally traded places with her, the pile of gold had tripled. Working for one more hour before quitting in exhaustion, Becky erased official markings on another twenty bars, turning the glittering strips into nugget-like lumps in the process. Cramps knotted her shoulders, turning muscle to wood.

Calling a halt, Crandall helped Becky to her feet, wrapped his arms around her, and sent her topside with a kiss. He tossed misshapen gold chunks into a nylon duffle bag and buried it behind laundry, locking it below Becky's berth. Tomorrow they would resume the job—with Kalani conveniently marooned on shore, they would have two entire days to themselves. By then, Crandall said, they would have figured out exactly what to tell him.

....

Chapter 68

Port Vila, June 27

Working non-stop for three days, they finished 420 bars. Crandall put all the untouched ingots in a small waterproof bag, removed a floor panel, and submerged the cache in the bilge. Kalani, he assured a dubious Becky, would not snoop in their absence. Gathering toiletries, swimsuits, and several changes of clothing in two backpacks, Crandall and Becky locked up *Sunshine* and took the inflatable to shore.

Kalani was waiting for them on the Waterfront Bar & Grill's dock with two bags of groceries at his feet. Three nights in a soft bed, fresh water showers, and days at the resort's pool had worked magic. The Hawaiian was in a festive mood.

"How was shore leave?" asked Crandall.

"Ono, brah. Da place is cool. Met a couple of Kiwi wahines on holiday. We gonna try the casino tonight."

Smiling paternally, Crandall wrapped an arm around the youth's shoulders. "Okay with me, it's your money. But remember the drill, Kalani. You spend the night on board, right?" He got a solemn nod. "Why all the groceries? Those girls coming for dinner?"

"Gotta eat, brah."

Becky arched an eyebrow. "Hope you're not planning to host any parties on board while we're gone." Kalani turned frosty. "No way. I'm saving my money for a little night action. Gonna score big."

"The house always wins," she cautioned sarcastically.

"Gonna be just like James Bond, you watch."

Crandall tossed keys and a stern warning to Kalani. "Lock up anytime you go ashore. You know where to find us if you need us."

The couple waited as Kalani loaded his bags into the rubber dinghy. As he motored from the dock, Crandall waved goodbye. "I'd actually feel better if we were staying on board the entire time," Becky said.

"Hey, we need a break as much as he does. Don't know if you caught it, but he didn't say a word about what we were hiding."

"I wouldn't be so confident. He'll want to know eventually, probably in the next few days when he's had a chance to think about it."

"Well, the only thing I'm thinking about right now is getting some food, catching a ride to the hotel, and going for a swim. Oh...and taking a shower. Talk to me after I've accomplished those goals." Slipping her hand in his, Becky tossed Crandall a sultry look. "We should probably shower together to save water."

"Excellent idea. Conservation of natural resources is a commendable thing, Becky. When in Rome..." She purred seductively. "Or when in Vanuatu..."

Hand in hand, the couple threaded their way upstream through a multi-colored, non-stop chattering river of locals and tourists. They stopped at a grocery store where Becky played peek-a-boo with the Chinese proprietor's granddaughter while Crandall filled their backpacks with imported canned goods. He added wine, fresh fruits, and vegetables. They left with three days' worth of food for their room's refrigerator. Backpacks bulging, the lovers strolled leisurely to the main road and hailed the first van they saw with a "B" in its license plate.

For two days, the couple was content to make love, sleep late, drink coffee, breakfast on their villa's tiny veranda, and lounge by the pool. The third day, they went into town for lunch, explored local shops for T-shirts and trinkets, drank cold beer under thatched roofed bars, and shared an intimate candlelight dinner in one of Port Vila's finest hotel restaurants—all while convincingly playing the role of a honeymooning couple. In the three days, Becky's mantra became, "I wish this could last forever."

The next morning, Becky stepped from the shower, wrapped a towel around her hips, and sat on the edge of the bed, concern written on her face. Elbowing the sleeping Crandall, she said, "Kalani knows."

"How do you figure that?" mumbled Crandall turning on his side.

"I feel it. He knows."

"Woman's intuition at work here?" he said, lunging across the bed for the towel. Squealing, Becky slipped from the bed, leaving Crandall with a fistful of terrycloth and a lustful grin. She headed to the bathroom wearing only rubber sandals. Unashamed of her nakedness, she began combing her hair. He propped himself on an elbow to watch her reflection in the mirror.

"I'm serious," she said, "he's not stupid. He knows."

Swinging his feet to the tiled floor, Crandall yawned, ran both hands through his hair. "Okay, let's say you're right. We'll do what you suggested. Offer him a ticket back to Honolulu and give him the three thousand he's got coming."

"How much would that leave us?"

Blinking to focus, Crandall mumbled figures into his beard. "With what I brought ...about twelve thousand."

"Is that enough for the…uh?"

"Sailing kitty? Yeah. Barring any serious mishaps we'd be in good shape."

"And what about not wanting just the two of us trying to handle *Sunshine*?"

"Other couples have done it. It's worth a try if it'll make you happy."

He crept behind Becky and threw his arms around her tanned body, nuzzling her neck as she closed her eyes and smiled. "I know what you're thinking, but we have work to do," she scolded gently. "Let's get back to *Sunshine*. We have one hundred bars to finish."

"I'm gonna shower first. You making breakfast?"

"Sure," she said, pinching his bare behind. Crandall yelped in delight and ducked under the nozzle's spray.

....

Chapter 69

July 1

Crandall came back to *Sunshine* after dropping Kalani ashore. He tied the rubber dinghy off the schooner's stern and passed groceries to Becky. She read his seriousness with one glance. "Why the long face?"

"It's Kalani. There's been a change in plans."

"Damn, I knew it. What's happened?"

Climbing the railing, Crandall took the food bags below, a glowering Becky trailing, pleading, "Talk to me."

"Let's go up on deck where it's cooler." They put away the groceries and went topside. Nestling next to Becky in the shade of the bimini top, Crandall dropped a bombshell. "He knows what we're carrying."

"How the hell..."

Shrugging, Crandall added an unsettling detail. "He showed me a scrap of gold. We must have dropped it when we put away the tools. He doesn't know every-thing, but he pretty much guessed what we're up to."

Smoldering, Becky spit her words. "I knew it! The sneaky little bastard. He probably picked the locks and went through our stuff when we were on shore. Maybe he looked in the bilge as well. Now what?"

"Good news first. Kalani says he'll take our original offer. Bad news, he wants to stay until we reach Fiji. Says he'd rather fly to Honolulu from there."

"How would that work?"

"Quantas runs a Sunday evening flight from Nadi Airport to Honolulu. Direct shot." Crandall laughed. "Funny thing is, he'd get home the day before he left Fiji because of the international dateline."

She was not amused. "Hilarious. Did he ask why you would offer to send him home at this stage of the game when he knows what we've got stashed aboard?"

"Nah, I pitched the homesick angle and the money."

Arms crossed, Becky stared icily. "He buy it?"

"Seemed to. Won't be cheap now that he knows about the gold."

"Too iffy. I don't like it. If he's not careful he's going to find out he's in over his head trying to pull this little shakedown of his."

Crandall threw an arm around her shoulders. "We could use the extra set of hands for that leg of the trip." Becky was unconvinced. "I still think he knows more than he's saying. He's being cagey."

"Look, Becky, the guy wants money, not the gold. And he wants to get home. We've got six days until we shove off. Let's see how it goes for the next few days. If you're still not convinced he's being straight, we'll think of something else."

"Like what, Plan B?" she growled. "There is no Plan B."

Moments of silence crept past, both lovers lost in their thoughts. Wind rippled the surface, sending a cooling breeze through the cockpit. Becky broke the spell. "Okay, we'll do it your way. But if he's screwing with us he'll regret it. We should be able to tell if he's playing us." She kissed Crandall. "I'll be a happy camper once he's off the boat. Just the two of us at last."

"Still a lot of ocean out there, Becky."

"But it will just be us. We can go anywhere we want and start over where no one can ever find us."

Crandall shot a lopsided grin at her. "And we can sail naked… just sunscreen, deck shoes, and a smile. Doesn't matter if you get soaked. Saves on all those wet clothes. Whadaya think about that?"

"I don't believe it," she snorted. "Be serious, Rick. We're on the verge of losing everything to this jerk and all you can think about is…what the hell did the navy do to you anyway? Sailors have a one-track mind."

Crandall collapsed in laughter. "Well, I certainly wouldn't expect you to run around the deck without clothes on while there are still three of us on board."

Somehow, his attempt at defusing the tension worked. Caught up in the moment, Becky sweetly cooed, "All the more reason to get Kalani to take the deal. Now if you'll excuse me, I'm going to work." She scooted below to finish her goldsmith chores, a beaming Crandall right on her heels.

. . . .

Chapter 70

Vanuatu, July 7

Reluctant to leave her island sanctuary, Becky, resigned to yet another long leg on the voyage, shut down emotionally the day they left. The subject of *Sunshine*'s hidden cargo was never raised among the three. As they cleared customs, Kalani was cheerful, busying himself with chores as they abandoned the harbor. The first day out of Port Vila, *Sunshine* made 100 miles, pleasing Crandall. It was not to last.

The next morning, clouds drifted like clots of blood in an orange sky, warning of something brewing over the horizon. "Red sky in the morning, sailors take warning," chanted Crandall from the stern pulpit. To add to the day's uncertainty, the sun rose, clouds broke up, and the sky cleared to a pristine blue in defiance of the mariner's proverb. Nothing happened until noon. Then, mysteriously, the wind died.

Unexpectedly becalmed, *Sunshine* slowed like a harpooned whale, wallowing in dark green water as if anchored in place. With Becky manning the helm, Crandall huddled over his laptop in the navigation center trying to divine reasons for the lull. He downloaded a satellite image to study weather patterns but learned nothing.

Conversation among the crew died the third day out of Vanuatu, leaving them almost 500 nautical miles from their goal, suddenly short of words and wind. Alone on a sea of polished green glass, *Sunshine*'s useless sails became limp as burial shrouds. Civility suffered in the heat. The three changed watches without customary banter. Kalani grew sullen. Becky wore a bored mask and Crandall gave up attempts to cheer her. To avoid Kalani's brooding stare, Becky showered with salt water only when he was below, sleeping. She and Crandall ate meals by themselves, exchanging a minimum of words.

On the morning of a fourth day with no wind and a listless crew, Crandall took matters in his own hands. He fired up the engine. Though Fiji still lay out of reach 500 miles to the east, he was determined to do something, anything, to get *Sunshine* moving. For three hours, the engine noisily clattered away, pushing the eleven-ton hull through a placid ocean.

Eventually, Poseidon abandoned his tease and sent them a series of squalls packed with stiff winds. Putting their animosity aside, the three again acted as a team, harnessing the wind the next four days. But the weather arrived with a cost. *Sunshine* lost its bowsprit to the waves and the headstay tore loose, shredding the new jib. Crandall jury-rigged a fix, using the anchor windlass to secure the headstay. The mishap marred the passage from Vanuatu, but Crandall was thankful to have made up four days of aimless drift. The morning came with rain. When winds slackened enough for one person to handle the helm, Crandall made more temporary repairs and insisted each of them stand watch no longer than two hours. "If you're not on duty, you have to be below in your berth, recharging." There would be no exceptions. Rest was mandatory.

In binoculars, Fiji's coast floated like a faint, tantalizing sliver of green on the horizon and they pressed on, Kalani at the tiller. He hailed Crandall, told him he wanted to talk. Twenty minutes later, Crandall went below, leaving the Hawaiian focused on holding *Sunshine* on course.

Shucking his foul weather gear at the foot of the ladder, Crandall staggered to Becky's berth and knelt, prodding her awake. It was two hours before her turn on watch. Groggy, she opened her eyes to find Crandall's face inches from hers. Whispering softly, he said, "Houston, we have a problem."

Raising herself on one elbow, Becky read concern, not panic, on his face. "Something's happened to the boat?"

"No. It's Kalani."

Becky fell back, covering her puffy eyes with both hands. "Not again. Please tell me he's only seasick."

"Wish I could, babe." A moan escaped her lips. "Okay, what's happened? Shit, as if I couldn't guess." Swinging her legs over the bunk's rail, she shook herself from sleep, mind racing, already sensing what Crandall was going to say.

"Kalani's changed his mind. Now that we're close to Fiji, he says he doesn't want to fly home after all. He wants us to head for Hawaii and drop him there. Say's he'll stay with us to make sure the gold is safely delivered. After that, we're on our own."

"How thoughtful of him. What bullshit. He wants some of it, doesn't he? How much?" Nodding, Crandall avoided Becky's eyes. "Says he's due a third share for the risk he's taking." Glaring, Becky balled her fists against her thighs. "A third! I knew it. That sonofabitch has been thinking about this since he found out about the gold. Our plan was to sail to South America and unload the gold up and down the coast. That's not going to work now, is it? I told you he'd pull something like this. I'm not surprised he waited until we put out to sea again."

"What do you think we ought to do?"

"You don't want to know." A menacing pause. "Actually, I'd like to shoot the greedy little prick. How long before we make Fiji?" Crandall stroked his beard, thought about the image in the glasses, his charts. "We should make the harbor at Suva tomorrow mid-morning. Why do you ask?"

"Just curious. Things can change. Should I talk to him?"

"He's pretty serious about this. I doubt you're going to change his mind if that's what you're thinking."

"I'm not sure what I'm thinking right now." Pushing off the bunk, Becky stood on the slanting deck, the white T-shirt barely covering her tanned thighs. She curled one arm around Crandall's neck, drawing him to her. Gazing into his eyes, she forced a smile, kissed him. "I do know this. I'm only worried about three things right now. Talking some sense into Kalani, getting the gold back, and…" She hesitated, her attention momentarily drawn to the open hatch leading topside, as if she expected to see the Hawaiian crouching there, eavesdropping. Crandall squeezed her hand. "And the third thing?"

"How all of this will affect you and me…our future."

"We're good, Becky. Remember what I promised? I'm not going to lose you again…not ever." She hugged him tighter. "Despite whatever happens?"

"Despite whatever happens." Crandall stood, one hand against a bulkhead to steady himself against the boat's roll. He pulled Becky close. "But nothing's going to happen.

I mean, how many people do you know who get that magical second chance? Remember that." He leaned down, kissed her.

"That was nice. Anyone ever tell you what a great kisser you are?" she asked.

"Well, there was this girl in Florida once."

. . . .

Chapter 71

Republic of Fiji, July 12

As Crandall predicted, they made Suva's harbor before noon. After clearing customs and immigration, the exhausted trio slept for ten hours. In the morning, Crandall piloted *Sunshine* along Fiji's coast to Port Denarau on the north shore. Marina workers replaced the splintered bowsprit and repaired the jib. The sailing kitty took a hit. All three stayed aboard the two days it took to complete the work. The second morning, while Crandall was onshore negotiating with the yard boss about the repairs, Becky cornered Kalani in the galley. "I don't know what kind of game you think you're playing, but if it was up to me this would be your last stop."

"And if it was up to me you wouldn't be here at all."

"You made that pretty clear when I came on board. But guess what, asshole? Your opinion doesn't mean squat. Rick wants me to stay. That's all that matters."

"Yeah, maybe you think keeping the skipper happy in the sheets will get you what you want. You don't think I know what you're doing? You're just using him, bitch."

"Who's using who? First you say you'll take the money and fly home from Fiji. Now you want us to throw out our South America plan just to get you back to Hawaii. And this after all Rick's done for you? You've got a lot of nerve, Kalani."

"Oh, that's good coming from you." He brushed past her to the ladder.

Becky followed him on deck, ready to do more verbal battle. Spotting Crandall about to board *Sunshine*, she retreated below to her bunk to regain her composure.

A scowling Kalani went forward as if nothing had happened and busied himself by untangling a coil of fouled lines. Neither of the combatants shared with Crandall what had just happened. An hour later, Crandall and Kalani went over the side to spend the better part of the afternoon scraping *Sunshine*'s hull, ridding her bottom of freeloading marine growth. Crandall felt the tension between the three of them, but was unaware of the turn things had taken. That evening, after a silent supper, Kalani turned in early. He slept on deck, away from the lovers. Becky, keeping her own counsel, said little.

All the following day, conversation was at a minimum. Water and fuel were topped off, saltwater-soaked stores replaced, bedding aired, and exit paperwork filed. That night, Crandall offered an olive branch to his crewmates without calling it that—dinner at Cardo's Steak House on the harbor. The meal seemed to ease some of the tension between the three.

At dawn, when they put to sea, however, it was as if the meal had never happened. Becky's apprehension returned. The realization of the distance yet to travel descended on her like a lead yoke. To her dismay, Crandall papered over his anxiety about Kalani's prior demands and she entertained doubts about her lover's loyalty. Seven hundred miles northeast lay Upolu, the smaller of Samoa's two islands, home to the capital, Apia. They were deliberately bypassing America Samoa as a caution. Apia was originally to be the final stop before aiming for South America, but things had changed. Kalani's insisting on returning to Hawaii first upset their timetable. It wasn't the only threat to Becky's dream.

The third day out of Fiji, Crandall awoke with a nagging headache. "Probably a touch of flu," he said. "Shouldn't have spent that much time in the water cleaning the hull." Halfway through next day's mid-morning watch, he asked Becky to relieve him. Hobbling his way below like a spent old man,

Crandall gobbled aspirin and slept through that day and the next, only leaving his berth to use the head. Alternating two-hour turns at the tiller, Kalani and Becky sailed on.

The morning of the fifth day, she found Crandall shaking uncontrollably. He could not get warm despite layers of blankets piled on him. Worried, she dozed next to him, his head cradled in her lap. When she left him to take her turn at the helm, she was shocked to find herself soaked with his sweat. Delirious with fever, he threw off the covers and slept naked to find relief. Kalani came below, covered Crandall with a sheet, and dragged his own bedding to the sea berth in the stern, away from his suffering crewmate. In minutes, he was asleep, snoring like a dull chainsaw. Twenty minutes passed. Crandall again shuddered in agony, clawing to reclaim blankets he had tossed at his feet. He was barely coherent. That afternoon, a cycle of white-hot fever and violent chills returned.

On the sixth day, Becky came down below to find Crandall semi-conscious, babbling incoherently, forehead on fire. A cold washcloth, one of several she began keeping in the refrigerator, was a temporary help. Kalani slept soundly, oblivious to the situation. She sat with Crandall for several minutes. *Sunshine* heeled, scrambling her topside to check the tiller's autopilot. After making a minor adjustment to the sails, Becky came back to Crandall's bedside. His half-lidded eyes blinked at her, prompting a smile, which he barely returned.

"I'm worried, Rick. What's happening?"

"Malaria."

"What? Malaria? How do you know for sure?"

A slow nod and the dreaded word again. "Malaria." She drew back slightly. "Is it contagious?" A shake of the shaggy head and a half-smile as if a child had asked a stupid question. "No," he groaned. "Just me. I own it."

"How long will you be like this? Do we have medicine? Can we find help in Samoa?"

Sighing, he turned to stare at her. "My locker. Plastic bin. Pill bottles. Bring them."

Up on deck, the main and foresail luffed, Dacron sails snapping in the wind, calling her. "Be right back." Becky climbed the steps. She was gone fifteen minutes.

Crandall felt the hull slow. When she reappeared at his bedside, he had fallen asleep. She went through his locker, found the plastic box, and sorted through the collection of orange prescription bottles. She set aside three promising ones: bottles with labels reading "malaria symptoms." When he stirred, she showed him the bottles.

"That one. Mefloquine," he croaked. "Water, please."

She tapped one pill in his palm, got him a bottle of water and asked, "You had malaria before?"

"No. A pharmacist friend fixed me up with medicine before we left Hawaii, just in case. Must have picked it up in Lae or Vanuatu despite precautions. Hope you've been taking your pills."

"I finished them weeks ago," she said.

He took a long drink of water, handed Becky the bottle, and rolled on his side, moaning softly.

"How long will it take before you're feeling better?"

Crandall didn't answer. He had fallen asleep on the rumpled sheets. Becky felt his burning brow. She let him doze and went into the galley to fix herself a sandwich. In the sea berth, Kalani's calloused feet poked from shadows where he had taken up residence since the first day Crandall's symptoms showed. *Coward*, she thought.

In two hours, Kalani would be back on deck for his three-hour shift. They were rotating daytime turns of three hours on, two hours sleeping. At night, they did two hours on and off.

It would continue that way until Crandall was well enough to share the duty. Weary, her muscles aching from her shift at the helm, Becky climbed the ladder and took her post at the tiller, a sandwich in one hand. She had an hour left on watch.

When she came below deck again, she'd wake Crandall and nurse him with a mug of noodles and broth. He had to get well. She needed his strength behind her. Kalani was growing surlier each day, ignoring her calls for help, showing up later for his turns on deck. When reprimanded, he snapped at her like a feral dog.

Is it coming apart now, she wondered. *So close to finishing this and we're slowly disintegrating as if we've been at sea our entire lives.* With Crandall ill, the days seemed one endless slog on an infinite ocean. Their GPS showed unmistakable progress but her emotions played tricks on her. She sometimes convinced herself *Sunshine* was dragging mammoth iron anchors along the sea floor. Starry nights, once a beautiful sparkling tapestry that delighted her, now seemed to hold back the dawn forever. Even the horizon seemed to begrudge the morning sun's efforts to float free. As was now his habit, Kalani climbed on deck thirty minutes late, rubbing sleep from his eyes. He checked the compass heading and took his place at the helm without a word. Becky retreated to the sanctuary of the cabin. "I hate living like this," she whispered to herself.

Her spirits lifted mid-week when she found Crandall sitting upright in his berth drinking hot chocolate she had made him on one of her earlier breaks. She wrapped her arms around him, smothering him with kisses as if he had risen Lazarus-like. "Whatever that medicine is," she crowed, "it's working miracles as far as I'm concerned."

Crandall managed a weak smile. "I wouldn't last one round in the ring with an eight-year-old right now. But I am feeling better." Between sips of cocoa he asked, "Show me where we are."

Becky passed the hand-held GPS to him. He read the fix, mumbled something in his beard, and lay back, drained from even that brief exertion. Nonetheless, he was alert and talking, which buoyed her. Crandall's eyes stayed with her as she changed from salt-soaked shorts into nylon pants and a hooded shell jacket. "Normally a sailor's butt is not a pretty thing after weeks at sea…but in your case…"

Becky finished dressing, heard herself laugh for the first time in days. "My, my, aren't we getting better."

"How about some dinner?" she called from the U-shaped galley. "Some pasta noodles, butter, no sauce."

"Sounds wonderful. I think I'm getting my appetite back."

"Good. I'll bring it to you when it's ready."

"I'd like to try eating at the table if that's okay. Make enough for Kalani, will you? He can eat at the helm." Frowning at the request, Becky didn't answer. Of all the things he might have asked, fixing a meal for Kalani was not something she wanted to do.

You haven't witnessed Kalani's treatment of me. She needed to talk with Crandall about him. Mutiny was a word that flashed through her head. *Is there such a thing as mutiny on a sailboat with just three people on board? Was she being too dramatic? Would Crandall think she was delusional? Paranoid? Three-on-a-match, two-to-one. None of it was good. They were three, maybe four days out of Samoa. After that, what?* Facing another 750 miles of open water north to Christmas Island on the way to Hawaii was too frightening for her to contemplate. *Just get to Samoa and spend some time on land. Restore some sanity. Get Rick healthy, even if it takes a week or two. Can't put back to sea with him like this.*

Each mile they sailed narrowed her options. If Kalani was thinking the same thing, he wasn't showing it. He wanted the gold, that much Becky was sure of. *He was playing cool, aloof, as if he didn't care.* She wasn't fooled. *Not yet, you bastard.* Crandall was the key. He had to be healthy to make her plan work.

....

Chapter 72

Samoa, August 2

Opolu Island's northern coastline floated like a welcoming green mirage on the horizon. Another half day of sailing and *Sunshine* would gain Apia, Samoa's capital.

For Becky, it would be Vanuatu redux. Solid ground under her feet, hotels, streets, people, cars, and trees. She smiled, thinking of houses, electricity, fresh water showers, and a clinic to properly treat Crandall's malaria. There was even rumor of a restaurant known for its Thai cuisine. In rising spirits, Becky gave up the helm to a brooding, silent Kalani and went below at dusk. Crandall was on his back, covers to his chin. She felt his brow. Embers of fever still smoldered, though the Mefloquine seemed to be doing its job. Lingering chills and fever would not let go quite yet. Along with dizziness confining him to his berth, Crandall suffered bizarre dreams—one of the drug's known side effects.

Becky made tea in the galley. She curled in the navigation station to study a map of Samoan waters, her fingers laced around the warm mug. She put away the chart, snapped off the light and stripped off damp clothes in the cabin's semi-darkness. After changing into jogging shorts and T-shirt, she felt her way to her berth and wearily crawled in, exhausted.

Becky's watch came and went without Kalani loudly clomping down the teak ladder to rudely wake her. She slept on, unaware of the hull heeling fifteen degrees to port, burying a rail in the waves. Oblivious to *Sunshine*'s new course, Becky lay in her damp poncho liner, exhausted, unmoving like a cocooned corpse.

At the tiller, Kalani made a deliberate, fateful decision. With a robust southeast wind on his starboard beam, he let the sails fill and took *Sunshine* knifing through the long swells. Apia's lights grew smaller by the minute until they were abruptly swallowed by the horizon. Only a dull reflection on the bottom of drifting clouds remained to mark Samoa's capital. Eventually even that glow died and *Sunshine* raced on in pre-dawn darkness, her masthead lights flickering like tiny blue stars high above the deck.

In the morning, expecting to find herself in Samoa, Becky awakened instead to an empty ocean. Standing in the hatchway, her elbows propped on the cabin roof, she rubbed sleep from her disbelieving eyes. "Where are we?" she yelled to Kalani. "What the hell happened to Apia Harbor? What have you done with Samoa?"

"Missed it," he said groggily. "Big storm came up when you was sleeping. No way to get in safely. Had to keep going." Knowing he was lying, she cleared the hatch, stood there gripping a handrail with one hand, the other one a fist. "You should have awakened me. We could have heaved to until daylight."

"I tried to wake you but you were out cold."

Another lie. Grim-faced, she shot back, "Bullshit."

"Suit yourself."

"What are you doing? How far off track are we?"

"No problem. I got us back on course."

"Okay, that's good. But now where, back to Samoa?"

"Christmas Island."

Becky lost it, shrieking, "That's almost fifteen hundred miles! Are you completely nuts?! We have to turn around! Go back!"

Unfazed, Kalani did not yield. "Only fourteen hundred now. No going back. Another three weeks and we'll be there."

"Use your head. We have to go back. Rick's got malaria. He needs a doctor. He could die. Don't do this."

"It's done. We get plenty water, plenty food. Skipper's getting better. He'll be okay, you watch."

"This is crazy, Kalani. I'm going below and telling him."

"Go ahead," he screamed. "You're the skipper's whore, so tell him. You'll see. Ain't no big thing."

With that comment, Kalani signed his death warrant. Becky's mind was set. Things had been heading this way since Vanuatu, when he had discovered the gold. The Hawaiian was a dead man, but the timing would be hers. No need for Crandall to know what she was going to do; he wouldn't agree to it anyway. Kalani had done her a favor by skipping Samoa. *Lot of open water ahead. No witnesses. Plenty of opportunity.*

She thought of Darryl. The way it ended with him had been tough. Still, once she had made up her mind, it was easier than she had imagined. Something like it had been in the back of her mind all those years. *What was it Ida had said back in Upsala? "Here today, gone tomorrow."* Waiting for the perfect opportunity was the hardest. With Darryl, she may have been the instrument, but a river in PNG had been a gift.

In the cabin below, Crandall sat on the edge of his bunk listening to fragments of the heated exchange. With one hand pushing against a bulkhead, he held himself upright, managing a weak smile when Becky came down the ladder. "Hey girl, what's happening topside?"

She changed from grim to cheerful in the time it took to reach his side. "Kalani's bypassed Samoa. Says he thinks it's better to keep going; hit Christmas Island, then on to Hawaii."

"Huh, don't know if I agree. Would have been nice to lay over a week. I should see a doctor and you need to spend a few days in a hotel room. See the town, you know."

"Would have loved that. Too late," she sighed. "He's determined to do it his way."

"He should have asked."

"You weren't in any shape to decide. I dunno, maybe it's for the best."

"Maybe. Maybe not. Don't like it," he said testily. "Last time I checked I was still skipper." She shifted gears. "Would it surprise you to know he thinks I'm the captain's whore?" Frowning, Crandall asked, "What?"

"Kalani said I'm the captain's whore. I said I was going to tell you about his changing course. You know, skipping Samoa. He said, 'Go ahead, you're the skipper's whore, so tell him. You'll see. Ain't no big thing.'"

Crandall reddened. "He shouldn't have said that, Becky. I'm sorry. Disappointed. Kalani probably thinks I'll just accept what he's doing. He can't treat you like that. I'll get him to apologize."

Seeing an opportunity, she planted a seed. "I don't think he will. I don't want his apology. Besides, it really doesn't matter. He's making all the decisions now. And you can't change his mind about Christmas Island if that's what you're thinking."

"We'll see about that. Since when does the pupil turn tables on the master, huh?" Too weak to stand, Crandall told her to open the safe behind the curtain at the navigation station. Following his instructions, Becky punched buttons on the keypad and opened the door. She rummaged in the steel box and held up a fist of paperwork, cash, and three passports. "This is everything that's in there."

"That's it?"

She felt inside the safe. "Yeah, just the money, paper, and passports, no gun."

Crandall, visibly upset, wobbled painfully across the slanting deck and sank down on the bench.

"What about the gun?" Becky asked. "What's going on?"

"I don't know, but I don't like it. Why would he take it?" He tugged at his beard. "How long do you figure he's been at the helm?"

"Ten, maybe twelve hours. Why?"

"He might have popped some pills to stay up that long. He's got to be ready to collapse. He's not going to be making good decisions if he stays up there. You're going to have to take the next watch, Becky."

"I can do that."

"I'll have to give you a hand if you get into trouble."

"You're not strong enough yet."

"Don't have a choice, do we?"

Sunshine suddenly heeled to port. Netting holding a row of paperbacks and music CDs tore loose, spilling them across the deck. Bracing herself, Becky waited for *Sunshine* to correct herself. A quick glance at the inclinometer mounted at the head of Crandall's berth read twenty degrees. Slipping into rain gear, she said, "I'd better go on deck to see what's happening."

"Watch yourself," cautioned Crandall. "If Kalani comes below, I'll try to talk some sense into him." She headed up the ladder, paused. "Don't push him too hard. He's in a bad mood. And if he has the gun…" Crandall waved her away. "He's got the gun. But nothing's going to happen. Go. Take over the tiller. Tell him he's relieved."

Crandall squirmed behind the mess table to wait. After rising and falling, *Sunshine* settled into steady rhythm. *Good, feels like Becky has the helm,* thought Crandall. *Now all I have to do is find out what the hell Kalani's up to without spooking him.*

Followed by a spray of water, Kalani invaded the main cabin, his foul weather coat glistening. The Hawaiian's eyes were red-rimmed, puffy from lack of sleep. He had been running on adrenaline too long and it showed. Fatigue furrowed his face, adding a veneer of hostility. Salt water dripped from his shaggy hair. Shucking his wet jacket and pants, Kalani hung them on a peg behind the ladder. From his lair in the sea berth, he could reach them quickly if needed on deck.

Crandall played a diplomatic card. "So you think we're better off heading northeast to Christmas Island, eh? Long haul. Not the route I would have taken. I'm curious, what made you change your mind?"

"Had to make a decision. Your wahine doesn't know shit about navigating."

"She's a fast learner, does okay for someone who's never sailed before."

Sullen, Kalani spoke without meeting Crandall's gaze. "I don't like women on board. Bad luck."

"Get over it. The ancient Polynesians had no problem sailing with women aboard." The anecdote fell on deaf ears. He tried another card. "Anyway, we have to figure out how to get back to some sort of cooperative sailing routine. Things have gone downhill these last few weeks. We've all been at sea too long."

Crandall's bid at conciliation was frostily ignored. Dropping his sodden deck shoes at the foot of his berth, Kalani stared listlessly across the cabin before slithering into his sleeping bag. Pushing his point, Crandall asked, "What did you do with the pistol, brah?" No answer. He eased from behind the table and propped himself at the foot of the sea berth. "Kalani. Where's the gun that was in the safe?"

Bolting upright, Kalani reached under his pillow, suddenly

flashing the shiny handgun in Crandall's face. "You wanna know what happened to the pistol?" he snarled. "Here it is! It's my insurance!"

"Insurance? What the hell for? You gone nuts? Give it to me before someone gets hurt." Waving the .357 carelessly as if it were a malevolent toy, Kalani snapped at Crandall. "I don't think so, brah. Only people going to get hurt are you and that whore."

"Knock off the name-calling."

"You don't think I know what you two are up to? You think I'm a lo´lo´, eh? You don't think I know you two wanted to get rid of me in Fiji? You missed your chance so you figured Samoa was just as good a place as any, didn't you? You want the gold for yourselves. Ain't going to happen, brah. I'm making sure I get my share. I earned it."

"C'mon, you know me better than that, Kalani."

"No! I thought I knew you. That was before your whore came on board."

Crandall put an edge in his voice. "Knock it off. Enough with the names. Give me the gun and we're square."

Pushing back into the darkened sea berth, Kalani let out a hyena-like laugh. "Oh, that for sure ain't gonna happen. You two try anything, and someone WILL get hurt. Now get out of my face. I need rest. I'll be sleeping with my finger on the trigger. Remember that. Don't make me use it."

Dumbfounded, Crandall stood in the cabin, out of cards.

....

Chapter 73

Silver Spring, Maryland, August 6

The question seemed innocent enough. “Well, Geoff, it’s been months, heard anything from our Australian friends lately?” Perched in a high-backed leather chair behind a desk, the questioner—a scowling man in a tailored Italian suit—stroked his goatee with manicured fingers. When perturbed, Buddy Daniels, former Green Beret colonel, was in the habit of smoothing his closely clipped beard.

Geoff Timmons, shaved head and black predatory eyes adding menace to his presence, stood at parade rest in front of the polished mahogany desk. He cleared his throat. “Not a word. All our emails are getting bounced back to us. Our blokes aren’t answering their phones.”

“What about our contact in Darwin?”

“Clueless,” said Timmons.

Staring at a bank of floor-to-ceiling windows, Daniels swept his gaze over the city sprawling below him and snorted in frustration. On the far wall facing him, a bronze Indian rider—Fredrick Remington’s “The Scalp”—dominated a long, low bookcase filled with military titles and army field manuals. Framed diplomas and signed photographs of politicians, generals, and action movie stars covered the wall above the bookcase, Daniels beaming in each photo. Sleek leather designer chairs were pushed against a sound-proofed glass wall, a small table with a carafe of ice water and cups between them. A striking antique woodcut of a wild-eye samurai hung on an easel next to the closed door. “Hard to tell what the hell’s going on out there without boots on the ground,” Daniels said without looking at his man.

"Extremely hard to do," answered Timmons.

"We've let this go too long," mused Daniels. "I should have been more proactive on this. That's going to change. You're going to have to go back to the field and get us something we can use, Geoff. Our wayward Aussies should have returned by now. And they'd better have a damn good reason for not contacting us. So help me, if they've skipped…"

"They're good people, Sir. My guess is something's gone off the rails."

"I don't pay you to guess. What about that chopper pilot? Remind me again what he said."

"Claimed he never heard from the boys. Said he was on standby but the call never came."

"You trust him?" asked Daniels.

"Colonel, I don't trust anyone."

"Good answer, Geoff." Spinning his chair to face the standing man, Daniels laced his fingers under his chin. "I want you to finish up what you're doing and head back to Minnesota sometime in the next two weeks. Kick ass and take names. At the least, I want some of my money back from that lying little bitch. Find the guy who put this trip together for her. He has to know something."

"I'm on it."

"Take the Gulfstream. I'll have Thi alert the pilots. Oh, and no reflection on you, Geoff, but this time take Spiros with you as backup."

Ushering his tracker to the office door, Daniels added, "There's a couple million dollars in gold out there somewhere and it belongs to me. Get it back. Do that and you'll find a nice bonus waiting for you."

"I appreciate the sentiment, sir."

"Don't thank me yet. You still have to earn it." Daniels laughed, his hand on Timmons's back. "If you need anything special stop by the armory and pick up what you want." Daniels barked at a curvaceous Vietnamese woman in a clinging white silk Ao Dai. The Viet was manning three wide-screen computers, each filled with a dozen streaming security videos. "Thi, darling, call Sly. Tell him Geoff and Spiros will need the plane sometime in the next ten days for unfinished business."

....

Chapter 74

For the next seven days, Crandall, Becky, and Kalani co-existed in a charged state. Weather wasn't a worry. Steady southeast trades kept them moving. Kalani and Becky pulled three-hour watches. They ate at their stations, slept when they could use the autopilot, and spoke only when necessary—even then, words between them were short, angry. Crandall shed malaria's symptoms and continued to improve, though too weak to handle sail. During daylight, he sat at the tiller, relieving the other two when they used the head or catnapped.

Kalani carried the pistol everywhere, the gun snug in a makeshift oilskin holster in his waistband. Each day, his paranoia about plotting crewmates increased exponentially. Becky said the Hawaiian had slipped over the edge. Crandall counseled diplomacy, patience. "Something will break soon, you'll see."

Less generous, Becky muttered darkly, "I hate the way Kalani struts around with that pistol in his belt. I hope he trips and shoots his balls off."

Meanwhile, she waited. Five days out, Becky finally got her opportunity. Revenge arrived disguised as a line of menacing squalls sweeping across the horizon. At first, she didn't recognize the oncoming storms as a solution to her "Kalani" problem. The two changed watches at dusk, with him going below to eat. At the helm, Becky spooned fat buttery noodles from a steaming mug, keeping one eye on boiling black clouds dancing their way. The weather was ugly. She tied off the tiller and went below to don foul weather gear. Crandall, hollow with fatigue, dozed in his berth. Kalani was spooning pineapple from a can and watching a surfing DVD on the laptop for the hundredth time, the .357 on the table in front of him within easy reach. Becky threw on a hooded waterproof shell and struggled into a safety harness. Planting a foot on the ladder's bottom rung, she warned, "Line of squalls heading our way. Might need your help to shorten sail if it gets out of hand." He grunted something unintelligible in response. Fuming at his petulance, Becky bounded up the ladder, latching the watertight hatch behind her.

The wind picked up, turning sails into taut scalloped shapes. Ragged whitecaps sprouted everywhere. Wind sheared off the tops of waves and *Sunshine* picked up speed. A wall of rain arrived, followed by another sweeping across the deck, drenching Becky. The boat dipped its port rail under water and kept it there, pounding over the back of swells. Waves rose up from the darkness, exploding in a fountain of spray against the port beam. Thrown off balance, Becky wrestled with the tiller, ducking as the boom whipped past, nearly decapitating her. Battling for control, she sent the boom back to its original position, filling the mainsail again.

The close call shocked Becky, but gave her an idea.

First, she had to survive the storm.

Sunshine bucked against the chaotic sea. Becky shrieked at the hatchway until Kalani, safety harness over his yellow rain gear, appeared on the top step, an anxious Crandall poised behind. She waved Crandall back. "Stay below! We can handle it!"

Kalani sealed the hatch behind him. Crouching, he faced Becky, one hand locked on a rail running the length of the cabin roof. The pistol, wrapped in oilskin, was jammed in his belt. Jabbing at the foresail, she screamed into the wind, "We're carrying...too much... sail!"

Nodding, Kalani grabbed his safety clip and steadied himself, craning his neck at a towering wall of shimmering Dacron amidships. He looked at Becky, then turned back, studying the billowing foresail, as if doubting her. The brief pause was all she needed.

Becky slammed the tiller hard left and ducked.

The heavy boom slashed like a huge out-of-control scythe, smashing into Kalani with a sickening, meaty thud. He hurtled over the railing, wide-eyed, arms flailing. Becky saw him pitch into the wild dark sea. Swept into oblivion. Gone.

It was no small feat to master *Sunshine*. Rain, driven by a howling wind, peppered the deck like buckshot, drenching everything. Summoning every reserve of strength, Crandall forced his way topside. He fought to shorten mainsail and foresail. That done, he flopped near the closed hatchway, pinned in place by his safety harness, too spent to move. "Where's Kalani?"

Shaking her head, Becky clung to the tiller with a death grip. "Lost! Overboard!"

Stunned, Crandall stared at the chaotic sea. In the cockpit, Becky, arms draped over the tiller, every muscle in her body throbbing with pain. When the squalls finished, they were left with a confused sea. Hours later, the waves lessened, then died to five-foot troughs and a manageable chop. She gazed at the horizon, her eyes dull with fatigue in the storm's wake. Given the storm's ferocity, there was surprisingly minor damage.

Leaving Becky alone on deck, Crandall crawled to his berth and slept as dead for eight hours. A gentle rain, more of a passing mist, arrived with dawn. With the sails reefed and the jib set,

Sunshine sailed herself—speed five knots, compass reading zero-two-five degrees.

....

Chapter 75

Republic of Kiribati, August 20

Other than a brief entry Crandall scribbled in *Sunshine*'s log, he and Becky did not talk about Kalani. The Hawaiian was gone, but how he died remained an unresolved issue. Once again, conversation became a casualty. They ate in silence, avoiding each other's eyes. She no longer crept into his berth. Sleep eluded both. Rotating two-hour turns at the helm, they made landfall at Christmas Island nineteen days after the storm. The last twelve hours of the passage, wind deserted them, leaving *Sunshine* agonizingly short of the goal. Not content to drift, Crandall fired up the old Mercedes and took the boat into anchorage. They stayed for a week before reluctantly heading to sea.

They made forty miles the first day, doubled their progress the second day and covered one hundred miles the third day. The morning of the fourth day at sea, *Sunshine* hit a band of light air that bedeviled Crandall's best efforts to coax more distance despite skillful maneuvering. Only occasional ripples disturbing the blue-green sea hinted at wind. He tied down the tiller and catnapped in the sun. He awoke when Becky came up the ladder with mugs of hot chocolate and a plea to talk.

"What can I do to make things right again? We're acting like strangers. I hate it. Tell me how to fix this."

Crandall stared into the mug, avoiding her gaze. "It's just

that…losing Kalani was something I didn't want to happen. Not like that."

"Are you blaming me, Rick? Please tell me the truth."

He finally lifted his eyes to her. "I know things were getting a little dicey, but…"

"You think I wanted it to end the way it did? Is that what you think?"

His eyes shifted to the horizon where a pod of porpoise arched playfully through low swells. "You made it clear you didn't care for Kalani. Didn't like the way he was behaving. Ever since Vanuatu, it was pretty obvious where you stood…with him knowing about the gold and all."

She followed his eyes to the porpoises, forced a smile at their antics. "Look at them. Not a care in the world. I'd like to be like that right now."

He was unmoved. "What happened that night?"

"I told you," she sighed. "We broached a couple of waves and I lost control of the boat. He lost his balance. Went over the rail before he had a chance to hook up his safety harness. It was so quick I had no chance to help him. It was all I could do to get *Sunshine* back under control."

"I know that's what you told me. It just sounds too…convenient, Becky."

She folded her shoulders inward, hugging herself, holding the warm mug against her cheek. A hint of tears formed in her eyes. Turning away, she fought to keep her composure. "You think I wanted Kalani dead? Is that what this is about? There were times when I felt like that, yes. But I never in my wildest dreams thought it would happen. Do you believe me?"

Crandall finished his drink, put down the mug, and glimpsed a frigate bird patrolling the cloudless sky one thousand feet above the sea. Keeping his eyes trained on the bird he said, "Three men are now dead because of that gold."

Becky interrupted, "And you think their deaths are my fault?"

"Let me finish."

"Sorry. Go ahead, say it."

"A guy has to wonder, Becky. The Lindquists go to PNG with you. You find the gold. They help you get it, yet neither one of them makes it out alive. You manage to survive and show up with the gold. I pick you up and we leave PNG."

Becky's tears began tracing paths down both cheeks. She bowed her head, saying softly, "I told you what happened to David, how he was shot by the Australians. And Darryl…well, he didn't make it across the river."

Turning his gaze on her, Crandall forged ahead as if the cockpit had become a courtroom. "I remember everything you told me about how they both died. I could probably accept that, did in fact. But then, there's Kalani and I have to ask if that's coincidence as well."

"He had your gun," she whimpered. "He was probably going to use it at some point. Maybe when we got close enough to Hawaii. Kill us both and take the gold for himself."

"You don't know that."

"Then why did he keep the gun?"

"He was frightened. Thought we were going to get rid of him so we wouldn't have to share the gold."

"He didn't need the gun. He was really weird that last week. You saw it. You know it's true."

A gust of wind filled the sails prompting Crandall to read the telltales and nurse the boat to port. When the sails luffed, rippling in the air, he eased the tiller back until the sails responded. Satisfied, he resumed his interrogation. "I admit I didn't know what he was going to do. I didn't completely trust him at that point. Wish I had tossed the gun after leaving Fiji. I wasn't thinking clearly by then."

"You had malaria, remember?"

"Yeah. Maybe that's when he started coming apart. It's a bit of a blur for me."

"Kalani's death was an accident. Believe me. If I could do things over…"

"That's a good question, Becky. What would you do if you could start again?"

"I might have just been happy to have found you again…and left it at that."

"Huh, we both might have been better off. I said I loved you."

"You still feel that way?"

"I do. But I've been doing some deep thinking, some soul-searching. I wonder if you can appreciate my predicament. Actually, it's our predicament. I have to be able to trust the woman I love, just like you have to trust me. Do you think that's a fair assessment?" Tearful, she nodded, wiping her swollen eyes with the back of her hand.

"Okay. It's a start. Take over the helm for a spell. I want to get something below."

Puzzled at his request, she scooted across the cockpit seat and put her hand on the tiller as Crandall disappeared in the cabin. He emerged minutes later, the laptop tucked under one arm.

....

Chapter 76

5° 27′ N, 156° 42′ W

He sat beside her in the stern and opened the computer. "Pay close attention to what I'm going to tell you. I want to explain some things." The glowing screen showed a nautical chart with waypoints plotted across a pale green expanse of ocean. Crandall hit a few keys, scrolling to the top of the display until the Hawaiian Islands popped into view. He shifted his gaze to her upturned face. "We're on a run almost due north. We're not sailing east to South and Central America as planned. His right index finger tapped Oahu's outline. "We're going back to Hawaii."

"But why?" she asked. "You said you had contacts in Ecuador, Peru, and all along Central America—places where we could start selling the gold without having to unload it all at once."

"Right. My plan was not to arouse too much suspicion. I thought we'd sail north to California and do more of the same. Then, back down the coast, through the canal, hit a few more contacts, and finally end up in Jacksonville."

"And now you're changing plans? Isn't that risky?"

"Hey, this whole idea was risky. Has been from day one."

"But we don't have to sail to Hawaii now that…"

"Now that Kalani's not with us?"

Becky sighed. "I didn't mean it quite that way."

"Well, it's true. But I have to go back. He has family there, an auntie. I promised him three thousand dollars to make the trip. I want to honor my commitment. It's the least I can do."

"What about your promise to give him a third of the gold?"

Crandall's eyes hardened briefly. "I never promised him that.

That's what he wanted, demanded. But it doesn't matter now. It's a moot point. He's gone. I'll pay the promised three thousand."

Worried, Becky asked, "Will we have any trouble in Hawaii?"

"I can't see it happening. I've logged our trip, including Kalani's death. That makes it pretty official. I'll report it to the right people. We've got nothing to hide. It happened."

"Does that mean you believe me, Rick? Please tell me you do."

"I'll get to that. First, I want you to use this route to Hawaii I've mapped out. The waypoints are all in there. I've got charts in the navigation station as well. You've done well in learning the basics of navigation. You handle *Sunshine* pretty damn well for a farm girl."

"I'm a midwesterner," she pouted, "not a farm girl. There IS a difference."

For the first time, he smiled. She took that as a good sign.

"Okay. You've got the course to Honolulu. Plotted. You're set, good to go."

"I understand. But why are you telling me all this?"

"You have to know these things. You have to be ready. If you want to sail with just the foresail and jib, that's fine. *Sunshine* will sail herself just fine with that rig. Might take longer but she's easily handled that way."

Crandall put away the laptop and took it below. She waited, curious. He came back on deck wearing a full-body wetsuit, complete with booties and hood.

"Why the wetsuit? Is there something wrong with the steering?"

"I'll get to that." Once again, he sat beside her. His tone softened. A look of ineffable sadness crossed his face. Taking both her hands in his, he said solemnly, "Becky, I told you I love you. I do love you with all my heart. I've always loved you."

She started to answer, "And I have always loved..."

"Shhh," he said gently, putting a finger to her lips. "Let me finish. You say you love me. I accept that. Now prove it to me."

"Anything," she whispered. "I'll do anything."

Crandall kissed her forehead. He stood, towering above her, his hands resting lightly on her shoulders. "You have the gold, Becky. It's all yours. You've earned it a hundred times over. You have a decision to make. I can't help you with it. Don't make this decision too quickly and don't make it lightly. Think about it."

"Don't talk like this. You're frightening me. What are you trying to say?"

Pulling himself up over the cockpit seat, he quickly stepped to the stern. Before she could speak, Crandall flipped the aluminum diving ladder into the water and lowered himself into the ocean up to his waist.

Becky scrambled after him, her hands gripping the stern pulpit's railing as she leaned from the cockpit. "Please, don't do this, PLEASE!"

Crandall stepped off the ladder, one hand still holding the bottom rung as he was gently pulled along in the boat's wake. "You know how to sail. You have a choice to make. You can keep all the gold for yourself. You know where it's hidden. I doubt folks in Honolulu will find it. You won't fit their profile, sweetheart."

Becky began crying, her breath coming in deep sobs. Tears streamed down her face. "You can't do this. It's crazy. Please, stop! Come back! Don't leave me, PLEASE!"

He let go of the ladder. "I can last for about an hour, maybe longer. If you really love me you'll come back for me. If not, I'll understand. I have to do this. I'm at peace with it. Goodbye, Becky."

Sobbing uncontrollably, Becky pulled herself into the cockpit, took the tiller.

Treading water, Crandall floated away, staring at the white

hull as it slowly sailed on. From the water, *Sunshine*'s masts stayed in sight until they too, vanished. A gentle swell lifted him, giving one last tantalizing glimpse of sail, then only the horizon. Forty minutes passed. He lay back, arms outstretched, the black neoprene suit providing buoyancy. The experience was proving deceptively pleasant. He had not expected that. Wonderful cumulus clouds drifted above him, changing shapes as they passed, screening the sun.

The noisy clattering of a laboring engine closing on him broke his reverie.

The Mercedes! Righting himself, Crandall dog-paddled in the green swells to fix the sound. Rising on a long unbroken swell, he spotted a white hull heading his way. Sails down, *Sunshine* was motoring right at him. He raised a hand, waved and was rewarded with the sight of Becky readying an orange horseshoe lifebuoy. She cut the engine, letting *Sunshine* drift close enough to hurl the line. Embracing the collar with both arms, he let Becky pull him to the boat. *Sunshine* lay dead in the water. Crandall swam to the stern and labored to climb the diving ladder to the deck. Weeping, Becky threw her arms around him. He pulled her tight against him without speaking. They stood like that for several minutes, both of them in tears. When she had calmed enough to speak, Becky berated him for what he had done. "How could you do that to me? Promise me you'll never, never, never do anything like that ever again!"

Holding her at arms length, Crandall broke into a relieved smile. "I promise. Can you understand why I had to do it? I had to know." He pulled her close. "It's all over. We'll never talk about this again. It's done."

Hot tears filled her eyes. "Never again. I couldn't survive something like that.

I don't want to let you out of my sight for as long as I live."

They kissed. Exhausted by his time in the water, Crandall flopped on the cockpit's bench seat. "Help me out of this wetsuit, will you?"

"I've a mind to let you do it yourself. It would serve you right to have to wear that all the way to Hawaii."

"C'mon, I'm practically an invalid. You know, the malaria."

"Seems to me you had no trouble getting into it." They both laughed as she ran the zipper down his back. She helped him peel off the suit. "I think I'm going to call you 'Malaria Boy' from now on."

"Fine with me. I'll milk it as long as I can."

Surveying the haphazard heap of Dacron sails, Crandall scolded Becky. "I'm gone a few minutes and you turn the deck into a rag pile. Sloppy seamanship."

She started to reply, but stopped. Burying her head in her hands, Becky knelt on the deck, breaking into tears again. "I couldn't handle the sails alone. I remembered what you taught me about the 'man overboard' drill but I just fell apart," she said between deep, wracking sobs. "I had to use the motor. What if I hadn't been able to find you?"

He lifted Becky to her feet and hugged her. "But you did come back. I had my doubts for a while. But I have to say, I was happy when I heard the engine. You got there just before the sharks."

"Sharks?" She paled at the thought. "You saw sharks?"

"No. I felt them below me. They were just curious. Eventually the word would have gotten around. Thanks for the lift."

She punched his arm. "Don't kid around like that. I'm still shaking over this."

He tied the wetsuit to a halyard to dry and looked around the deck. "I'll run the sails aloft. You take the helm. We've got a lot of sailing to do." She didn't move. "Well, what are you waiting for?" he barked, slapping his hands together. "Chop, chop, girl. Hawaii beckons."

"Are you traveling like that?" She laughed, pointing to him.

Realizing he was completely naked, Crandall joined in the laughter. "Didn't I say we could sail like this?" He went forward to raise the foresail and jib. That done, he loped past her and raised the mainsail. Light winds breathed enough life into the sails to turn *Sunshine*. He skipped across the deck, whistling at Becky as he scrambled below to find clothes. She heard him singing some bawdy sea chantey in the cabin and smiled.

I've got him back, she thought. *We're finally free.*

....

Chapter 77

Cannon Falls, Minnesota, September 18

Hints of fall, oddly premature and unwelcome, were already nibbling away what was left of a record cold, wet summer. Overnight the blanket of hillside sumac flanking Morris's winding driveway burst into scarlet. Indian Summer had proved a no-show and it wouldn't be long before maples and birch would mimic the sumac. Waves of orange, yellow, and crimson would sweep through the woods then turn leaves to brittle, mottled browns before they fell. From his den window, Morris spotted lumbering green combines running arrow-straight sweeps through standing corn. The soil in the broad valley had finally dried enough to hold machinery and the farmers were hard at it. Two neighbors on adjacent horse farms had already made their "snowbird" preparations and would be gone in two months.

Soon, Morris would reluctantly begin packing up the house. A new Realtor had proved herself within sixty days. The buyer, an impossibly young surgeon new to Mayo, who wanted to try his hand at a hobby farm, was anxious to close before school started. At the insistence of his Realtor, Morris had knocked five thousand off the asking price. "Do you want to get out from under your house or not?" she had asked. "Then drop five and let me do the talking." Thoughts of winter added to the urgency of selling and Morris had capitulated, only to hear the woman congratulate herself. "Didn't I tell you? Wasn't I right about pricing it to sell? I'm never wrong on where my clients should be on price." Her boasting didn't help his sour attitude. The mouthy harpy, plus the bizarre unfinished business of his PNG trip, the disappointing summer, and the thought of coming snow, drove Morris to brooding silence. He had toyed all summer with the idea of fleeing to Phoenix, San Diego, or Florida. In the end, he opted to return to Florida—a place he knew well. He was investing as a silent partner in a fifty-five-plus community. Once he made up his mind, selling the house had been the sole reason keeping him in Minnesota. What could make him stay? Certainly not the winters.

One late-night phone call from Upsala nearly derailed his plans.

"Thought you should know we had visitors," began John Soderlund. "They left Barbara Wickstrom's house not more than an hour before my wife and I got home. We had been in the Twin Cities for the theater."

"Who is 'they'?" asked Morris, pacing between packing boxes in his kitchen.

"Two guys. They came to see Barbara, said they were FBI. Scared her half to death, Amy Larson too. They asked a lot of questions about Becky."

Morris had a bad feeling. "What did they want to know?"

"It's more about how they asked. They took their time and they weren't polite according to Amy. These two guys turned the place upside down looking through Becky's old room. Amy tried to call 911 but they took the phone away from her. They took it away from her. Her own phone. How can they do that?"

"Because they weren't FBI. Did she ask for identification?"

"She was too scared. Amy answered the door. They marched right in like they owned the place and started asking questions. When we got home and found out what had happened I called the sheriff. They've got a deputy over there right now taking statements. These thugs trashed Becky's room. Tore apart her old computer. Damn thing didn't even work. That was the first thing we checked when she disappeared. What should we do? Barbara's not doing well with this."

Morris thought for a moment. "Sorry about that. Go over to Barbara's and tell the deputy to check with the FBI in the Twin Cities. Have him call to see if the feds actually sent somebody out there. I doubt it, but he'll need to ask. Then, see if they have someone who can do a sketch or some sort of composite of these clowns. You'll need to take a look at the pictures too."

"Why? I told you we got back too late to see these guys."

"I know, but my hunch is these guys are connected to that first visit Becky had in January. It's a stretch, but if I'm right, you might be able to ID one of them. How's Mrs. Larson handling it? Did either of them give up Becky Lund?"

"They didn't tell them anything. Amy's a tough old bird. She's pissed more than shaken. Angry she didn't get their license plate."

"Probably a rental. They would have used fake IDs. But you might mention that to the deputy while you're at it. My guess is they were probably driving some sort of SUV. For some reason, guys like that get off on using those. There are bound to be a lot of them at the airport rental firms but it's worth trying."

"You sound pretty sure they're out-of-towners."

"Have to be. Like I said, I bet it's got something to do with that guy who first visited her, the one you saw. Becky told me he worked for some relative back east who was bankrolling her trip. Sounds like that was a cover too. I'd like to believe she didn't know about this, that she was set up by people who got wind of the plane's find. I just can't figure out how this ties in. Damn, it's frustrating. Too many loose ends. Look, I'm kinda busy myself right now. I'm planning on folding up my tent here in the next three weeks. My house finally sold and I've got a closing set. But I think I should drive up there day after tomorrow and say my goodbyes."

Soderlund sounded relieved. "That would be great. We'd be glad to see you again. Even Amy Larson would welcome you with open arms right about now."

Morris laughed. "That's an image I'll try not to think about."

Soderlund's voice took on a flat tone. "Hey, one more thing to think about."

"Which is?"

"Have you considered that these guys must know about you? If they're looking for Becky, they may come for you. Have you thought of that?"

"Thanks for the reminder. They might know of me from my connection to her. We only talked once before the trip to PNG turned into a sure thing. Our second meeting was when she told me some uncle had offered to fund her. Has to be the same people. I'll keep an eye open. You said these guys left Barbara's house an hour before you got home. How long have you been home?"

"Twenty minutes."

Morris did the math. "I'm about a hundred-fifty miles from

Upsala. They'd take I-94 to Highway 52. I've got almost an hour. I'll be waiting in case they show."

"You should call the cops before those two arrive."

"I don't think so. I'll handle this myself."

"Watch yourself. They probably won't be gentle with you."

"I wouldn't expect them to be. I've got to go. I'll call you tomorrow. Expect me the day after." Morris put down the phone and went into the kitchen to make fresh coffee. While it brewed, he went to his bedroom closet. Reaching to the back of the top shelf, he took down the Beretta 92, slapped in a fifteen-round magazine, jacked a round in the chamber, and flipped on the safety. He poured himself a mug of hot coffee and went through the house turning on all the lights except for a small study at the front of the house. Sitting in the dark, he sipped coffee, the Beretta on the desk in front of him. From his vantage point Morris studied headlights streaming south on Highway 52 through a pair of binoculars.

Fifty minutes passed before he spotted them. A black SUV slowed in the right-hand southbound lane and turned west on the County Road 86. Morris kept his eyes glued to the big car, saw it take the frontage road and begin climbing the gentle grade toward the forested knob where his house sat overlooking the valley. The SUV switched to parking lights for the final two hundred yards past the cul-de-sac. There was no doubt they were coming for him.

Morris threw on a dark hooded sweatshirt and slipped out the kitchen door to the cedar deck. He padded down the steps to the side of the house. Beretta in hand, he moved quickly, circling back toward the front of the house where a stand of pine served as a windbreak among hardwoods. From his vantage point behind a towering oak, he could see everything. He didn't have to wait long.

His visitors parked the SUV to block the driveway. Two white men in heavy overcoats got out, glanced around, and warily approached the front door. The pair stood under a porch light. The shorter of the two, a stocky, dark-haired weightlifter type, repeatedly punched the doorbell. The second man, taller and wearing black gloves, pounded on the door. "Mr. Morris, federal officers. We need to ask you a few questions, sir!"

Shrugging, the two glanced at each other. The short guy peered in the lighted windows, his hand jamming the doorbell. Bathed in the light, the pair made perfect targets. Fifteen yards away, Morris crouched, his body hidden behind the gnarled oak. Steadying the Beretta with both hands, he called out, "Gentlemen, I wouldn't move if I were you. I'll drop both of you if I have to."

Surprised, the men pivoted toward the dark woods and slowly raised their hands shoulder-high. The taller one with the bullet-shaped head bellowed at the pines to Morris's left. "We're federal officers, Mr. Morris. We're here to ask you a few questions. Nothing more. If you're armed, you're making a serious mistake. Don't compound your error by threatening government agents."

"Cut the government agents bullshit! You big brave boys just came from Upsala after threatening a woman in a wheelchair. You were dumb enough to assume my friends wouldn't call me. That's your first mistake. I seriously doubt you're terrorizing invalids while on government business! I'm not in a wheelchair, assholes, but you both might end up in one. Your call."

The men on the porch awkwardly turned in Morris's direction, unsure of his location but desperately hunting with their eyes.

"I know you're here to ask about Becky Peterson. I can't tell you anything. You know as much as I do, maybe more. She disappeared in PNG. I have no idea where she is…or where the two brothers who went with her are. I'd like to know their whereabouts myself. Ain't going to happen, apparently. Nobody knows where she is. Barbara Wickstrom certainly didn't know. If you're so bright, you figure it out. Why would I still be here if I knew where she was? Whatever business you have with her is your problem. My advice is for you cowboys to pack it in and go back to whatever pond you climbed out of. Call it a win for the home team tonight."

The tall one started to slowly lower his hands. "Morris, be reasonable, we're not looking for you. We want to talk to Becky Peterson. We thought you might tell us where we could find her."

"Keep your hands where I can see them! Didn't you hear me? For the record, I don't have a clue where she is. She didn't leave the island with me."

Both men raised their arms, palms showing. A minute of deadly silence passed. "Look, this is getting us nowhere, Morris. Okay, so you don't know where she is. What if we accept that and move on?"

"Good choice, gentlemen. I suggest you go back to your vehicle and get in. Then drive away. I'd hate to lose patience and shoot two armed intruders who came calling at night. I'm sure the local sheriff would commend me for defending myself. We do have the right to carry in this state…or maybe you boys didn't know that. Thought you'd come out here to work your magic on the simple folks in flyover land, huh?"

Morris knew by now the two had likely fixed his position. It was getting dicey. If the pair split up and came at him from two directions he would be lucky to get one, let alone both. He could tell they were discussing their options. To his great relief, the strangers turned to face the lighted porch, their hands still high above their heads, and began backing down the steps.

Morris took the opportunity to move quickly to another tree as a precaution. His field of fire was perfect if the pair tried anything funny. The taller man reached the vehicle and opened the passenger door with one hand, the other still held high. He slid in the seat and shut the door. His shorter, broad-shouldered accomplice continued backing around the rear of the vehicle, arms overhead. He too, opened the SUV's door with one hand and carefully settled in the driver's seat. The car started and began backing up. While the vehicle turned in the driveway, Morris kept the SUV's shape centered in his sights.

Perspiration soaked his sweatshirt, running down his back, suddenly chilling him in the night air. He went back in the house, killed all the interior lights, slept on the living room floor and left the yard lights burning until dawn.

In the morning, Morris called Soderlund to tell him about his visitors and to thank him for the timely warning. "I must be getting old," he said. "I never anticipated those people coming after me. If Becky's alive, she's in a nasty fix. Those two didn't strike me as the kind of people who stop looking. It's obvious they're working for someone." Morris gave Soderlund the rental SUV's license plate and asked him to phone the Morrison County sheriff's office. "I'm not in the mood to talk to any of their deputies right now," he said. The next day, he drove north and spent the afternoon with Barbara Wickstrom to reassure her the pair who had terrorized her were unlikely to return. After a late lunch, he drove home for a meeting with his favorite Realtor. It had something to do about a home inspection she was arranging with the buyer.

. . . .

Chapter 78

Honolulu

Hawaii seduced Becky the moment she roused herself from a three-hour nap and came topside to find Oahu's lush green hills beckoning from the horizon. "You should have awakened me an hour ago."

"I enjoyed watching you sleep. Besides, you needed it."

Wrapping herself around Crandall's shoulders, she breathed deep, convinced she could smell floral scents wafting from the shore. "It's more beautiful than I imagined."

"Yeah, it's exotic, colorful, and overcrowded all at the same time. You'll love it."

"I love it already. I can't wait to walk on real grass again. To sit in the shade under a tree, any tree."

"Technically we've got forty-eight hours to go before we're cleared to go ashore. Sorry, but we'll have to sleep on board two more nights." She kissed him passionately.

"I don't care. We're here. We made it. I just hope I'm not dreaming."

"I'll introduce you to Honolulu traffic, then you'll know you're not dreaming."

"I don't care. Even traffic sounds good to me."

Crandall laughed. "Be careful what you wish for."

To avoid customs until the following Monday, they had arrived on Saturday. Crandall went ashore and made three calls. The first one went to Tony Chun to arrange for a temporary loan of the mechanic's spare pickup truck that night. Chun agreed. "I can leave now. I'll have my auntie's boy follow me to the harbor and give me a ride home. I'll meet you in the marina parking lot and give you the keys. See you soon, brah."

"Works for me, Tony. Mahalo, eh?" With Chun on the way, Crandall's second call was to Customs to let them know *Sunshine* had arrived and would wait for processing on Monday morning. The last call was to the state agriculture department. He got an answering machine and left a detailed message about where they had been.

It was dark when Chun arrived. The men had a hurried reunion in the parking lot with a promise of a bigger party by week's end. Crandall got the truck keys and no questions. To Chun, Crandall was ohana—family. Family didn't need to explain.

That night, Crandall used a wheelbarrow to move the gold to the truck's cab. The vehicle was parked within eyesight of *Sunshine*'s slip. He and Becky kept vigil all night. They ate aboard and took turns watching until Monday when agents from Customs and Agriculture came aboard to process them. At noon, they were done with the formalities. Crandall secured the boat and sent Becky to babysit the truck while he made another call. He phoned an old navy buddy, a retired carrier pilot who lived in Manoa, and arranged for the use of his bachelor friend's one-bedroom downstairs apartment. The flier said he would leave the key in the mailbox while he ran errands.

They loaded a backpack with laundry and the laptop and left the marina. After stopping at a grocery store, they headed for Huelani Drive in Manoa Valley. When they reached the house, they found a note and an envelope with a key for the lower-level unit.

After unloading groceries, Crandall went back for the battered canvas duffle bag containing the gold. He carried it on his shoulder down stone steps set in moss covering the tiny side yard. Inside the apartment, he dropped it behind a loveseat in the living room. Becky was already in the bathroom, a trail of clothes scattered across the tiled floor. While Becky showered, Crandall checked the computer for gold dealers on Oahu. He began making phone calls to compare prices. The storeowners were wary, but he eventually compiled a list of six dealers, four in Honolulu, one in Pearl City, and another in Kailua on the windward side.

They would start tomorrow in Kailua and work their way back to Honolulu along the coast. Maybe lunch at the Crouching Lion in Kaaawa and then downtown Honolulu. She'd get her wish—to see traffic. Pearl City could wait another day or so.

Crandall headed for the bathroom. He left the door open to the living room where he could keep an eye on the bag behind the sofa. Becky was clearly enjoying herself. *No need to waste water*, he thought. He rapped on the glass door and saw her face light up.

....

Chapter 79

To avoid arousing suspicion, Crandall unloaded three ounces at each gold dealer's shop, promising more if given a fair price. No questions were asked. In two days, he reversed his route, trading a half-pound at each store, ending in Pearl City where the rotund Chinese owner asked for more. On the next go-around, he sent Becky in to each shop with six ounces before pulling the plug. Not wanting to push their luck, the pair agreed to leave Hawaii the following week. They threw a raucous goodbye luau in Tony Chun's backyard and returned his pickup truck.

They sailed to the San Juan Islands, selling two pounds to

local jewelry makers along the coast. Stopping in Bodega Bay, the pair turned more gold into cash at a local goldsmith's boutique shop, then sailed to San Francisco and did a lucrative business for two weeks. Sausalito proved a good market. Becky rented a car and they drove north to Novato and Santa Rosa, unloading gold as they went.

"Maybe we should try dentists next," quipped Crandall as they stopped for lunch in Menlo Park on their return south. They dumped more gold in Palo Alto and San Jose, in shops eager to buy. Over the mountains in Santa Cruz, artisans snapped up more of their hoard. They doubled back to San Francisco and made an unplanned stop south of the city on El Camino Real. A sullen, bearded gold buyer running a seedy-looking "Cash 4 Gold" shop practically wet himself to buy a half-pound from Becky. "Can you get more?" he growled. When she shook her head and pocketed the cash, he glowered. His partner, a burly gray-haired hulk with a ponytail, followed Becky from the store. Crandall locked the car door behind her and headed into the city. "Time to move on. That guy looked like he was after the goose with the golden eggs. He may have friends. Maybe we should think about heading to Los Angeles."

Staring out the window at fog-shrouded Golden Gate Park, Becky pouted. "Ugh. I'm so tired of living out of motels and hitting every dinky shop we can find. We'll be sixty years old by the time we're done selling."

"Ninety pounds is a lot of gold to spread around. We've sold off a lot so far."

She reached for his hand. "I know. I'm sorry to be a bitch about it, really. It's just so tiring doing it this way."

Squeezing her hand, Crandall offered a compromise. "Okay. How about this. Let's blow northern California and do the southern coast thing for a while. We'll get a car and head over to Vegas. Unload a lot of it there and get married. Maybe do Reno as well. After that we head back, pick up *Sunshine*, and sail down the coast. Whatever's left we'll sell in Panama and Belize."

"What did you say about Vegas?"

He played dumb. "We'll get a car, sell in Vegas, and…"

"No, I definitely heard the word marriage."

"Why not? I think we make a good couple, don't you?"

"I accept. And I love you for suggesting it."

"Maybe one of the dealers will trade a couple of rings for some gold."

She laughed. "I'm sure they'd be happy to do that." She planted lipstick on his cheek. "It's so perfect. What about Mexico?" she asked.

"Too risky. Plus, I don't have any contacts there. I do know Panama and Belize. You'd love those spots. They're romantic. Exotic."

"And then what? I'm ready to settle down for a long time, maybe for good. What about Palm Beach? Or Jacksonville. Your dad lived in Jacksonville, didn't he? You've got your navy disability. We'll have lots of cash by then."

"Have you thought about the Keys or the Bahamas?"

"Sure. I could be happy either place. If we found some quiet town where no one would bother us."

"Yeah, but would you stay happy?" She caught his eyes with hers. Serious. "Anywhere I go, I want you with me."

"Bottom line?"

"Bottom line."

"Okay. Here's what we'll do." He recited a proposed itinerary. "Hit Los Angeles and Vegas, skip Mexico, go through the canal and stop in Panama and Belize if need be. From there we cross the Gulf, sail the Keys, and end up in Jacksonville."

Becky cocked an eyebrow at him. "Seriously?"

Crandall pounded the wheel for emphasis. "Absolutely. You say the word and it's a done deal." She leaned across the seat and cupped his chin, kissing him. "I love you more each day."

Crandall kept his word. They took *Sunshine* south along California's coast, docked at Long Beach's Shoreline Marina, and spent the next two weeks spreading twenty pounds of gold from Santa Barbara to San Diego. They tied the knot in Vegas in a tacky chapel with an Elvis impersonator crooning off-key at a pink baby grand. Champagne and a night in the Venetian's wedding suite followed. Selling more of their dwindling hoard, the newlyweds banked more cash and headed south. It took them a month to salt Panama and Belize with what was left of the gold. Banks in both countries were more than happy to accommodate the handsome couple from el norte. Now newly minted millionaires, the pair finished a run across the Gulf, skirted a tropical storm aiming at the Keys, and ended in Jacksonville.

Within a month, escorted by a motherly silver-haired Realtor, Becky fell in love with the perfect furnished house on shaded Yacht Club Road. The home nestled in a wooded lot facing the St. Johns River. The owners, two retired doctors in their eighties not sure about selling, were abroad for two years. With the Realtor's encouragement, Becky convinced Crandall they should rent with an option to possibly buy.

It was a good fit. Becky reinvented herself. They mingled with old money at the nearby Florida Yacht Club and eventually got themselves sponsored as members. Tennis, a pool, and dining were now just steps away. That winter, Crandall found a marina downriver at Green Cove Springs and had *Sunshine* completely overhauled, inside and out. He and Becky made new friends among Jacksonville's moneyed sailing crowd.

It was everything Becky had hoped for, with one exception.

Though she kept the thought to herself, in the back of her mind she lived each day waiting for the proverbial "other shoe" to drop. She did not have to wait long.

....

Chapter 80

Jacksonville, Florida, November 28

Dale Morris stood on the bow of his friend's sailboat, mooring line in hand. When the hull's bumpers kissed the pier, he leaped to the dock, pulling the line taut. A tall sun-tanned man at the helm yelled, "Am I good?"

"You're good, Frank!" Morris looped the nylon line around the stout cedar piling and went aft to snag the stern line. The boat's owner, Frank Kennedy, and another day sailor named Ted, a chubby, grinning bearded man in an Auburn sweatshirt, began flaking the mainsail. The pair folded the Dacron sail in perfect accordion pleats over the boom. Morris nimbly stepped on board and lent a hand with the sail ties as they finished. The men slipped a blue cover over the mainsail and were done.

Three women—all blondes, tanned, athletic, and chatting non-stop—emerged from the companionway loaded with plastic bins. Morris crossed to the dock and took containers as the women passed them over the rail. The pile of coolers and bins kept growing. Kennedy, the tall man, ran a hand through his thick silver hair. "What a fantastic day, Dale. Thanks for helping out. We should do that more often."

"I'm game, Frank. Call anytime you need an extra hand."

The round man in Auburn colors winked at Morris. "What Frank's really talking about is your saving his ass, Dale. You filled in for a blind date no-show who was supposed to keep Lady Gwen amused."

"Aha," said Morris. "And all this time I thought Frank liked me for my ability at crewing his boat." Waving away the bearded man's comment, Kennedy said, "Ted's always a kidder, Dale. Just ignore him."

"I tried," said Morris. "He was determined to get me next to Gwen every time I looked for a place to land."

"She's a keeper," nodded Frank at the women who were hustling two carts filled with bins and coolers along the dock. "Watch yourself, Dale. She likes you. She's high maintenance, and what Gwen likes, Gwen gets."

The men ambled along the pier behind the blondes. Morris said, "I'm on hiatus from women for now." Lagging behind the other two, Ted, blurted, "Thinking of joining a monastery are you?" Morris laughed. "Believe it or not, there is a season for everything, including women."

Frank abruptly stopped to gaze at a sleek white sailboat tied stern first in one of the slips. "Wow, what a beauty. That's a lot of stock options floating there, gentlemen."

"That's an Alden, isn't it, Frank?"

"I think you're right, Teddy. One classy boat. Beautiful."

The trio resumed walking, following the women across a paved boat storage lot to a parking lot next to the tennis courts. They gathered at Kennedy's black SUV. Morris helped stow gear, coolers, and plastic bins into the yawning cargo area. The group tossed light banter back and forth, promising each other, "We must do this again."

Handing Morris a business card, the blonde named Gwen cooed, "Call me sometime, stranger. I'm not in the book but that's my business phone. I'll school you about political polling if you want to be bored over lunch."

Blushing, Morris scanned the card and pocketed it. "Thanks. I enjoyed meeting you, Gwen. I'll take you up on that. Polling sounds fascinating, politics not so much."

She laughed, perfect white teeth flashing in a flawless tanned face, purring, "What a smoothie you are, Dale. Yeah, I had fun. Frank and Doris are great friends. Theo's always a hoot. His wife is a saint." She offered a hand. "Well, gotta run. It's been fun."

He took her hand. "Likewise. Thanks for letting me come along at the last minute."

The perfect smile again. "What a gentleman. A rare breed. I won't hold my breath, but call me for coffee if you'd like. Cheers." She turned and walked to a red convertible, blonde ponytail bouncing.

Morris offered a wave as she wheeled from the lot. Blonde Gwen didn't look back.

His car, an aging Beamer, was parked in the corner of the lot, nose to the hedge screening the tennis courts. He surveyed the shiny, new expensive models parked nearby, not one of them over a year old. *Definitely not my style*, he mused. Morris slipped into his seat, started the engine, and lowered both windows to let the day's heat escape.

A Lexus, tires squealing, turned off Yacht Club Road and zoomed across the asphalt. The car jerked to a stop in an end stall next to the boatyard. A shapely, dark-haired woman in tennis whites got out of the Lexus and wrestled a pair of grocery bags from the trunk. The young woman turned and for a split second, her eyes caught Morris staring at her. She hurried across the paved lot toward the pier. Glancing back once, she kept going. Morris killed the engine, got out of his car and followed. Pausing next to a parked trailer mounted with a fishing boat, he saw the woman head toward the boat he had admired earlier, the one Teddy and Frank had called an Alden. Jogging to the middle wharf with its eight slips, Morris stepped on the dock and yelled to the ghost, "BECKY!"

On the pier, the woman froze, then disappeared.

Quickening his pace, Morris went the length of the wharf to the last slip where the schooner's stern pushed against soft white rubber bumpers. His quarry had vanished. Morris paced alongside the boat, yelling again. "Becky! It's Dale! Dale Morris!" No response. Walking to the end of the pier and back Morris grew agitated. *She has to be on that boat.*

"Becky!" A woman's silhouette flashed in a cabin window. "Talk to me," boomed Morris. Wearing sunglasses, the woman poked her head from the companionway. "Please go away or I'll call security."

"Becky Peterson. Becky Lund. I know it's you. It's Dale. I don't believe it. What are you doing here?"

"I'm warning you. Leave me alone."

"What the...what happened in Papua New Guinea, Becky? Where did you go? We thought you were dead."

"That's it. I'm calling the police."

"Wait! Just tell me what happened over there! Why the disappearance? Are you in some kind of trouble?"

Behind Morris a deep voice said, "You're the one who's in trouble, mister. What the hell do you want?" The voice belonged to a bronzed, bearded man in jeans and a sweatshirt. Morris judged him to be thirty years younger and fit. Stepping back to size up the man on the dock, Morris held up his hands, palms out. "Who are you?"

"This is my boat and that's my wife you're bothering."

"Wife? I know her. Her name's Becky. Becky Lund," said Morris.

"Doesn't matter what you think her name is. She's my wife. You should leave."

A gray-haired man in blazer and tie, trailed by two rent-a-cops likely summoned by the woman, was hustling across the boat storage yard. Morris was in decent shape but he was outnumbered. A brawl would draw real cops. The security guys came up behind the boat's owner and the huffing, red-faced guy in the blazer.

"Okay, no problem," said Morris. "Maybe I've mistaken her for someone else. My friends and I saw your boat…it's an Alden isn't it?"

"So you know your boats. Yeah, it's an Alden. What does that prove?"

"We thought your wife was someone we know who crews an Alden."

"Who's 'we'? I don't see anyone else but you. You need to leave. NOW!"

"Okay. I'm done here. Mistaken identity. My error. No problem. I'm leaving peacefully." He took a step toward the trio, cast a last look at the darkened cabin, thought of leaping aboard to confront the woman he knew as Becky Peterson. *What would that prove?* He slowly walked between the men on the dock. The security guards stepped aside to let Morris pass. The pair followed, staying several steps behind him all the way to the parking lot. One of them jotted down his license plate. They didn't leave until he exited yacht club property.

Driving home, Morris kept telling himself he wasn't crazy. The woman he had seen was the same Becky Peterson—*no, Becky Lund*—who had followed him in the jungles to find a missing airplane. *Why had she done that?* The people in Upsala had initially confounded him by telling him the woman in question was named Becky Lund. *They had to know the truth. They hadn't lied to him. Becky Peterson had died in the same car accident that crippled her mother. This woman was Becky Lund.*

When he got to his Lakeview condo, Morris called Kennedy and asked him if he could find out the name of the owner of the impressive Alden schooner. "Give me a day. I'll make a couple of calls," he promised.

Morris hung up. *I'll wait to see what Frank turns up and take it from there.*

....

Chapter 81

Once Crandall was certain Morris was gone, he boarded *Sunshine* and went below to the main cabin. Becky threw her arms around him. "Am I glad to see you. That was Dale Morris, if you hadn't figured that out by now."

"I thought so. How the hell did he end up here?"

"Of course! How could I have been so stupid? I forgot he lived here. He told me that when we first met. He's found us, Rick. I'm sorry to have this catch you off guard."

He hugged her, stroking her hair. "Not your fault. He blindsided us both. Think he'll give up at some point?"

"What if he finds out about the gold?"

Crandall laughed. "What gold, sweetheart? It's all gone, remember? It doesn't exist anymore. Maybe it's not going to be Jacksonville after all. If Morris lives close enough to show up like he did, I think that's too close for us to feel safe."

"I know. I'm confused right now. I mean, we've made a life here," she said.

"I feel we've put down some roots. I'd hate to leave."

"Might not have a choice," he said. "Maybe it would be smart to get away and figure out how to handle this before we do anything rash. You okay with that?" Becky nodded, too upset to answer. Crandall held her tight to still her shaking. "What would you say to getting a group together and going up to Savannah or Charleston?"

"I'd love it. Can we leave tomorrow?"

Crandall roared. "My spontaneous wife. Always joking."

Becky settled in his lap, arms around his neck. "I'm not joking. Morris won't leave us alone now that he knows where we are."

"Well, in any case, it would take us a few days to get out of Dodge." Crandall, his brow knitted in a V, took two beers from the refrigerator, offered one to Becky. "Crew wouldn't be a problem. Ginny and Oz are getting antsy. I could tell from their comments the other night at dinner. They're experienced. They'd be fun. There's nothing to hold them here. We'd take *Sunshine* of course. Drop off the map. Disappear again for a spell. I'll get working on this." Crandall went to the boat's navigation station and pulled out a set of charts. "We could get up to Bermuda for a couple of weeks. That'd give us time to think, what to do, you know? Sound like a plan?" She sipped her beer, ran the chilled bottle across her forehead, nodding in agreement. "We'll start with Savannah and after that, play it by ear." He leaned down, kissed her gently. "Consider it done, Ms. Crandall."

....

Chapter 82

True to his word, Kennedy called the next afternoon and left a message about the boat's owner on Morris's answering machine. "Here's what I have. Guy's name is Rick Crandall. Member of The Florida Yacht Club in good standing. Pays his bills on time.

Navy carrier pilot. Served on the USS Carl Vinson in Operation Enduring Freedom in 2001. Retired with a disability. Wealthy. Couple of the guys at the club with major hull envy told me Crandall had his Alden overhauled downriver last year for a truckload of cash. Rumor is he inherited a lot of money. Not sure how, since his dad was career Navy. Maybe from his wife's family. Everyone speaks quite highly of him. Wife's name is Rebecca. Bit of a cipher. Plays tennis at the club twice a week. No kids. Other than the tennis, she keeps to herself. My Doris knows her from some charity events at the club. Says she's quiet, nice. That's about it. Don't know if that helps but that's what I found. Call me if you have more questions. Oh, by the way, we're having a small gathering at our house next weekend. Gwen will be there. Call if you can come. Talk later."

That night, Morris called Soderlund in Upsala and dropped the bomb, telling him of his bizarre encounter with a very-much-alive Becky. Her former neighbor ran through several stages—disbelief, bewilderment, and finally anger. Morris knew them all, had cycled through them himself as he tried to process what had happened dockside. "I'm no private detective," he told Soderlund. "I don't know what else to do. No one in law enforcement back home seems interested enough to pursue this. The cops down here would laugh me out of their office so I'm not going to them with this." Soderlund suggested the FBI but Morris dismissed the idea. "Been there, done that," he said curtly. "I called them after I met you. They were about as helpful as your county sheriff."

"I'll stop by Barbara's tomorrow and break the news."

"You might want to rethink that. I mean, does she really have to know?"

"You're not suggesting I lie to her?"

"Of course not. Just don't tell her the whole story. The truth might be too hurtful. Let her think Becky Lund's gone for good."

Soderlund thought about it for a moment. "I see your point. I'll need to mull that one over for a while."

"Take your time. I'm going to give one more shot at Becky. If she doesn't respond I'm done with it. I'm certainly not going to spend my days chasing someone who obviously doesn't want to be caught. Let the bad boys give it a try. I'm just about done with this. Let's face it. This woman's gone to extraordinary lengths to stay lost. You understand what I'm saying?"

"Not really. But we'll try it your way. Keep me posted if things change."

"Of course. I'm not hopeful she'll respond and come clean, but you never know. She does have one thing in her favor, though."

"Oh, what's that?"

"The cowboys looking for her don't know she's alive or where she is."

Soderlund finished the call. "Thanks for turning my world upside down. Seriously, I appreciate your letting me in on this. Take care."

Morris put away the phone and sat at his kitchen counter to compose a last-ditch plea to Becky Lund. The effort took him most of the night until he was satisfied. He went to bed, certain he had done everything he could to make sense out of the mystery.

....

Chapter 83

The Florida Yacht Club, two days later

Morris pulled into the club's driveway and signaled the parking valet. The youth, a bleached-blonde surfer type in a powder-blue polo shirt with a club logo, hustled to the driver's door and reached for the handle. Waving him off, Morris handed the kid a twenty-dollar bill folded over a beige envelope with script on it. "Just dropping this off. I'm in a bit of a fix. Turns out I'm not able to make my tennis date with Ms. Crandall, Becky Crandall. Do me a favor. Make sure she gets this, okay? She's probably waiting for me down at the pool."

Beaming, the valet took the envelope, pocketed the twenty. "Yes, sir. You got it."

"Appreciate it," said Morris.

He drove away, eyes glued to his rear-view mirror. The youth disappeared through the club's front door. Morris went home to his condo in Lakeview, got himself a cold beer, and went out on the balcony overlooking the river. He settled in a cushioned wicker chair, propped his cell phone on an end table, and sipped the beer, waiting.

At the club, Morris's messenger found his quarry in a chaise lounge, knees drawn under her, an iced tea in one hand, paperback in the other. A sheathed tennis racket lay under the chair, two unopened cans of fresh balls next to it.

The youth offered Becky the envelope. "Ms. Crandall, ma'am. It's for you. The gentleman's apologies. He can't make the tennis match."

She glanced up. "Tennis match? What gentleman?" Tossing the book aside, Becky took the letter, turning it in her hand.

"Who gave this to you?" The kid didn't hear. He was already halfway across the concrete apron surrounding the club's wading pool.

The envelope was addressed in a masculine scrawl. She put down the tea, scanned the pool and tent pavilions for signs of life. A dozen leathery blondes were baking in the sun at the shallow end of the pool. Two waiters were setting up tables under a shelter. Four toddlers splashed in the wading pool under the eyes of their chatting mothers.

Becky knew instantly who the note was from. *If I don't open this it doesn't exist*, she told herself. *That's stupid. Of course he knows. He found me, didn't he?*

Running a blood-red nail along the flap, she read the simple white note.

> *Becky, Fate is strange, isn't it? Guess I was meant to find you again. Did you forget I built a house here in another life? There was no doubt in my mind that it was you when we met the other day. Not by accident, was it? You obviously don't want to make contact so I'm not going to force it. I'm not stalking you if that's your concern. It's not me you have to worry about. There are a couple of bad actors looking for you. They've already been to Upsala. They weren't gentle with Barbara. The same two paid me a visit. These guys are professional. My guess is that they work for the man who gave you money for the trip. He's probably not inclined to let you off the hook. He may think you are dead. We all told him that. We thought it was the truth. That may be your only hope. I'm owed an explanation about what happened. Your people in Upsala certainly need some sort of closure. Whether you decide to give them that is up to you. It would be the right thing to do. Some of us spent agonizing moments wondering what*

happened to you. We gave you up for dead. I don't know how you managed to survive. That in itself would be worth hearing. I'd be happy to buy the beer and just listen. Think about it. Keep your guard up in case your "benefactor" doesn't stop looking. Despite what's happened I hope he gives up the chase for your sake. I enclose my phone number. I hope you'll call. Believe me when I say I am genuinely glad to see you made it out alive. Dale

Morris waited, his phone nearby. Only when the sun set, throwing shadows across the river, did Morris reluctantly gather his empty bottles and cell phone. He went inside and sat in the darkened living room waiting for the call he hoped would come. Close to midnight, he ambled off to bed. Just to be sure, he parked his phone on the nightstand as he had done the previous two evenings, and tried to sleep.

Awake at five, he made himself fresh coffee and went out onto the balcony in the chilly dawn. Leaning against the iron railing, the river below dark and deserted, he told himself, *Did you really think she was going to call? Fool. She's gone.* Lifting his coffee mug in a toast, Morris said softly, "Here's to you, Becky Lund. Despite everything, I wish you a happy ending to whatever story you're writing with your new life."

EPILOGUE

In the village, the old chief, sclerotic and failing, succumbed within a month of the untimely deaths of his two sons. They were shot and killed during an argument over a woman or land—or both. The cause remains unclear and the culprits have not been found. Simeon became the new headman. His ascension to the office was due to both his lineage and his knowledge of the outside world.

In Upsala, Barbara Wickstrom continued to heal from the accident that claimed her daughter. Under Amy Larson's watchful eye she abandoned the wheelchair for a walker. Following that miracle with another, she took up a cane and set a new goal of walking completely unaided by year's end. She plans a spring garden next year.

Missionaries Brad and Dorothy Wood stayed on in Papua New Guinea. Two years after the disastrous expedition, a generous unexpected gift from an anonymous benefactor enabled them to build a small clinic and school in Simeon's village. The elders recently gave the Woods permission to erect a church. Barring any delays, construction is expected to be completed before the rainy season. Wood still looks for downed aircraft. The bones of the American flyers remain at his mission station. The U.S. embassy in Port Moresby has refused to accept the remains because being removed from the original crash site had, in the military attaché's words, "compromised" the evidence. Wood is hopeful the next JPAC recovery team to visit Oro Province will stop to hear the story of how the bones came into his possession.

After sailing up the coast and wintering in Bermuda, Crandall and Becky returned to Florida. They declined to renew their lease on the rented house and set off for the Keys. From there it was a long, leisurely cruise in the Gulf with stops along the coast, one of which was Galveston, where Crandall was treated for a malaria relapse. From Texas, they sailed for Belize and stayed for two months before passing through the Panama Canal. On Central America's Pacific coast, they fell in love with Costa Rica's Guanacaste Province and bought a beautiful oceanfront home. Twice a year, they throw huge parties for friends, ex-pats, and locals: Fourth of July and September 15—American and Costa Rican Independence Days. *Sunshine* is moored in a nearby marina where Crandall is a familiar figure. When not working on his sailboat, he can be found surfing with new friends at good breaks up and down the coast. A goofy-foot, he is known for his smooth longboard style. Becky has found a calling—maybe her penance—tutoring children in a local school. She considers every moment with Crandall a continuation of their honeymoon. Becky has never contacted Morris or the people she left behind in Upsala. She is settled, content at last.

In Jacksonville, Dale Morris watched the condo development collapse around him due to mismanagement. He somehow emerged financially unscathed and orchestrated the purchase of the six-unit building in which he now lives. Morris keeps a twenty-six-foot boat at a dock on his doorstep along the St. Johns River and has become an accomplished deep-sea fisherman. He does not miss Minnesota winters.

Sometimes, after entertaining friends at dinner, he will join guests for brandy on the balcony overlooking the dark river. While they chat, Morris will be lost in thought, thousands of miles away, his head filled with images of jungle trails and the half-buried silver fuselage of a P-38 Lightning.